Memories of a Fading Empire

Memories of a Fading Empire

J. Leslie Evenden

Media, Pennsylvania, July 2020

Copyright © J L Evenden, 2020

ISBN 978-0-578-75089-7

FICTION/Historical/Ancient
Keywords: Britannia; Roman Empire; Dark Ages

Published by WiltonLogic LLC
Media, Pennsylvania, USA

"All you had was glory… All the rest was unbearable toil and a plethora of unpleasantness, receiving a delegation from your enemies, judging court cases or sending instructions to your subordinates. There's always a rebellion to deal with or an attack from one of the peoples bordering on your empire. Your lot is fear and suspicion of everything. Other people may count you happy. You'll be the only one who denies it."

Lucian, *The Ship*, from *Chattering Courtesans and Other Sardonic Sketches*, translated by Keith Sidwell

❧ Prologue 407 CE ❧

Londinium was emptying at last. The line of soldiers, baggage carts and camp followers stretched over the bridge and halfway to Durobrivae. General Flavius Claudius Constantinus, recently hailed as emperor, as Constantine III, was leaving with his troops to stake his claim in Gaul. Most of the city folks were glad to see him go. Admittedly, the troubles which had preceded his acclamation had been bad for business. And, so long as the hordes of soldiers and camp followers who had swamped the provincial capital had cash in their hands, there had been money to be made. However, when the cash began to run out, the general had been forced to concede it was time to set the men marching. His supporters, those who had staked their fortunes on his success, were expecting a return on their investment in his campaign. The camp followers would have to make their own arrangements.

He had promised law and order and an end to the barbarian invasions that had disrupted trade, terrorised Gaul and threatened the families and estates of the wealthy patricians and officials who divided their time between Belgica, Gaul and Britannia. They, in turn, had been glad to make loans and provide supplies on credit, on the understanding that when Flavius Claudius Constantinus completed his seizure of power, the lucrative offices, the well-padded supply contracts and the basing of legions would all be decided on who had supported him and who had not.

"No gain without pain. You have to spend money to make money," he had pointed out. "Failure is not an option," he had assured them, patting them on the back and thanking them for their contributions.

Cassius Astrebanus watched them depart, his hands on the shoulders of two young men, his sons Vitellus and Drusus. Beside them stood Apollinarius, the lawyer, and their mutual friend Claudius Cornelius.

"*Alea iacta est*," muttered Vitellus, watching Constantinus receive the salutes of his men.

"The die is cast. You said it, my boy," concurred his father.

"Better make an additional offering on the way home," suggested Claudius Cornelius.

"You could try praying to this new god, Jesus," observed Cassius. "My wife does. It could help." Claudius Cornelius, a little unsure of Cassius' own position on religious matters, shook his head at the gullibility of women. Claudius himself was a widower, with a daughter to marry off. It would not be a good moment to cause offence.

"Honorius claims to be ruling in his name, this Christus," said Apollinarius, his tone also unsure. "I do hope we don't have to rely on the intervention of the gods," he added with a nervous laugh.

"Your wife is still in Treviri?" asked Cassius, as if changing the subject.

"She felt it safest there."

Cassius stroked his thin beard.

"Your son?"

"Also."

"Looks like you are hedging your bets, my friend," observed Claudius Cornelius.

"Like I said," replied the lawyer, "you can't rely on the gods, not in these times."

"We've done what we can," said Cassius, turning away from the parade. "Now it's up to the general."

There were those who doubted, as always, though few of them in Londinium. Those in the far provinces, who owed their posts to the previous regime. Men who wrung their hands as the legions marched away, leaving their regions open to predation by opportunists from over the seas or over the frontier. Men who were far enough away from Flavius Claudius Constantinus and the troops who had raised him to power that they could ignore his demands for loyalty and requests for money. Their days were numbered, reflected the spectators watching the final soldiers depart over the bridge. Constantinus stepped down from the viewing podium and vanished into a throng of officers. The doubters would get what they deserved when Constantine III consolidated his power, when the legions returned.

❧ Chapter 1 ☙

There was a sharp knock against the door frame, and the curtain covering the opening twitched aside.

"Master, wake up," came a voice. I woke with a start, though the request was not directed at me. The room was almost completely dark. Only a faint strip of moonlight seeped in through the shutters. I could see my father stir, then sit up.

"What is it?" he asked, still groggy from sleep.

"Master, I heard a sound from the river meadow, the cattle." The man paused. We had let the cattle out of the winter barn just three days ago. My sister and I had laughed to see the clumsy animals running and leaping in the meadow, enjoying their freedom and the prospect of fresh grass after being closed in, half starved, all winter. "I went to investigate," the man continued.

He did not need to say more. My father was wide awake, stepping off the bed and looking around for his breeches.

"What's going on, Annius?" asked my mother.

"Something or someone has been disturbing the cattle."

"Were there wolves? I was dreaming of wolves," said my mother.

"No," said the man in the doorway. "There were hoofprints, horsemen."

My father was still looking for his clothes. He should have opened the shutters to let in a little more light, but clearly his mind was already on his stock.

"Do you want me to fire the beacon?" asked the man.

"How many horsemen, do you think, Ryn?"

"It was hard to see the traces, master, in the moonlight, and they had been trampled by the cattle."

"Give me a guess."

"About half a dozen, no more. They didn't even manage to take all the beasts with them."

"We can deal with them ourselves," said my father. Now he had found his clothes and was pulling them on, tucking his undershirt into the breeches, reaching for a woollen overshirt.

"Ride round by Willow Bottom and Little Trickle and roust out Dell and Carr." I knew Dell and Carr. They were tenant farmers. "I'll round up the men and the boys. Tell them to meet us by the bridge."

At the word "boys", my ears pricked up.

"Does that mean I can come, Father?" I asked, sitting up.

He glanced across at me. "No, Marcus. You're still too young. You stay here and help the girls round up the strays."

He could not see how my face fell. I was fed up with being too small. I could ride a pony. I even had a wooden sword and had been practising with Ryn in the farmyard.

My father left, but by now my mother was awake, stepping from the bed, trying not to rouse my sister who had slept through the disturbance. Our home, Umbrosa Farm, was a long, narrow house, with a passage that ran from the main entrance where my father had his workroom, the whole length of the building to the kitchen and the storerooms. I followed my mother to the kitchen, finding that end of the house in turmoil, with the newly woken maids standing around aimlessly and the overexcited stable hands and yard boys popping in and out in the dim light.

My mother took charge in a moment.

"Build the fire up," she ordered. "Where are the saddlebags, Wes?" The latter question was addressed to one of the stable hands. "Are you men planning to be out all day in the hills with no food?"

"No, mistress," said the youth, bowing his head and slipping out into the yard. In a moment he was back, but before he returned my mother had already begun to gather bread and cheese and dried fruit from the storeroom ready to fill the bags.

I was in the way, of course. Somehow small boys are never welcome in the kitchen at times like these, so I dodged through the open door and out into the yard. The noise and bustle outside were more to my liking. Horses were being led out of the stables and dogs were running around, yapping and barking with excitement. My father was striding about checking the equipment, making sure each man had his sword and a hunting spear. Wes appeared from behind me, from the kitchen door, carrying the saddlebags, throwing one over his horse and handing out the others. My father gave a command, indecipherable words to my ears but clear in their meaning to the men, who swung themselves up onto their horses. A couple of the bigger boys, together with Old Tom, heaved at the bar of the gate and swung it open. My father and his men trotted out into the first light of dawn, and we who had nothing better to do followed them. We watched them take the road down towards the river. We could just make out the shapes of Dell and Carr threading their way along the field tracks towards the bridge. Ryn already stood there waiting. The group gathered for a moment and then, kicking their horses into movement, crossed the bridge and vanished into the shadows on the other side.

My mother had not had time to wish my father a safe day and tell him to take care of himself, and I could see it made her nervous. I watched as she took a little of the bread and cheese that remained and made her way to the front of the house to the family altar just inside the door. There she stood for a moment with a bowed head and then placed her offering in a flat dish in front of the small stone carving honouring our ancestors, the men and women who had cleared the farm and built the house, my grandfather and his father who had befriended the Romans and earned our family a little wealth and a position of respect in our community.

She returned to the kitchen, her head still bowed, as if her thoughts were on my father leading his men up into the hills on the heels of the Welsh raiders who had stolen our cattle.

Once it was light enough, she chased me out to join the boys and the farm girls rounding up the strays, who were now enjoying the unexpected opportunity to explore the roads and paths that led off into the fields and woods. It was lucky that it was too early in the year for the crops to have come up, otherwise the beasts could have caused a good deal of damage. As it was, we cut ourselves switches from the hedge and spent the morning searching the lanes for the missing animals and driving them back to the meadow, where Old Tom had repaired the wattle gate cut down by the thieves.

It was dark before the men reappeared, slowly making their way down the road which descended from the hills, driving cattle in front of them. One of the maids spotted them first. She had spent a good part of the day fretting down by the bridge. Her man was amongst those who had ridden off in the morning. Not Dell and Carr: they were married. Perhaps Ryn or Wes: they were the favourites amongst the maids. In any case, we could hear her calling, and we ran down to the bridge. To everyone's relief none of our friends had been seriously injured, although Ryn had dislocated his shoulder wrestling with one of the thieves.

I heard my father telling my mother about it later.

"They rode off when we caught up with them and left most of the cattle behind."

"How many did they take with them?"

"Four head."

Our men had captured one of the raiders. He had been knocked off his horse in the melee. Ryn claimed the credit as an excuse for his injury. No one was inclined to dispute it. The Welshman had hurt his ankle and had been unable to remount or run off, so he had been bound and slung over Carr's horse and brought back. He was tied up and left in the woodshed.

In the morning my mother went over to inspect the prisoner. She took some warm oats to make a poultice for his ankle and a beaker of boiled willow bark. We followed her, peering through the door as she tended to him. He was a disappointment. I am not sure what we expected, but he was just a short, skinny, thin-faced man, indistinguishable from the men who lived around us.

"He'll mend," said my mother to my father. "What'll we do with him?"

"I'll send him back once he can walk," said my father.

"Wouldn't it be better to take him into Walcastrum and sell him?" asked my mother. "That way, we would receive some compensation for the cattle they stole."

My father shook his head.

"I don't think so, Phila. If we start selling captives, who knows where the stealing might turn? Cattle rustling is bad enough, but I don't want the border plagued by kidnapping and murder."

When the man's ankle had healed, he was sent on his way with a bag of food, some ale and a message to his friends that next time we would not be so merciful. They left us in peace for the rest of that year.

A few days later there was another disturbance in the yard, this time in the form of my father's friends, Chief Gallius and Chief Nautius. I had seen them before but discounted them as too old and haughty to be of much interest. They were greeted at the front of the house and led into my father's workroom. When my mother took in some refreshments – I think she went as far as to fetch a flagon of Gallic wine from the cellar – I took the opportunity to slip into the room and sit down in a corner, my back against the wall and my legs curled up. I had never intruded on my father's business previously, but the raid by the Welshmen had piqued my curiosity. I suppose I had grown a little older during the winter and more curious about the affairs of adults.

"You were lucky," said Gallius, sipping at his wine. "Only four bullocks."

"Thanks to Ryn being alert. I never asked why he was up at that time of night."

"Better not to be too inquisitive."

"You lost cattle, too, earlier in the month."

"One of my tenants. His entire herd was stolen."

My father sighed.

"Do you think we need to call out a posse and make a show of strength?" asked Nautius, helping himself to a dried plum.

"I'd be willing," agreed Gallius.

They looked towards my father.

"I don't see the point," he said. "We don't know who took our cattle. They're as slippery as eels. We could spend days riding around in the hills without even seeing a Welshman or any sign of our stock."

"We'll see them right enough in the autumn at the cattle market," said Gallius.

Nautius grunted. "Fat and sleek from feeding in the hills."

"Selling us back our own animals."

I could see my father's eyes glancing back and forth between his two friends.

"It didn't use to be like this," said Gallius, "when I was a boy."

"Nothing did," acknowledged my father, "but what can we do about that?"

I had heard the story before, but it was only now, this winter, that I had begun to pay more attention. Years ago, when my father and Gallius and Nautius had been boys, the Romans had been the rulers. They kept order and made sure that everything and everyone performed as they should. That usually meant to the advantage of the Romans, though there were plenty of others who benefitted. Britannia was a long way from Rome, and the governors and their friends escaped much supervision. The less ambitious and greedier men were content to enrich themselves, but as the competence and influence of the emperors of Rome declined, the more ambitious and least perceptive started to aspire to being emperors themselves, given a chance. Several of them went as far as to collect the legions, ship them over to the continent and then get soundly beaten. That was a problem. Once gone and once defeated, as invariably happened, the legionaries did not always come back. After a while the emperors in Rome concluded that they could avoid the problem of rebellious governors of Britannia if they did not appoint one in the first place, though that left a power vacuum tempting to other ambitious men.

The few remaining soldiers, small groups of auxiliaries – Goths, Vandals, Scythians and Dacians from all around the Empire – had no desire to sit in wind and rain in the Welsh mountains or the hills of the far north, abandoned by their superiors and surrounded by hostile natives. They were tempted by cosier billets. As soon as they had a chance, they too found reasons to leave for warmer climates. At first the Welsh did not notice what had happened, but when a few venturesome individuals approached the gates of the old legionary camp in the hills and there was no challenge, they went in and found it was empty. The Romans, the legions, the auxiliaries, the tax collectors and moneylenders, the bar owners and whores had all gone. To their great surprise, the Welsh had finally triumphed. After a while the rest of the Britons also realised there were no Romans around, true Romans from Rome. The Britons, some of whom vaguely imagined they were Romans, had been left on their own without being given a chance to make any preparations. My grandfather had been one man who had picked up the responsibility. When he grew old and weary, my father had stepped into his shoes.

"My job is to keep the peace, not stir up trouble," said my father.

"Yes, but who gains from the peace?" asked Nautius, an irritated tone in his voice.

"Sometimes you need to stir up trouble if you want to make a change," added Gallius.

"Those bastards in Corinium, living easy and getting fat on our effort," said Nautius.

"Taking our money, and what do we receive in return? Tell me that, Annius!"

"Is that you sitting there, Marcus?" asked my father suddenly, turning around and peering into the shadows.

"Yes, Father," I admitted, standing up.

"I think it is past your bedtime. Off you go now." He smiled kindly, and Gallius and Nautius smiled too.

"Phila, the boy is running around wild," said my father a few days later. "It's time he began a proper education, not just sneaking into my workroom when my back is turned and eavesdropping."

"We'll never be able to find a tutor out here," replied my mother.

"I have been thinking," said my father in a confident tone. "I learned all I needed from Grandfather."

I noticed my mother grimace slightly.

"You could teach him to read and write, Phila," suggested my father.

"And you?"

"Latin and history."

"We'll see how much he learns of that," answered my mother, "with all the spare time you have on your hands!"

Not that my mother had time on her hands, either. It was my mother who constantly supervised the house and the farmyard, checking the animals, ensuring that the wood was cut and stacked, supervising the girls' spinning and weaving, ordering the slaughter of livestock and making sure the merchants delivered all the tasty extras and useful tools that we needed for a comfortable life. She had the task of ensuring that our home – a home not only for our family but all the servants too – ran smoothly. Now she had to teach me to read and write as well.

As my mother anticipated, however, my studies of Latin and history did not make much progress. My father was perpetually away. Sometimes he would be at home in the evening when I went to sleep and be gone in the morning when I woke up. If he disappeared during the night, he would be back the following day or the next one, tired and sweaty. Sometimes he took a couple of his closest men with him. Sometimes all the able-bodied men from the estate saddled up, grabbed whatever weapons they could and disappeared in a cloud of dust or showers of spray. Now I realised they might be riding up into the hills pursuing Welsh thieves.

At other times we knew my father was going on a journey long before he left. Neighbours, like Gallius and Nautius, would come over to visit and sit huddled with him for hours. The servants would be chased off to clean his best clothes. His travelling necessities would be carefully packed up. Then he would be seen off, accompanied by a couple of the housemen, with waves and best wishes. When he left like that he was usually away for days, sometimes weeks. My father was an important man. People needed his help. Men listened to his advice. That was why the neighbours were always visiting. That's why he was always away, solving people's disputes, helping them, giving them advice. Even the governor relied on his judgement. It left little time for teaching a son Latin or history, although that does not mean he taught me nothing. His claim to have absorbed all he knew from Grandfather had a little truth to it.

❧ Chapter 2 ☙

I was about seven years old when my life was completely upended. My father had been away on one of his long journeys and had arrived back just two days before. I thought the way he greeted me had been a little strange, but I concluded he must have just been tired. Since his return he had been sitting in his workroom with my mother, who emerged now and then to issue orders to the servants. I was chased out of the way. My questions were brushed aside. It never crossed my mind that I was the intended victim of this feverish activity until I was called in from the yard and told that my father wanted to speak to me. How very odd, I thought, especially when I saw the severe expression on his face.

My father spoke in a pompous tone I had never heard him use before: his business voice, I later learned. My mother looked on, her eyes damp, almost on the verge of tears, but forcing a smile from her mouth.

"Marcus, my son. I have some good news for you," my father pronounced. "My good friend, Governor Publius Julius Ursinus, has agreed to take you into his household and educate you alongside his own sons, Gaius and Lucius."

Before I could even begin to register what he had said, my mother burst out, "Oh, Marcus, you will be educated like a real Roman! I'm so proud."

At least, in later years, I always assumed she must have said something like that, because, in reality, my mind went blank at that moment. I did not burst into tears. I just stood dumbstruck. I simply could not comprehend my father's words.

Of course, I knew there was a world outside the farm, but up to that moment my universe had consisted of our house, the farmyard, the fields and woods round about and, beyond that, a spice of the Welsh and a few fairy tales whispered by the kitchen fire. Who was this Ursinus, and what did he want with me? And his sons, what did I care about them? How had the Romans become involved? I had no desire to be a Roman.

In a moment my head began to clear and my senses to function again, and I heard my father saying, "…and we leave tomorrow." With that, panic took over.

My first sight of Villa Verdaris was like a dream or one of those fireside fairy tales, though I was wide awake, seated beside the carter on the front of our farm wagon. As we crested a rise in the north–south road, I saw the house stretched out down the hillside in a series of terraces, white plastered walls with a red tile roof, a high tower rising in the centre and the whole building sparkling in the sunshine. A long driveway, with carefully trimmed trees exactly spaced along each side, led up to the main gate. Shadow and sun, shadow and sun fell over us as we rolled up the road under the archway and into a courtyard, which seemed to spread out in front of us, almost endless compared to the yard at home. When we came to a halt, a pair of stable hands ran out and took the reins from the carter. A tall man, dark-haired, tanned and dressed in a long white robe, stepped from a door in the main building and greeted my father. I recognised their words as Latin, but they spoke so quickly I could not follow. The tall man looked down at me, patted me on the head and smiled to my father, who turned and told me, "This is Master Nikos. He will be your tutor while you are here."

The two men exchanged a few more incomprehensible words, and my father disappeared inside the house. The tutor spoke again more slowly, but even then I could not understand. My father's attempts at education had been too desultory in that regard. Nikos shook his head, seemingly in disappointment, but his tone remained friendly. He called out and, after a moment, two boys came running from the stables, one taller than I was, perhaps ten or eleven years old, and one of about my own age. They must have been hiding, I thought, observing me from some secret place. Now they examined me curiously. The tutor spoke to them. I still did not understand a word.

The older boy grimaced, frowned at the tutor and then turned to me, holding out his hand and saying in British, "Hello, my name's Gaius Julius Ursinus. Welcome to our home."

The younger boy piped up, "And I'm Lucius."

"Don't mind him," said the older boy, indicating the tutor. "He doesn't understand British, do you Nikos?"

The tutor spoke again in Latin, leading Gaius to turn to me and roll his eyes.

"He says he understands us perfectly well but chooses not to speak British. I don't believe him. I don't think he knows how."

The man spoke again, gently but firmly.

"He says that only peasants and servants speak British and that educated people should converse in Latin. Do you know how to converse in Latin, Marcus?"

I shook my head.

"Well, you will do soon." The boy paused. "Do you actually know any Latin?"

I was too nervous and ashamed to reveal to these two strangers the little that my father had managed to teach me. I simply shook my head again.

"Well, never mind," said Gaius. "Neither did we once, and now we speak it like Romans. Better than the Romans," he added determinedly.

While we had been talking, the carter had unloaded my belongings, and several servants came to carry them into the house.

"Nikos," said Lucius. "Can we show him his room and the children's quarters?"

He obviously had more faith in the tutor's ability to understand British than his brother. Nikos gave up his effort to keep the discussion in Latin, revealing that he could, in fact, speak British, albeit with a heavy accent which I had difficulty following in the early days.

"We will in a moment, Master Lucius. First we will go and introduce Master Marcus to your father and mother."

We passed through a door, out of the bright sun of the yard, and into the dark, cool shadows of the house. Just inside the door was an alcove where an oil lamp was burning. I recognised this was the shrine to the *lares* of the house, the family gods, and probably a long line of ancestors of the Ursinus family, just like the one we had inside the entrance at home. I was surprised to see, amongst a row of small statuettes, a gold-coloured cross. Someone in this wealthy household must be a Christian, I realised.

We continued down a short passageway into a corridor that opened out along the full length of the building and disappeared round the corners at each end. All the way along the floor ran an intricate pattern of black-and-white tiles. To my eye, it seemed to stretch forever. On one side of the corridor was a series of rooms, on the other a colonnade, and through it I could see a courtyard containing a garden with a fountain in the middle. Neat hedges lined paths paved with oyster shells and gravel, separating beds containing flowers and herbs of many types from small trees trimmed into spheres and cones. The far end was blocked by a wall with a gate in the middle. Through it I could just glimpse another garden stretching on down the hillside. It was magical.

We walked together along the corridor and, turning the corner, saw a door standing open a little way further along. I could hear voices, one of them my father's, the others those of strangers. Gaius and Lucius ran in, and Nikos ushered me after them. I saw my father and, with him, a man and woman, probably around my father's age. The man wore a short tunic of white cloth. His legs were bare, and he had sandals on his feet. The woman wore a long white dress, drawn together at the waist by a thin leather belt and made of a material so fine I could see the shadow of her body through it. My father, in contrast, stood in his usual travelling clothes: a jerkin, trousers and boots. He looked like a farmer, and the two others were more like gods. So, these were real Romans, I surmised.

I glanced around the room. The walls were filled with wooden shelves divided into compartments, and in each compartment were scrolls and parchments. To one side stood a large desk with writing implements and a couple of unrolled documents, as if the owner had been interrupted in his work. And this is how Romans live, I concluded.

The two boys were speaking, both at the same time, and the man had to quieten them down with a firm tone. He turned to me.

"Welcome to our house, Master Marcus. I am happy to have you in our home as a friend and playmate for my sons." He spoke in British, a clipped and clear accent. The woman said nothing, but she smiled in a friendly manner. I assumed she was the boys' mother. The man gave a discreet signal to Nikos, and he ushered us out of the room.

That was my first meeting with Publius Julius Ursinus, deputy governor of the province of Britannia Prima – governor in practice since no one had arrived to replace the last man when he returned to Rome. In those days, whenever the deputy governor asked for something to be done in the northern region of the province – he never gave orders; that was hardly necessary – it was my father who ensured that it was carried out. Since such matters had always been dealt with promptly and effectively, Publius Julius acknowledged he owed my father a small favour in return, and since it suited them both that I should have a "proper" education, that was the deal they had struck.

With two sentences, we boys and the tutor had been dismissed, and we returned along the corridor with the patterned floor, across the front of the villa again and around the corner at the other end. As we did so, a door opened and two girls peered out, dark-haired and dark-eyed. I had learned that Gaius and Lucius had two sisters, Ophelia, tall and slim, and her younger sister, Hypatia. I was introduced, and Nikos whispered a few words, at which the two girls laughed and retreated behind the door.

"We'll see them at dinner," said Gaius, "but they don't study with us."

"And they certainly don't learn to fight with swords like us," added Lucius.

Once I started to settle in, I began to build up a clearer picture of my new home. As I had seen when I arrived, the villa was made up of three wings, each of two storeys, constructed of stone and brick. We children kept to the east wing where we had our schoolrooms, separately for the boys and girls, and a small dining room. Above were the bedrooms, with the boys' room at the far end. On the opposite side of the garden was the west wing, where we had first met Publius Julius. This was the most luxurious part of the house and we children rarely went there. Aside from Publius Julius' study, there were rooms for meeting guests and dining. They were lavishly decorated, with fine mosaic floors and beautiful paintings on the walls. Joining the two wings were the rooms that the deputy governor and his wife occupied, the steward's office and the estate treasury.

Behind the villa were two yards, the main yard containing the stables, the milking parlour, the weaving shed, the dairy and the kitchens. In the corner, there was a tower from which you could see the entire valley. Beyond the east wing was another yard surrounded by buildings: barns and workshops, used for activities best kept away from the house for fear of fire or unpleasant smells: the bakehouse, the smithy and the slaughterhouse. A colonnaded path led down the hill to a bathhouse.

Nikos taught us reading and writing in Latin and Greek, rhetoric and poetry, as well as arithmetic and geometry. Of course, Lucius and especially Gaius were already well ahead in these studies compared to me. However, they did not show off or bully me on that account. Far from it. Gaius was kindness itself and often helped me with my lessons, parsing grammar and making sure my verse scanned properly when Nikos challenged us to write poetry. We read Homer in Greek and Virgil in Latin, and we soon knew more about the history and habits of the Greeks and Romans than we did about those of our own province, whose inhabitants had been so careless not to describe themselves in writing. It did not strike us as strange when Britannia was mentioned by Caesar, Tacitus or other writers, and their descriptions bore no resemblance to what we could see with our own eyes. Somehow these masters perceived wonders invisible to us.

We rarely crossed paths with the girls. The books we used contained all sorts of material unsuitable for young ladies. As Lucius had correctly pointed out on the first day, they were not taught to fight with swords or spears, to run or lift weights. Instead they spent the afternoon in the weaving shed, spinning or learning embroidery and sewing. We sometimes came across them helping in the kitchen, the dairy or the bakehouse, but we did not stay long.

The blacksmith was more exciting and told better stories, and no girls were allowed.

We did not see Publius Julius or the children's mother much. They were too busy with their own affairs, governing and entertaining. In the summer they often had guests at the villa. The dining room would be lit up with candles and oil lamps, and filled with loud talking and laughter, and music would echo around the garden. I would sit in the shadow of the colonnade and watch the figures on the other side. As Gaius grew older, he was sometimes invited to join these gatherings. I assumed that it would be an exciting experience, but he reported back that the parties were exceedingly boring. Nobody took any notice of him. On the rare occasions when he was invited to speak, it was to recite poetry from memory for the entertainment of the visitors.

Now and then, the guests brought their children with them, and these were lodged with us in the east wing. Great care was taken to arrange a children's version of the dinner being enjoyed by the adults across the garden – girls and boys together – with the intention that Gaius and Lucius, and Ophelia and Hypatia, would become acquainted with the sons and daughters of friends and relatives who were potential marriage partners. Whether I was included in those plans is unclear to this day. However, my participation was not without consequences.

One afternoon in particular, Gaius, Lucius and I returned to the villa after an expedition in the fields in the company of Nikos. We had been translating the *Eclogues*, and our tutor felt that rustic surroundings might stimulate our imaginations. To be honest, the peasants we saw bore little resemblance to those described by Virgil, perhaps because we were living in an all-too-real Britannia rather than an idealised Arcadia, and our peasants were genuine field workers and not princes and princesses in disguise. Nonetheless, we had spent an enjoyable afternoon throwing sticks and chasing rabbits, and perhaps a little Latin had sunk in. I still recall that afternoon whenever I open the *Eclogues*. The associations that come to mind are less than bucolic.

As we came out of the entrance hall and turned towards the east wing, laughing amongst ourselves, we noticed a pair of strange boys sitting in the garden. The larger of the two had his nose in a book, and only his pudgy neck and carefully parted hair were visible. The younger sat on the ground at his feet, idly throwing small stones into the fountain. We stopped in our tracks and stared. Nikos was the first to react, and he stepped down into the garden to greet them.

The elder boy looked up from his book at the sound of the tutor's voice.

"I am Vitellus Astrebanus," he said in flawless Latin, "and this is my brother Drusus." The younger boy flung a last stone into the pool and stood up, brushing dirt from his tunic.

I perceived a certain stiffness come over Gaius. Usually he would rush over and welcome any newcomer to the villa. He was the son of the master, of course, and it was part of his upbringing to be hospitable to guests. In this case, however, I quickly saw that there was no sign of welcome.

"Master Gaius, Lucius, come and greet our visitors," said Nikos. Gaius stepped forward stiffly and held out his hand in greeting. The other clasped it briefly, and the two exchanged cold glances.

Nikos waved me over.

"This is Master Marcus Silvanus, a friend of the family."

I held out my hand, but the pudgy boy merely bowed his head in acknowledgement. The younger one, however, had fewer inhibitions, and he came up to me, looked me straight in the face and took my hand in his.

"My father has business with yours," said Vitellus Astrebanus addressing Gaius and ignoring the rest of us. "I suppose we will be staying a few days. Really we should have gone to Londinium, but my aunt is sick."

"She's having a baby," said Drusus, and Lucius and I laughed. Gaius did not, merely giving Vitellus an ugly look.

"You must be thirsty," said Nikos hurriedly. "We are. Let me call for water."

The next two days were amongst the most uncomfortable I spent at Verdaris. Lucius and I got on well enough with Drusus, but there was an air of implicit hostility between Gaius and Vitellus Astrebanus.

"I hate him, and I hate his father," said Gaius one evening after the Astrebani boys had retired to their room for the night. I was surprised, as he generally had kind words for everyone.

"Why?" I asked.

He looked at me for a moment, as if searching for an adequate explanation.

"I don't know," he said at last. "I just know his father is chief of the Durovenes, and our father is chief of the Dumantes. I know he lives on the Agridurnum estate and has friends in Londinium and Camulodunum. It's obvious he sees us as country people, even though our father is governor and not his. Isn't that enough to hate someone?"

For a boy of his age, maybe it was.

"What is so special about the Agridurnum estate?" I asked.

Gaius frowned. "It's supposed to be the richest estate in Britannia."

"It can't be as good as Verdaris," observed Lucius, sounding defiant. Gaius looked at him with a sad expression but did not reply.

"Drusus seems pleasant enough," I observed, feeling the irritation.

"He's a little brother. This doesn't involve him," said Gaius. We left it at that, and the following afternoon the Astrebani, father and sons, had departed as abruptly as they had arrived.

Around that time there were many visitors to the villa, alone or in family groups. Years later, for example, Milesia Cornelia told me she had visited Verdaris as a child, although I did not remember her.

"I saw you sitting quietly, observing everyone," she said, "but you didn't notice me watching you."

I suppose I had been nine or ten years old at the time, and a girl of eight had not been worth my attention. You cannot blame me for my mistake.

The nearby town of Corinium was the provincial capital where the governor and his administration had their offices and where the council met. Gaius, Lucius and I were expected to attend these meetings on occasions, in the company of Nikos. The centre of administration was located on the west side of the forum in the public basilica. The other three sides of the forum were made up of shops and the offices of various merchants. The basilica was a large columned hall with a raised platform in a rounded apse at one end. On festival days the raised platform was used for speeches, or musicians and dancers passing through town could put on shows there. A range of rooms on the far side was occupied by the provincial administration, officials and their scribes and clerks. The largest of the rooms was the council chamber.

"One day you will have to speak in the chamber," said Nikos. "It's important that we visit Corinium to listen to the proceedings of the council and learn about the weighty matters discussed there."

Since we only visited on special occasions, I suppose we saw the best side of the council, although even that was not particularly exciting for impatient youths. We sat on the very back bench in the furthest corner and barely understood what was being discussed. I was not impressed by the attendees or their rhetoric. The seats around the chamber were filled with fat merchants from the town and landowners from around the province, some obviously rural and others, I guessed, wearing the smartest and latest fashions from the mainland. The most striking figure was probably the Christian bishop, but only because he wore curious, embroidered robes. They may as well have been Pliny the Elder or Cato Senior from our schoolbooks as people who were making decisions which would affect our everyday lives.

On one visit we were walking from the Ursinus town house towards the forum when we heard a commotion in the street. I was astonished to see my father riding into town at the head of a delegation from the north. To my surprise, I recognised some of the landowners whom I had seen visiting him at home. Behind them came half a dozen armed men. I spotted Dell and Carr amongst them. I remember how tough they looked compared to the townspeople. My father's clothes might be plain, but they were tidy and well made, not fashionable and luxurious but not foolishly rustic either. When we saw him in the council chamber, he stood solidly and looked people in the eye. I noted the governor gave him time to speak, and his voice filled the room, not stiff and pompous, as I had feared, but clear and decisive. I saw the landowners and merchants, even those I did not know, listening to him, paying attention, nodding in agreement. And when, after a great deal of heated discussion in the chamber, we watched as they left town, their horses carried saddlebags filled with coin and silver to be used in the ever-niggling conflicts with the Welsh. From the snippets I could follow, it was evident that the southerners of the province had concluded it was better that my father and his friends were paid to deal with the irritating bandits from the hills rather than allowing them to disturb the peace and their prosperity, even if it hit them in their money bags.

I never thought of my father in quite the same way after that day. He might be sweaty and tired, gruff or joking at home, but seeing him in the council chamber I began to understand how a man who got things done for the governor had to look, sound and behave. I began to grasp why I had been sent to Publius Julius Ursinus to learn to think and act like a Roman.

„ Chapter 3 ‟

Ophelia was the first of the children to leave Verdaris. She was the daughter of an important man and had to accept that her future would be decided by her parents. She was to marry the son of a rich landowner in Britannia Superior. Packed onto a cart decorated with greenery and blossoms, together with her clothes and favourite possessions and accompanied by her father, mother, Gaius and a train of servants, she set off to her new home. I thought I saw a tear in her eye as she looked back towards the villa. I had never had much to do with her, and though the east wing was quieter and felt emptier without her, I did not miss her or think much about where she had gone or dwell on what had happened to her. When Gaius was sent to London, to one of Publius Julius' lawyer friends to train for that profession and prepare for the time when he would take over his father's position, it was another matter. There was even talk of sending him to Rome for a final polishing. There were real tears in my eyes and in his when he left, and I felt that part of me left with him.

Three of us remained: Lucius, Hypatia and I. Of necessity, we were thrown more closely together since we were roughly the same age. Hypatia started to join us in the classroom, and with Nikos being careful which subjects he took up, she studied alongside us. By then, I had been seven years in the household of Publius Julius. I was no longer a child, and it was time for me, too, to end my schooldays and begin my adult life. My father had already warned me that he would need me at home at harvest time, and as the summer came to an end, one day Ryn rode into the yard at Verdaris with a spare horse. I packed up my few belongings, bade a formal farewell to Publius Julius and, with a wave to Lucius, Hypatia and Nikos, left, I thought, never to return.

The winter after I came home from Verdaris was the first time my father opened up to me about his worries with the Welsh.

"This can't continue," he said. "We are spending more and more time and money on trying to keep them out, and the situation is only getting worse."

He stared into the fire.

"There must be a better way," he continued, more to himself than to me. "We should be friends and neighbours, not enemies."

Once the winter had lifted, the snow had melted from the mountains and fresh grass had started to spring up, the Welsh began their raids again. Our farm and our tenants were not spared, and as my father had feared, both sides had become more desperate. Many of the farmers had become defensive and hesitated long before letting out their cattle, often bringing them back into their yards at night. In response, the Welsh grew increasingly bold and attacked the farms themselves. One day my father returned from a meeting with his neighbours with a sorrowful look on his face.

"It's going too far, Marcus. Two nights ago, they attacked Yrso's farm. They didn't just drive off his cattle, but they robbed the farmhouse and carried off his wife and daughters too."

"What happened to Yrso?" I asked.

"Dead," said my father.

"What's next? Are we going to take retribution?"

"Vengeance, Marcus," said my father, "is a fool's way. It will only lead to more killing. I've been thinking all winter and I have an idea, but I must persuade the council to go along with me. In seven days we'll have a council meeting in Walcastrum, and this time you must come with me."

Walcastrum, our local town, had been founded as a military camp where the north–south road crossed a bridge over the River Wal on its way to Deva Victrix. Over the years a small town had grown up around the camp, and it proved a convenient meeting place for local landowners and farmers to bring their produce to market and discuss the business of the day. A small basilica was built, and as the province prospered these informal meetings had been formalised and a local council had been established. My father, and his father before him, had been leaders of this council, and with that came the responsibility of relaying the concerns of the northern part of the province to the governor and his officials in Corinium.

I had to sit at the front of the council chamber alongside my father. I was expected to keep silent, but I was at least treated respectfully by the other members instead of ignored, as we had been in Corinium. My father spoke, reviewing the raids so far that spring.

"I'm sure many of you – just like my son – would like to take revenge, to ride up into the hills and take a life for that of Yrso, and perhaps several more as a warning, to take women in recompense for Katha and the children. But where will it end, my friends? You know as well as I do. One week, two weeks or perhaps a month will pass, and where there were twenty Welshmen, there will now be fifty or one hundred, and where one farm was robbed and burned, ten or twenty will suffer that fate until the whole border is laid waste. I can't allow it. We pride ourselves on being better people, civilised, reasoning and thoughtful. In some cases, even Christian."

"We're not going to turn the other cheek, are we?" came a voice from amongst the audience. Others growled in agreement.

"I did not say that," my father emphasised, "although there may be wise men who say we should, in the interest of keeping the peace."

"It'll just encourage them if we do nothing," came another voice.

"I'm not proposing to do nothing."

"Well what are you proposing? Get to the point, Annius."

"More money from Corinium?" asked someone.

"Forget it," said another.

"All the money in Corinium won't solve this problem," said my father, "not least because I don't think they have any for us."

"Where are our taxes going, then? To the hidden world, to Hel?"

"Let's put that aside, friends, and consider that we must solve this problem ourselves."

"You already said that," came another voice, tinged with frustration.

"Gentlemen!" Gallius stood up. "Let Annius have his say. I've heard his proposal, and I think it's a good one."

"Let's hear it, then!"

"I propose we speak to the Prince of Gwent and ask his assistance in bringing his countrymen, his subjects - at least nominally - to heel."

There was a half-stifled gasp in the room.

"Friends," said my father. "It isn't long ago that this border was at peace. The Welsh were simply another tribe, like the Durovenes. We did business with them. We lived in peace with them."

"Since when did we live in peace with the Durovenes? If it hadn't been for the Romans, we would have been at each other's throats long ago," muttered the man behind me. Perhaps my father did not hear him. If he did, he ignored the comment.

"Some of you in this room even have Welsh mothers and grandmothers. Don't forget that," he continued.

There were more interruptions.

"The legions always knew how to deal with troublemakers."

"That was in the time of the old prince, not this fool they have on the throne now."

"I know," said my father. "Prince Owain has been a grave disappointment, but I've heard he is sick, probably dying, and his son Dewi is a strong and determined young man. This is an opportunity for a fresh start, and with our support the new prince could put an end to this trouble."

"With our money, you mean."

"Yes," said my father, "with our money, if necessary. Or would you rather spend it ransoming your wife?"

There were a few rough laughs around the room. I was not sure what they found amusing in my father's question.

"I have something else to say," he went on. "I have listened to the talk in Corinium, and there has been little good news lately. Pirates attacking the east coast again, even over-wintering in Britannia Superior. Some unscrupulous individuals appear to be employing them to further their own interests."

"That's not our problem," grumbled Nautius this time. "The citizens in Britannia Superior have brought it on themselves. As for the legions, there has been no sign of them in Britannia Prima for years. We've had to get by without them. Let the people of Britannia Superior do the same. In any case, from all that I have heard, they've been nothing but trouble. They obey no one but their generals, and hardly even them."

"Not our problem today, perhaps, but what about tomorrow? What about the day when Saxons come pouring through the woods from the east and Welshmen down from the hills to the west?"

"That will never happen."

My father turned to me. "Marcus, you were in the governor's house last year. You were at the council. What did you hear?"

I was caught out by his question. I tried to think. I had not been worrying about politics then, only about doing my lessons. Then I remembered a rumour I had heard.

"Con... Ger... somebody or other... I don't remember his name. Maybe there was more than one. He thinks he should be emperor, could do a better job than the present one," I stammered. "With the help of barbarians. Yes, Father, I heard Publius Julius discussing it with one of his Londinium friends."

"And what was their reaction?"

"I don't know," I stuttered. "They saw me listening and changed the subject."

Gallius stood up again and turned to face the council members.

"Friends, I don't see that there's any harm in talking to this new prince in Gwent. At the very least we can suggest a meeting."

There were murmurs of "We want action, not talk!", "Give peace a chance!" and such like, but enough men in the council were willing to listen to my father. The opposition voices died down, and he and Gallius were authorised to write to the Welsh prince.

I complained to my father on the way home.

"I felt embarrassed," I said, "when you suddenly asked me to speak in the council. I wasn't expecting it."

"I didn't mean to embarrass you," he replied, "but you should expect it. Remember, Marcus, you've had an education and exposure to the world that no one else in the northern council has had. You need to be able to use it."

"But how was I supposed to guess what you would ask?"

"Think about what happened, and don't get caught out again."

I do not know what was in the letter, but it was obviously well timed and sufficiently well baited. We received a reply confirming that the old prince had indeed died. His son, Dewi ap Owain, now claimed sovereignty over the areas where the cattle thieves lived and operated. He would be happy to receive a delegation from his neighbours. There was a flurry of activity around Umbrosa as my father struggled to assemble men with sufficient status to impress the new Welsh leader without appearing to bully him and without costing too much in terms of gifts and expenses. Above all, we could not suggest the Romans were making a return.

On the way into Wales, I found myself riding beside a young farm hand, tall, well built, with a broad smile and red hair and a curious accent to his voice. I did not recall him as one of the boys I had known before I left for Verdaris.

"I've seen you involved in a couple of pursuits this spring," I said, by way of opening the conversation.

"My master has been raided twice already," he replied.

"Your master?"

"Rollfus."

"You don't sound as if you are from these parts?"

"No," he replied, "I'm a North Briton, you could say. My mother and father were killed by Irish pirates when I was a boy. My brother and I barely escaped with our lives. We fled south, hoping for a better life."

"And did you find one?"

"Now we have. We were cold and hungry when we came into town, into Walcastrum. An old lady saw us begging in the street and took care of us. She's passed now. Rollfus' aunt."

"I remember her," I said. "She was a kind-hearted woman, so Mother always said."

"She was. When Rollfus came to the market a couple of weeks later, she persuaded him to take us on as farm hands."

"It was a good decision, I think." I smiled at him. "I've noticed you can handle a sword, too."

"The way the world's going, we all need to. I always think that it's a pity my dad was not a better fighter."

"I don't see your brother with us?"

He laughed good-humouredly.

"We rolled dice to see which of us would come, and I won."

"Your brother stayed at home?"

"I think he has his eye on Ulla, Rollfus' daughter. I think he fixed the dice so he could have a few weeks to work on her while her father's away and so's his own nosey little brother. I'm Cull, by the way."

"Marcus," I said.

"Ah, the chief's son, am I right?"

"For what it's worth," I said.

We took the old Roman road, crossing the River Flowen and passing into the territory of the Welsh.

"Is your father expecting a hostile reaction?" asked Cull as we rode along. He pointed up the road.

"I suppose there's always a risk that a hot-headed local might mistake us for a threat," I replied, straining my eyes in the same direction.

"Look ahead," said Cull. "Who are they?"

Half a dozen soldiers on ponies were trotting along the road towards us. Their pace suggested no threat, and as they approached we could see their swords were sheathed.

"They seem smartly dressed and organised," observed Cull.

"Let's hope they can find somewhere for us to sleep for the night."

"It'll be our own beef we're eating for dinner, no doubt," added my new friend with a laugh.

The princes of Gwent had taken over an abandoned Roman army camp and made it their home. While the Welsh had never accepted the Romans, never submitted to Roman rule, they were not slow to exploit them, even after they had gone. The old camp was an excellent fort surrounded by stone walls, and Prince Dewi or his ancestors had converted the commandant's house into a comfortable hall. The whole edifice had an air of organisation and self-sufficiency, leaving no doubt in our mind that Dewi ap Owain was a prince who knew his business.

Based on this first impression, I had expected the prince to be a grizzled old rogue, but to my surprise he turned out to be only a little older than I was, with a young wife and two sons: a boy of about four named Owain and a baby, Merwyn.

Cull and I were far back in the party, but we could hear him greeting my father and Gallius.

"Welcome, welcome, my friends. I'm so sorry that it's taken such troublesome business to bring you here."

I could see the leaders clasping each other in embraces with the best will in the world.

"My father, God rest his soul," continued the prince, "suffered a long sickness, and these brigands have been taking advantage. While he was still alive, there was little I could do without appearing to anticipate his death." I saw my father nod gravely in agreement. That would have been most unsuitable.

The prince led the way into his hall. We followed, the prince speaking all the time.

"But now you are here, and we can be friends. Chief Annius, Chief Gallius, I am sure you can help me bring an end to this anarchy, and it will be a benefit to everyone."

As is so often the case, the help involved the exchange of gold and silver. I was not present for all the discussion but was delegated to wrestling matches and hunting with Dewi's entourage. Both sides took care to divide the success in these sports on an equal basis.

Later in the day I found my father and Gallius pacing the former exercise grounds of the legionaries.

"We will pay him a subsidy," said my father, bringing me into the conversation.

"He promised to use the money to hold back the mountain men who are responsible for the raiding, by bribes or by force," added Gallius.

"The warriors I have wrestled today seemed quite ready to use force," I noted.

"You're right, Marcus. I'm glad we didn't choose to make an enemy of Prince Dewi," said my father.

The visit was ended with a feast. The eating and drinking were accompanied by interminable harp playing and songs detailing the lives and deeds of Prince Dewi's ancestors back into the legendary past. Towards the end I was surprised when the prince caught my eye and, a glass of wine in his hand, called out and offered a toast.

"Master Marcus," he greeted me. I was slightly taken aback to be addressed at all in front of my father and Gallius. What was behind his smile? Diplomacy, flattery, some unknown Welsh custom, or was he simply playing the devil?

"Your name came up in our discussion today."

I could not help frowning, feeling embarrassed.

"I heard you'll soon be in need of a wife."

I must have betrayed my surprise.

"Don't look so shocked. You're a handsome young man, and before long you must start a family of your own. My sister, for example…" He pointed across the room to a dark-haired young woman sitting at the table opposite. "Unfortunately for you, she's already promised to Prince Connor of the Kavanaghs. She'll be away over the sea to Hibernia before the winter gales set in, otherwise…"

He looked thoughtful for a moment.

"You have a sister, too?" he asked. I suppose he knew the answer already.

"Yes," I replied. "She has just passed ten years."

"A little old for my sons, but some time we should try to find a way to link our families," he continued, glancing at my father. "It's the best way to keep the peace."

He raised his glass to me again and turned to speak to someone else. I suppose another young man might have felt proud at being addressed like this. I felt disconcerted. The Welsh have a reputation for magic, for trickery, for being more in touch with spirits and ghosts, for seeing the future, than we Britons. At least, I reflected, my sister and I had been saved from being offerings for peace on this occasion.

❧ Chapter 4 ☙

The Welsh prince kept his word. The night raiding and stealing died away, and I was impressed by the value of good relations with neighbours. That did not mean we forgot we lived in frontier territory. On the contrary, every farmer and landowner had to supply weapons for his men and ensure they were trained to use them. I was present at the council meeting when my father returned from Corinium after he had informed the provincial leadership of our bargain and asked for support to pay for it. I already knew before he rose to speak that his news would not be good.

"My friends, we will not be getting any assistance from the provincial council," he announced.

The sound of angry voices erupted throughout the chamber as frustration boiled over.

"Why do we have to keep paying taxes to the province?"

"We get nothing in return!"

"How do they expect us to pay bribes to Prince Dewi and to fill their purses?"

"This has gone too far!"

For a moment I saw an expression of doubt cross my father's face as if matters were slipping out of his hands. Then Gallius stood to speak on behalf of the disgruntled voices.

"You've done your best, Annius," he said, "but enough is enough. I suggest we hold back our tax payments this year and wait for the consequences." There was a chorus of cheers.

My father looked disappointed. I knew this was not the course he wanted to take, but I could see his fellow chiefs and landowners were furious. It was useless to protest when they resolved to use the taxation receipts to pay Prince Dewi, and the administration of Britannia Prima could have what was left over. That would not be much.

My father remained silent for much of the journey from Walcastrum to Umbrosa Farm, lost in thought. About a mile from home, he looked across to me, a sad expression on his face.

"I feel trapped, Marcus, between our friends here in the north and my duties to the governor."

He hesitated before going on.

"It seems that we must have a conflict, one way or another. We can't satisfy both the governor and Prince Dewi."

"Do we have to?" I asked. "The prince has kept his word. Our farms and fields are safe, and now we can sleep easily. What does the governor have to offer?"

For a moment a glint of irritation appeared in my father's eyes.

"I thought you would have learned, all the years you spent in his classroom! The Empire and the governor offer a peace far more valuable than quieting a few cattle raiders – *Pax Romana* it used to be called. It's easy to forget how fragile peace is when it's taken for granted."

With those words, he turned his gaze back to the road and lapsed into silence.

Governor Publius Julius Ursinus and his allies could not let the assembly decision pass without a reaction. A tax collector travelled up from Corinium with two clerks and instructions to make new assessments on the principal landowners. My father recognised the man from his visits to the provincial capital and, to oblige him, gave him an opportunity to speak in the assembly. The tax collector pointed out in the strongest possible terms that we had not paid our full taxes.

"We've sent our tax money to Prince Dewi of Gwent," said Gallius, "and he has put it to better use than you ever have."

The tax collector looked strained. I thought he had cunning eyes and a greedy face. His clerks looked pale and nervous. They were just doing their jobs.

"There will be severe consequences if you do not pay in full, I promise," the collector threatened, before calling for his horse.

His bluster led nowhere. In the following year there was no repeat visit, no hint of a new assessment, and so, emboldened, Gallius and his allies once again withheld the tax quota. My father felt ashamed to attend the provincial council. He hesitated to visit Corinium, except when business absolutely required it. When he finally did make the journey, he returned looking gloomy and worried.

"The northern landowners aren't the only ones taking matters into their own hands," he told me. "The merchants of Litorina have refused to hand over their full taxes."

"Why?"

"They heard what we'd done and then excused themselves by saying they needed to improve their defences against pirates."

"Do you think someone is trying to stir up trouble between the north and south?" I asked. "That would be a disaster."

He shook his head.

"I don't think so. The merchants have no tribal loyalties. They are only worried about their money bags."

He took a draught of his ale before continuing. "In any case, the troublemakers have bigger fish to fry. I heard there has been another revolt in the east."

"I heard," I said, "some rumours in Walcastrum, in the market, while you were away."

"They are true. This Constantinus you mentioned in the council," he said, giving me more credit than I deserved, "with more ambition than sense, puffed up by the lawyers and moneylenders in Londinium." He sighed. "I heard that he has proclaimed himself emperor and taken what remains of the legions with him to Gaul."

"Will he succeed?"

My father shrugged.

I could not help asking, "Is that where our tax money has gone, to fund a revolt?"

"Publius Julius promised he wouldn't take sides, but with the legions marching and the moneylenders calling in their debts…" He left the rest unsaid. "People from the east say that barbarians are already taking advantage of the poor defences. That's what has made the merchants so anxious."

"But those places are far away. Gaul, Londinium…"

A pained look crossed my father's face.

"It will be a sad day, my son, when that's all people think. Then the world I've known will have come to an end."

I was always sorry to disappoint my father and especially bitter about that occasion. It was his last journey to Corinium. When the winter weather came early, he was seized by coughing and fever, but he still insisted on riding to a council meeting in Walcastrum. On the journey back the weather took a turn for the worse, and it began to snow heavily. Soaking and freezing, he stumbled home in the middle of the night and took to his bed. His coughing and wheezing grew worse. Despite all the efforts of my mother and the medicine woman, the fever grew stronger and he grew weaker, his breathing shallower, his eyes sunken. On the evening of the third day after his return, he left us.

His death still feels painful today. Even after everything that has happened since, I still feel uncomfortable thinking about it. It seems so unnecessary that he should have driven himself into the grave on such meaningless business. At the time it felt as if a great weight had crushed my family. My mother wept for days, too grief-stricken to take care of the house. I wandered round in a stupor, not knowing where to turn. The household and the farm hands went about their tasks dejected and in tears. A stream of neighbours came to pay their respects, and we managed to hold a dignified ceremony despite the appalling weather. My father's body was cremated and his ashes placed in the family mausoleum beside the road out of Walcastrum, the mausoleum he had ridden by so many times during his life. He was not the only man to die of that disease during the winter, and to our horror my sister developed the same symptoms. We kept her warm and safe, the medicine took hold and to our great joy she recovered. Seeing my sister return to health helped lift us out of our despondency. The world had not come to an end, and as the spring nights became lighter, we pulled ourselves together and began to plan our life without my father.

My father's friends joined us in grieving, paying their respects at the funeral, filling our ears with praise for him as a good man and for his work on behalf of our community. However, not long after, Chief Nautius paid Umbrosa Farm a visit. My mother met him at the threshold, but after a few polite words of condolence, it was clear that he wanted to speak to me.

"Marcus," he said, "I understand this is a difficult time, but unfortunately the world outside does not stand still. Your father is badly missed by the leadership of this province. Gallius and I – and we are not the only ones – look forward to seeing you take on his mantle."

"But I can't do that," I protested. "My father was an experienced man, with many years of service. I'm far too young. I've hardly taken part in the council. Besides, I have the farm and the estate to look after."

Nautius smiled and reached out to me, tapping my arm.

"You're a young man, but we all were once and we've all had to learn, just as your father did. Look around you. Your mother has been running this farm for years while Annius was away on business. Once she has overcome her grief, she'll be glad to do that again. It'll be better for her that she does. Besides, you have excellent servants and tenants to support Mistress Philomena. No, Marcus, you're required in the council more than on the farm."

It felt hard to be told I would not be needed in my own home.

"Besides," he continued, "I'm not suggesting you take on your father's role as leader. Of course, that would be impossible, although there are already some who believe you might have the governor's ear in a way that we provincials do not after all your years in his house," he added.

"Hardly," I said. "We barely exchanged a word."

"Nevertheless, Marcus, I've been speaking to many members of the council. I reckon that the majority are in favour of electing Chief Gallius as our spokesman. He has the wealth and experience to take on that role. But" – he wagged his finger at me – "we expect you to be present at our meeting. We'll be disappointed if you're not."

In our society, the elders and traditions are still respected. Disappointing the other chiefs would have been unacceptable. I duly made my way to Walcastrum along the same road my father had taken on his last journey and, with a heavy heart, took my father's seat in the council chamber. I kept my peace and voted for Gallius as leader.

Chief Gallius was a man of uncertain temper, and what respect he may once have had for the provincial administration and

Governor Ursinus quickly evaporated. Once chosen, he departed to attend the provincial council, but when he returned, his irritation was evident.

"I swear I'll never set foot in Corinium again," he announced to the council. "That thief and robber we call governor refused to recognise my position as your representative until I paid him for the honour."

"I think that has been the custom previously, under the Empire," one of the older members suggested.

"Well, it's going to stop now."

"Perhaps the governor thinks it would be a way to collect the taxes we have withheld," proposed another.

Gallius banged his fist on the table.

"I don't care what that man thinks. I propose we ignore the provincial council entirely. We should uphold our alliance with Prince Dewi and mind our own affairs. The provincial council be damned."

The summer passed, and another winter, and soon it was spring again. A year had gone by since my father died, and while we missed him every day, the farm and the estate continued in the time-honoured manner. Where once my father's word had been final, I had become the head of the household, and the servants and tenants offered their advice and the benefit of their experience to me and expected me to make decisions. The fields, the crops, the horses, cattle and sheep all had their own rhythms which needed to be respected whatever the tragedies and joys that took place in the world of men.

❧ Chapter 5 ☙

In the late spring of the year after my father died, I was surprised to receive a message from Corinium inviting me to attend the provincial council. It was carried by a liveried servant and sealed by Publius Julius Ursinus himself. After I had read it, although I understood the words, I was confused by the implications.

"Why has this message been sent to you and not Chief Gallius?" my mother wondered when I showed the letter to her. "It's true that Annius was the delegate for the north of the province, and his father before him, so of course it should be your post by rights." The assembly had not shared her view, but I was careful not to press the point too hard.

"I know that, Mother," I insisted, "but the governor must realise we have selected Chief Gallius as our representative. He's so much more experienced than I am."

"Perhaps Publius Julius thinks you would be willing to pay the fee that Gallius has declined?" My mother had no high opinion of Gallius and thought him stubborn and provocative.

Gallius was not a man to have as an enemy, and this summons had an air of being a further way to insult him. Even though he had not attended the provincial council for more than a year, I still thought it best to consult with him before accepting the governor's invitation.

If he interpreted the message as offensive, he covered his feelings well.

"Waste of time," he said, looking at the letter. "If you want to trail down to Corinium and spend your days blethering with those fools, you're welcome. I don't plan to pay a *sestertius* to the governor, and I would advise you not to either. His pockets are bottomless, I tell you."

He rested a heavy hand on my shoulder.

"Marcus, no good will come of it," he insisted. "The governor and his cronies have long since ceased to be of any benefit to the north, and they're only asking for tax payments and kickbacks. Maybe if you go instead of me, you can hear them out, but just remember, you've no authority to speak on our behalf and you're not to agree to any additional tax collection."

I had no difficulty in agreeing with Gallius that I would keep a modest profile. Except on special occasions, even my father had usually only taken a couple of retainers. I decided that I would ask Cull and Ryn to ride with me. With such a small retinue, it would be obvious that my attendance was as a modest farmer and not as the leader of a representative delegation.

From Umbrosa it took three days to reach Corinium. We arrived in the evening, passing by the long row of ancient and elaborate family tombs which lined the approaches to the town. Entering through the north gate, we took a room at an inn, the Fox Tavern. It has always been a favourite of visitors from the north. In those days the landlord was a man named Will, who had grown up in Walcastrum, so he knew when conversation would be welcome and when to leave you alone. I think Will's son, or maybe his grandson, keeps it now, although I do not know how he manages to make a living these days.

The provincial council meeting was scheduled to start at noon, so after rising I spent an hour walking around the town. The streets did not seem to be as lively as I recalled from before. Numerous shops were shuttered, and here and there houses had sunk into disrepair. The construction of the new Christian church appeared to have made no further progress. I made my way towards the basilica. Once again, I was surprised. Where the side rooms had been filled with clerks and scribes last time I visited, now they were almost deserted. A single lawyer sat in one office with his clerk. When I enquired, he introduced himself as Aurelius, the city magistrate. The tax collector's office was empty, and in the office of the census, scrolls and documents were scattered about in disorder. Looking at the mess, it was hardly surprising that no one had come to demand taxes from us in the last year.

It had been a long time since I had attended the provincial council in Corinium with Gaius and Lucius and our tutor Nikos. I remembered the packed council chamber and the heated debates. Since then I had heard my father complain many times about the useless discussion, wasteful spending and endless demands from the governor and the Empire. Communications with the council had almost completely ceased since my father's death and Gallius' assumption of the role of leader in the north. I also knew that the relationships between the provincial government and local leaders in other parts of the province had soured, as pleas for money continued but services deteriorated.

In a confused and uneasy state of mind, I made my way to the council chamber. I was anticipating an intense debate. The same half-circle of seats faced a raised dais. They had been packed on those previous occasions, but now they were almost empty. On the left two older gentlemen were sitting together. I recognised them as the merchants Marius and Fabianus with whom my father had had business in earlier times and who had occasionally visited Umbrosa Farm. When they saw me come in, they stood up and called out a greeting.

"Marcus, what a pleasant surprise. We were sorry to hear about your father," began Fabianus. "I'm glad to see you've taken his place on the council. He was always so proud that you were learning alongside Gaius and Lucius Ursinus. Hopefully you'll bring some of that classical education to the chamber."

"But I'm not a member of the council," I stammered. "Chief Gallius is the representative for the north. I'm only here because I was invited by the governor."

A frown creased Fabianus' brow, and he exchanged an almost imperceptible glance with his friend.

"He has his reasons, no doubt," commented Marius quickly. "In any case, we haven't seen Chief Gallius for months, and I suppose Publius Julius wants to hear from the north, even if it's from a young whippersnapper like you." Marius chuckled, and the two merchants patted me on the shoulders.

"Marcus," added Fabianus, "when you see how this council is functioning at the moment, you'll realise that whoever turns up is part of it, no matter their official position. Marius and I are the representatives for Corinium. Do you think that would ever have happened in the old days – a pair of merchants?"

"We're the only ones left with any ready money, Fabianus," muttered Marius with a grimace. "That's why we're on the council. To get soaked."

"Well, let's wait and see who else appears. That gentleman over there, you should go and speak to him, for example."

Fabianus pointed across to the other side of the room towards a burly man, somewhat older than me, dressed in a tunic and heavy cloak. His blond hair was clipped short, and his face was weathered. He appeared to be paying us no attention, but following the advice of my father's friends, I crossed the room to speak to him. He looked up when I came near, a combative expression on his face.

"Hermanus, captain of the auxiliaries. And you?" He spoke in Latin, but with an obviously foreign accent.

I explained who I was and how I had been invited by the governor.

"I invited myself," said the captain brusquely.

At that moment, before we had a chance to speak further, a side door opened and Publius Julius Ursinus strode in. As usual when on official business, he was dressed in a toga and wore a laurel wreath around his head to emphasise his authority. He took a quick look around the room and climbed up to the dais. Once settled there, he gazed around once again in a more careful manner.

"Ten of us, at least that is a quorum – better than last time," he muttered, barely audibly.

Marius raised a hand. "Captain Hermanus is a member of the military. He cannot be included in the council quorum."

"Marcellus sent me an excuse and I do not see any other representatives from Litorina, so the captain must stand in for the town. He is included in the quorum," growled the governor and put an end to that interruption.

I was rather surprised that there were so few people present. There was space for at least forty people on the benches, perhaps even fifty at a squeeze, and I remembered the council chamber being full. Was my memory wrong? Had I been so easily impressed as a schoolboy? Had so few people been the source of all my father's complaints? I expected the doors to open and a crowd of latecomers to surge in.

The governor turned to me.

"I am glad to see that you have been able to come, Marcus. Your father is sorely missed. He was a faithful member of the council, and God knows we need more of those."

I opened my mouth to speak, but the governor had already looked away, so I held my tongue.

Marius spoke up again.

"Laurentius is at sea, Your Excellency. He expressed his regrets."

"Laurentius is always at sea and has avoided paying his dues," grumbled the governor. "Lucius Scipio also sent his regrets, and

Honorius died during the winter. The Astrebani have not had the courtesy to inform me what they intend to do. Soon there will be no one here but me."

"Crusus was killed by pirates last autumn." The soldier, Hermanus, spoke up. "With Laurentius away and Crusus dead, there were no civil representatives from Litorina."

"That's exactly why I counted you in, Captain," said the governor, "and with young Marcus here, that is a quorum, and I think we can turn to business."

With that, an uncomfortable silence fell upon the room. The governor cleared his throat.

"The first item on the agenda is, once again, the poor financial state of our province. We have received no subsidy from the Empire to pay the auxiliaries again. The entire burden will fall on the province, although I think we can agree that the auxiliaries are an imperial responsibility."

"It hardly seems reasonable that the province should take the whole expense," said Marius. "We didn't ask for them to be stationed here."

"You recall, no doubt, that we received a notice from the administration in Rome that we would have to shoulder the burden ourselves. It seems they have bigger problems to deal with," said the governor.

"Still, it seems excessive," a voice echoed from the other side of the chamber. "Especially for those of us who pay our taxes."

"Some people might be paying," said the governor. "Others appear to have decided they know better how to spend the money than this council."

I felt a slight sting aimed at us northerners. I raised my hand. All eyes swivelled towards me.

"I'm sure I can convey a message back to Walcastrum. No one recognises the importance of our military more than we do."

I saw Hermanus look towards me and make a brief bow before addressing the governor.

"We need money for training and maintenance of the weapons so that my men don't have to spend all their time farming and plying trades simply to feed their families. I'm sure you're all aware that in other parts of Britannia unpaid soldiers have turned to robbery to supplement their pay."

"And revolt," I heard the governor mutter.

There were the sounds of throat clearing and coughs from around the room.

"I assure you that my troops are better disciplined, but regular payment would help keep order," the captain continued.

There was silence in reply.

"Very good," said the governor abruptly. "We all agree to a disbursement from the public treasury for payment of the auxiliaries. Let's now turn to the subject of the state of the roads." He began to look around the room until his eyes fell on the man who had spoken up earlier. "Chief Statorius, I believe you had something to say on this subject from the missive you dispatched to me recently?"

Everyone was dependent on efficient transport of their farm produce, so it was easy to agree to put aside tax money to keep up the roads. On the other hand, the Christians would have to fund the building of their church themselves. Other worshippers could do what they could to satisfy their own gods.

"The quantities of corn in public storage are adequate for the subsidies, Your Excellency," reported Fabianus, "which we should be thankful for, given the poor harvest of the last year. There have been no requisitions by the army in recent times, which probably accounts for the surplus." He looked over at the officer. "I think, perhaps, Captain Hermanus, since you have been kind enough to join us today, Master Marius and I could have a word with you before you return south. We may not be able to offer any circuses, but some bread is a distinct possibility."

His attempt at humour was wasted on the few men in the chamber.

No tax money would be sent to Rome, though no one seemed to recognise the irony.

"I don't even see why that item is on the agenda," protested Marius. "I thought that the Empire had cut us off."

"That does not mean we have cut them off," replied the governor firmly.

If we do not send our share to the Empire, I thought, how can we expect anything in return, but I kept my opinion to myself.

With that, the meeting closed and each participant went his own way.

Or at least most did. As I walked back to the inn, I heard steps behind me, and a voice called my name. It was Captain Hermanus. I stopped and waited for him to catch up.

"I'm sorry for my surly behaviour earlier. I really don't like this type of council meeting. I always feel out of place."

I could understand. I felt out of place myself. Why was I having to defend the behaviour of the Walcastrum council when Gallius should be here doing it?

"It seems to be difficult to find representatives for the towns," I observed.

"Nobody's willing to put themselves forward, especially with the fee that the governor expects. I wasn't planning to come myself until I heard that Crusus had been killed. Then I decided it was better that someone from Litorina should attend. Crusus had always been a friend to the military."

"Still, it seems you have been missing out on your share of the corn," I pointed out.

"That was earmarked for the legions, not us. Crusus did his best, but the auxiliaries were always lucky to receive anything at all."

"I thought all the legions had left with General Constantinus?"

He paused for a moment. "Most of the auxiliaries too, but mine and a few other garrisons were left behind. That doesn't mean we have a right to a corn ration. I'm thankful you spoke up on our behalf. It'll put off trouble for a little while if the merchants follow up on their promise."

It seemed to me that Hermanus might doubt his troops' loyalty more than his words in the council had suggested.

"Will you join me for dinner?" I asked. "My friends are waiting for me at the Fox Tavern."

"Gladly! I met your father once or twice," he said, as we walked through the darkening streets, "although I don't think we saw eye to eye. He was always concerned with the defences against the Welsh. My orders were to defend against pirates and sea raiders."

"My father had good reason to worry about the Welsh," I pointed out.

He broke me off. "If you'd seen what I have, you might think differently. My family comes from Germania. My father had a small farm."

"My father had a farm too," I said.

"This was a very small farm," Hermanus emphasised. "I didn't want to grow up being a farmer, so me and my friends, we all joined the auxiliaries. First, we were in Gaul and Hispania and fought the barbarians, then finally we were transferred to Britannia. After the troubles in Gaul, I thought I had come to paradise. How many others do you think there are like me on the mainland who have deserted the legions or the auxiliaries, who are ready to take up arms… for nothing more than their own gain?"

We reached the inn and greeted Cull and Ryn, hungry and ready to dine.

"I've heard that the Empire has given up on Britannia. At least that's what the governor seemed to be saying," continued Hermanus, as we settled to our table.

"I was sent here before all that happened. Now I think they've forgotten about us. We're not the only ones, the auxiliaries stationed in Litorina. There are bands of auxiliaries and retired soldiers abandoned all over the provinces, in the east and the north as well. We've just been left to do the best we can. Nobody here trusts us entirely, but many of my men have British wives. I do myself, and three small children. We have our lives here, too."

Cull raised his beaker and tactfully offered a toast to Hermanus' wife and children.

"I don't think any of the auxiliaries have intended to cause trouble," he continued.

"But I've heard all sort of stories of robbery and rape."

"It's hard to survive when the pay doesn't turn up. If you're the only men with good weapons, who's going to stop you?"

"Your commanders, your good morals?"

"Morals don't put food on your table. I'm not so young, and I've become used to the discipline. Many of my men are younger and more impetuous. When they hear how pirates and brigands are robbing and stealing and living the high life, you must admit, it looks like a tempting alternative to army regulations and short rations."

Fortunately, our own rations arrived at that moment. They were plentiful, and we showed exemplary discipline in applying ourselves to consuming them. After a short silence Hermanus began again.

"For all their talk, merchants like Marius and Fabianus couldn't put up much resistance. They would have to pay us off one way or another. I promise you that it's much better to pay a proper wage and keep the soldiers under orders than allow them to become bandits and have to bribe them not to rob you."

I could believe it. I knew how much it was costing to pacify the Welsh.

"I manage to keep them in line, even when times are tough. I tell them the pirate life might look inviting, but it's usually short and brutal. Much better to be in a safe bed with your girl and little ones, even if you do have to hoe a row of cabbages now and then to make sure there's food on the table."

I could see Cull and Ryn nodding.

"Other than paying their salaries," I asked, "what else could we do to help keep the auxiliaries motivated?"

"If the Christians were better organised and restarted construction of their church," said Hermanus, "then they would need labourers who knew how to build walls. There's no one like a soldier for building walls. It's the first thing you learn in the army: how to dig ditches and put up walls." He laughed for the first time that evening, and we were glad to join in.

We parted on friendly terms and little did I know how important that chat over dinner would be.

Cull and I had intended to leave for home early in the morning, and I had just told Ryn to start readying the horses when a man appeared at the tavern with a message for me. From his uniform I concluded he must one of the governor's servants.

"Master, His Excellency wishes to meet you before you leave."

I made my way through the streets to the Ursinus town house where I had stayed on the occasions during my school days when we had visited Corinium. As boys, we entered and left by the rear gate, but this time I marched up to the front entrance and gave my name. I had expected to have to kick my heels in the anteroom along with a bunch of other petitioners, so I was surprised to be received by an old porter who quickly led me to the governor's private office.

He greeted me warmly when I was shown in.

"Marvellous to see you again, Marcus. I was so saddened to hear of your father's illness. Now that my own boys have left home, the place seems so quiet without you noisy youngsters."

I was slightly perplexed by his friendly tone but tried not to show it in my expression.

"I was happy to be able to attend the council," I said. "I'll pass on a report to Chief Gallius when I return. Hopefully I can persuade him to take a more active role."

"I wouldn't do that," said the governor quickly.

This time I was unable to prevent a quizzical look from passing across my face. He must have noticed it.

"I mean, he has not paid the dues. He is not eligible to attend until he does," said the governor.

"But he's our chosen representative, Your Excellency," I protested.

"Rubbish," said the governor. "Your father always did a first-rate job, and I am sure you could, too. I was impressed by your intervention yesterday. Most mature and judicious, unlike some of our older members, who should show more wisdom and states-manship."

"I'm not sure..." I began.

"I will not hear of it. And do not worry about any dues. Your father paid all the dues necessary with the work he put in over the years. Of course, if you could find a way to make a donation, it would help to smooth matters with the other members."

My father's dedication to his duty had led him out travelling when he was ill and cost him his life, I reflected. That was surely more dues than any son should have to pay.

"I like to have intelligent young men around me, Marcus. You received the best education you could in my household. I feel you are almost a son to me, too."

"I'm very grateful for those kind words, Your Excellency."

"Of course," he continued, almost as if he were not listening, "there is much that needs to be done, and I am sure you are man enough to do it. Bear that in mind."

With that, he bade me farewell and wished me a safe journey.

When I returned to Walcastrum, I reported what I had seen and heard to Gallius. I also reminded him how worried my father had been in recent times.

"Perhaps we shouldn't be so complacent about the lack of support for the administration," I suggested.

"Thank you, Marcus," he said abruptly. "The barley seems to be coming on very well, don't you think?"

❧ Chapter 6 ☙

A month or so later I was surprised to receive another summons from Governor Ursinus, this time to meet him personally, not in his official place of work or even in his town house in Corinium, but at Villa Verdaris. My mother, my sister and I read and re-read the letter, speculating on the implications. I had not visited Verdaris since I had left as a boy. Only very special and important guests were invited to the villa. My father had been one of them, but not even my mother could rationalise how I qualified. This time I did not consult Chief Gallius before I left.

Immediately I rode through the gate of the yard at Verdaris, I had the same peculiar feeling that I had had when I visited Corinium. The villa seemed more eerily quiet than I remembered. The governor had always had servants to attend him and, even at his country estate, a throng of petitioners would be asking for favours. No longer, it seemed. My horse was taken by a single stable boy. I was guided to the governor's study by a carefully uniformed servant, but otherwise there seemed to be curiously few others to be seen.

I had only ever been in the governor's study on one occasion: the very first day I set foot in the villa. I remembered it as a luxurious room, and it still was. There were painted plaster panels on the wall depicting elegant men and women, gods and goddesses. On the floor was a detailed mosaic, and in the middle was a picture of a man, or perhaps a god. Around him trailed vines and grapes, figs and other exotic fruit. The room displayed the plenty and luxury appropriate to Publius Julius Ursinus' heritage, wealth and position. As I took my seat, the servant poured some wine for us both and left.

I examined the governor discreetly but carefully. Although I had met him so recently in Corinium, I had been a little overawed by the occasion and had not paid much attention to his appearance. In his own home, of course, he was not wearing his toga and laurel wreath, and without the uniform he had lost some of his air of authority. He seemed older than I pictured him, his face more worn. His short hair was grey and thinning. Perhaps he had lost weight, too. Once, he had been a somewhat frightening character, stern and strong, the epitome of a stoical aristocrat. Now he had begun to look strained, more of a tired old man.

"Marcus," he began. "As I mentioned when we met before, I am sorry about your father. He was a fine man, a man of honour and a gentleman of the old school. Your family has ancient roots. Your ancestors and my ancestors fought the Romans together, and then when they recognised that further fighting would gain nothing, they made peace, took the best of civilisation from the Romans and made it work for our people. This province has prospered as it never did before thanks to men like your forebears and mine."

His words had an unexpected air of flattery about them.

"Times have been changing, however, and not for the better," he added. "Your father has passed on, and even I am becoming older." He smiled weakly, as if he did not really mean what he said. "As I think you may know, my elder son Gaius has obtained an appointment with the administration of the Empire in Arelate."

I did not know this.

"Your old comrade Lucius had the good fortune to marry the daughter of an important official in Londinium, an old friend of mine. Now Antoninus has been called to Rome, and Lucius and his wife will travel with them. I myself have shouldered the burdens of the governorship and the administration of this province for many years. With my sons leaving, I have decided it is time for me to put these responsibilities aside – for a while, anyway. My wife and I can take the opportunity to visit Rome ourselves. That will open up the chance for a younger man to experience the duties of governing. My decision to travel is firm, but some problems remain, and I have asked you here today to offer you an opportunity to help me."

I was considerably surprised by this short speech. It was astounding enough that a man in the governor's position was telling me he was planning – no, had already decided – to abandon his post and leave the country, even if it was just temporarily, but what had this to do with me?

"I'm sorry to hear it. I hope I can be of help, Your Excellency," was all I could manage to say before he continued.

"Marcus," he said. "You are an intelligent young man, of a good and respected family in this area. You spoke well in the council meeting and showed that you understand the problems facing the province. You know yourself that certain chiefs and landowners have been refusing to pay their taxes, and this has caused difficulties for me and for the administration. When I was young, the legions held the power in this land, and we civilians did as we were told. They took our land when they wanted it, and they took our corn and cattle and horses, but they paid well and gave employment to our poorer people in the fields and workshops. I heard that you took dinner with Captain Hermanus. There are many lesser men than our captain who have let their soldiers turn to robbery, who have colluded with the pirates or who have taken private money to do the business of whoever pays most. Our people need the auxiliaries to stay loyal, and for that we should respect an honourable commander like Hermanus."

He paused for a moment. I was having a little difficulty in following his argument.

"I have told you that I have made my decision to travel, but I must delegate my responsibilities while I am away. Britannia Prima will still need a good man to exercise authority. I have made up my mind to name you as acting provincial governor, my deputy so to speak, in my absence. It is within my power to do so, at least until a new governor is appointed by Rome, should that become necessary. I am sure you see that your honour, your family's honour and the honour of your ancestors gives you no choice but to accept this responsibility. When I have the opportunity, if I hear you have done well, I can argue on your behalf for a permanent appointment."

I hoped my mouth did not gape, but my mind was so blank that anything could have happened. How could I take on such a post? I was hardly the age when I would even be eligible.

"I realise," continued Publius Julius, again without waiting for any response from me, "that you are a young man and probably feel unsure about taking on these responsibilities. I am guessing you consider that there are older, more experienced men who might resent your elevation. Perhaps you are concerned that you will have difficulty in persuading people to follow your instructions, obey your orders."

I suppose I must have nodded. This was exactly what I was thinking. After all, he was having trouble exerting his authority himself. He continued with a half-smile.

"I ask you this. Where were these men last month at the council meeting? Too sick, too far away, too busy with their own affairs, anywhere but taking the responsibility for the province. If there is anyone who feels they have earned this position, then they can petition the emperor and point out your faults and their own competencies. In the meantime, someone has to take charge when I am away."

He took a sip from his wine glass. Mine still stood untouched. If I had tried to take a drink, I would probably have choked.

"Now I come to a more sensitive suggestion, but one I believe will ensure your success. I am proposing that you take my daughter Hypatia as your wife. You have known her for many years. You played together as children, and now she has reached the age of marriage. I must tell you that she does not want to leave this home, and she dislikes the idea of travelling to Rome. I have tried to reassure her, but she insists on remaining. She has heard too many stories of barbarian invaders and shipwrecks from her friends, undoubtedly exaggerated by women's chat. The only way that I can assure her well-being is by allowing her to stay, and if she is to be safe, I must find her a suitable husband. She is an intelligent young woman, Marcus – perhaps too intelligent – and given to excessive contemplation. I believe you would be a suitable husband for her, and you would be a suitable master for this house in my absence. My wife, I am glad to say, agrees with me."

I was stunned. The governor's daughter as a wife, master of the luxurious Villa Verdaris, even if only for a short while. I could feel my heart pounding and my breath catching in my throat. What was he saying? This felt unreal, a dream or more exactly, perhaps, a nightmare.

"Your Excellency, I hardly know what to say," I stuttered foolishly. I do not think he was listening.

"I have two conditions, Marcus, and I do not think you will object to either. I propose to adopt you into my family so that you will take my family name, Ursinus, as your own, following the example of our emperors, no less. Let us not be modest. Unfortunately, honesty and competence are not sufficient for a leader, as they once were. Being a member of my family will provide you with the appropriate social status for the role. Marcus Lucullus Ursinus. It has a certain noble sound to it, don't you think? With that name, no one will interfere with your position. No one will feel they have a better claim as my deputy than my own adopted son. My second condition is that you ensure the profits from this estate continue to me and my family while we are away, after you have deducted reasonable living expenses, of course. I will formulate this condition into a legal document, fairly witnessed by appropriate parties," he added with a generous wave of his hand.

What was I to do? He turned towards me with an oddly expectant expression. I could not just accept the offer in that moment, even if I could see no other choice than to accept.

"Your Excellency," I stammered, "you have made a most wonderful offer to me, a young and immature man, recently fatherless. I'm most honoured and overwhelmed. I hardly know what to say. May I beg of you a short time to put my thoughts in order, at least to talk to my mother, before I give you my answer?"

He gave me a benevolent look. He was a great chief offering one of his minor followers a position of power and influence. He knew it was impossible to decline such a proposal.

For a moment I thought I saw a look of relief pass over his face. It occurred to me that he had been saying something that had been preying on his mind for a long time and that he was comforted to have put his thoughts into words. Having me as a son-in-law might not be the solution he really wanted, but in the circumstances it would be satisfactory. If the worst came to the worst, he was still the governor, still the chief. He could always return, take up his position again and relegate me to subservience. In that event, as his son-in-law, I would just have to do as I was bidden. Now he could afford to appear generous and flexible.

"Of course, Marcus. Your dear mother. Send her my kind regards, by the way. I understand this will mean a big change for you, with a lot of new responsibilities. The province, a large estate and its many tenants and, above all, the duties of a husband to a spirited young woman and perhaps soon a father yourself. As I have told you, my decision concerning my own future has been made, but as yet I have not decided when I will depart and for how long. I think it is only reasonable that you journey home, to the home of your ancestors, and pray at your family shrine for guidance. I will wait for your answer for ten days."

"Thank you, Your Excellency," I said in as humble a tone I could manage. I stood up, shaking. I had to steady myself so as not to knock against the table and spill my glass of wine, still untouched. I bowed low and backed out of the room, not just as a show of humility, but because I did not want to feel Publius Julius' gaze on my back.

I carefully closed the door behind me. I stood motionless, my hand against the wall to help me stay upright and took a couple of deep breaths and tried to calm myself. After a moment I began to feel a little better and set off along the corridor towards the passageway leading to the yard and to escape. Somehow, I had to make it to my horse, get on it and leave without making a fool of myself. However, it was not so easy to escape unnoticed. Just as I passed the door to Marcella's private parlour, it opened and Hypatia stepped out. She must have been waiting. She must have known what her father had been doing.

"Marcus," she said softly, "may we speak before you leave?"

"Of course." I heard my voice emerge as if from another person altogether. She beckoned me into the parlour. We were alone. She sat down on a bench, looking tense and stiff. I did not want to sit beside her. After the conversation with her father, it felt like an unwarranted intimacy, and I searched around for an alternative. Out of the corner of my eye I saw a carved wooden chair, the chair her father often occupied when we were brought in to say goodbye and thank you as children. I hesitated for a moment, and then took it.

"Marcus, I know my father has been talking to you," she began. "We've been arguing about this in the family for months. Gaius has already left, and Lucius is now leaving. My father and mother are getting older, and the position of governor has become more of a strain as the Empire has cut back its support. After the revolt in Londinium… I've seen how tired and anxious he has become. He's always admired Rome, but all his life he has been working on the Empire's behalf here in the province. He would so much like to travel with Gaius and Lucius and see the world before he's too old. He'll go, you know, and if you don't accept the post yourself, he'll have to appoint someone else, someone older, someone selfish and stupid and lacking your sense of responsibility."

She sighed, and her large brown eyes seemed to fix on me.

"But that's not really what I want to say to you, Marcus. Did he tell you I don't want to leave? I'm frightened to leave. I want to stay here. This is my home, here at Verdaris, here in this beautiful countryside, with our friends and neighbours. In Gaul or in Rome I would just be another rich man's girl, prey for any ambitious person, and with these lawless times who knows what could happen? Marcus, I won't go! Do you understand? I'm not going. I'm not old. I'm not tired. I'm not strained. I'm just beginning my life, and I want to lead it here. But that's not the only thing, not even the most important. Marcus, I've always admired you. You're so calm, so intelligent, you speak so well, you're beautiful. Even when we were small, and Ophelia and I played at families, I always wanted you to be my husband. Please, please accept my father's offer. Please come and live here and make Verdaris a home for a family with me."

Tears began to flow down her face, and all the stiffness went out of her body, a sad and lonely girl with a desperate hope for her future. Her dreams had turned into a nightmare, I thought, outside of her control. Anxious and overwhelmed as I was, I had to choose my words very carefully.

"Hypatia, I've always respected you," I said. "I know you are a kind and gentle girl, who has grown into a beautiful young woman. I would not cause you hurt, but I came today not knowing why your father had summoned me or having any inkling of what he has just told me. This has been a complete surprise to me. I almost don't know what to say. My own father is not long in his grave. I've no one to turn to for advice but my mother. Your father has given me ten days to return home to talk to her and to pray before my family shrine and seek the guidance of my ancestors. I have to do that before I can give you an answer."

She straightened slowly up, rubbing her hand across her eyes.

"Your father was an honourable person, Marcus. Your mother is too. They're known throughout the province for their goodness and kindness to everyone, rich and poor. Perhaps your household gods already gave your parents guidance years ago. They sent you here to learn with my brothers so that you could be equal to them, and you are. Better even. I've been praying already, praying to Lord Jesus to look over me and to look over you. Can we pray a moment together for God's help in making the right decision?"

She reached out to me and placed her hand on my forearm. I was unsure how to respond. I was not a practising Christian. As if detecting my hesitation, she slipped off the bench and knelt on the floor, beckoning me to do the same. She took my hands in hers. I felt the warmth flowing through them; what man could resist?

Hypatia bowed her head in silence, and we knelt together, still for a moment. Even though we had exchanged no vows or promises, I felt as if we had been irretrievably joined together by a force greater and mightier than we were.

She let go of my hands and stood up, and so did I. I took a deep breath and put my arms around her. After a moment I kissed her cheek, stepped back, gave a small bow and left the room.

The stable boy fetched my horse. He watched as I mounted, my legs still weak. He must have wondered what had brought me to Verdaris and why I was leaving so quickly in such a state. I let the horse carry me through the gate, down the driveway and a mile along the road until the villa had disappeared from view. Then I dismounted and sat on a rock with my head in my hands for a long while until I felt calmer and stopped trembling.

❧ Chapter 7 ☙

I had not pictured my marriage being arranged like this. I had imagined discussing suitable matches from neighbouring families with my father, young women selected to create the best alliances and then haggling over the dowry. My father had managed his business well, and for a provincial family we were quite wealthy, as my mother was keen to point out.

"Our family is one of the best in the north of the province. You would be a fine match, perhaps even good enough for the mythical Welsh princess that Annius hoped for," she said. "I don't understand what the governor is up to."

"I have been caught up in a bigger game," I replied, "though I think Hypatia's feelings are genuine. I could feel them myself when I held her hands."

"You should never have done that," said my mother.

I had reflected on my behaviour and my feelings in Marcella's parlour on the long ride home. Hypatia had only been a girl when I last saw her. Now she was a woman, changed. It made all the difference.

I deflected my mother's curiosity.

"Publius Julius Ursinus seems to have given his plan some thought," I said. "He took care to invite me down to the council."

"To be inspected," added my mother.

"He looked tired and strained, like a man who had had enough, who did feel it was time to retire," I said. "His sons are successful.

Why shouldn't he take the opportunity to leave while retaining his honour?"

"Men like that never do."

"Plenty of others have attempted worse in recent years, although it's true that most of them have failed and met an ignominious fate."

"I only wish Annius were here to advise you," said my mother, and after a moment added. "She seems a nice girl, from what I've heard."

I have always respected the Christian god. Gods have powers to influence the affairs of the world in ways that suit their purposes, and I assume that the Christian god, and his son Jesus the Christ are no exception. Hypatia had prayed to her god for guidance, and perhaps in his own inscrutable way, he answered her prayer.

On the third day after my return, a horseman trotted into the yard of my parents' house, obviously tired from a long journey. He asked for an urgent audience with me. One of the servants showed him into the study, my father's old study still full of his belongings which I had not yet had the courage to rearrange. To my surprise, the horseman turned out to be Captain Hermanus. I had not seen him or spoken to him since we parted after dinner at the Fox Tavern. I did not realise he knew where I lived, or indeed had any interest in me whatsoever beyond being a potential ally on the council. Looking back, it feels as if he unwittingly took on the role of God's messenger, improbable in form as they often are.

I greeted him as warmly as I could in the circumstances. He was sweaty, and I could see that he was exhausted and probably hungry. I had already dined, but I immediately sent the girl away with an order for food and drink for him.

"Please take a seat," I said.

"I have been sitting all day," he replied. "I would prefer to stand for now." He took the opportunity to stretch his legs and pace back and forth across the room.

I wondered how to start. It seemed banal to ask, "What brings you here?" or "How can I help you?" but I did not have to. The captain watched the maid leave the room to fetch the food and then turned to me.

"I have heard a rumour," he began. "The governor's steward has been in Litorina, asking about shipping, and one of my men was talking to his servant in the stables. He came to me straightaway with some curious information. Is it true? Is it true that the governor is leaving, retiring from his post as governor? Is it true he has asked you to take his place?"

This time my jaw did drop. Had rumours started to spread throughout the province before I had even had time to make my decision? I put my hands to my face and took a sharp intake of breath, letting it out in a sigh.

"Hermanus, I take you to be my friend. I don't think you would have ridden day and night to this end of the province if this wasn't of importance to you, so I'll give you an honest response. I can't answer for Publius Julius. I ask you not to say a word to anyone else. Servants' chatter can easily be dismissed, but chatter by people like you and me is taken seriously. He has told me he plans to travel, probably to Rome, and has asked me to act as his deputy while he is away."

"Gods! And what do you intend to do?"

"I don't think I have any choice but to accept. To be truthful, I don't think I had any choice from the moment the words left his mouth. I don't know when he plans to leave or for how long. I suppose there's some formal process that must be gone through, but he suggested I could stand in for him while he's gone or until the emperor appoints a new governor."

Hermanus stopped pacing and came to a halt in front of me.

"Give me your hand." It was an order, not a request. I held my hand out.

He grasped it and fell to one knee.

"I promise you my loyalty when you become governor, and I'll serve you the best I can. I swear to the gods."

What was I to say in return?

"Bless you and thank you for your support, Captain. I accept, of course, but I'll not be governor myself. I'll only be a stand-in for Publius Julius."

He stood up and suddenly gave me a hug, and a laugh spread over his face.

"The emperor, whoever he is now, won't appoint a new governor. The Empire's finished in these parts. It's you and I who're going to have to deal with this business, and perhaps the others who care enough to show up to the council. Publius Julius knows that. I saw it in his eyes at the last meeting. Four members present and a couple of ruffians like us – the Empire has dissolved in front of him."

My mother came in with the food, a smile on her face but a look of concern in her eyes, curious to see this stranger. It had been many years since a military man of Hermanus' rank had set foot in the house. The captain turned to her with a look of gratitude.

"My lady, thank you! Let me at that food and drink!" Then he laughed and added, "Thank the gods for mothers… and wives too, Marcus!"

He grinned when he saw the expression on my face. "Don't ever dismiss servants' gossip, Marcus. They often know more about what we're up to than we do ourselves."

About half a mile from Umbrosa Farm, a spring emerges from the hillside and flows down into a still, almost circular, pool surrounded by trees. A few stones mark the place where people long ago came to worship a spirit, I suspect the goddess of the earth, the source of all life. In the days when Umbrosa was my home, many of the country folk went down to that pool to make offerings to the spirit for a good harvest or the safe delivery of a child. I assume they do so even now. The day after Hermanus left, I needed to find a quiet place to think and reflect and, almost without making any conscious decision, made my way along the path through the fields to the old spring. I sat down on the soft grass in a gap between a couple of trees and gazed at the calm pond, my thoughts on the challenges which faced me. I must have been daydreaming because, all of a sudden, I seemed to see an image on the surface of the pool. Three old women were spinning thread. It was clear to the "dream me" that they were spinning the thread of life. As I watched them spin, one of the women contrived to make a knot in her thread, while the other two went on spinning and twisting the yarn together unperturbed. As they worked, the knot disappeared amongst the newly spun yarn, out of sight but still present. Then the vision dissolved as the wind ruffled the surface of the water. As my mind cleared, I recognised that I could never anticipate all the tangles in the thread of life. I could only live the fate that had been spun for me and accept it, knots and all.

I had not brought a specific gift for the spirit, but I realised I had my purse and keys attached to my belt. I opened the drawstring of the purse and pulled out a coin. I looked at it for a moment and saw the emperor of the Romans staring back at me. Would I ever hear from him, I wondered? Then, with a flick of my wrist, I tossed the coin into the pond, and he disappeared beneath the surface.

❧ Chapter 8 ☙

Hypatia Ursina and I were married in the dining room at Verdaris. A Christian priest from Londinium presided over the occasion, once he had ascertained that I had been baptised years ago when I was a child, probably in the same pool where I had lobbed the emperor's image just a short time before. I have noted that the Christians are very careful about keeping records.

The dining room was the largest room at Villa Verdaris, and it was as filled with guests as good taste permitted. My marriage was not just a religious ceremony or a domestic celebration but also a political statement. Everyone who was anyone in Britannia Prima had been invited. Chief Gallius had made excuses and stayed away, but my father's friend, Chief Nautius, made the journey from the north. Chief Marcellus travelled up from his estate close to Litorina, and Marius and Fabianus, the merchants from Corinium, and solid local men such as Paulinus Bredonius and even old Sextus Statorius from the eastern marches of the province were present, amongst others. These men and their families were to play important roles in my life, but at the time to me they were just cultivated dignitaries: friends of the governor or old associates of my father. They might be a little suspicious of the governor's motives, but they were happy to celebrate an event linking two notable families. Publius Julius had said nothing publicly about leaving but, as I had heard from Captain Hermanus, rumours – quite accurate rumours – had begun to circulate. The wedding guests may already have been making calculations that the man of the future, whether they liked it or not, would be Marcus Lucullus, the new son-in-law and adopted member of the Ursinus family. However, if they did, they kept it to themselves.

There was also a hint of tribal politics in the guest list. I should have realised, but to tell the truth, I had never paid much thought to tribal matters. Britannia had been a tribal society long before the arrival of the Romans and remained so despite three hundred years of Roman rule. In fact, the Romans had maintained, even encouraged, the tribal system in Britannia. It kept us native inhabitants divided and provided them with opportunities to play off one group against the others. My family belonged to the Dumantes tribe, who had lived in the north of the province of Britannia Prima for as long as anyone could remember, or even weave into stories. Throughout the period of Roman rule, our tribe had always had the dominant position in the province. Even when the governor and his staff had been sent directly from Rome, the tribal chief of the Dumantes had been the Empire's closest local ally. After the recent history of revolts, and the absence of an imperial appointee, that influence had only grown. Publius Julius Ursinus, as chief of the Dumantes, like his father and grandfather before him, had to all intents and purposes become the government. This did not satisfy everyone in the province. The Dumantes were not the only tribe making up Britannia Prima, and tribal rivalries provided a ready pool of resentful men and women. In the south of Britannia Prima, there was a second powerful group, the Durovenes, which included many rich landowners who had long harboured ill feelings towards the Dumantes. Chief Marcellus represented what might be called the accommodating faction, making his presence at my wedding especially welcome.

According to Lucius Ursinus, there was simmering frustration amongst certain important members of the Durovenes that I was rumoured to be stepping into Publius Julius' shoes. There were others who thought it was their turn, especially Vitellus

Astrebanus, who had just succeeded his late father as head of their leading family. I remembered the time I had met him as a child. Vitellus had not attended the provincial council on any of the occasions I had been there and, from what I heard, spent most of his time in Londinium. Naturally, neither he nor any of his fellow Durovenes ever came to the north of the province, not even Chief Marcellus. They valued their skins too much to take that risk. To some extent, I could understand their annoyance. If I am to be honest, Vitellus had a good case he could make. His family were wealthy, and since their estate, Agridurnum, lay on the east side of the province, he had good contacts with Londinium and even Gaul and Belgica. I was well aware that Vitellus had a lawyer's education and friends amongst the leading families in Britannia Superior. There must have been many people, including perhaps Vitellus himself, who thought that he should be marrying Hypatia Ursina. Hypatia hinted as much as an explanation for his absence from the wedding ceremony. On the other hand, Londinium and Camulodunum were regarded with suspicion by many in Britannia Prima, and there were plenty of people glad to see the Durovenes kept in their place. There were enough men and their wives happy to attend my marriage to remove any doubt about the support for my new status.

After the ceremony Hypatia and I travelled up to Umbrosa Farm, almost as far away as you could be from the troubles of the big world. We could focus on the small world of the home and the farm, and on becoming comfortable as a couple. Hypatia may have been dreaming of having me as a husband for years, but I had not imagined that she would be my wife. I had not even been giving much thought to marriage. I had enough on my plate with the death of my father and taking over the family estate.

One day I was lying in bed, staring up at the roof. I must have had a worried expression, because suddenly Hypatia was leaning over me, looking down into my face.

"What's the matter, Marcus?" she asked.

"I don't know. I suppose I'm worried how I'll cope when your father leaves."

She sat up straight on the bed beside me, her legs tucked under her.

"Marcus, we're a team now. We'll do this together." She sighed, unconsciously drawing her hand through her hair and pushing it over her shoulder.

"I know I must seem to be a spoilt rich girl. I can see how hard your mother and sister work to keep this house in order, to keep this farm running. Everything the servants do, they can do just as well. Sometimes I feel ashamed of myself, of my lack of skills, but I promise I'm going to learn."

She looked thoughtful for a moment.

"I already began to realise I might have to adjust when Father began to send his people away, or rather when they left of their own accord. I was just dreading the day when someone who had a really important job left."

"Who do you mean?"

She giggled.

"The milkmaid, or the man who cleaned out the pigs. Suppose they had just upped sticks and gone. Do you think I could have milked the cows or cleaned out the pigs?"

"Did any of them really leave?" I asked, a little anxiously.

"I don't think so."

She gave me a serious look.

"And just in case they do, I'm going to study hard with your sister."

I laughed.

"Well you're definitely too late for your lesson today. Di will have certainly made sure all the cows have been milked by now, while we've been asleep."

"You're cruel," she said, laughing back. "I suppose today I'll have to practise cleaning the pigs instead. All afternoon, up to my ankles… with Ryn." She stopped for a moment. "But seriously, Marcus. Farming is a challenge for me, and soon you're going to have a tough time dealing with the lawyers and politician and merchants."

She pursed her lips, and the laughter disappeared from her face.

"But understand, I know those people. I know how they think. I know their strengths and weaknesses and their family secrets. Mother and I used to hear all the gossip, though Father thought he knew best. Living up here with your cows and sheep, you can't even pretend you know best. You need me, Marcus."

"You're right," I sighed. "I'm quite aware that I don't know any of those people. I know more about Cicero and Augustus, and I have to hope some of that classical education comes in useful."

She looked doubtful for a moment.

"I think you'll do better to trust me than your old books," she said. "Just as I have to rely on you to pick up a shovel and help clean those byres out."

With that, she jumped at me and began to pull me off the bed.

What a difference it made to hear a happy woman's laugh in the house! I saw how Hypatia drew my mother out of her grief with her silly questions about farm life, matters my mother and sister took for granted but which were new to her. What a difference it made to the cook and the housemaids to chat and gossip with their new mistress! They could show off their skills to her, and she was generous with her admiration.

Another hot afternoon, Hypatia and I were sitting on the riverbank in the shade of a willow tree. Nominally we were fishing, but Hypatia was gazing up at the hills on the other side of the valley.

"I don't know anything about Wales," she said. "I don't think anyone at Verdaris or in Corinium cared very much about the Welsh. They seem a lot more important here, when you know they're living so near, up in those hills."

"You can thank my father that we haven't made closer acquaintance with them," I said. "Stealing our cattle, for example."

"Probably it's thanks to your father that nobody in Corinium ever bothered about them very much. He just took care of all that." She looked at me. "Now you're going to have to do it."

"Nautilus already hinted as much," I answered.

"How far do you think it is to the very end of Britannia?" she suddenly asked. "I mean, the North Britons. I know nothing about them. Do they ever come here?"

"They sell us salt," I said.

"But the really wild, really north North Britons."

"You mean wilder than Cull?"

She gave me a sudden, sharp look. "You're right, I should ask him. You just know the theory."

"I know Agrippa once sailed all the way round Britannia, so there must be an end somewhere."

"Book learning again," she said and smiled. "Hey, Marcus, have you ever even been to Litorina, looked out over the sea?"

"No," I admitted.

"Not even when you lived with us?"

"No. We never went much beyond Corinium. I remember Nikos was going to take us to Aquae Sulis one time, but then it rained for several days, so we never went."

"You've never been to Agridurnum either, then."

"No."

"You can't understand the Astrebani until you've been there, just as I don't think I will ever understand the Welsh unless I climb up into those hills. Those people are so rich they don't know what to do with it all" – she looked thoughtful – "except cause trouble. And there are villas like that all along the south, one rich family after another, and I've been a guest in them all."

She looked across at me.

"Perhaps I should have married one of those rich boys."

"Why didn't you?" I asked, trying to sound light-hearted.

"Because they're just like me, and you're not, and that's why I love you. Every day's a fresh start. Let's hope it goes on like this forever. Come and give me a kiss, and then prove to me you can catch fish."

What a difference it made to the tenants to find their wives and daughters cheerful after a visit from the new mistress! They admired her clothes and her hairstyle, and they tried to copy her by adapting their dresses in the Londinium fashion. The men, like Dell and Carr, were pleased that the estate was in good hands. Before long, their master would be the most powerful man in the province. No one promised that gold would fill their pockets as a result, but equally no one would mess with them when their master was governor, and that would make their lives a lot easier.

Do not imagine we spent all our time on bucolic passion. There was time for fun, but there is always work to be done on a farm. Between chores and romance, time passed and still there was no message to tell us when Publius Julius and his family would depart.

"I wish we would hear from Father," Hypatia said, anxiety in her voice. "I'm surprised we haven't. I wrote to Mother, but she hasn't replied."

"Do you think your mother would like to come and visit us here at Umbrosa Farm?"

She looked doubtful.

"I don't think she would be as open-minded about the rural life as I'm trying to be," she said. "That was half the problem, if

I'm honest. She grew up with luxury, and she's used to it. She thought Ophelia and I should do the same. I don't know how she'll manage on the journey all the way to Rome."

She sighed, and I put my arm around her.

"Marcus, I do hope they're all going to be safe. Can I put a little cross amongst your *lares*, so I can offer up a prayer for them?"

"Of course," I said.

"Your ancestors won't be offended?"

"I'm sure they'll be charmed," I said and gave her a sly look. "Though I'll have to go down to the offering pool and throw in a large pot of gold."

"You don't have a large pot of gold, Marcus, so don't fib."

"Do you wish I had?"

"No," she said, with surprising vehemence. "They bring bad luck."

Hypatia was certainly making an effort to adapt to rural life. I think she was beginning to find herself at ease at Umbrosa Farm. It was small but comfortable, and my mother and sister were welcoming. Our people were unfussy and unpretentious. They had been treated kindly all their lives, and they knew how to treat others the same way. In contrast, Villa Verdaris had always been on display to the world. It was a powerful man's home, large and luxuriously decorated. It was built to impress, and in that it certainly succeeded. It had been filled with people who needed to impress and who needed other people to be impressed by them. Publius Julius Ursinus had grown up as the son of the governor and tribal chief, and it came naturally to him to follow in his father's footsteps. Perhaps Publius Julius and his sons needed to be the centre of attention. I wondered if they had decided to abandon the fading traces of the Empire in Britannia and look for new positions over the sea to maintain that flow of admiration, reputation, glamour, luxury. How were Hypatia and I going to fill the space left by Publius Julius and his family? We spent unnecessary time speculating on the risks we might face. Fate and the actions of others made the decision for us. We could have spared our breath.

❧ Chapter 9 ❧

Hypatia and I actually had no more than a few weeks to settle in at Umbrosa, though it seemed much longer. Then, out of the blue, a message arrived imploring us to come to Verdaris as soon as possible. A carrier brought it from Walcastrum, and he left before we could question him.

The message was addressed to Hypatia, and she examined the small roll with a look of surprise.

"Why has Barnulf, the steward's son, written to us, and not my father or even Beinnie, the steward himself? I hope that there's nothing wrong. Father has been so strange recently and Mother so anxious."

"We'll leave at once," I said, seeing the expression on Hypatia's face, "but not alone."

I rode over to Rollfus' farm right away to ask Cull to travel with us while Hypatia and my mother prepared the necessities for the journey. We took the road south with a certain amount of apprehension, but no amount of concern or imagination could have prepared us for what we found.

The great courtyard at Villa Verdaris appeared deserted when we entered. A stable boy cautiously emerged from one of the buildings and took our horses. He only answered our questions with a dumb look and a shake of his head. We were crossing the yard to the house door when a young man stepped out. I did not recognise him, but I felt a startle from Hypatia.

"Mistress Hypatia, Master Marcus, you remember me – Barnulf?" He looked anxiously at Hypatia. "I am the son of your father's steward, Beinnie."

Hypatia gave a nervous response to his bow. He took a deep breath before speaking again, as if he had been preparing for this moment with dread.

"You might wonder why I am greeting you and not my father or your esteemed parents, but I have to tell you that your father and mother left Verdaris three days ago to travel to Londinium," he said in long stream.

"They left without telling us," Hypatia muttered, largely to herself, gripping my arm.

The young man must have heard her.

"I'm sorry to have to tell you this. I wish that you had heard some other way."

He had an anxious look in his eyes. His voice was strained and trembling, and he seemed to be forcing himself to continue a recitation.

"The master informed my father that he would be leaving to visit Master Lucius in Londinium. He told my father to arrange carts to be brought here. The house people were ordered to load the furniture and valuables onto them, as much as they could pile. Five days ago the carters left, and then the master and mistress, your father and mother, followed after. They didn't leave any instructions behind them."

His voice faltered. His gaze dropped.

"My father has fallen ill with worry, and I was left to decide what to do. I thought it best to ask you to come… and you, Master Marcus," he added.

Hypatia's face was ashen.

"Why have my father and mother just disappeared like this without telling me, without leaving a message?"

She tugged at me, pulling me through the door and into the house, seeming to hope we could find something that would tell us more, a letter or one of the house servants with a message. The first thing I noticed was that the household gods remained in their nook, but the Christian cross was no longer amongst them. We walked from room to room. Some appeared untouched, exactly as they had been when we left, but the personal apartments had been stripped bare of furniture, clothes and decorations. Barnulf followed us in silence until Hypatia turned to him with a questioning look.

"The silver and gold were the first to be loaded, mistress," he commented nervously, unsure if that was the answer she was expecting to the question she never asked.

Publius Julius' study was one of the rooms that appeared untouched, at least at first glance. His desk and chairs were still there. Only a few dust marks showed where items had been taken: a small statue, a few books. Even his pen and seal lay where he had last used them. The shelves around the room were tidily stocked, but when I looked carefully, I noticed that there were a couple of places where some scrolls appeared to have been rearranged and left untidy.

We wandered dazed through Hypatia's parents' apartments, through their servants' apartments and through the rooms we had used as children. Everything personal to Publius Julius and Marcella had gone, as if they had decided to leave no trace of themselves. We found nothing from them to tell us why they had left so abruptly or of their future plans. With their personal servants gone, there was no one even to ask.

Hypatia was the first to snap out of the trance.

"Barnulf, is my father's old messenger Sergius still living here?" she suddenly asked.

Barnulf had been deep in his own thoughts and jumped at the sound of her voice.

"I need to check in the village, Mistress Hypatia. Recently the master has been using a messenger from Londinium, a servant of Master Lucius, but I don't think he sent Sergius away. I think he still lives in the village."

"Send someone to find him and bring him here right now. I want to speak to him," she said in a commanding voice.

Sergius was a middle-aged man who had often travelled on business for Publius Julius when I lived at Verdaris. He arrived after a short delay and gave a hesitant salute on seeing his employer's daughter.

"You know the route to Londinium? You are familiar with the city?" These were as much statements as questions, and without waiting for confirmation, Hypatia continued, "You know Lucius' home? The places where my father did business?"

Sergius acknowledged that he did with a silent bow of his head.

"Then, Sergius," said Hypatia, "take a horse from the stable and make your way to Londinium immediately. You must search high and low for my father and find out where he has gone and what he's doing. I don't understand this, and I need to know what's going on."

"Yes, mistress."

"Take whatever money you need," she added, turning to Barnulf, expecting him to deal with the matter. The steward's son left, looking almost relieved to have something to do.

The messenger touched his forehead and departed behind him. As he left, Hypatia turned to me, suddenly angry.

"This is unbelievable. How can they have abandoned me like this?"

I tried my best to comfort her, but it was almost useless. We were both too shocked.

"Something must have pushed him over the edge," she went on, ignoring my soothing words, speaking to herself. "I know he seemed strained, but has he taken leave of his senses?"

"He seemed to enjoy being the governor," I observed, feeling a little foolish. "I always thought it was strange that he was ready to step down in the way he did. Perhaps he knew he was sick and chose not to tell anyone? Perhaps he had premonitions of some terrible fate in dreams or a warning from the gods or a witch or an oracle?" I suggested.

Hypatia looked me straight in the eye.

"Marcus, you are babbling. I was living here with him up until a few weeks ago. I would've known if there was anything like that. My mother would've known, and she would've told me. No, I know there have been problems, but I didn't expect this. Whatever's going on here, they've both chosen to hide it from me, and I don't like it."

I felt it was better to keep quiet for the time being. Publius Julius might not have publicised his plan to leave, but he had not hidden it either. We had known, his friends had known, by now the administrators in Corinium must know, so why disappear suddenly in this peculiar way? Nothing made sense to me.

In the evening we asked Barnulf to call together the remaining servants. They stood, their heads hanging low, in the dining room, the scene of our wedding just a few weeks before.

"You must speak, Marcus. You're a man. You're the master now," whispered Hypatia. "They'll expect it of you."

"But what should I say?"

"What would you say to your own people? What did you say when your father passed away?"

I looked around the room. Some eyes met mine; others avoided my gaze. A few people possibly remembered me as a scrawny schoolboy. Most of them had only seen me briefly at the time of the wedding. What were they thinking, I wondered, as I asked them to continue to do their duties? I said that Hypatia and I would speak to each of them in the coming days to find out their needs, and if there was anything urgent to be done, they were to tell us right away.

For two days we put all our effort into restoring the villa into some form of order. Hypatia spoke to the womenfolk, and I spoke to the men. We asked them to make sure the slaves kept doing their work, the cows were milked, the crops tended. Water needed to be drawn and firewood cut and stacked for the winter. Life must go on.

The first night we slept in a guest room, cold and a little damp. We had left Umbrosa in a hurry, so we had brought hardly any clothes with us. Fortunately for Hypatia, her old rooms were untouched, and many of the personal items she had left behind were still there. My needs were fewer, and I would not have been interested in wearing Publius Julius' finery even if he had left it. By the second day the female members of the household began to be ashamed to see their mistress's husband walking around in stained travelling clothes, and they stitched together a new tunic, jerkin and leggings, so at least I was now dressed like a respectable farmer.

"Marcus," said Hypatia. She was checking the fit of the new clothes when her hands fell to her sides. "We've not been thinking clearly enough."

"What do you mean?"

"We've been in such a desperate hurry to ensure that this house and the estate are in order that we've forgotten about the town house."

I opened my mouth to speak, but she went on.

"That's not all. We've been so worried about our own personal situation that we've forgotten the needs of the province. Since my father is unwell or has been taken by some folly, then you must now step in as governor."

An icy feeling spread down my back. Of course, it was not only the man, Hypatia's father, who had disappeared, but also the governor of the province. What might have happened in Corinium if people had realised Publius Julius had left abruptly in this strange way?

"Who was in charge before, Hypatia, when your father was away?"

"I don't know. Aurelius, the magistrate, is competent, but I must be honest with you, I've not seen my father's usual associates for a long time, long before we were married. I think everyone was biding their time, shunning him, perhaps, or waiting for him to leave the scene."

I was gripped by apprehension. A power vacuum in the province would be a disaster, especially when there were others who would be ready to step in. Could there have been rioting in the streets, murder and looting in Corinium, or was Vitellus Astrebanus already sitting in the governor's office? We had no choice but to leave Verdaris to look after itself.

I called Cull to me to act as the messenger.

"Ride north," I said. "Tell my mother that we are well, but we have to take care of some matters and cannot return immediately."

He nodded.

"Then," I continued, "round up half a dozen of the most trusted men – men like Carr and Ryn – and ride as fast as you can to meet us in Corinium. Tell them they should come fully armed."

Once he had left, we took Barnulf and a couple of the more muscular farm hands to make up a small troop and left for the provincial capital.

As we made our way to Corinium, our fears began to subside a little. On reflection, it was not unusual for the governor to be away from town, and possibly no one had yet noticed that something was amiss. In the summer he often spent weeks at a time at Verdaris, conducting his business from the estate, travelling to the east or visiting family and friends. And besides, since Verdaris was less than a day's ride from Corinium, if there had been serious trouble, the news would probably have reached us already.

Nonetheless, we were relieved to see that life in the provincial capital was continuing as customary when we rode in through the north gate. At the Ursinus town house, there was confusion and a little worry but no chaos. When Hypatia questioned the staff, it soon emerged that the situation was similar there to Verdaris.

"He asked me to order a wagon," said the porter.

"When?"

"About ten days ago. Then everything from the master and mistress's rooms was loaded on."

"Where did it go?"

"To Litorina, mistress." The porter hesitated. "There was something else a little strange, mistress." He looked away, avoiding our gaze. "The master told us to take everything from his office, all the papers, books and records, and pile them in the yard and burn them."

"Did you do that?"

The man looked a little ashamed.

"We did as we were told, my lady."

When we went into Publius Julius' workroom, we saw that the furniture was still there, but everything else had gone – books, papers, decorations, even his personal mementos. We had already been worried about his state of mind. I cannot speak for Hypatia, but now I only felt complete bafflement. We barely needed to exchange words before I left the house with a sinking feeling and set off through the town to the basilica.

As I made my way through the streets, Corinium appeared to be at ease, enjoying a summer evening. The air was warm, and while the town was no longer thriving the way it had been some years ago, the food stalls were still open, and there were people enjoying the setting sun with wine and a meal, the typical habits of town dwellers who had limited cooking space at home. There were children playing in the forum, and some young men were huddled over a board game under the arcade. No one took any notice of the rustic figure slipping into the basilica. Presently, a watchman, an old soldier with a wooden leg, appeared and asked me my business.

"What are you doing here? There ain't no one here at this time of night!"

"I'm looking for Master Aurelius, the magistrate."

"He's gone home long ago. Now clear off!"

"I have urgent business for him. Can you tell me the way to his home?"

He gave me an annoyed glare.

"You can wait for tomorrow. He'll be here then… if he has time for you."

"It's urgent." I wondered what ruse would make him react. "I've come from Verdaris. The governor sent me with a message."

The man gave me a dirty look, but he swallowed my story. Somewhat reluctantly, he gave me the directions, and I made my way through the darkening streets to the lawyer.

Aurelius' servant answered my knock on the outer door, glanced at my clothes and began to close it in my face. I tried the same trick.

"I've come from Verdaris. The governor sent me with a message."

"I've never seen you before."

"The usual guy is sick," I said quickly. "Master sent me instead, since I was delivering some hay in town." It seemed plausible to me, and fortunately it sounded sufficiently truthful to the doorman. He scowled but told me he would go and check if his master had time for me, if I really had such urgent business that I had to disturb him at his dinner. After a short while the man came back.

"You can step inside and wait here in the entry hall. The master will be with you shortly," he stated curtly.

The lawyer himself appeared from inside the house a few moments later, drying his hands on a cloth, dinner evidently finished. For a moment he did not recognise my face, only seeing my rough clothes in the dim light of the house. Then an expression of shock and surprise spread over his face.

"Master Marcus, sir. I… I'm sorry. My man told me there was a farmer waiting to see me."

"I apologise for disturbing you at home, Councillor Aurelius," I began, "but I felt it was urgent that I spoke to you. Hypatia and I have just come from Verdaris. We have discovered that Governor Ursinus and his wife have left for Londinium in some haste, leaving no reason or explanation."

Aurelius frowned.

"We've also found that the governor has emptied his town house," I continued. "He burned the contents of his workroom before he left."

The lawyer's frown deepened.

"I… I was a little concerned that the governor did not seem his normal self – stressed and anxious – in the last couple of months," he mumbled. "That wasn't like him, although I must say, when I think about it, in recent years he had lost some of his… usual poise." He scratched his head and looked at me doubtfully. "He was a powerful man, Master Marcus. I mean, it wouldn't have been wise to ask too many questions, to have pried into his business. I didn't want to antagonise him."

"I think he worked hard at keeping his face," I said to mollify the lawyer. I needed him on my side.

Aurelius shook his head with a bewildered expression.

"You say he left abruptly? I heard talk in the forum of him moving his possessions. I thought he was taking some of his property to Verdaris. To Londinium, you say? That's very curious."

"It's more than curious, Aurelius," I said, somewhat severely. "It's downright disturbing. Hypatia and I have had several days to think about this and to try to sort out the confusion he left behind at home. We're starting to worry he's left the affairs of the province in the same mess. When outsiders hear what has happened, as they inevitably will, there could – there will – be major trouble unless we find out what has happened right away and deal with the situation." My voice rose in a disconcerting mixture of anxiety and anger the more I imagined the scenario.

"What do you want to do?" Aurelius was now starting to sound worried himself.

"Fetch a couple of your trusted men, ones who know how to keep their mouths shut. I suppose as a lawyer you have some. I suggest we go to the basilica and examine the provincial offices immediately."

The evening was cool, but now beads of sweat had appeared on Aurelius' brow. He was a man used to writing and arguing with words, not a man of action, and I could see that he was feeling out of his depth. I was out of my depth too, but I felt I had to act quickly.

Aurelius called back into the house, and a couple of servants were dispatched into the gloom. We paced about, saying little, until footsteps returned, signalling the arrival of two of Aurelius' most trusted clerks. He introduced them: Flavius and Theo. The four of us set off for the basilica through the gloom, the clerks carrying blazing torches.

By now the forum had emptied out except for a few wine drinkers who recognised Aurelius as he passed by and called out some jokes about working late. We went into the basilica, dismissing the watchman as he stumped up. We strode down the interior aisle, our voices hushed, our footsteps echoing through the empty building, past the rooms of the town scribes to the provincial offices. Last time I had been here, the census office had been unoccupied, though I had seen it was filled with the records, even if some loose scrolls had been left lying around. When we looked in this time, the shelves had been cleaned out. The scrolls had gone.

"Had you not seen this, Aurelius?" I asked.

He shook his head, admitting that he had not been paying attention to the census office recently. "There's been no one working in these rooms since last autumn."

"But this must have been cleaned out recently?" I said. "I'm sure the records were here when I attended the council meeting in the spring. The room was a mess, but it was still full of documents. Surely those were the census records for the province, and now they've vanished."

"I know. I'm sorry," muttered Aurelius. "I haven't seen the treasurer, Tullianus, for months. I suppose someone must have been here recently during the night."

I sighed. On the few occasions I had met Aurelius previously, he had appeared to be a competent administrator, but now he seemed to have been blind to what was going on around him. We sent one of the clerks to fetch the watchman back. In a short while he returned, almost dragging the watchman behind him.

"Do you know who this is?" Aurelius asked the watchman, recovering a little of his composure. The unfortunate man played stupid, hardly surprising given the way he had greeted me earlier. He only shook his head.

"This is Marcus Lucullus, the son-in-law of His Excellency Governor Ursinus. He is the new deputy governor while the governor is away."

The watchman looked doubtful, cringed and bowed his head. "I'm sorry, master. I thought you were just a lost countryman."

You're not far from the truth, I thought and then raised my voice. "Now, tell me, have there been men in this office during the night?" The watchman was wary, hesitant.

"The governor said I was to tell no one," he mumbled.

"Do you know who they were?" The man shook his head silently, his eyes on the ground.

"Very well, you can go without telling us more," I said, satisfied. "Continue with your duties."

I turned to Aurelius. "It's obvious that the governor was involved. It doesn't matter who specifically cleaned the place out. We can assume they were acting on his orders. I suppose we'd better check the other offices."

The tax collector's office was similarly empty, and when we came to the governor's office, it had been cleared out too. As we surveyed the corridor, it was evident that almost all documentation relating to the provincial government had gone: the correspondence, the tax records, the census records, charters and grants, who owed money and who money was owed to.

"My records are still here," said Aurelius with a sigh, perhaps fishing for a little approval. "The results of recent lawsuits, marriage records, and so on."

That was something to cling to, I supposed, my heart sinking because the rest could only be considered a disaster. Could the public records have all been burned like Publius Julius' personal records? If so, we had serious problems.

At that moment the watchman came limping back, bowing and touching his forehead.

"Master, I just remembered."

I felt ready to strike the man, to take out my frustration, anger and, to be honest, fear on him, but I managed to restrain myself.

He snivelled slightly and still would not meet my gaze.

"In the stable yard behind the basilica, they left some large chests. I suppose they were going to come back for them, like they did the others, but they never did." He waved his hands aimlessly. "They're just by my room. I could show you if you want."

Of course we wanted to see the chests, although how much would be visible in the pitch black of the stable yard was open to question. We followed him through the empty basilica and went out into the night to the back of the building. There was a small yard containing a couple of lodgings – one of which was the watchman's home – a stable and a set of latrines for the use of the clerks and scribes. In one corner of the yard were three wooden chests, each bound in iron and closed with a lock. We tried lifting one. It was heavy, but not too heavy for the four of us to carry. We had no idea what they could contain, although evidently they had something to do with the night-time activities which the watchman had been careful not to reveal. We lugged them, one by one, back into the lawyer's office. By now it was late, almost midnight, and it did not seem as if there was any more we could do until morning.

"We need a locksmith to open the chests," observed one of the clerks, "or else we're going to have to force our way inside."

"We won't find one at this time of night." The other stated the obvious.

"Let's call it a day," I said. "We'll reconvene here early in the morning."

We closed up the office and went our separate ways, each, I could guess, deep in anxious thought.

I spent a sleepless night and so, it seemed, did Hypatia, even though I could not bring myself to tell her the full extent of the situation at the basilica. Before leaving for the offices, I wrote out a message for Hermanus, found one of the house servants and told him to grab a horse and make all haste to Litorina to find the captain. In the letter, I instructed him to leave a few of his soldiers in the camp with his deputy, the *optio*, and to march the rest to Corinium as quickly as possible. After that I set out for the basilica where the mysterious chests still waited.

When I arrived, Aurelius and his clerks were already in the tax collector's office. They had roused a locksmith who was standing talking to them while they all stared down at the chests. The locksmith was shaking his head as I came in.

"I've never seen chests like these before. They look like antiques. Where did you find them?" We avoided giving him a straight answer.

He crouched down and began to examine the locks.

"I'm not sure," he said. "These could be from Londinium, Gaul or even Rome." He straightened up. "I don't know that I can help you. Whatever was in these, it must have been stored there a long time, and whoever owned the contents did not want other people getting in. What do you think it was?"

We again gave no answer but instead sent for the blacksmith.

Eventually a heavily built man ambled into the basilica carrying a large sledgehammer and a meaty fistful of metal punches. After a consultation with the locksmith, he creased his brow, selected a punch and placed it in the keyhole of the first chest. Then, satisfied, he swung a hefty blow. The punch was driven into the lock, forcing the lid of the chest upwards. With a few more strikes, the wood splintered and the lid creaked up. As it opened, rolls and scrolls unravelled and tumbled out across the floor. Aurelius and his clerks gathered them up and began to examine them.

"Legal documents and tax records," the magistrate observed. He unwound a scroll and frowned. "I can investigate the legal material, but we would need an expert to look at these financial documents."

I waved a hand as a sign to the blacksmith to attack the locks of the second and third chests. The results were the same. When we opened them and checked the contents, they were also filled with a jumble of documents.

"We will need someone trustworthy to look at these," I said. "Who could that be?"

"I think the merchant Fabianus is an honest man who understands finances," said Aurelius, so Fabianus was sent for.

While we waited, we picked through the documents, but I could make no sense of them. While they were evidently provincial records, they had all been mixed together, as if they had been dumped in the chests by someone in a hurry, someone who just wanted to hide them or carry them away for disposal. The presence of the locksmith and the blacksmith precluded much speculation, but no one thought to send them away. In a while Fabianus appeared, shambling along and accompanied by his son, a younger version of the father. Both were stocky with trimmed hair and beards and undefinable work clothes, neither Roman nor British but of deceptively good quality.

"Fabiansson," the younger man said, by way of introduction and without a hint of irony.

The two merchants took a few of the papers from the chests and scrutinised them.

"These are records of payment. Some of them are payments the province has made, and some of them are payments the province has received. Some look like tax receipts, although others may be loans. They're a complete jumble. Someone will have to sit down and sort them out carefully. To be truthful, there might be records of some loans I have made mixed in here," said Fabianus.

"I can take a look," said his son. He turned to Aurelius, presuming he was in charge. "You know, I have suspected for a while that not all has been well. I talked to Laurentius last autumn and we could make no sense of it, but who takes any notice of merchants? We can't go about questioning the authorities."

I would have liked to know more, but he began to look around at us all and suddenly spoke again.

"Where do you suppose the actual money is?" he asked.

Aurelius looked doubtful. "I'm only responsible for legal matters, not the money."

The watchman was sent for once again. He appeared, looking sleepy after his disturbed night and, by now, quite scared.

"The treasury's in the cellar under the building, masters. I never go down there. I just check the door's firmly closed at night."

"Show us the way," I ordered, and the watchman hobbled off along the aisle and round behind the raised dais at the other end of the basilica hall. A flight of steps led down into the ground, and at the bottom was a wooden door, which appeared firmly closed.

"Stand back," commanded the blacksmith and put his shoulder to the door. It flew open.

"It wasn't locked," observed the watchman with a hint of surprise in his voice. "It should've been locked."

Torches and lamps were sent for, and finally we went in. By now, there was quite a crowd peering into the darkness. The cellar was dark and damp, and at one end there was a second door. This one was obviously locked, as there was a hinged clasp with a padlock attached. The locksmith turned it over in his hands while the blacksmith retired to fetch his tools, and once again the sledgehammer was applied. The lock resisted the first blow, but by the third and fourth it began to sag, and by the fifth the clasp was hanging free. The blacksmith dragged at the door, and it swung open. We all peered inside. There was nothing to see. The treasury was empty but for cobwebs and a few loose coins lying on the floor. We went inside: Aurelius and his clerks, Fabianus and his son and I, with the blacksmith, a couple of curious scribes, the locksmith and the watchman bringing up the rear. We could see marks in the dust, which could easily have matched the three chests we had just opened. There was similar, fainter evidence of places where other chests must once have stood. Fabianus picked up a couple of the coins.

"Good silver," he commented. "Whoever cleared out the treasury must have dropped them and been in such a hurry they just left them." He scanned around the room as the shadows from the torches played over the walls and caught faint metallic glints scattered on the floor.

"You might just have thirty pieces of silver here altogether," said his son. "It's a good job none of us are superstitious Christians, or I would be seriously worried."

I felt sick. My immediate instincts told me that this was an impossible situation. I should escape, flee back to the north to my familiar world. We could ignore Corinium and the rest of Britannia. I should leave these men, who had been blind or ignored what was happening, to their fate. Why should I care when they did not seem to? But then, looking round the room in the flickering light, I began to notice that they did care. Fabiansson's feeble attempt at humour was a way to cover his own horror. His aged father was leaning against the wall, fighting for breath. Aurelius' white face betrayed his distress. They must realise the significance of the empty treasury far better than I did.

We exchanged looks. We did not have to be Christians to be worried. Someone had looted the provincial treasury, and then, it seemed, the governor or his associates had systematically destroyed the records. A wave of anger swept over me, directed at the treasurer and the census taker, but as it did so a second wave of dread and trepidation quickly followed. The governor was my father-in-law and the man who had placed me in my current position. The pilfering we had discovered could easily be used as a weapon against me. Even if I imagined I could run away back to Umbrosa Farm, I would never be allowed to. I was married to Hypatia. I had accepted a favour from Publius Julius. I was adopted into his family. In his absence, in the absence of anyone else to blame, his enemies would be my enemies, and I would be a suitable scapegoat and sacrificial victim if they could not lay their hands on him or his accomplices.

The blacksmith, the locksmith and the night watchman were finally sent on their way. Could we trust them to keep quiet? Probably not, but what alternative did we have? Perhaps we could have locked them up to silence them, but then someone would have missed them, come searching for them. Someone would find out what we had done and raise a hue and cry, and that was the last thing we needed. Instead, Aurelius and his clerks, Fabianus and his son and I retreated into Aurelius' room. Little was said. I knew what was going through my mind; I could only surmise what the others were thinking.

Just a few weeks before, we had agreed in the council to use the tax money to pay the auxiliaries and for other government business. Now we had found there was no money. What would happen when the auxiliaries found out the treasury had been looted? Hermanus would be betrayed and could lose his authority. Dozens of angry, armed men could be on the loose in the land. Supposing someone else could pay the soldiers and turn them against me and my family? There were plenty of candidates. The Astrebani were reputed to be rich. They had no love for the Ursinus family. The other Durovenes chiefs were rich. They had proven to be mean and short-sighted when it had come to funding the auxiliaries previously, but if they saw a chance to turn them into a private army, perhaps they would untie their purse strings.

Once our tongues had been loosened with the help of a flagon of wine that Aurelius sent for from the forum, I was relieved that the men gathered in the basilica seemed willing to back me as their leader, at least for now, though we still hardly knew one another. Plunging the land into disorder would harm them as much as it would harm me, perhaps more. The only way we could keep opportunists and challengers away was to give the appearance that everything was in order and it was business as usual. And, while we were keeping up that facade, we had to try to track down the missing treasure or come up with a plan to replace it. If we did not, then any one of us might conclude it was better to cut and run.

❧ Chapter 10 ☙

While we had been investigating the chests and the cellar – I could not really call it a treasury anymore – life outside had begun its normal, comfortable routine. The scribes had started their work in the offices around the basilica, the shops had begun to open up and the forum to fill with people. Countryfolk came into the square, setting out their wares for sale, and a few early topers were already sampling their first wine of the day. Aurelius took his usual place in the magistrate's office and began to deal with the routine legal matters, though today he worked alone. His closest clerks were sequestered next door in the tax collector's office, along with Fabiansson, to sort through the chests of documents.

I slunk into Publius Julius' office, which I reckoned was mine now, to contemplate the next steps we should take. I knew so little about how the province worked, where the money came from, where it went. Where would the lack of physical coins have its first impact? Who would be expecting to be paid and kick up a fuss if they were not? How much coinage would we need to keep them satisfied? If people began to believe there was no money and then came to the conclusion that chaos was about to break out, before long chaos really would break out. We had already heard of the proliferating panic in Britannia Superior. That could easily spread, especially when there would be plenty of people ready to take advantage. I recalled how quickly uneasiness could expand from the times when the trouble with the Welsh had been at its worst in my own part of the province. This would be tenfold worse. I could imagine the result now.

I began to feel angry. Angry at the officials who had betrayed the trust placed in them and angry at Publius Julius who had deceived me and deceived his daughter, who had put us in a position where our very lives were in danger. I had some idea where he had gone, I reflected, but where in the world was the treasurer, Tullianus? Where was the census taker? They should be held to account, made to pay for their lack of responsibility, their greed and selfishness. There was little I could do at that moment to fill the coffers with gold and silver, but by the gods, I could try to make those two face justice. I stuck my head into the treasurer's office.

"I need some assistance."

The younger of the two clerks stood up.

"Theo, governor. Can I help you?"

"I want to find the tax collector and the census official. Where could they be?"

"They both have houses in the town," said the clerk. "You could check them first."

"Show me the way," I ordered.

The young man thought for a moment.

"They might have country villas too, but you would have to ask Aurelius or one of the merchants. Humble clerks like me are never invited to officials' villas," he added.

"Let's check their town houses first," I said, cutting him short.

We trudged through the streets until we reached a part of the town close to the walls. One of the houses in this quarter had evidently belonged to Tullianus, the treasurer. The door facing the street was closed, so we knocked politely. There was no reply. We gave it a push, but it did not move. We stood and listened, but we could hear nothing from inside. Theo led the way down a narrow alley until we reached the back of the house and the servants' entrance. We knocked again, with the same result, but this time when we leaned against it, the door swung open. We stepped inside what appeared to be a storeroom. It was empty. A thin layer of dust covered the floor. We continued through the house and peered into the kitchen. It was also empty, aside from a few cheap pots standing in a niche in the wall. It did not look as if there had been anyone at home for a while. We walked out into the atrium. Weeds were sprouting up between the paving stones, and the flowers and small bushes in the garden were dead. The pond was covered with floating plants and rotting leaves. We examined the other rooms in turn. They were all empty, except for a stray cat, which slunk off as we drew near.

"How long has it had been like this?" I mused.

"Perhaps Tullianus just decided to retire to his country villa," Theo suggested.

"That will have to be investigated in time, but I can't imagine he would leave his town house in this state. Let's go and check on the census official's home."

To reach it, we crossed the town again, and to my surprise I found that the house was located just a short distance from the Ursinus town house. The few windows were high up in the wall so that burglars could not climb in, and the front door was closed. However, this door opened with a squeak when we pushed against it. We went in and were met by a scene not so different from the one we had found in the tax collector's house, even down to a scurrying cat. The place was deserted, perhaps since the winter. In one of the rooms at the back, we found that a fire had been built in the middle of the floor. There were a couple of old blankets and some gnawed bones lying in a corner. There was a stink of stale urine. Apparently, a squatter had been living there, but even that seemed to have been a while ago. So much for holding the tax collector and the census official to account. All the evidence indicated that both of them had left town back in the autumn when they were last seen in their offices.

I looked at Theo.

"Theo, where do you live?"

"In a room above the Golden Lion tavern," replied the young man, "but my wife is expecting a child, and so we were hoping to find somewhere bigger."

"Welcome to your new home," I said, gesturing around. "I'm appointing you the provincial record keeper, and I presume that this house goes with the job. In any case, a governor has the right to confiscate the property of traitors, and these two characters fit that description perfectly. I'll send around a couple of servants to clean the place."

The young man stared at me.

"Governor, I can't do that."

I was not sure whether he was referring to the job or the house. My answer was the same either way.

"Someone has to, and if Aurelius trusts you, then I must. Go home and tell your wife about your new accommodation. Call in at the locksmith on the way to fix the door before you have any more squatters. Then return to the basilica and continue your work on the records."

As Theo dashed off to tell his wife, I made my way sadly back to the basilica. What a mess! How long had this been going on? Who else had been involved?

Fortunately for me, for all of us, I should say, Fabianus had been considering the same questions.

"I went back to my warehouse after our meeting," he reported in the early afternoon when he rejoined us in the basilica. "I keep my own financial records there. I don't have good news."

He looked around at our worried faces.

"In the spring I loaned a substantial sum of money to the provincial government. I expected that it would be paid back from tax revenue after the harvest."

"That's not unusual, surely?" asked Aurelius.

"Definitely not. However, that was not the only loan I've made recently. In the past I've been repaid promptly, but I'm still owed payment from last year."

His son broke in.

"That's what made me speak to Laurentius, Father. I was wondering whether there were unpaid debts elsewhere."

"And were there?" I asked.

"Unfortunately, yes. Laurentius had heard complaints from some of his business associates in Belgica. Until recently Britannia Prima's credit has been good, but in the last year or so, lenders have had to whistle for their money."

Fabianus frowned. "We've seen this morning that there's no chance of any loans being repaid from the treasury. If I demand money now, then you'll just tell me you can't pay, and I'll lose everything I'm owed." He looked serious. "I'll just lose my money, and that's part of the risk of doing business. Publius Julius is no worse than a ship that has sunk or a poor harvest, but if a rumour starts that the government is bankrupt, that soldiers cannot be paid? If the small merchants who have been supplying the governor or the provincial council hear that they have all lost their money, then riots could break out."

"It can hardly be the first time that has happened?" said Aurelius.

"Not at all. That's why we know precisely what will happen: buildings set on fire, warehouses raided, homes looted and, without paid soldiers, no way to stop it."

We stood quiet for a moment, imagining the scene, until he continued. I silently gave thanks that Cull should be on his way with reinforcements.

"I have another worry, too. There are landowners and local chiefs who owe me money, plenty of them. What if they decide to take matters into their own hands?"

"Hypatia and I have the same concern," I pointed out.

"I'm glad we agree then. We have to work together. I want to keep the situation stable. You want the same."

"What are you proposing?"

"I'm not entirely sure." He paused for a moment. "When I was walking over here, it occurred to me that there's still a good stock of corn and other foodstuffs in the public granary. You remember, Marcus, I mentioned it at the council meeting."

"I do."

"Well, in the past this was kept on hand to feed the legions, as a buffer against famine and also to give out as free bread on holidays and feast days to the citizens and townspeople. Of course, people would be pretty upset if the free food disappeared, but these days there are fewer people living in Corinium, so the need is less. And there are no legions. That's probably why the stores have filled up."

"But you promised food to Hermanus and the auxiliaries?"

"I did, and especially in this situation we must keep our word. However, I've heard that the harvest is promising to be good."

"If there's no bad weather, it should be a bumper harvest," I said, with the emphasis on the word "should".

"It would be a risk," said Fabianus, "but suppose we sold off most of the stored food. The prices in Gaul are good at present. The stocks from the previous harvest always begin to run low at this time of the year."

I waited to see what would come next.

"I would be willing to buy the grain for a reasonable price," the merchant continued, "which will refill the provincial coffers in the short term and give you time to find a more enduring solution."

I was no merchant then and never have been. As the son of a landowner and farmer, I did not entirely trust merchants. It was hard to know whether Fabianus was making a reasonable offer or merely finding a way to profit from our misfortune. On the other hand, I had seen the growing crops around Umbrosa Farm, and those around Verdaris also looked healthy.

"Governor," said Fabianus deliberately. "I can imagine what you're thinking – can I trust this merchant? Isn't he just out to make quick money? Until recently you were a farmer. You had to think like a farmer. You were from the north of the province, so you had to consider what was best for your people in the north."

He looked me in the eye.

"But now you're the governor for the whole province. You must consider everyone: farmers, merchants, soldiers, innkeepers and bath attendants, everyone who lives here, north and south, rich and poor, honest and dishonest. We have to help each other."

I could see Aurelius nodding in agreement.

"I've seen what happens when people don't trust one another. I have friends and business contacts in eastern Britannia, in Britannia Superior, in all parts of Gaul, in Belgica and Germania. My family and I will be the first to suffer if disorder breaks out. Who do people think have money? Merchants. Who do people think have stocks of food and drink? Merchants. Who do people turn on and rob and kill first when times turn bad? Believe me, it's the merchants. I'm the last person who wants to make matters worse. It's dishonesty, selfishness, covering up and lying that has got us into this situation. My offer to use my contacts to sell the grain is a sincere one. The treasury is empty, and I can supply you with coin immediately. I would rather do that than have the mob break into my home and take my silver from me by force. If we work together honestly, we can solve this problem."

He looked at me fiercely. I did not know what to reply, but my thoughts were interrupted by a knock on the door. I had no servant to open it, so I had to get up and look out myself. Standing there was Marius, the other elderly merchant who had been sitting beside Fabianus in the last council meeting.

He looked into the room.

"Ah, Fabianus, my friend, you're here," he cried out and turned to me. "Governor, I'd heard you had arrived and that my friend Fabianus was over here meeting with you; I didn't want him to get the first chance of any favourable deals." The old man chuckled.

"It's no time for joking, Marius," said Fabianus quickly. "Come in and sit down. You're needed here on a serious matter."

"Don't worry, Marius," added Fabiansson. "I wouldn't want to swindle my father-in-law. Priscilla would never forgive me."

The merchant quickly filled in his friend on the discoveries of the morning. The old man blanched when he heard about the empty treasury. Evidently he had also lent money to the provincial government.

Fabianus fixed his gaze on me again. "You see, we're all in this together. If I try to make a dishonest deal with you, then Marius will suffer, and if he or anyone else tries the same, then I will."

"Very well," I said. "Should I be like King Solomon and split the baby in half? Both you gentlemen are in the same situation. You're both owed money and probably there are others, too. I will trust you, Fabianus and Marius, to arrange for the sale of the grain store, but you must leave enough to provide bread for the people and for the auxiliaries."

The merchants nodded in assent, with heavy sighs. What choice did they have? When I explained the plan to Hypatia, she quickly pointed out that we had little choice either.

"We're as broke as the provincial administration, Marcus. Father and Mother took everything of value. We need to fill our coffers too."

I must have looked anxious.

"I realise it's a gamble, Marcus, but I've checked the granaries at Verdaris," she said. "They're full, thankfully. We can sell some of our grain too, if the merchants will buy it. If we do that personally, then perhaps people will have confidence in what you're doing as governor."

❧ Chapter 11 ❧

Cull and my men arrived in Corinium a couple of days later, followed quickly by the auxiliaries. The soldiers were quartered in the old legionary camp outside the town walls and immediately put to work repairing the barracks and cookhouse. It was not long before Captain Hermanus appeared in my office. He looked concerned.

"I have to be straight with you, Marcus," he said. "The troops are unhappy. They were supposed to be paid at midsummer, but no money came. My men haven't been paid since the New Year. I've lost a couple of them already, and it's as well they've been moved up here rather than remaining in Litorina. It's not as easy to slip away to Gaul."

In a few words, I explained to him what we had discovered. The expression on his face grew more anxious.

"Marcus, I've seen what happens when the troops are not paid. They're armed men, the only armed men in the province. I know I said they're good, disciplined troops, but how long will that last? It would be a disaster and, in that case, letting them desert might be a better option, but then what?"

I smiled and stood up.

"It's not quite so bad yet, thank the gods. Come with me," I said, placing a hand on his shoulder. He did not seem at all reassured.

We stepped out into the aisle and went into the treasurer's office. There sat the newly installed treasurer, Flavius, the older of Aurelius' clerks.

"Flavius," I said, "please take Captain Hermanus down to the treasury and make sure he gets the back pay for the auxiliaries. We need the army on our side!"

"With pleasure, Governor," said the smiling new treasurer, taking a key from a chest behind his desk. "but you'll have to come with me." He handed me a second, similar key. "I've changed the locks on the vault. Now both of us are needed to open the door."

"I'm not sure that would have helped prevent the theft," I grimaced, "when it looks as if there was a conspiracy, but lead the way."

Hermanus left for the camp a short while later with a leather satchel of coins. He had seen with his own eyes the renovated chests, one of which, we revealed, contained real money sent over by Fabianus and Marius from their private stores. I did not think it would be wise to tell him the other two chests were still empty.

Soldiers spending money in the shops and taverns would help quieten any remaining rumours, or so I hoped. But I recognised that that was not enough, so I nailed up a proclamation that there would be a public feast and a parade in the town to celebrate my new position. News of the feast spread fast, and the public square was soon buzzing in anticipation. The profits Hypatia and I had made by selling the grain from Verdaris would soon be spent, but as the emperors had found out years before, free food and entertainment were an excellent way to keep the populace happy.

The following day Theo and Fabiansson asked to see me in the governor's office with a summary of their findings.

"Sorry, boss," said Fabiansson, with an unhappy expression on his face, "but we've come to some dismal conclusions."

He set down half a dozen scrolls and a wax tablet, with rows of numbers scratched across it, on the table and we gathered round.

"Many of the documents we have found refer to payments and expenses relating to the provincial administration. Some people have actually been getting paid – friends of the governor, mainly."

He pointed to the next row of text.

"We also found documents recording the loans from my father, from Marius and from several other local merchants, loans made to the provincial government."

He looked up at us with a grim expression.

"Most of this money was quickly transferred to various moneylenders in Londinium, apparently as repayment for other loans. Here are some examples." He tapped on the scrolls.

"But they still kept records of all this?" I was a little surprised.

"Even crooks have to know who they're paying off," said the merchant, "and I use the word 'crooks' specifically, since there are no records that these Londinium financiers provided funding for the province."

"Where did the tax money go?"

"That remains to be seen. In addition, the amount of money recorded as spent cannot account for the empty treasury. The rest seems to have gone up in smoke."

"We're going to keep looking," said Theo hopefully. "It's possible that some documents are still missing."

Fabiansson was more sceptical. "We haven't finished going through all the records yet, and it's still possible that careful checking might uncover other legitimate expenditure, but I think you'd better start facing the possibility that much of the treasure has simply been stolen. What happened to the missing chests, the ones whose dusty imprints we could see in the cellar, for example?"

"Perhaps they were empty," I suggested hopefully.

Fabiansson looked at me the way a schoolmaster might look at a particularly stupid pupil. I had to face the truth.

"The abandoned houses of the tax collector and the census official point to two of the culprits," I admitted. I dreaded to think who the third might be.

The messenger Sergius returned that same evening, apologising for having taken so long. He had last seen us at Verdaris and had expected us to find us there.

"I rode up to Londinium," he began. "I've made that journey many times over the years, so I had a pretty good idea where the governor usually stayed when he was in town and who his business contacts were. First, I checked the houses of his usual friends, but none of them were home. Then I went to the lodgings he used when he was in town unofficially, but he'd not been there either. After that I went round to the house of your brother, Lucius, but it was also deserted."

Hypatia looked pale and tense as he continued.

"I paid a visit to the lawyer's office where Master Lucius was partner, but they told me your brother had last been seen three days before. No one had heard from him since. They told me he had seemed very distracted recently."

"What did you do then?"

"I was unsure. Not only were Master Lucius and the governor missing, but I picked up a nasty feeling of unease in the city that hadn't been present before. On the surface nothing seemed to be different. Merchants and lawyers were going about their business, farmers and countrymen still stood in the marketplaces with fruit and vegetables, but there were rumours of trouble."

"That's what I have heard too," said Hypatia. "I've had letters from my friends telling of bands of armed strangers, robberies and hold-ups along the highways in broad daylight, gossip of evil omens and prophecies of doom."

Sergius nodded. "Exactly, but those rumours are always going around. I never paid them a lot of attention. If you ask me, the city is a lot quieter and safer now that the general and his soldiers have left." He sniffed heavily. "Like I said, I was more worried because several members of your family had just disappeared without leaving any messages. It's not like the governor or Master Lucius. I thought it best to check on Mistress Ophelia next, even though that meant a journey out of the city."

Since she had married, Hypatia's sister had been living with her husband's family in the city of Verulanium, some miles north of Londinium.

"It took me the whole day to get there, and I had to ask the way when I arrived since I've never visited before. In the end, I found the house, but it was empty as well. I asked around the neighbourhood and sprinkled a few coins; you know how it is with servants. That way, I found out that the family had left earlier in the month. The slaves had all been sold, the servants paid off. The goods had been loaded onto wagons, and the whole family had left town, all very abruptly."

He paused to let his news sink in.

"Talk was that Mistress Ophelia would be travelling with her family to Gaul to visit her brother. The women I spoke to told me that their own master and mistress were also considering selling and moving. What would become of them, they wondered, if they lost their homes and livelihoods and were thrown on the street?" Sergius shrugged. "Of course, I was sympathetic to them. I mean, just look how many people have left Verdaris in the last years – begging your pardon, mistress. I know it wasn't your fault."

"Please just tell us what you found," said Hypatia edgily.

"Sorry, miss," said Sergius hastily. "I made my way back to Londinium slower and more thoughtfully than I left, I can tell you. What was going on? The entire Ursinus family, with the exception of yourself, had vanished, gone up in smoke. I know the governor said he was planning to travel south, but why had the entire family left so furtively like this?"

Exactly, I thought, but I was beginning to have my suspicions.

Sergius took a draught from the ale which a maid brought in and continued.

"I thought it best to continue the strategy of talking to servants. It's only chat, I know, but sometimes you can pick up nuggets. I went and searched out some of my old contacts in the servants' quarters of your father's business partners, people I used to share a meal and a drink with in the old days. They were glad to see me, I can tell you, and glad to talk. Yes, they confirmed that they had seen the governor in the last few days, together with Master Lucius. He was at the moneylender's office to pay back loans he had taken out, so they said, but oddly, he handed over gold and silver goblets and plates rather than coin."

That explained where the better tableware had gone.

"My friend had been there while they weighed them out – paying by weight of metal, not the actual value of the objects. He thought it was very strange. On the other hand, the moneylender had been delighted to rid himself of the Empire's coinage and replace it with silver and gold which could be chopped up into bullion."

"What was the name of the moneylender?" I interrupted.

"Sergentius," said Sergius. I was scarcely surprised. A moneylender by the name of Sergentius featured in the records that we had found in the chests.

"I heard the same had happened with several other moneylenders," commented the messenger, "and there was some very odd business with merchants. For example, Master Lucius sold off a large quantity of good-quality furniture at bargain prices. From what I heard, the merchants hardly knew what to do with it. With all the talk, there are very few clients who want luxury furniture for their villas the way the world is now. Perhaps if a new governor is appointed from Rome, he'll need to fill up the palace, but otherwise?" Sergius' voice trailed off. He took another drink.

"Well, to cut a long story short, I found out that the governor and his family had gone around the city disposing of almost everything they had."

"It's what you would do if you were planning to travel to Gaul," said Hypatia, a little testily. "You can't take wagonloads of furniture."

"Exactly, miss, that's what I thought," said Sergius quickly. "So I set off on the south road towards Dubris. As I rode along, I asked at various inns and hostels after a family by the name of Ursinus, and I was soon able to confirm that your father and your family really had travelled along the same road several days before. I pushed my horse as hard as I could, but when I arrived in Dubris, I found they'd sailed the day before and were now presumably on the other shore. To be honest, miss, looking around the town, I could see that your family was not the only one which had decided it was time to move on."

He frowned.

"I thought I'd done what I could for you, miss. I thought it was best to return home and let you know."

"Thank you, Sergius. You've been very thorough. You may go back to Verdaris, and make sure you rest in case I need you again," said Hypatia, her voice trembling. When the messenger had left, she turned to me.

"It doesn't make sense, Marcus. If they were travelling to Gaul, just as they planned, why this mystery, why this secrecy?"

I think Hypatia had been fearing the worst.

"I'm sorry," I said, "but I have to tell you that your father was in serious financial trouble."

I had to reveal more of what we had discovered, without emphasising the possibility that her father had been involved in embezzlement. She sat silently, hunched over, listening to my explanation.

"It's me who should be sorry," she said at last. "I should have realised."

Later that night she lay beside me sobbing. I did what I could to comfort her. Poor girl. She had been deceived by her father and mother and left alone with the consequences. And where did it leave me? What did it mean to have been delegated the responsibility of ruling the province by a man who was probably a thief and a fraud? How secure was my position in that case?

There was a little solace for Hypatia a few weeks later when a message arrived from her sister:

Dearest Hypatia,

The last few days have been such a rush and excitement. Cornelius has been going out of his mind, but the children have been wonderful. They think it is such an adventure, which it is, for all of us.

We have arrived in Remis safe and sound and are now staying in a comfortable hostel. Father is meeting with his business friends, and we are waiting for a caravan of merchants and religious pilgrims who are going to take the road south to the city of Lugdunum and then on to Arelate. We will be leaving in a few days, and we are so looking forward to seeing dear Gaius once more. I will write again when we arrive.

Your loving sister, Ophelia

It feels ungrateful to say so, especially in light of what I discovered later, but I had already come to the conclusion that the further away Publius Julius Ursinus and his family were, the better for Hypatia and me.

Over the coming days, as the implications of the governor's flight sank in and as our researches into the jumbled heap of documents continued, we could begin to form a picture of what had taken place. As far as we could tell, in the good times under the Empire when taxes rolled in reliably, there was always sufficient money to fund the lifestyle of the governors and their associates.

"I have read enough stories in Tacitus and Suetonius to know how provincial governors squeezed their territories to boost their fortunes," I said to Theo and Fabiansson, "but that was history, long ago."

"Expectations haven't changed," said Fabiansson, "but the financial circumstances have."

The luxury and expense I had seen as a child were what Publius Julius and Marcella had been brought up to expect. Hypatia, too, for that matter.

"When the Empire began to pull back," Fabiansson continued, "when subsidies no longer arrived from Rome and men like your father and his neighbours stopped paying taxes, the surplus left over for high living dried up. The governor must have had to begin borrowing money to fund his lifestyle. When it became difficult to pay back the loans, he seems to have started to divert money from the provincial treasury."

"It looks like Tullianus, the tax collector, and the census taker were willing collaborators," said Theo. "Probably helping themselves, too."

Fabiansson nodded in agreement.

"When they saw the writing on the wall, they likely divided the last money between themselves and fled." He turned to me.

"Neither my father nor Aurelius have been able to find a trace of them through their friends in business or the law. We just have to assume they are lying low, perhaps overseas, perhaps under assumed names."

I sighed.

"When the officials disappeared, the whole scheme must have unravelled entirely for the governor," I said. "He must have found out, like we have, that there was no treasure in the treasury to repay his loans. He must have realised he had arrived at the road's end himself and been forced to start the whole process of uprooting his family and leaving."

"He wouldn't be the first governor to cash in his riches and retire to a warmer climate," said Fabiansson. "If he could only cover his tracks, it would all seem so reasonable."

"But he didn't," I protested. "It's all so obvious!"

Fabiansson looked me in the eye. "Maybe he underestimated you – all of us. Maybe he thought you would give up. Maybe he thought if he got away to the mainland, it wouldn't matter."

"It does matter," I said. "We're not going to let this defeat us."

It was a dubious honour, in the circumstances, to organise a parade and feast, but it had to be done. I could not give the impression of being stingy. The money we had gained from selling the grain had to be showered around by putting on a show. In the morning there were wrestling matches and running races. Men, women and children streamed in from the countryside in the hope of winning prizes. In the afternoon came the parade itself. The statue of the emperor was taken out of the temple, dressed in purple robes and carried around the town on the shoulders of the strongest volunteers. The town band, which I had discovered was on my payroll, marched in the lead, followed by the auxiliaries in full uniform, with Hermanus on horseback at their head. Behind them strode Father Martin, the Christian priest, bearing a cross. I came marching after the priest wearing a toga, the first time in my life I had dressed up like that. I was followed by the dignitaries from the town and province in descending order of importance. Hypatia, my mother and my sister came after them, with household servants throwing small coins to the crowd. When all was done, the emperor's statue was safely returned to its niche in the temple and the spectators and participants gathered in the forum where wine, beer, roasted meat, bread and cakes were served, free to everyone.

There was a certain comfort in walking through the crowd as the townspeople ate and drank, seeing the happy faces, accepting congratulations, being thanked by the public and forgetting about the troubles that faced the province. I began to feel that possibly I was capable of being governor, at least in the eyes of the populace of Corinium. I was also beginning to understand how Publius Julius ended up as he had.

❧ Chapter 12 ☙

Unfortunately, the townspeople of Corinium were only a small proportion of the entire population of Britannia Prima, and one successful festival could not disguise our challenges. Nonetheless, I felt our fortunes had taken a turn for the better. Our hopes for a good harvest were justified. As summer turned into autumn, the good weather held and the crops began to be harvested, starting in the south and day by day proceeding northwards throughout the province. But, while the crops were gradually gathered in, the money in the treasury continuously trickled out, to the upkeep of the baths, to the travellers' hostels along the main roads, to the basilica and to the salaries of the clerks and officials. One damp and slightly chilly day in early autumn, my closest advisors and I gathered in the council chamber to review our progress.

"The finances of the province remained precarious," I said, though my colleagues knew that as well as I did. "We have to find a reliable source of income. I'm afraid that means more taxes."

The lack of enthusiasm was obvious. Not only would new taxes be unpopular, but our records were in chaos, and we had no trustworthy means of doing an assessment.

"I remember once when my soldiers went without payment," began Hermanus, "years back when I was fighting in the civil wars in Gaul."

"You mean the same wars which led to the legions being withdrawn from Britannia," said Aurelius. Hermanus nodded in agreement. It took us a little while to realise that he was not simply distracting us but working his way round to a constructive suggestion.

"We had gone without pay for so long that we had no money for food. What was I to do, as the officer in charge of the detachment? I could order my men to requisition the food, a polite name for robbery."

"It used to happen all the time here," Fabianus commented as Hermanus continued.

"Exactly. We would've been acting in the same way as the brigands and barbarians we were supposed to be combatting, and it would hardly have improved our popularity. Or I could come up with a way to find money and food which at least appeared legitimate."

"So what did you do?" asked Aurelius, suspecting illegality.

"I had a great idea. I set my troops out at either end of a bridge close to the encampment, the only convenient way to cross over a fast-flowing river. Then we exacted a toll from everyone who passed over."

"But that was extortion all the same," objected the lawyer.

"Of course it was," said the captain, "but since it affected everyone equally, or maybe even the rich and strangers more than the poor, the locals were willing to accept it… especially when the men began to buy food and drink from them. Maybe we should use a similar strategy?"

"We don't have any large bridges over unfordable rivers, so there's no way that idea could work in Britannia Prima," said Aurelius, taking Hermanus' suggestion literally.

"The River Wal," I commented, no better, "is deep and swift at Walcastrum, and there's only one bridge, though on reflection blockading it wouldn't do my popularity any good with my fellow northerners."

There was a gloomy silence until Fabianus, looking around the room, said, "It's precisely what the Empire has done on the frontiers forever. We could do it. There are really only two large ports in the province, Litorina and Porta Siluria, and of these Litorina is by far and away the busiest. Soon the surplus grain, hides from slaughtered animals and other produce from the harvest will be flowing to these ports to be carried to Gaul or Hibernia."

He glanced around the room before continuing.

"Why not do as Hermanus suggests and station the few officials we still have at the ports, along with the auxiliaries to back them up? Since the wealthy heads of households will never turn up in Corinium to volunteer information about their property, as they used to in the old days, why not tax them when they come to us?"

Hermanus was sent back to Litorina with a group of auxiliaries, along with Theo and a couple of scribes. They blockaded the routes into town, noting down the size and value of the goods carried in. The northern frontier was my responsibility. I could predict how much opposition there would be to effective tax collection since I had been part of it not long before. If I could persuade the northern leaders to agree to the tolls, it would set a precedent for the rest of the province. A visit to Walcastrum would also provide an opportunity to redress another longstanding omission. According to tradition, the governor should visit all the major towns around the province from time to time to hold an appeals court. Townspeople could bring their complaints and ask for a review of their legal cases. This had been a duty which Publius Julius had neglected. It had been years since he had appeared in Walcastrum to hear cases. Fulfilling my duty to hear appeals might be a cheaper way of gaining good publicity than the public feast in Corinium.

I knew I needed impressive support going north, so the remaining auxiliaries were ordered to repair and shine their armour. I did not have the gall to wear armour myself. I was not used to wearing a soldier's uniform and Hypatia thought I would look ridiculous. However, Hermanus kindly lent me his spare officer's cloak, and the camp armourer managed to attach an impressive decoration of plumes to an old helmet, which was polished and hung from my saddle. I hoped it gave a sufficient impression of military authority.

We set off on the high road, quite like the old days, and strangely enough, when we had marched enough for each day, the scouts generally found the remains of a camp that the ancestors of our auxiliaries had laid out. In some places there were only a few ruins in a field, and before pitching our tents we had to re-dig the ditch first excavated by legionaries in earlier times. At other sites there were still a few stone buildings and rough walls standing. There we could move into the best-preserved quarters and shelter for the night. I was relieved that some of the older soldiers had experience of campaigning in difficult conditions. These set the tone for the younger men. I was also relieved to recall that the camp at Walcastrum, while it had been abandoned for many years, was still relatively intact, so once we arrived the troops would have proper housing. I hoped the northern leaders would be pleased to see the auxiliaries fixing up the old *castrum* that gave the town its name.

After five days' march, we entered the town. I rode in the lead. Behind me came the mounted auxiliaries and behind them, the foot soldiers. News of our arrival had been sent ahead, not least because I wanted Chief Gallius and the mayor of Walcastrum to arrange a suitable welcome. As it was, the streets were filled with gawkers. Nothing like this had been seen for years: a troop of Roman soldiers marching up from the south. Some of the older folks almost had tears in their eyes as they recalled the scenes of their youth. Children ran alongside shouting and cheering the procession. We paraded into the forum. The troops came to a halt and set up in formation; Chief Gallius and the mayor were waiting for us. I dismounted and they greeted me. I would not say it was done warmly, but at least it was done with respect. They knew why I was there, and they grasped what message the military display was intended to convey. I invited them to inspect the troops with me, and we walked together along the rows of standing men. I exchanged words with one or two whom I had met previously when they had been doing guard duty in Corinium, and then I gave the order for them to march off to the camp. As their footsteps died away, I walked with the mayor and the council leader towards the basilica.

"Very impressive, Marcus," said Gallius, a little sourly, as he watched the troops leave. "I never expected to see legionaries in Walcastrum again, even if these are just a bunch of auxiliary Goths. I suppose they could fight if they had to."

"They have been fighting since they were children. That's what Goths are brought up to do," I pointed out. Gallius gave me a dubious look.

"You seem to have made a promising start down in Corinium. The message you sent implied you are expecting us to begin contributing taxes again to pay for it all."

"We all have to," I said. "There've been almost no taxes coming to the provincial government for years."

"And with good reason."

"There are legitimate costs," I said. "I know there were extravagances during Publius Julius' time, but I'm not planning on continuing those. You know me. I grew up here. I don't need fancy luxuries, just a roof over my head and food in my belly. That's the way it's going to be from now on."

"We know you," said Gallius. "We knew your father, and he brought you up well. But you also know we have our expenses up here, and we have had precious little help from the south for years."

I waved my hand in the direction of the departing soldiers.

"You see now that there's help if you need it. If we can stop the waste and improve the finances of the province, I can recruit more auxiliaries. We could keep a permanent garrison here in Walcastrum. That would give the North Britons something to think about and impress our friend, Prince Dewi."

"And you propose to charge tax on our trade?"

"Yes. I propose to set up a toll on the Wal bridge. Probably the North Britons have had a good harvest like us, so they can make a contribution if they send goods south. We are already putting the tolls in place in Litorina, so don't think the southerners will escape. We're also setting up a toll at Porta Siluria."

"And if we send goods north?"

"Why not?"

"This will have to be discussed in the full council," said Gallius. "When I heard you were coming, I called a meeting – for tomorrow before you open the appeals court. In the meantime, I suggest that you go and check up on your fancy soldiers and make sure they're not getting into any trouble."

"You forget, Chief Gallius." I smiled. "I have a mother and a sister not many miles from here, and I plan to visit them first. I have to make sure that Umbrosa Farm can contribute its fair share to the taxation." With that I left.

My old home looked well. The barns were full, and the winter stores were being gathered. My mother looked happy and my sister radiant. I heard that the son of a local landowner, a young man named Tulloch, had begun to sound out the possibility of marrying the neighbouring girl who had so suddenly become the sister of the governor. It seemed that the interest was returned. It would be a relief for her to be married to a man she knew and liked before politics began to play a role. Just now, I was a new piece on the playing board, and many people were waiting to see what I was worth. If I survived, my sister could well become a pawn in a bigger game. She did not deserve that. She was a northern girl, born and brought up amongst her own people, and she deserved a happy life. I had known Tulloch since childhood. He was good-hearted and kind, a knowledgeable farmer and respected by his peers. His father had always been tough but fair, an old friend of my father, and I was sure his son would turn out the same way. Both Tulloch and his father would be good men to have on my side.

I hinted as much to the landowner when I returned to Walcastrum on the following day for the council meeting.

"Diana mentioned your son has been round courting."

The older man grunted. "I hope your sister's not the one out hunting," he said, proud to show a little classical learning.

"My father would have been pleased to see our families allied," I replied.

"We'll see about that. Let's hear what you have to say about the taxes, lad, before we start talking about young folks courting."

That gave me a hint of the distance that had already begun to separate me from my old acquaintances, a distance which became all the more evident when I presented the taxation proposal to the assembly.

"I'll be paying the taxes just like everyone," I emphasised, "not just from Umbrosa Farm but at Verdaris as well. Previous governors may have awarded themselves the privilege of avoiding taxes, but I will not, and I don't expect anyone else to demand it."

The lack of appreciation was obvious, so I continued.

"Some of the old administrators had difficulties in adjusting to new times," I went on. "Their habits and expectations were outdated and extravagant and led to wasteful expenditure."

"We know," grumbled more than one voice.

"However, I should remind you that there are services which will soon be missed if they can't continue: the soldiers you saw yesterday, good roads, law courts, and so on. I've brought in new people who understand that times have changed. These men need regular salaries to stay honest, and so we need taxes – taxes collected on a regular basis. That way, I can ensure that the administrators are rewarded fairly and reasonably, and I will make sure they put the good of the province first."

The northern leaders looked sceptical. They knew that Publius Julius had left abruptly. Some of them might even have heard rumours of the mess we had uncovered. On the other hand, I knew that a few must have passed the old legionary camp on the way to the meeting, since I had heard some muttered comments when they thought I was out of earshot. They had seen the soldiers clearing out the ditches, removing weeds and cutting down the saplings that sprung up around the barracks. One old gentleman had already sidled up to me and asked whether we needed any roof beams, as he had a piece of forest that he was planning to cut once the frost set in. I had smiled and replied that I assumed I could count on his vote for the tolls since I supposed he wanted to be paid for his timber!

The main concern was the old one.

"We have the extra expense of dealing with the Welsh. You know that. You were there when Annius closed the deal."

"We have all benefitted from the peace," I responded.

"That's true, but they still need to be paid each year."

"I was there, and I was present when the sum was debated in council." I knew exactly how much was being paid. "I'll grant you this concession," I said. "The northern council can deduct that payment from the tax revenue before the rest is sent south to Corinium. Is that fair?" I glanced around the room. They were not exactly smiling, but there were murmurs of agreement. They imagined they had won the argument. I made a mental note to send Theo up to verify their accounting.

Only the need to adjourn and open the court at midday brought the debate to a close.

On the way out, I pulled Tulloch's father over.

"Now we have dealt with the taxes, you should allow Master Tulloch to visit Verdaris."

"I'll do it as soon as the harvest is in and we don't need him at home," he answered, more ominously, I thought, than necessary.

The appeals court was my first time judging cases, although previously I had attended the regional quarter sessions with my father. It had been years since there had been an opportunity to petition the governor, and the queue stretched around the forum. There were servants and masters, peasants and farmers, shopkeepers, tavern owners and jilted lovers complaining about everything from broken contracts, boundary disputes, shoddy building work, straying animals and workshops polluting the neighbourhood to unpaid dowries, unfair inheritances and abandoned children. All aspects of human life, in fact. Some of the complainants were self-confident and loud; others were reduced to nerves, hardly able to speak, quite regardless of the rights and wrongs of the case. Nobody ever said that going to court was entirely fair, I reflected.

For the most part, I could see that the magistrates of Walcastrum had tried to be just. Many of the people complaining were merely unhappy with the outcome. These were easy cases to dismiss. Others, I sent on to Corinium where I would have more time to consider them. As the day drew to a close, I began to realise I would never clear the backlog, and I would have to return on a regular basis. If Walcastrum was a precedent, a place where I could count on being listened to with some respect, how much more difficult would it be in Litorina or Competum Novum, towns where I had never set foot and no one knew me?

The following day I set off back to Corinium, leaving most of the soldiers to complete the renovations at the camp. I was relatively satisfied with the outcome and my performance. I had the deal with the northern leaders, stamped and sealed, in my saddle bag.

I had hardly had time to see Hypatia once I arrived in Corinium. News of objections to the novel taxes by some of the southern landowners had already arrived. I was forced back on my horse to head south and put in a personal appearance. I would have to look and sound convincing without the benefit of a military parade, but I hoped that the acquiescence of the northern council might carry some weight. As I neared Litorina, I was impressed to be overtaking wagons and packhorses carrying goods towards the coast and seeing merchants transporting foreign products inland. At least the merchants and shop men of the province appeared to be prospering, I reflected. On the edge of the town, just outside the main gate, a roadblock had been set up, manned by auxiliaries who were inspecting every horse and cart. Unsurprisingly, there was grumbling in the queue for inspection, mutterings about overbearing officials and outrageous taxes and complaints of government oppression, but despite this the line was moving slowly forward in an orderly fashion. I trotted past the waiting carters and drivers for whom, then, I was just another anonymous rider. I saw how the clerks were taking careful note of the contents of each cart, recording the name of the owner and how much tax would have to be paid. When they had paid their dues, the carters would be given a pass that would be checked when they left town.

I briefly greeted Hermanus at the auxiliary camp but decided my first priority would have to be to visit the tax office in the port. When I arrived, I found, to my surprise, Chief Marcellus deep in discussion with Flavius.

"Marcus," he said, in a tone of equal astonishment when he saw me come in. "This blockade you've set up is a bloody nuisance." I guessed he thought I was still somewhere on the northern frontier, and he was not the only one who had made that miscalculation.

"It seemed to be moving smoothly when I rode in," I replied.

"You can't believe how many complaints I have been fielding," he answered.

"You know it's necessary," I said. "You were in Corinium when we last discussed taxes. It was a shambles."

"Always a bloody shambles in Corinium… has been for years," said Marcellus.

"I'm trying to make a change," I said, "to get things organised and efficient."

He grunted sceptically.

"I know how you feel," I continued. "I've just returned from Walcastrum, and my own people gave me a hard time."

"Deserved, no doubt," said Marcellus.

"They agreed to a toll on the Wal bridge," I said, "though I had to set aside money for the arrangement with the Welsh." I tried to look innocuous as I asked, "Is there anything similar I can do to help you and the landowners down here?"

For a while he simply frowned reproachfully without speaking.

"Deal with the bloody pirates," he said at last. "Can't send out a fishing boat these days without a band of Saxons coming and making off with it." He grumbled to himself for a moment. "Fortifications are in a mess. No one has made any repairs for years. Your father-in-law didn't care. No bloody pirates at Verdaris, I suppose. Too far inland. Something needs to be done!"

"Exactly!" I agreed. "We need to build up our defences, recruit more auxiliaries and maybe even set up an early-warning system along the coastline. All of that will take money – money we can only obtain through taxes."

I stood as if thinking, hoping he would pick up the thread, but he didn't, so I was forced to go on.

"Supposing the southern landowners could agree on a plan together with the citizens of Litorina to strengthen the coastal fortifications, set up a watch, maybe arm a boat or two. You know, Marcellus, it's just as important to safeguard the south from pirates as it is to protect the north from cattle raiders."

He gave me a shrewd glance, suspicious of my motives, I would guess, but I could see he understood what I was suggesting.

Not all of the southern leaders were as understanding, I soon discovered. In the early afternoon of the following day, three heavily laden ox wagons arrived at Litorina along the coast road. They joined the queue for inspection. Just as they reached the head of the line, an elegantly dressed young aristocrat galloped up and began to argue with the soldiers. As it happened, Hermanus and I were chatting nearby, watching the operation. Hearing raised voices, we hurried over to see who and what the problem was. I was sorry to see that the new arrival was Vitellus Astrebanus.

I had hoped to avoid direct confrontation, but Astrebanus was yelling at the soldiers.

"You've no right to stop my carts. I refuse to pay these illegal tolls. This is daylight robbery," he snarled at the clerks. Then he noticed me, uttered a curse and yelled, "You're no better than a bandit."

There was no calming him down, though I tried to reason with him.

"We've all paid taxes through centuries of the Roman Empire," I pointed out. "I admit I've not been paying for years, like most other people, but now I've seen that I must change, and I'm paying the new tolls."

He ignored my words and instead cursed on, pointing his finger in my face.

"I don't give a damn. You've no right to impose any taxes, and, damn you, I'm not going to pay them. You're nothing but a sham governor, so-called Ursinus."

I sensed my anger rising and my hand reaching involuntarily for my sword. I felt Hermanus restrain my arm.

"No, Marcus, don't make this personal. Keep it a conflict between those who are willing to follow the laws and those who think they are above them."

With an effort, I joined my hands across my chest.

"Why not just pay the old taxes, then, Chief Astrebanus?" I said. "You can send them directly to Corinium, just as our fathers did. That should settle your concerns about legality." I tried to sound conciliatory, which was hard enough. "Aurelius will provide the appropriate documentation. I can even send the tax assessor over to your estate once the harvest is completed and make sure everything is done fair and square and according to the book."

Of course, that did not suit him either, not least, I suspected, because the old taxes would have cost him a lot more than paying what was due now.

"Just let me get down to the quay, damn you. It's a free world, and you've no right to stop me. I'm not moving until those obstructive bastards let me and my wagons into the town."

All the while he was shouting, more carts had been arriving, and a crowd of drivers, carters and farm workers began to gather, jostling and shoving, some shouting at him, some at me and the soldiers. I began to worry that if we did not settle this soon, the situation would get out of hand. Behind the crowd, people began to call out.

"Hey, you! We've had our passes stamped and we want to go home."

"You, big guy! Who do you think you are, you arrogant idiot, better than us?"

That earned them fresh curses from Astrebanus and his men. Hermanus decided to send to the camp for more soldiers to unblock the road and keep order. Carters stuck at the back of the line began to come forward and argue with Astrebanus' men.

"Get out of the way if you're not going through!"

"What do you take us for?" came the reply. "You're just a bunch of cowards, no better than grovelling slaves."

Words began to turn to jostling and blows, and the auxiliaries had to step in to separate the quarrelling men. I had had enough.

"Chief Astrebanus, if you and your men don't move out of the way, I'm sorry, but I'll have to arrest you. This is no longer a matter of paying taxes but of creating public disorder."

"You can't arrest me, you jumped-up northern nonentity. I am the chief of the Durovenes, like my father before me, and you are just a miserable farmer's son from the backwoods." The soldiers edged nearer. Astrebanus glared furiously, and then, thinking better of the situation, he turned, shouting abuse over his shoulder as he left.

"You'll be hearing from me," he yelled. "I know I have the law on my side. I'll drag your miserable arse in front of the *vicarius'* tribunal in Camulodunum, and then we'll see who is arrested. I'll send an appeal to Rome. And I'm not paying your damn taxes. I'll take my corn to Dubris, and you just try to stop me."

"That's fine," I said, simply relieved to see him go. It would cost him a great deal more to cart his produce across country to Dubris than it would to have paid the toll. Not only that, while we had been standing arguing, the scribes had been careful to make a note of his name and how much grain was in his wagons, and they had entered it into the assessment. His tax avoidance would be on the record for all to see, including his neighbours who had paid and who did not have the option of wasting money trailing to Dubris.

With a great effort and additional foul language, the three wagons were extracted from the queue, manhandled around and the oxen re-hitched. As they finally disappeared back along the road to the east, the other carters shook their heads in disbelief. It would be days before that corn reached a port, and it could already have been sold and loaded onto a ship. Some people's pride got in the way of good sense.

The line edged slowly forward once again.

❧ Chapter 13 ☙

In Publius Julius' time, the Ursinus town house would often be thronged with petitioners and people seeking favours. The anterooms and the atrium were public places. Often there was no other way to approach the governor than to wait. When Hypatia and I started using the house, I discouraged this convention by spending most of my time at the provincial offices in the basilica and making myself available for court hearings and governmental business during the day. However, there was also the business of the estate to be conducted, and so we occasionally had visitors in the evening: Barnulf, Fabianus or his son, sometimes Marius or Aurelius. I was not surprised when, late one day during the following winter, a servant told me an unknown man had come to the door asking to meet me. I was surprised when the flickering oil lamps revealed the stranger to be Drusus Astrebanus. Since his older brother had confronted me at Litorina, the Astrebani had continued to refuse to pay their taxes, and Theo's clerks had been repulsed by armed retainers when they visited Agridurnum to make an assessment.

"I have an urgent business matter to discuss with you," Drusus said when the servant led him into the atrium.

"In that case we should go into my workroom," I suggested. "Can I offer you wine?"

"There is no need," he answered abruptly.

He did not take a seat, but once we had gone in, he pulled a sheaf of documents from a bag he was carrying inside his cloak. He placed them on my desk. I picked one up to look at it.

"What are these?"

"They are promises to repay loans taken out by Publius Julius Ursinus. As his heir, you are responsible for them."

"His heir?" I said, confused. "He isn't dead, as far as I know, so I can hardly be his heir."

"Nonetheless, you are responsible for his estate," Drusus replied.

I took up several of the documents and examined them. By now, I had seen plenty such scrolls, and these looked genuine – city documents. They could not be recent, either, since they were written on imported papyrus.

"These are made out to different people, not to you or your brother."

"That's right. My brother bought them up from various men who were owed money by the governor. They were glad enough to part with them, especially after the governor disappeared. How fortunate that you've put your finances in order and we can now make our claim." Drusus smiled smugly.

I leafed through several more of the papyrus sheets, totting up the amounts listed. How had it been possible that Publius Julius had borrowed and spent such sums?

"Are these all that you have?" I asked, stalling for time to think.

"My brother asked me to bring these to you. I'm not at liberty to say whether there are others. It's not relevant to the business I have with you today."

I said nothing for a moment. I was too shocked to feel anger. The silence prompted him to continue.

"You'll see, Marcus, that the dates for payment on all these loans have long passed. We expect you to repay them in full, and immediately."

How was I going to be able to do that? It was impossible, especially in the middle of the winter. To pay these debts, it would be necessary to sell the town house at least, perhaps even Verdaris.

"Drusus!" came a sharp voice from the doorway. It was Hypatia. "I heard voices and wondered what stranger could be visiting us."

"No stranger, mistress," said Drusus.

She eyed him coldly.

"What are these?" she said, noticing the sheets on my worktable and picking one up.

I watched to see what she would make of them.

"Old loans taken out by my father," she mused, turning to Drusus. "Why have you brought them here now?"

"The due dates are passed, and Vito is expecting them to be paid."

She laughed. "Drusus, these are duplicates. My father paid off these debts years ago. Your brother has made a mistake."

"I don't think so, mistress," said Drusus.

"I assure you that is the case," said Hypatia. With a quick gesture, she gathered up the documents and dropped most of them onto the tiled floor. Before Drusus could react, she touched the remaining sheets against the flame of a lamp. The dry old documents blazed up in an instant, and as they did, she threw them down onto the heap that lay on the tiles.

Drusus yelped with shock and dismay as the stack caught fire.

"What have you done?" he squealed.

Hypatia looked him calmly in the eye.

"We have been through all the records, Drusus. We have checked. The debts have been paid. We don't owe you or your brother anything, no matter how many papyri and parchments you've accumulated."

The pile on the floor was reduced to ashes as we watched. Hypatia rubbed at the remnants with her foot, stirring the fragments around. Several of the documents had seals attached, and she quickly bent down and gathered them up.

"We don't want these falling into the wrong hands," she said. "I'll take care of them. So nice to see you again after all these years, Drusus. I'm sorry that you've been disappointed. Goodnight."

With that she left the room, taking the fire-damaged seals with her.

Drusus and I looked at one another. I do not know which of us was more shocked by what had just happened. I do not know how he would explain it to his brother, but I feared Vitellus' response. After a moment of icy silence, he gave me a brief bow and turned to the door.

"This will not be forgotten," he hissed over his shoulder, and he vanished into the dark of the atrium.

When I found Hypatia in the parlour, she was sitting on the floor crying, with the old seals scattered around her. I bent down and asked her what the problem was. She shuddered.

"To think I might've had to marry that man, Vitellus Astrebanus."

While I recalled that there had been speculation that Vitellus might have expected to marry Hypatia, I had never before heard anything to suggest it was more than speculation.

She looked up at me.

"I'm sorry, Marcus. I should've said something earlier, but it has weighed on me. My father and Vitellus' father planned the match when we were children. Neither of us knew it then, of course, and even the best plans don't necessarily come to fruition."

I knelt down beside her and took her hand in mine.

"You know how it is, how marriages are arranged to suit the families. I'm sure it seemed a wonderful idea to unite the two most powerful families in Britannia Prima," she sighed. "Perhaps we'll be faced with the same type of decision one day. I hope we do a better job."

There was little I could add to that, and she continued.

"I would like to say I was resigned to it, that I had no choice but to marry Vitellus, except with time I realised I loved you, that I wanted to be your wife, just as I have always told you. Then I sensed some disagreement between my father and the Astrebani. My father was upset, and he became more upset every time Cassius Astrebanus and his lawyer friends came to visit. My mother seemed to be sick, so agitated, quite different from how she had always been. Now, of course, we know why, but I was just a girl, and I saw things with a girl's eyes. After you left us, Vitellus began to act as if he owned me. Probably he thought he did."

She made a gesture towards the seals.

"I knew that Gaius hated him from the start, and I started to hate him too. How could I marry a man whom I hated? How could I let a man like that touch me, lie with me? It would be impossible. I prayed to God and to Jesus that they would save me from that fate, and then Our Lord gave me courage."

I was silent. She looked at me again.

"Father came to me and told me that it was time to make the wedding arrangements. I said I would never marry Vitellus. He insisted I would. He, my father, had agreed to the marriage. I told him I would rather kill myself than live with that man. That I would die like Saint Agnes rather than marry a nasty, evil man like Vitellus. He was shocked, but I could see in his expression that he understood. Perhaps he had come to hate Vitellus and his father, too."

"Was he angry with you?" I asked.

"He tried to be, but his heart wasn't in it. Maybe he had given up and realised where everything was leading already then."

"What do you mean – the loans?"

"Those, but not only those. I think they were trying to blackmail Father to join their conspiracy."

I must have looked puzzled.

"The Astrebani and their allies supported Flavius Claudius Constantinus, the general who claimed to be emperor. They had financed his rising, paid for his troops."

"But the rising failed. Constantinus is dead. And your father didn't get involved, right?"

She shook her head.

"Exactly. Father was always loyal to the Empire." She wiped a tear from her eye. "They laid out a fortune for nothing. I think they may have needed Father's money to repay loans they owed, and one way to get it was through me. Imagine how bitter they must be, how much they want revenge against Father."

"What did he say when you refused to marry Vitellus?"

"He said if I didn't plan to marry him, then who would be good enough for me?"

She paused and looked up at me.

"I told him I would marry you. Marcus, I said. Marcus Silvanus, the son of a man who has been your faithful friend and supporter all your life. The boy whom you brought up in your own house with your sons. Wouldn't he better for me than Vitellus Astrebanus?"

She swallowed and looked away.

"I saw an expression come over his face as if he had never contemplated the possibility. Maybe he was faking it, but I don't think so. Did your father ever talk to you about marriage, Marcus, before…?"

"No," I said. "We never got around to it before he fell ill."

"You should be glad you are not a woman."

"What happened then?" I asked.

"Nothing, for a while. Then he said he had spoken to you at the council and that perhaps it wasn't such a bad idea after all. Somehow, I think he was relieved. You can guess I was. I didn't want to kill myself, though I would've done. I wanted to live, but

I wanted to live my life with someone I could love, not someone I only hated. With you."

She started to rise to her feet, and I held her hand to help her up.

"I was right. Everything I said was right, and everything I did was right. I just hope our daughters will have the guts to tell us if we try to marry them to men they despise."

She rubbed her sleeve across her eyes, kissed me and said, "Let's go and see if they have the dinner ready."

The whole incident with Drusus had been so short and dramatic that I had not been able to memorise all the names and sums on the documents I had seen, but afterwards I could still recall sufficient information to check some of them against the records Theo had assembled. I was almost sure that the loans were genuine and had never been repaid. I was still concerned that Vitellus Astrebanus had more debt letters in his hands. If the Astrebani had managed to amass notes of credit to the amount I had seen, then they had certainly had Publius Julius in a stranglehold, and selling his daughter to them would have appeared a tempting solution.

It seemed unlikely, almost impossible, that Hypatia's suggestion to her father that she could marry me was sufficient motivation for Publius Julius to select me as a son-in-law. It seemed out of character for the man in whose house I had lived for so many years to bow to the will of his daughter. It seemed implausible that he had suddenly developed a soft heart, whatever his opinion of the Astrebani. It would have been less surprising if I had earned a knife in the dark to remove me as a hindrance to his plan, to his desperate need to solve his financial problems. Why, then, was I not lying in a shallow grave somewhere in the foothills of Wales? What had he seen when I attended the council that made him agreeable to Hypatia's proposal? There were times when I wondered whether I was simply a useful fool or a disposable tool. That I could be fed to the Astrebani to buy him time to escape or to lure them into a trap. It was all the more surprising, then, that we had had no word from Publius Julius or any other member of the Ursinus family, not even a direction where to send the money we had promised him, little though it was. It was inconceivable that they could all be lying low in silence, but strangely, after the letter from Ophelia, there had been nothing. The thought began to grow in my mind that it might one day become necessary to take more active steps to solve the mystery myself.

I heard nothing more from the Astrebani in the immediate aftermath of this incident either, but I had the uneasy feeling that Vitellus had not gone to ground or been bluffing about appealing to Rome to overturn me as governor. I also found out from Hypatia that he had married a woman in Londinium, a woman named Milesia, the daughter of one of the principal citizens who had fled to Belgica in the wake of Constantinus. I hoped she was happier with the match than Hypatia would have been.

Beyond that brief thought I did not have time or energy to waste on the personal affairs of the Astrebani. My life had been busy enough as it was. Hypatia and I had neither money nor interest in acquiring a herd of flunkeys to fill up empty rooms. Our guests were few, and those who did visit had modest expectations. Though Verdaris was thriving and the household bustling, the house was far too big just for a family, and it often felt cold and uninviting. We decided that the east wing would be converted to farm buildings and the luxurious bathhouse down by the stream would be abandoned and replaced with a smaller one, attached to the house. No more business would be conducted around the plunge pool, no more voices enthusiastically exchanging the news of the Empire, no more groups of lightly clad ladies gossiping amidst the clouds of aromatic steam. Villa Verdaris became less a grandee's country mansion and more an effective and, hopefully, prosperous farm.

In the spring our daughter had been born. The child was blessed by Father Martin, our Christian priest, and given the name Silva. Shortly afterwards my sister was married to Master Tulloch. Father Martin was persuaded by Hypatia to make the journey north to add his benediction on the happy occasion. To my surprise, an unexpected visitor appeared at the feast, no evil wizard come to spoil the luck of the couple, but an envoy from Prince Dewi ap Owain. As I gave him a warm embrace, he apologised that the prince himself did not make the journey. Were the Welsh becoming our friends rather than our enemies?

ঙ Chapter 14 ଓଷ

Although Christianity had been the official religion of the Empire for many years, Britannia was far from Rome and the old religions had held their own. Even at Umbrosa Farm, when the servants and slaves were in need of good fortune, they went to offer trinkets at a small altar, roofed over in stone, by the tree-shaded pool in the stream. I still made a point of going myself now and then and casting in a few coins. I needed all the luck I could scrape together.

Father Martin, the Christian priest, was a modest man who lived in Corinium. Attached to his house was a stable which had been converted into a small church where believers could gather each seventh day. Hypatia attended the worship when we were in town. The priest also catered for the needs of the Christian community in the surrounding countryside, riding from house to house on an old mare, holding services in villas where family members practised his faith.

In the late autumn of the year after Silva was born, I was walking from the basilica to the Ursinus town house one chilly evening, wrapped in a plain wool cloak. By then, many people recognised me, and one or two greeted me, though others continued on their way without acknowledgement. As I passed the travellers' hostel close by the forum, there was an unusual commotion in the street. A procession was approaching from the south gate. Mindful to avoid attracting attention, I backed into the shadows to watch. The group riding up South Street clearly signalled someone of importance. I had not heard any rumours of official visitors. I was sure that if a replacement provincial governor had been appointed by Rome, the news would have come in good time. For a moment I feared it could Vitellus Astrebanus flaunting his wealth. In front rode two robust-looking men wearing white cloaks, but the symbols they carried reassured me. One had a cross and the other, an ornate object resembling the carved crook Father Martin used in his role as shepherd of the Christian flock. Behind these two rode a stout, older man resplendent in an elaborate cloak with an embroidered hat. Across the front of the cloak, once again, spread the Christian cross. This man was followed by a further pair of sturdy individuals, one with short-cut blond hair but clean shaven and the other with dark skin, a rare sight in Corinium. Behind the riders came a small cart drawn by a mule. With the driver sat two demure-looking women in grey gowns, their heads covered by shawls. Soon every urchin and unoccupied adult was rushing towards the hostel to take a look. I remained concealed until the group passed inside and the gate was shut behind them. A fascinated buzz spread throughout the crowd. Who were they, and what did they want? They seemed to be Christian, but I overheard whispers that the men carried weapons hidden beneath their cloaks.

I was not entirely ignorant of the ways of the Christian Church in its strongholds in Southern Gaul and Rome. The merchants had been dinner guests at Verdaris and told marvellous tales about their experiences on the mainland. We used to have a bishop ourselves in Corinium a few years ago, a pompous Greek, I recalled. I also knew that many such leaders behaved as, and thought themselves equal to, lords. But now our priests and churchmen in Britannia were of humbler stock, typified by Father Martin. Who was this individual, and what was he doing here?

When I mentioned what I had seen in the street to Hypatia, she smiled discreetly, suggesting she knew something I did not.

"That must be the new bishop," she said.

For a moment I felt a little irritated, but she smiled and gave me a hug.

"Dear Marcus, I only found out a couple of days ago myself. My friend, Felicia, spotted the same group travelling from Dubris and sent a messenger on a quick horse. I was as confused as you were at first."

"Felicia is lucky enough to have a husband, I assume?"

"Of course."

"And he didn't remark on these people and send me a message?" I complained.

"I don't think he paid them any attention, dear."

"Your women friends are running the province, I suppose," I grumbled.

"Of course we are, Marcus. Haven't you realised by now? But I wonder what the bishop plans to do."

"I shall make enquiries in the morning," I said, somewhat coldly, primarily thinking of my meal. In that, I was scarcely better than Felicia's husband.

My curiosity was satisfied, although my concerns were not stilled, later in the evening when there was a hurried knocking on the outer door and a worried-looking Father Martin was shown in.

"I thought I'd better speak to you, Governor, my lady," he said, glancing nervously between Hypatia and me. "I was summoned to the hostel, or rather I should say one of the cooks came to find me. This bishop sent his men to find any local priests. My friend ran to warn me at once." The priest gave a weak smile. "I had heard about the travellers, the man dressed up in fine clothes carrying a cross, so I thought it best to go and meet him."

"That was wise, Father," said Hypatia.

"His name, he said, is Bishop Matthias."

"That's what I heard too," said Hypatia, "but who are the other people? Did you find out anything about them?"

"They are his deacons, my lady, the tough-looking characters. I didn't meet the womenfolk."

"I see," said Hypatia. "I will send a message to the hostel tomorrow, and perhaps I will have better fortune and learn more. Did Bishop Matthias tell you why he had come?"

"He said the bishop of Senones had heard that Britannia was in the grip of pagans since the death of the previous bishop and sent him on a mission."

"I see," said Hypatia again. "And Bishop Matthias is in charge of this mission?"

"Yes, my lady. He grilled me about the Christian practices in Britannia Prima. He said my answers had proved unsatisfactory, and I was dispatched to arrange a meeting with the governor for tomorrow."

"That was the word he used? Unsatisfactory?" Hypatia raised her eyebrows.

"Yes, my lady. I don't think we are unsatisfactory."

As I listened to this exchange, I was in a dilemma. This bishop sounded like a self-important and haughty individual, implying that our priest was not a good Christian. His appearance and behaviour might have been appropriate in the days of Publius Julius when pomp and show were all of the essence. How was I to deal with him? I could try to meet him like for like. I was the governor, and I could put on a show if I had to, as I had in Walcastrum. I could dress myself in a toga and dust off my laurel wreath. I could order Hermanus into full dress uniform to march the auxiliaries into the forum on parade. I could distribute sums of money, now that the provincial treasury had been somewhat replenished, and fetch out a crowd to sing in jubilation and shout my name and put him in his place. The cost would not be excessive anymore. But what was the point? I had made a promise not to be extravagant. Jesus of the Bible started life as a carpenter's son, born in a stable. His friends were fishermen and a tax collector. The bishop needed to be reminded of that. Besides, the basilica was cold, although it was too early in the year to light a brazier in my office, and I would greatly prefer to be wearing my warm cloak than a toga.

"Thank you, Father," I said suddenly. "You may return to the bishop and let him know I will give him an audience in the morning in the basilica."

The priest departed, and I exchanged uncomfortable looks with Hypatia. There was an expression in her eyes that warned me not to say more.

I did not need any warning of the bishop's arrival the following day. Even though my office was deep inside, I could hear a growing hubbub outside in the basilica. I sat working on some papers with a clerk, determined not to make the first move, when Theo came into the room. His assistant had run in from the forum to report that the bishop was on his way. His deacons were marching in formation, singing a Christian hymn, while the bishop himself was blessing the crowd which had gathered to see the show. Moments later the sound of tramping feet could be heard in the *curia* outside my room.

As the clerk opened the door, two of the deacons strode into my office, and the bishop followed. The others remained outside in the aisle, on guard, no doubt. We stood facing one another, wondering who should bow first. Theo had the wit to break the ice by bowing deeply himself, and the two clerks followed suit. The bishop was then forced to acknowledge their bows with a slight inclination of his head, and I was able to pretend that he had been bowing to me and gave him a quick nod of acknowledgement. The deacons remained impassive throughout this small ceremony.

The bishop looked me up and down slightly disdainfully. Possibly he was unsure if I was the governor. I supposed he had been expecting an elegant gentleman of his own age, rather than a young man wearing a leather jerkin and woollen trousers, wrapped in a plain cloak. Certainly, he had dressed very well himself, wearing a different cloak and gown from the one I had seen the day before, but it was just as finely embroidered, and there was a jewelled cross hanging from a chain on his breast.

"I apologise, Your Excellency. You have caught me here at work with my tax collector. We are a poor province and we need to take care of our money, little that it is."

He looked around the room and cleared his throat as if he was taking his time to choose his words.

"Governor, your province may be poor in money, but His Excellency the bishop of Senones has heard that it is rich in souls who should be gathered to the one true religion. I am here on a mission, Governor, sent in haste by His Excellency, who has your province in his thoughts and prayers. His concerns led him to dispatch me, together with others of great faith, my deacons, Justin and Baxter, to revive the Christian Church in this land."

He paused as if expecting a response.

Was I to thank him and the bishop of Senones for their consideration, or argue that the souls of the people in the land were at peace worshipping whichever gods they felt best met their needs?

Since I did not reply, the bishop was obliged to continue.

"His Excellency is aware that there has been no bishop in the city of Corinium for several years, although it is the capital city of this province. He heard that work on the Christian church has ceased, that it stands half completed, an infamy, while the Christians of this city are forced to worship in a quite unfitting location. The priest, Father Martin, confirmed this to me yesterday evening."

I felt the need to defend the father.

"Father Martin is a good man. He works hard to meet the needs of the Christian community."

"He may be a good man, Governor, but he works alone. However hard he works, he can only have limited success in spreading the Word of the Lord. It is my duty to bring everyone under the protection of Christ."

"Whether they like it or not," I muttered to myself.

"Our Church must be strengthened and built on new foundations. I have no desire to cause offence to those who look to Father Martin and perhaps other simple men of faith for guidance, but my mission is to spread the grace of Our Lord to those who have not received your priest's message, who have not heard the Good News, and who are thirsting after the Word of God."

I was a little unsure to whom and what the bishop was referring, but the man was clearly serious, and I did not want to cause offence either.

"Your Excellency, you are welcome to Corinium. I hope you will find fruitful ground for your mission," I said, breaking into his flow with a firm voice. "If I can help you, I will be glad to do so, providing it does not cause trouble in the province. I myself am baptised a Christian, and my wife Hypatia is one of Father Martin's flock."

"Governor, on the way through the city to your office, I saw many idols still standing in the city and evidence of offerings to idols in the travellers' hostel itself."

I thought of the *lares* in the entrance hall of my own home. "People give thanks for safe arrival at their destination," I protested.

"Christianity has long been the one and only faith of the Empire, and yet I see evidence of worship of false gods with my own eyes. How can this take place with a Christian as governor?"

"The Empire has long ceased to have any influence over this province, Your Excellency, and, as you have so cogently pointed out, you Christians have neglected us for a long time. People seek help and comfort wherever they can in these difficult times. I am the governor for all people in this province whether they are

Christians or not. It is not my business to tell them who to worship."

For a moment the bishop looked a bit hesitant.

"Well, that is a sorry situation," he spluttered, obviously deflated. "I had expected better."

"Sorry or not, it is the situation we find ourselves in," I answered brusquely. "If you and your deacons, and the holy sisters I saw accompanying you yesterday, can persuade people to follow the Christian way through good example, through preaching and good works, then no one will be happier than me. On the other hand, I have lived here all my life, and I know the faith that people have in their own ways, old and misguided though they may be in the eyes of many."

I smiled encouragingly.

"I would be happy to accompany you on a walk around the town, and we can inspect the site of the church and perhaps pay a visit to Father Martin's humble chapel," I suggested. "Just a moment while I arrange a fitting escort." I whispered a few words to my clerk. He nodded and left the room.

While we waited, I told the bishop a little of what I knew about the history of the church building. Hypatia had told me that the construction work had been started by Publius Julius as a wedding gift to Marcella.

"At first the building progressed well," I explained. "But with the troubles over the years and the poor financial state of our province, and despite the good intent of several of our most prominent citizens, work, unfortunately, came to a halt."

I gave him a compassionate look.

"I'm sorry, Bishop, but I've not felt able to use our limited public money for the construction. My Christian friends, including my dear wife, persuaded me that God's work would be better achieved by feeding the poor and taking care of the sick."

The bishop had been clearly straining to speak during my explanation.

"But people must be able to see the glory of God!" he cried. "If we praise him and glorify him, then blessings will descend upon us, and the hungry will be fed and the sick healed by his hand," he added, convincingly.

I was spared the need to reply by the return of the clerk and the sound of boot nails on the flagstones outside. A command was barked out, and we could hear the stamp of feet and an exchange of words with the bishop's men standing outside the door.

"I think the escort has arrived," I observed and invited the bishop to follow me out of my office. In the hallway stood Hermanus and a small squad of soldiers. He saluted briskly as we stepped out of the office, and the escort formed up.

The site of the church building was really a sorry one, in truth. Publius Julius had arranged for the old temple of Jupiter to be cleared so the foundations could be used for a new church. He had not dared to touch the temple to the deified emperor which stood beside it. That might have been interpreted as support for one of the rival claimants who had sprung up in recent years, Constantinus being only the last of these. At the east end, construction had progressed to the point where the walls were about ten feet high, but round the rest of the building the stonework reached little higher than a man's waist. In recent years the site had become a dump for rubble and old timbers. The remnants of masonry had been used as the back walls of a series of small workshops. The bishop shook his head, then walked into the outline of the church, up the weedy pavement – skirting the heaps of rubbish – and knelt briefly at the place where the altar would have been.

We all tramped back through the town, somewhat disheartened and followed by a curious throng, until we reached Father Martin's house. The soldiers held back the crowd, and the bishop and deacons were ushered into Father Martin's yard. To one side was the stone stable which had been converted into a small church with a cross erected outside. The bishop crossed himself, dipped his knee and went in. I always thought the chapel was rather cosy. The windows were set high up and let in enough light so we could see the walls decorated with biblical scenes. A local painter had done the job. I recognised Jesus dividing bread in one place and triumphant on the cross above the small altar at the east end where two candles burned. Perhaps this was not much for a bishop from Gaul, but I felt sympathy for Father Martin.

After the bishop and the deacons had prayed and sung a short psalm, we left and, somewhat frostily, went our separate ways. The escort marched briskly off to the camp, and Theo and Hermanus accompanied me back to the basilica. This pompous-sounding stranger was promising to be a real headache.

When I returned home at the end of the day, I found Hypatia sitting in the reception room, and to my surprise, the bishop was seated there as well. He was no longer wearing his finery, but instead a plain grey wool habit and leather sandals, a glass of wine in his hand. He appeared a great deal more human: a middle-aged man, tired from his journey, anxious about his duties in a strange country and perhaps glad to sit in a warm room with a friendly face.

I called for a glass of wine myself while he thanked me for the tour around the town. He confessed that while he had knelt in prayer at the little altar in Father's Martin's church, a voice inside had reminded him that he was merely a servant of the Lord, and that his task was to do the Lord's work wherever it took him.

"The bishop has been telling me his story," said Hypatia. "How he grew up as a prosperous landowner in the south of Gaul."

That was not hard to imagine, I reflected.

He took up the story. "I ridiculed my mother's religion. I thought the poor should do as I told them and help me become richer." He looked down for a moment. "One day I was out riding around my domain when a great light appeared before me, not dissimilar to that experienced by Saint Paul. I was shocked, overwhelmed, struggling to dismount from my horse. It was all I could do to stagger to the side of the road and fall to my knees."

He looked up at us.

"When I recovered my senses, I felt like a changed man, determined to follow the ways of Our Saviour. I sold my lands and estate, freed all my slaves, giving each of them a small sum of money so they could start on their own, and then I donated the rest to the Church."

I suppose I should have been impressed, but I suspected his mother might have slipped something into his lunch that day long ago. However, I kept my thoughts to myself and kind interest plastered on my face.

"At first," he continued, "I worked as a humble monk, but eventually I was called to become the abbot of the monastery."

A good decision, no doubt, I thought.

"Unfortunately, I gradually fell back into my old ways and once more became proud and arrogant. Then the bishop picked me out for this mission to Britannia Prima, which led me to your town. I was determined to impress, and now I confess I entered the city full of pride, while Christ himself rode a mere donkey into Jerusalem. I have treated you, Governor, in an excessively arrogant manner."

He bowed his head.

"But while I was praying in that humble chapel, I saw the good faith of the priest and the others gathered together, and I was reminded that Christ is neither proud nor arrogant."

I felt a little ashamed of myself for my suspicion. I realised he meant well, even though he seemed to be speaking in riddles half the time. I asked him how we could help.

"Your Excellency, I was discussing that very problem with your lady wife when you came in," he smiled. "My missionaries and I need somewhere to live. I had imagined there would be a monastery or some other religious building where we could stay, but how mistaken and disappointed I have been."

Hypatia spoke up.

"They can't stay in the hostel. It's difficult for them, and it's embarrassing for the other travellers when they want to relax and have fun if the place is filled with holy people."

I could see her point. I knew the kind of fun the travellers preferred. I would be pretty annoyed to find the place infested with disapproving Christians myself.

"There are several abandoned houses in the town that your group could occupy if they are prepared to put up with a bit of discomfort," I suggested.

"My men and I would gladly do that, but what about the ladies? They have already suffered greatly during the journey."

"They can stay here," said Hypatia quickly, "until the lodgings have been put in order."

"I am so grateful. I had begun to fear for our safety and spiritual well-being." He turned to me. "I assure you that my men and I can renovate any building you could find for us. The deacons are men of God now, but in the past they trod the paths of evil." He smiled apologetically. "Now they have been called to serve the Lord, but they have many practical skills which would be useful in construction and renovation. They handle axes and hammers with expertise."

At that moment the servant came to the door and announced that dinner was ready. I could not help but smile to myself when I saw the contented look which came over the bishop's face as he walked beside Hypatia into the dining room.

Later that night she snuggled up to me.

"Thank you, Marcus. I could see you were boiling inside. But don't worry, I'll work on him. You see, in a few months, the bishop will be our friend, and I think you'll find him a good man to have as an ally."

☙ Chapter 15 ❧

Hypatia was right, of course. Once the bishop had found his feet, he became a valuable advisor. He had the benefit of a classical education and a knowledge of history and politics. He shared Hypatia's ability to get along with the snobbier landowners, and especially their wives, in a way only someone born to that life could. He travelled around the province spreading the Word and, at the same time, snapping up gossip.

"The tribunal in Camulodunum is up for sale," said Hypatia. "Everyone knows that."

"They have never had jurisdiction over Britannia Prima, not since the provinces were divided," said Aurelius.

"It doesn't matter," said the bishop. "If someone in Rome decides their word carries weight, it could swing the case in Vitellus Astrebanus' favour."

We were sitting in the summer room at Verdaris, although it was already early autumn. Dinner had just been completed, and the wine jug stood on the table. One of the boys Hypatia was training filled the glasses once again. Aurelius and Theo were there. Fabiansson, Bishop Matthias and Hermanus made up the rest of the party. It was a council of war of sorts.

"Especially if it is backed up by gold," said Fabiansson, "and I have heard that Astrebanus has been ensuring it is." He took a drink. "That's not all he has been doing," he added. "I have heard that he's hawking your father's old debts, Hypatia. Big debts."

"How did you hear that, Fabiansson?" I asked.

"Laurentius and Drusus crossed paths in Remis. They have thousands, so he said."

"It's a lie," said Hypatia, placing her hands on her belly where our second child was already evident, almost as a protection. "Father paid off his debts."

Fabiansson looked at her questioningly, careful not to contradict her directly. He had seen the same records I had.

"It doesn't matter," he said, "so long as people believe they are unpaid. The Astrebani can use them to raise money, to hire men, to pursue lawsuits, to make your life a misery."

"Why haven't they done it already?" asked the bishop, concern in his voice.

"They tried," said Hypatia suddenly. "Drusus came to us, waving his papyri, and I burned them."

There was a hushed pause.

"Bravo," said Fabiansson finally, "but it won't be over so simply. Sufficient people believe your father still owes large sums of money. So long as they believe that and so long as there are assets" – he looked around – "such as this beautiful house, then the Astrebani can continue."

"How can we stop them?" I asked.

"We can't beat them legally," said Aurelius. "They know all the tricks. The lawyers will mostly side with them."

"We can't beat them with money," I said. "Every *sestertius* we earn goes back into the farm and the estate. The little we have left over from the outrageous taxes," I added, provoking strained laughter from around the room.

"We can't beat them with force, so long as they are lurking in Agridurnum," said Hermanus. "They certainly have enough retainers to defend the estate. Just look at the reception they gave your tax assessors."

"Or if they remain out of our reach on the mainland," added Fabiansson. "I'm worried that Drusus is trying to gain support from the Britons who have fled from Britannia Superior in the wake of the Constantinus fiasco."

"I don't hear much sympathy for them around the province," said the bishop, "even in the south."

"That's very reassuring to hear, Bishop," I said.

"Too many people had their fingers burned by Constantinus," said Aurelius.

"Most people I have met are impressed by the way our governor, and his colleagues of course" – the bishop smiled around the room – "have managed to keep our province calm when all around is stormy."

"I have to be on constant guard against those storms," I said.

"Indeed, indeed," said the bishop. "We must all pull together to keep the boat afloat, so to speak," he added.

There was quiet for a moment, each of us wondering, perhaps, what our role in the crew was. What would our fate be if the waves did start to break over the side? At last Hypatia broke the silence.

"We can beat them with cunning," she said emphatically. "We can beat them because we want to win more than they do, and because they are greedy and ambitious."

"How can we do that, dear?" I asked warily.

"Everything they're doing takes time: buying support, pursuing lawsuits, making an appeal to the emperor. I heard Father complain so many times about how long it took to get anything done in Rome, and that was before the letter."

"The letter?" asked Theo.

"The letter telling us that we were on our own," said Aurelius. "It was in your father's time, wasn't it?"

"Yes," said Hypatia. "I think that was one of the events which contributed to his problems. He always counted on support from Rome, and then they abandoned him."

"There are men who still think Rome will intervene. They are keeping quiet - waiting to choose sides when they hear who the emperor supports," said Aurelius.

I saw Hermanus grimace. I knew his opinions on that likelihood.

"We must force them to choose sides before any response comes from Rome," said Hypatia, "while we have the upper hand!"

"Do we have the upper hand?"

"We have the auxiliaries," said Hermanus. "So long as you keep paying them, so long as I'm their captain, they'll be on your side."

"You have your own men from Umbrosa, and the chiefs in the north would join you if it came to a fight," said Hypatia. "Prince Dewi, too."

I put my head in my hands. God forbid a time would come when we allied with the Welsh against fellow Britons.

"You have me and my father," said Fabiansson. "We may not count for much in high society, but now that Marius has passed on, we have the majority of the trade from Britannia Prima to the southern lands. Besides, Hypatia" – he smiled to himself – "if the Astrebani have loans of your father's, there are plenty of gentlemen in Britannia Prima who owe us money."

"You can count on me, too, my lady," said the bishop, glancing over at Hypatia. "I have appreciated the assistance the Church has received in this province. I only wish the same were true in Britannia Superior. I was quite dismayed when I visited Verulamium. They are lost souls, I am afraid."

Hypatia turned to me.

"You see, Marcus, we have a lot of powerful people on our side, and that's not counting my friends." She looked around. "We must come up with a ruse that is so provoking that the Astrebani will not be able to resist. Vitellus will have to make a move, and we can break him in public."

"Declare independence from Rome," said Aurelius. "Make a public declaration that the laws and authority of Rome are no longer valid in Britannia Prima. Base your declaration on the letter, base it on the absence of a *vicarius*, base it on there being no governor sent from Rome, so you have no choice."

"Back it with force," said Hermanus.

"No Welsh!" I said.

"No Welsh," said Aurelius, "but the plebs."

"The plebs," said Hypatia, with almost as much distaste as I felt for the Welsh.

"The people of Corinium. No matter how many armed men Astrebanus has, imagine them set on by the mob. They would be torn to pieces."

"Let's hope you don't have to go that far," said the bishop. "I have seen the mob in action, and it is to be feared."

"Precisely," said Aurelius icily.

I admit I had my misgivings about this proposal. I had given my word to Publius Julius that I would serve as his deputy, and it seemed presumptuous to proclaim independence unilaterally. Supposing he was to return? I was surprised that Hypatia was so solidly behind the plan and took an active part in setting it in motion. Likewise, I was still unsure why the bishop was willing to support me.

"Your dear wife recounted to me how she had prayed to Our Lord for help and he had brought you to her. You are part of the Lord's plan, Governor Ursinus, whether you are aware of it or not. We all are," he added.

"In Gaul and in Italia," he explained, "such a mish-mash of barbarians and unbelievers has spread across the land that the Church has had to become the fount of authority in place of the

Empire. The bishops have found themselves forced to take responsibility, both temporal and spiritual."

Both Hypatia and the bishop criss-crossed the province that winter drumming up support. The only substantial opposition came from Statorius. As usual, he was far enough away from trouble to be happy with the status quo.

"He asked, 'Why stir up trouble where there is none?'" said the bishop. "I replied, 'I am sorry, sir, but I think trouble will be coming whether we like it or not,' but he did not seem convinced."

It is never a good idea to blow your own trumpet too hard, on that I concur with the ancients, but even I braved the snowy roads and visited Walcastrum.

"We're behind you," said Gallius. "We've no interest in seeing the Romans back and definitely no interest in allowing any Durovenes in power. I'm not sure what those Astrebani are up to, but you have to put a stop to it."

My mother said the same. So did Prince Dewi when I wrote him a carefully worded and highly secret letter. I felt as if I was collaborating with the enemy as I put pen to parchment, but times were changing, and I had to adapt.

"I wish we could be certain what happened to Father and Mother," said Hypatia suddenly one day while holding our new daughter, Amanda, to her breast. "It would be so much better for the children, and it makes me especially anxious as the declaration of independence is approaching. What would we do if Father suddenly appeared? Of course, the family would be happy, but what about the province?"

"It makes me uneasy too," I admitted, "but if I believe Aurelius, any agreements made before the announcement would no longer be valid."

"We gave our word though, and that's personal."

"I know," I said, "but surely we would have had a message if they were planning to return."

"Why hasn't Ophelia written again?" It was a subject she had pondered many times before. "I just feel they must have had some sort of trouble. It makes me so uneasy. It would make me sad to think they were so far away and still did not write, but to imagine something terrible happening. I can't, Marcus, I can't."

I put my arm around her.

"What can we tell the children when they are older and begin to ask?" she continued.

I had no good answer.

"We promised to send them money, too, remember, for seven years."

"The profits," I pointed out. "And there have hardly been any."

She sighed.

"Maybe when this is over," I added, "when everything has calmed down, we can try to find out what happened to them."

"What are we going to do about the Astrebani if they take the bait?" I asked. I had gone through scenarios in my mind.

"Banishment would make most sense," said Aurelius, "based on precedent."

"Confiscation of their goods to the emperor," suggested Theo.

"But we won't have an emperor."

"Banishment and confiscation of goods," mused the bishop, who had joined us in my workroom in the basilica.

"We could donate the goods to the Church?" suggested Aurelius. "That would remove the emperor from the picture."

"It would be most gratifying," said the bishop, "but should the Church accept goods in those circumstances?"

"Declare them outlaws too," said Theo. "That way, every man's hand would be against them, and there would be no incentive to support them in the future."

"Where would we banish them to?" I wondered. "We don't rule over Bithynia or Parthia or any remote regions where we could send people. It would just be asking for more trouble if they were sent to Hibernia or they decided to hightail it to Pictland. Can you imagine?"

"A remote island?" suggested the bishop.

"The Isle of Wight is too close."

"And too rich."

"One of those little islands off Cornwall or Wales would do."

"Then we would need help from Prince Dewi or Prince Cormac."

"Prince Dewi has already promised his support," I said without thinking.

Their heads turned towards me.

"You have been in contact with him about this?"

"I have," I admitted. "Not about banishing the Astrebani, of course, but about staying neutral, at least."

"No stab in the back," Aurelius reflected. "That's a relief."

❦ Chapter 16 ❦

In the late spring of the fourth year after Publius Julius' departure, I sent out an invitation calling one and all to a gathering in Corinium at midsummer for a celebration and feasting. I wrote personally to those whose appearance was deemed to be essential.

"*Alea iacta est*, if I may steal some well-worn words," said Aurelius, as we watched carriers with the first message clatter away across the cobbles towards the south gates.

"It didn't end very well for Caesar," I pointed out, "or his allies."

"History never repeats itself exactly. Wasn't it Herodotus who said that?"

"I don't think so," I replied, "but let us hope this does not end in a farce."

"Better a farce than a tragedy," concluded the lawyer, as we returned to our workplace.

Invitations were sent to all four corners of the province to ensure that every significant landowner and chieftain was aware of the event and could only blame themselves if they were not present.

Was it really necessary to take any of these steps? Was anyone going to challenge me as governor? Bishop Matthias, who had the best connections on the continent, seemed to think it would make little difference. The Empire had already left us to ourselves. Even so, I suspected he calculated that breaking political links to Rome would leave the religious connection undisturbed, perhaps even strengthened. He did make it clear he would be very happy to see the temple to the emperor, so inconveniently placed next to his growing church, demolished.

My main desire was to eliminate doubt, to unite the people of the province, bring the tribes together, provide a clear leadership. There were men who still saw me as merely the delegate of the real governor and were biding their time, withholding their support in the hope that a replacement would arrive from Rome and their party could triumph at my fall. There were probably women who shared that opinion too, I suppose, but their voices were only heard in their own halls and bedchambers. There were men who we suspected were actively plotting with Vitellus and Drusus Astrebanus. Above all, there was always the risk that someone, claiming to be removing an illegitimate ruler, would try to grab power himself. That would plunge the province into the same chaos submerging Britannia Superior, and I was determined that it would not happen in Britannia Prima. My closest collaborators agreed. It was time to put an end to the false hopes and flush out the malcontents. The invitation was not the first step in the plan we had drawn up. It was only the first visible step.

As midsummer approached, local leaders from across the province began to arrive at Corinium in anticipation of a celebration. They found accommodation available in the town, with stables for their horses, sleeping lofts for their retainers and food and drink for all visitors. The town walls had been whitewashed, and companies of smartly dressed soldiers patrolled the streets, their armour polished, their swords and spears sharpened. Not least, the Christian basilica stood proud and complete, its bell tolling the hours for prayer, with the deacons chanting and the splendidly dressed bishop officiating at the services, a smiling Father Martin ready to welcome converts for baptism by the river.

Midsummer's Day began with a parade. Fortunately, it was a bright, sunny morning, not too hot, but without a cloud in the sky. The old image of the emperor – everyone had forgotten exactly which of them it represented – was taken out of the temple and carried through the streets in the accustomed manner, accompanied by flutes and drums and a troupe of young women dancing with garlands and ribbons. However, instead of being returned to the temple to be honoured with a sacrifice, it was taken in through the great doors of the basilica and placed on a pedestal in the apse at the far end. It was no longer the image of a god in a shrine, but simply the statue of a man, placed on public view to remind us of our past.

The forum filled with people excitedly waiting for the feasting to begin. They would have to wait until I had made a brief speech before the free food would be served. The tribal leaders stood at the front, by the steps of the basilica. Their followers filled the square, with the workmen, women and children of the town straining behind, peering out from side streets and alleys. There was a faint smell of cooking in the air, the sun shone down and expectations grew. Bishop Matthias stood to one side on the steps, dressed in his finery, his crozier in his hand, his deacons – also splendidly dressed – behind him. Hermanus stood on the other side, leaving room between himself and the bishop. His armour dazzling, a crested helmet on his head and a spear in his hand, he looked as if he had stepped down from one of the monuments of the old Romans. His deputy, Optio Gracchus, stood one pace behind him, dressed in a similar manner.

Between the bishop and the captain, the basilica door was open. The bright sunlight kept the interior in shadow. The bishop looked up. The sun had risen to its peak. The church bell began to ring, signalling that midday had arrived. The bishop banged his crozier on the ground. Silence. Hermanus barked an order. Two files of soldiers appeared, marching in strict ranks from the interior of the basilica. They passed between the bishop and the captain and, in a sequence of smart steps, formed a line across the front of the basilica.

The bishop stepped forward.

"Citizens of Corinium, tribesmen of the Dumantes and the Durovenes and all our friends," he began.

From inside the basilica I could not hear exactly what he was saying, but I had a good idea. The Britons had never completely accepted being ruled by the Romans. I am sure I heard him invoking the names of several long-lost fools who had committed slow suicide by leading revolts: Boudicca, Caractacus and others now nameless, and telling how our people had been exploited by the Empire and their treasures carried away. Now an opportunity had arrived to show how great we were, to regain the independence which our forefathers had lost long ago. Our country would become rich and prosperous without depending on the Empire and, of course, I was the man to lead us to this glorious future.

I was nervous. I could feel small beads of sweat trickling from my armpits, although it was quite cool in the shade of the building. My hand was clammy as I clutched the ceremonial spear we had constructed. I was trying to look dignified but did not feel that way. Hypatia had a concerned expression. I guessed she was thinking of our children waiting at home. Then she stepped towards me and straightened the cloak which hung around my shoulders. She put her hand to my cheek and gave me a smile.

At that moment the bishop reached the climax of his speech and it was time for me to make my entrance onto the stage.

"Citizens of Corinium, tribesmen of Britannia Prima, please welcome the man who has led you to your present peace and prosperity and who, with God's blessing and our prayers, will continue to lead us to an ever more prosperous future as independent Britons: Governor Marcus Lucullus Ursinus!"

This was the critical moment. Would there be cheers or hisses, thumbs up or down? I stepped out of the darkness onto the basilica step. One pace behind me came Hypatia. Both of us were dressed in the finest British clothes we were able to create. My sword was around my waist, and in my hand I had a spear that we had gilded so that it flashed golden in the sun. A great cheer echoed around the forum.

From the hard work and the miles put in by Hypatia and the bishop, I had counted that the majority of the leaders standing before me would be favourable. I also knew that there were people in the crowd who hated me. Now we were reckoning that they could no longer hide their anger, that it would burst out in public, if not right here in the square, then later as the wine and ale began to flow. Then it could never be hidden again.

As I stood on the basilica steps listening to the cheers of the crowd, the smell of roasting meat began to drift over the forum. I suspected that the people on the periphery were starting to feel hungry after the bishop's speech. I had only intended to say a few words, welcoming them to the celebration and wishing them enjoyment of the meat and drink. I did not even have the chance to start. There was a disturbance at the front of the crowd, and a man stepped forward.

"Usurper, traitor!" he yelled. "Criminal, thief!"

It was Vitellus Astrebanus.

"Silvanus," he continued, using my old family name, "you are just an upstart and an imposter. You have been one since the day you seduced Hypatia Ursina and deceived Publius Julius into accepting you as her husband." He turned to face the crowd. "This man has imposed taxes on us with no right; this man has stolen our corn and our meat to feed his minions. This man has trampled roughshod over our traditions and our rights. Now he has revealed himself as a traitor to our emperor, a cheat and a liar, leading our people on the path to ruin."

He probably was not alone in that opinion, but what astonished me was how he continued.

"I am the rightful governor, and here I have the proof," he shouted, pulling a scroll from his gown and waving it in the air.

Many of the leaders at the front were clearly puzzled by this outburst. This was supposed to be a festive day, not a time for insults and quarrels. However, I could see some questioning looks. What was this document Vitellus Astrebanus had produced? They began to back away and leave a space around him. At the same time a group of tough-looking men began to push their way through the crowd, Astrebanus' retainers from their appearance. Vitellus himself began to shake his fist, wave the scroll and shout, but what he was saying could no longer be heard as the crowd at the back began to become annoyed by the disturbance and the delay to the feast. I let him continue for a while longer, in part because I was unsure how to respond to his claim to have a letter. We had not anticipated that development. My hesitation gave his followers an opportunity to push to the front of the crowd and stand by him, confronting the soldiers. Here and there it was possible to see that they had weapons concealed beneath their tunics. I did not want a fight to break out, a general melee between the Dumantes and Durovenes, or an angry mob to develop.

I stepped forward and looked down at Astrebanus, speaking only loud enough for him and those around him to hear.

"Chief Astrebanus, I am sure you would not want to be responsible for a riot. Let's not keep these people from their food."

Astrebanus looked around, a little unsure of the mood of the crowd from where he stood between the line of soldiers and his own followers. I turned to the bishop and waved my hand. He once again banged the ground with his crozier and shouted for silence in the voice he usually reserved for condemning sinners.

Perhaps in his mind that was exactly what he was doing. Outwardly, he called out a prayer of thanks for the food, and the band struck up and began to march into the marketplace, pushing a path through the crowd and making room for a host of servants to lay out the feast. Closest to us, Astrebanus' men shuffled uneasily, perhaps hungrily, while the chiefs looked on, frowning and wondering what was going to happen next.

With the crowd distracted, I once again turned to Astrebanus.

"You claim to have proof that you are the rightful governor? Have you received a commission from the emperor?" I said. He waved the document once more. From the corner of my eye, I could see Hermanus observing the crowd.

"A letter from the emperor?" I said, desperately improvising. "You must certainly let us see it. Come nearer and show us the document."

The bishop stepped towards me.

"It's a falsification. It must be. I've not heard anything about this through the Church, and I would certainly have done so."

I held up my hand.

"Let him come here."

Astrebanus moved closer, slowly, hesitatingly, as if he had lost confidence in his boasting. I waved my hand to encourage him.

From a distance the document looked impressive, a parchment scroll with several weighty seals attached along the bottom. If this was a real document from Rome, then I had just taken a step in defiance of the Empire. I had just become a traitor.

Hermanus leaned over and whispered in my ear.

"I don't see his brother."

"How did you receive this document, Astrebanus?" I asked.

"It was sent to my home, of course!"

"Why not here, to the governor's administration and the lawyers?"

"Because the emperor is quite aware that the administration of this province is in the hands of a group of rebels," he sneered. "Why would he have any communication with you?"

"And where is the messenger who brought it so that we can interview him?"

Astrebanus hesitated for a moment.

"He left straightaway so he would come to no harm from you and your cronies."

"Did you speak to him?"

"No. He left the letter with my… brother."

"This seems very strange," said the bishop, reaching out his hand in the expectation that Astrebanus would give him the document. Astrebanus took a pace forward, then a second, and held out the scroll so the bishop could take it.

The moment he moved, the soldiers closed behind him, separating him from his followers.

"You are under arrest and will be tried by the tribunal of the independent province of Britannia Prima," I said curtly.

As they heard their leader threatened, the followers of Astrebanus moved forward menacingly, starting to draw their weapons. The remaining auxiliaries took a pace towards them. They halted, confused, now trapped between the remaining chieftains, most of whom had been invited to dinner with me in the evening, and the menace of the auxiliaries.

"What have I done wrong?" Vitellus protested. "I have merely claimed my rightful position." He waved his hand towards the scroll, still visible in the bishop's hand.

"You are charged," I said, "with treason and with leading a band of armed men against the governor of Britannia Prima. You will be tried by the tribunal and sentenced according to the law that you have so diligently used to undermine order in this land. Come now, before I have to humiliate you further by binding you."

He had little choice. His followers were trapped. The populace had turned to the feast. Any allies he had in the crowd were holding their peace, not wanting to be associated with failure. Escorted by soldiers, he was quickly led into the basilica, through the chamber and down into the crypt, where he was locked up with guards placed outside. I doubt more than a few people at the front of the crowd ever saw what had happened.

His retainers seemed sufficiently intimidated to give no further trouble. They probably did not know why they were there, and with the disappearance of their leader, they had lost their way. A few defiant ones gave me hostile looks; the cowards hung their heads. Hermanus was still scanning back and forth.

"I don't understand it," he said. "There is no sign of Drusus. You would have thought he would be here backing up his brother." He looked back for Optio Gracchus, but as the plan dictated, he was no longer there.

I took three strides down the basilica steps and eased my way through the row of soldiers.

"I have no quarrel with you," I said to Astrebanus' followers. "If you swear loyalty to me, I will allow you to go back to your homes in peace. Now leave your weapons here and return to your lodgings. Don't cause a disturbance." To my relief, there was a clatter of iron and steel as they dropped their hidden weapons, evidence, if nothing else, of Astrebanus' intention. A path was made through the crowd so they could slink away. They were followed by the remaining soldiers who ensured that they returned directly to the house where they had been staying. Once inside, the doors and gates were closed behind them and guards placed.

As the retainers were ushered away, I saw Hermanus catch a couple of the soldiers and disappear into the crowd. Later that day he told me he feared that Drusus Astrebanus might have taken men to the Ursinus house, where the children and servants had been waiting. To his relief, when he arrived, the staff were singing merrily and starting to lay out the meal we were giving for the honoured guests.

The man with the most critical role at this moment had already departed. Optio Gracchus had slipped into the shadows the instant Vitellus had stepped forward. Unseen by anyone, he had left the rear of the basilica where a horse waited. While attention had been focused on the drama in the marketplace, he reached the legionary camp where a dozen further mounted men were waiting. With a sign, he indicated they should take the road east to Agridurnum, to the ancestral home of the Astrebani.

For the townspeople, booths and tables serving food and drink had been set up in the forum and the main streets. All sorts of showmen, jugglers and dancers thronged the arcades, some invited and some hucksters and tricksters who had picked up news of the festival and converged on the town. Men selling baubles and trinkets were also taking full advantage of the gathering. The minor tribal leaders and small landowners were invited to dine in the basilica under the watchful eye of the now-human emperor, with the bishop as host. For those who were not regular visitors to Corinium, this would be an occasion to remember and discuss for years to come. A well-chosen few were to be entertained in the atrium of the Ursinus villa, where Hypatia would preside over a feast with selected delicacies and better class entertainment.

For a moment, however, that was forgotten as we gathered around the bishop to examine the scroll that Astrebanus had handed over. He unrolled it, and our eyes followed his hands. The document certainly looked impressive. The vellum was top quality, the wording was drawn exquisitely and the row of seals was striking. My heart was in my mouth. Did this really mean that the emperor had appointed Vitellus Astrebanus governor, the man we had just locked up in the cellar of the basilica? I watched as the bishop read through the document, nodding his head. Aurelius appeared from the shadows.

"Optio Gracchus passed me on the way to the barracks and told me that Astrebanus produced a document. May I see it?"

We made space so that he could stand alongside the bishop.

"The formulations are correct, if a little archaic," he said. "It is sealed 'Honorius'. It could be correct."

"It's a forgery, and a clever one," said the bishop confidently. "If the emperor had appointed a governor of Britannia Prima, he would not have sent a mere letter like this with a cowardly messenger who crept away without anyone seeing. There would have been a delegation, a show of imperial pomp and strength. I have heard nothing of this through the Church, and at the very least the man who brought it would have been obligated to speak to me."

Suddenly everyone was speaking at once.

"What do we do?"

"What will happen now?"

"We continue as if we had never seen this letter," said Aurelius. "We have just proclaimed ourselves independent, and even if the emperor has named Astrebanus governor, he has no province to govern over. The emperor will have to come here and enforce his appointment."

"Kill him," said Hypatia, breaking her silence in a quiet voice, hardly above a whisper. "We need to eliminate this man once and for all. Get him out of the way. He's a threat to all of us."

A few of us eating and drinking in my atrium that evening were well aware that business would not be over with a successful feast for the leaders of the Durovenes and the Dumantes or the oaths from the followers of Astrebanus.

"This has gone too far," said Hypatia when I had a chance to be alone with her. "If he had merely insulted you and played the lawyer as he has done before, we could have spared his life and sent him away. But he has produced this letter, and that is an altogether different danger. It doesn't matter if it's real or false; there are people who will want to believe it's real."

We drank sparingly and gently suggested to those who did not have to rise early to leave and join the exuberant feasting in the town. We could hear music and dancing and the shouts and cheers of people in the surrounding streets. For those who did not have more serious matters on their minds, here was a chance for a little anonymous fun under the cover of darkness.

☙ Chapter 17 ❧

The tribunal met at dawn, the first tribunal of the newly independent province with the worst possible work to be done. It consisted of Aurelius, Bishop Matthias and Fabianus. The early hour ensured that the courtroom was free of the inquisitive public. Vitellus Astrebanus was escorted in by soldiers. He seemed to be shivering. The cellar had been cold, but I doubted that was the reason.

"Vitellus Astrebanus, you are accused of forgery, treason and conspiracy to murder," said Aurelius. "You have also presented us with this document" – he tapped his hand on the podium – "falsely claiming it is a letter from the emperor proclaiming you governor. You led a band of armed men to interfere with the proclamation made by Governor Ursinus and threaten his life. Do you have anything to say in your defence?"

He hung his head. "I am the rightful governor. The letter proves it."

I was puzzled. He really seemed to believe it.

Aurelius spoke up. He had no interest in considering Astrebanus' state of mind.

"Vitellus Astrebanus, you are simply condemning yourself with the words you are uttering here in the court. You have previously refused to recognise Marcus Lucullus Ursinus as governor of Britannia Prima. You have refused to pay justly apportioned taxes. You have threatened Marcus Lucullus with invalid lawsuits for debt. You have mischievously pursued an invalid lawsuit through the courts of Britannia Superior to Rome dishonestly claiming you have a right to be governor. You have bribed the tribunal in Camulodunum to support your case. You have insulted Marcus Lucullus and his wife in the public forum and called into question their honour and integrity and the sanctity of their marriage. Finally, yesterday, you led a group of armed followers with the intention of causing harm to Marcus Lucullus and his wife, along with a host of other people present. Do you deny any of these charges? Do you expect any mercy from this court?"

"I don't recognise the validity of this court! I am the legitimate governor of this province, and you have no right to try me. I am a citizen of the Empire. I demand to be tried in Camulodunum by the *vicarius'* tribunal. I demand the right to appeal to the emperor!"

I heard the tone in his voice. He seemed quite convinced that his claims were justified. He must believe the letter is valid, I reflected, even though the correct process had hardly been followed. Letters from the emperor concerning official business did not arrive with an anonymous courier to a man's private residence. And yet where had the letter come from, with its florid wording and fancy seals, if not Rome?

Aurelius looked down at him.

"This court no longer recognises the right of the emperor or any other court to judge cases from Britannia Prima. Your appeal is invalid. Enough! By insisting you can still make such an appeal to the Emperor of Rome, you have condemned yourself."

Aurelius turned to me.

"Marcus Lucullus, did you see this man in front of you yesterday?"

"Yes," I answered. "He pushed through the crowd at the head of a band of armed men. Fortunately, the actions of the soldiers prevented him from committing any actual violence. I ask that that be taken into consideration."

Aurelius shifted his gaze to Gallius, who was attending as the second witness and accuser.

"I saw the same," he said without being asked.

"Thank you. That is sufficient." Aurelius glanced at the other two judges, and they nodded.

"Vitellus Astrebanus, we find you guilty of conspiracy to murder, leading a group of armed men in an insurrection. We find you guilty of forgery, and we find you guilty of treason."

He took a deep breath and continued.

"Vitellus Astrebanus, you are sentenced to death by execution, and the sentence will be carried out immediately."

With that, he stood up and the two other judges rose beside him. The soldiers grasped hold of Astrebanus and began to manhandle him out of the courtroom.

He looked around him, as if searching for help. Such a pathetic figure: a lawyer, a man of pen and parchment, not a warrior. I suppose I could have had him sent into exile, somewhere nasty and bug-ridden or rife with deadly diseases, or else tried to convince him to commit suicide like Seneca. But the elite in those far off days had a greater sense of honour, and I was not ready to take any risks. He was also a rich man and a clever man, although apparently deluded. He could use his riches to support his delusion and continue to undermine the integrity of Britannia Prima. Hypatia was right. Aurelius was right. Reluctantly, I had to agree; now was no time for mercy.

At least your family and your followers are fortunate I'm a magnanimous man, I thought, as I followed the group out of the courtroom, through the basilica and into the yard. I have had a classical education and have learned some vestiges of virtue. It might not be much comfort to you, and I wonder what you would have done if the boot was on the other foot.

He was led out into the courtyard, where a group of soldiers were waiting in front of the stables. A large wooden block had been hurriedly set up and a quantity of sand strewn around. The deacons were standing nearby, the rough-looking Baxter holding a large wooden cross. When he saw them, Astrebanus began to scream and curse and struggled to free himself. He was held firm, dragged towards the block and his head forced down, but he would not keep still. If we were not careful, someone was going to be injured while the man received his sentence. Deacon Baxter pushed forward, moved one of the soldiers out of the way, took the butt end of the cross and struck Astrebanus on the side of the head. He immediately sank to the ground, senseless. His head was place on the block, his body propped up and the axe fell.

The sun had not yet risen over the roofline.

"I hope we don't have to do that again," said the bishop, raising his hand in a benediction. "The whole matter was distasteful and, I feel, not entirely in accordance with scripture."

"At least we gave him a trial," said Aurelius. "I don't think he would have done the same, given the chance, bringing a score of men with concealed weapons into the forum."

It was my turn to shiver.

It was not until later in the day when I was on horseback on the way towards Agridurnum that I realised we had made a foolish mistake. Not in executing Vitellus Astrebanus – that had been necessary – but in doing so without establishing the whereabouts of his brother.

◦ Chapter 18 ◦

Optio Gracchus and his cavalry troop had set off immediately on the eastern road once Vitellus Astrebanus had made his move, and they reached Agridurnum Manor, the Astrebani villa, by early evening. It had been essential to travel quickly, to arrive before any of the retainers could slip our guard in Corinium and reach home with a warning.

Gracchus and I have had many opportunities to discuss the events of that day in the years that followed and to reflect on whether everything we did was necessary, and whether we could have done more, especially because of the way events turned out. As it was, from what he told me, the cavalry cantered in through the open gate of the villa unopposed, through the outer yard, surrounded by stables and the like, and into the inner court where the domestic buildings were located. They slammed the outer gate closed and barred it. The archway into the inner court was blocked and guards were posted. Gracchus and the rest of the troops ran into the house, swords drawn. Astrebanus' wife and his child, a boy of about six years, were caught inside, along with his house staff, his clerks and diverse hangers-on. By nightfall a tense silence had fallen over the villa.

In the morning the farm workers were ordered to go about their business in the outer yard, taking care of the animals, and such tasks. No fires were to be lit and no one was to enter or leave the inner courtyard. As they began to open the stables, suddenly, out of nowhere, there was a scuffle and a shout and three horses with men on their backs bolted out of one of the barns. The sentries by the gate stood their ground, trying to block the way, but they were no match for the mounted men. One of the horsemen quickly dismounted, ran to the gate of the outer yard and drew the bar back. The others led his horse forward until they were clear and he could leap back on, give the horse a kick and disappear down the east road in a cloud of dust. Slowly, Optio Gracchus and his companions realised that Drusus Astrebanus had escaped.

We have been through these events many times since. Gracchus acknowledges that he was not careful enough. It was hot; there were too few guards. Agridurnum was an immense villa and they had not searched it thoroughly. Someone must have missed the men sneaking into the stables. The optio reacted, but too late. By the time our men set off in pursuit, Drusus Astrebanus and his companions had long gone. All that was left to do was to tend to the wounded guards and slide the bar back in place.

And so it remained until we arrived with the infantry: Hermanus, the deacons Baxter and Justin, and I. Hermanus heard out his deputy, cursing under his breath. No one had thought to search for Drusus. We had assumed he would be with his brother. The optio and his troop had already left before we realised that Drusus was not in Corinium. Our only reassurance was that he and his companions had fled to the east, away from the provincial capital, Verdaris and any places where he could cause immediate damage. Hermanus looked grim. No one could expect pleasant treatment after the flight of Vitellus' brother.

Dealing with the mistress of the house was my business. All I knew was that Vitellus Astrebanus had married the daughter of a prominent lawyer from London. I recalled that the woman's name was Milesia and his son was called Constantinus, after the infamous general, I assume. I had never met her, but Hypatia had told me her father had died not so long ago, leaving his daughter a great deal of money, some of it no doubt squeezed from Publius Julius.

I strode determinedly along the corridor to the room where they were being held. This time I had even put on a military uniform to add to the atmosphere of intimidation, and the hobnails of my boots crashed on the tiles. Behind me marched two soldiers bearing spears. The flight of Drusus had set my emotions surging. What other nasty surprises might be waiting?

The guards outside the room where the mistress was imprisoned sprang to attention as I approached, raising their arms in salute. I opened the door and stepped into the room. Vitellus' wife was standing by the window. His son was seated nearby on a divan. She was tall, almost as tall as I was, with black – raven black – hair arranged in the Roman fashion. I still remember she was wearing a long tunic of grey silk, and the light from the window caught her face, accentuating the contrast between her pale skin and her dark hair. A moment later her grey eyes met mine. It felt as if someone had stabbed me in the chest. In an instant I could understand how, in the old legends, mortal men were transfixed and turned to stone if they accidentally caught sight of a goddess, because something similar happened to me. I felt as if I had stumbled into the presence of Diana or Minerva. Milesia's gaze had rendered me immobile and speechless. I could tell you today that she looked beautiful, because now I know she is. I could say she sounded intelligent, dominating, because since then I have understood that she is that too, but in the moment itself, I found I could say nothing.

She stepped towards me, and I involuntarily took a step back. Perhaps I was worrying that she might pull out a dagger and stab me, but I do not think so. No, it was her aura, her presence, that forced me back, and instead of stabbing me, she just reached out and touched my arm, ever so gently, while she spoke.

"He was a fool, Marcus," she said, in a quiet voice, "always busy with his lawsuits, always scheming and plotting. He didn't realise that he could never win any more than he already had. Power, wealth…"

She paused and seemed to examine me.

"And you…" I stuttered, managing to find a voice, overwhelmed by her like some young fool encountering his first beautiful woman.

"And me?" she smiled. "Yes, his power and wealth, and me… and his boy, but he wasn't satisfied."

She sighed and took a step back, letting her hand drop, half turning from me.

"I don't say that he deserved what happened, but every move they took, Vito and Drusus, every decision they made, led inevitably to this outcome." She swept her hand around. "And here is what they have achieved. It's not the result they fantasised about, with Vito's dreams of power and glory, of governing, but it's the one that the Fates had spun for them."

Suddenly she looked back at me again, gripping me with her eyes. I was frozen like a statue.

"And you, too. You are simply following the path the gods have laid out for you. You can't step off the way. You can't retreat, only continue forward, one stumbling pace at a time. I don't blame you for what you have done. You had no more choice in this than my husband and his brother, although all of you thought you were deciding every move yourselves. No, Governor Ursinus, in fact the thread of the Fates bound you together, pulled you tighter. Every step was inevitable."

I have heard people describe her as a witch. I have even heard others say she is a saint. In truth, she is a woman whom people were easily bewitched by, her steady eyes, her calm voice, the impression she understood you. I know. I am one of them.

She fell silent and dropped her eyes. In the absence of her gaze, her voice, I felt released and sensation began to return to my body. My arms and legs could move once again. From being frozen, a sense almost of desire came over me. She was the wife of my defeated enemy. She could be mine to have, to possess. But the bishop had forewarned me. He had met her. He had seen enough of the world. He was a man who had grown up and lived in Gaul, where kings and chiefs and leaders of men followed each other in quick succession, each taking from the last and falling victim to the next, driven by a lust for power, for wealth, for luxury and for women. Milesia was a danger, not an opportunity, he said. She was too dangerous to leave alone, too dangerous to allow to remain.

I broke the silence.

"Lady Milesia, since everything is inevitable, what is to be your fate?"

"You will send me away, my lord, you and the bishop. You are a man of virtue, you suppose, and the bishop, a Christian. You will not kill a woman and a child. Instead you will offer us as sacrifices to your gods of virtue and Christianity and hope for their blessings. You will separate me from my boy, and you will send us away."

That was, of course, our plan. The bishop had already identified a small monastery, a holy house, in the remote south-west of the province on the border with Dumnonia where she was to be sent.

"Where has Drusus gone?" I asked abruptly, hoping to seize the initiative.

"I don't know where he is," she answered. "He was here when Vito and the retainers set off to Corinium. He did not tell me his plans." She smiled. "He did not trust me."

I bowed to her, now forcing myself to back away.

"You are right, Lady Milesia, that you will be sent into exile. You should make preparations for yourself and your son. My men will supervise you and your servants."

With a wrench I turned my back on her and left the room, but when I was outside, I realised I was trembling as the tension in my body sapped away. I stood still for a moment, then shook myself, pulled myself together and went to find Baxter and Justin. The sound of the hobnails on the tiled floor now felt ridiculous.

The deacons were supervising two girls who bobbed when I came up – Milesia's companions – and a pair of servants who had already begun packing clothes and bedding into chests for the journey. I left them in peace to complete the job and continued into the courtyard. Already, furniture and wall hangings were being carried from the house to be burned in the yard. It seemed such a pity just to destroy everything, but we had sworn that neither I nor any other man would profit from the fall of the Astrebani. I did not want people accusing me of having eliminated Vitellus Astrebanus only to enrich myself. Gold and silver, ivory and jewels were placed to one side under guard. I ordered one of the soldiers to fetch a chest, selected a few of the valuables and placed them inside.

"Take this to the deacons," I said, "and ask them to include it in Mistress Milesia's baggage."

She had foreseen her fate. She appeared resigned to it. If she was going to cause trouble, pursue a feud, raise a rebellion, she would do it anyway, somehow. Her husband's wealth, her father's wealth, assuming the rumours were true, was now in our hands. She did not need humiliating by being left destitute.

In the evening food was served, and the men gathered round the fire of burning furniture and roof beams torn from the villa. Inside, Milesia, her son and companions spent their last day in their home. In the morning the weather was fair. As dawn broke, two oxen were fastened to a wagon and the baggage loaded on. Milesia was led out and, with a certain amount of dignity, seated herself alongside the wagoner. I kept my distance as her son and the companions were assisted onto the wagon and did their best to make themselves comfortable for the long journey west. A dozen cavalrymen under the leadership of Optio Gracchus formed up. Alongside him rode Deacon Baxter. The optio gave a command, the wagoner cracked his whip and the gates of the courtyard swung open. The oxen took the strain, and the wagon creaked into motion. It slowly passed through the gate and down the driveway into the distance.

While Milesia's future might not have been enviable, the fate of the other captives was considerably worse. Once their mistress had left, they were taken from the barn, roped together and led away along the road to Litorina, to Gaul and the slave markets of the south.

The dismantling of the house continued. Piece by piece, the roof was removed, and then the walls were toppled. Only the barns and farm buildings were left standing. When the work of destruction had been completed, the farm workers were called together.

"From now on Deacon Justin is your steward," I announced. "You will be working for the Church. Those who are not already Christians will be baptised. Live in peace, and you will not be harmed."

From the rubble remains of the villa, Deacon Justin selected a few carved stones as an altar. Two beams were fastened together to form a cross. As I had promised, the fall of the Astrebani would not profit a single man, but the Church of God and Jesus Christ, his son.

I feared vengeance. I feared that the Durovenes would see my actions not as a re-establishment of order, carried out for the public good, but as an illegitimate attack by one tribe on the chief of another. I did not expect an armed uprising, but rather a dagger into the stomach while walking in the forum or an assault on Verdaris, directed at my family by angry followers or hired swords. Cull and I carried out careful inspections both at Umbrosa Farm and Verdaris to strengthen the defences and make sure no one could break in with a surprise attack. We began to train the field hands and tenants of Verdaris in the use of weapons, the way my father had trained the men of Umbrosa. I feared Drusus Astrebanus stepping out of an alley with a knife. For a while I took to wearing a leather jerkin covered with metal plates. It was heavy and uncomfortable. I looked and felt like a statue of Julius Caesar.

While I made these private efforts, I also took care to make a public show of strength. Some of the valuables we had confiscated were used to recruit additional auxiliaries. We set up small watchtowers along the southern coast of Britannia Prima and kept them continuously manned, sending out patrols to march from tower to tower along the south road. On the face of it, the towers and patrols were to guard against pirates, one of the major fears of the Durovenes, but they also served as a show of strength and as eyes and ears for any trouble that might be brewing.

Fortunately, over the course of the Empire, the Durovenes had trusted in law and order, grown rich and enjoyed living in comfort and opulence. Drusus might now have a legitimate claim to be considered the leader of the tribe, but they were not willing to upend their peaceful and prosperous existence by raising rebellion or employing assassins. They saw the armed patrols as a sign of security, not a threat. There was grumbling and the threatening of lawsuits to retrieve certain tribal regalia taken from Agridurnum, but no violence. In the autumn the tribesmen gathered together and elected Marcellus as their chief, and by some miracle the regalia of the Durovenes was found undamaged in Bishop Matthias' treasury and returned in time for the installation ceremony. I thought it best to stay away.

To all intents and purposes, Drusus Astrebanus had gone up in smoke, but his disappearance only fuelled fantasies. He had been seen in Litorina. Men loyal to Drusus had passed by Agridurnum in the night. A fire in a haystack on the Verdaris estate was blamed on him. Aurelius and Fabiansson listened for rumours, and out of these spooks and spectres a pattern began to emerge. Drusus

Astrebanus was alive and well in Belgica, living amongst the exiles from Britannia Superior, his childhood friends, the lawyers and shady moneylenders that he and his family had used to wage a hidden war against the Ursini. He and his family may have suffered a defeat, but everything indicated that he had not given up the war. Possibly the spooks and spectres were only delusions, or perhaps they were portents of events still to come.

❧ Chapter 19 ☙

The plotting and scheming of Drusus Astrebanus and the antics of a few disaffected exiles were little threat to the peace of Britannia Prima. That was the consensus amongst my colleagues. The majority of the landowners, chieftains and wealthy individuals of all classes were happy to cultivate their acres, lord it over their subordinates and enjoy a life of ease and luxury. The peasants and townspeople were more interested in scratching out their living than rebelling. Rich or poor, they only had to look east to see the alternative. However, thoughts of Drusus and his allies left me perpetually on edge. There was no need for an armed band to inflict suffering on my family. A single individual could cause irreparable harm. There was no need for a conspiracy to drag my name and that of my family in the dirt. Whispers in the right ears would be sufficient to question my credibility and my authority, to sustain the memory of Publius Julius and to give doubters an excuse for withholding their support. This was not a matter of government policy. It was personal.

Though several years had passed, Hypatia remained concerned that she had heard nothing from her family after her sister's last message from Remis. With two daughters growing up, she fretted that the little ones would never know their aunts and uncles and that she could not tell her own mother and father about their grandchildren. She talked about this often with me, and I surmised she must also have shared her worries with the bishop, because one day he appeared unannounced in my office in the basilica.

"Marcus, please forgive me for not having told you beforehand, but I have been trying to be of some assistance to Lady Hypatia. She has spoken to me so often about her family, and her worries about what has happened to them, that I took it upon myself to make some enquiries. Your dear wife told me that the last she heard from her family was a letter sent from Remis, so I wrote to my brother in Christ, the bishop, to ask if there were any records of the Ursinus family in the city. A little while ago he wrote back confirming a stay by the family of Governor Ursinus. Beyond that, he informed me that the records showed they left with a group of other travellers towards the end of August four years ago to journey south to Lugdunum."

"We have not heard from them since then," I replied.

"Just so," said the bishop. "Without consulting Hypatia, I must confess, I wrote again to my brother, Bishop Sebastianus of Lugdunum. Only yesterday I received a reply. Imagine my surprise that there was no record of the Ursinus family having stayed in Lugdunum. I had to come to speak to you immediately."

"It's possible they took another route," I offered. "Or hurried on to Arelate. I believe that's where my brother-in-law Gaius is living."

"That's my hope, too," said the bishop, "but still, it would have been possible for a message to reach you, as you can see from the success of my own efforts. It is strange that you have heard nothing."

"Publius Julius may have feared the response. You know the situation he left behind. He was in disgrace and had brought shame on his family."

"But for Lady Hypatia to be abandoned by her family, it seems unnatural, unchristian, and the ladies at least were believers?"

"That's true, Bishop. Do you have plans to do more?"

The bishop sighed. "I had thought to write to some other friends in Gaul, but where should I start? There are so many bishops and monasteries, and Governor Ursinus might not have made contact with them. So instead of writing, I wonder if it might be better to send one of my deacons to see if we can find evidence of where they went. Deacon Baxter is a knowledgeable man, and although he is originally from Africa, he can speak the languages of the barbarians as well as Latin. I thought to send him to meet Bishop Eusebius at Remis and then travel on to Lugdunum. However, I felt that I needed to consult you first."

"I'm very grateful for your concern, Bishop," I said. "but I must talk to my wife before we take that step."

In fact, since Hypatia was at Verdaris, before I had a chance to speak to her, I mentioned the bishop's proposal to Fabiansson.

"It's interesting that the bishop has brought up the subject, as I was in Litorina just recently and met Laurentius. He told me that there are people around Drusus Astrebanus who are also trying to discover the fate of your father-in-law. Their motives, I'm afraid, are not honourable. To put it bluntly, money is at the bottom of the matter."

I might have guessed.

"As you know," he went on, "your father-in-law sold his possessions and had accumulated a considerable sum, in gold and silver, sufficient to fund his new life and keep him in ease. No one knows what has happened to that wealth. Some of it, one can assume, was sent ahead to Gaius Ursinus, but Publius Julius must've been carrying a significant amount with him to pay for the expenses of travelling, if nothing else."

"And Drusus' pals want to get their hands on it?"

"Exactly. There are men who used to live in Londinium who maintain they're still owed money by the governor. I suppose you could claim they have a stake in finding him. But there are also men around Drusus Astrebanus who would like the riches in compensation for the confiscation of Agridurnum and to fund rebellion and disruption in Britannia Prima."

"My guess is the two groups overlap and share a common interest."

"Yes, and it's not yours."

"Are you suggesting we should go after the lost wealth, too?"

"Everything I've heard indicates it would be a waste of time. Your enemies have already made a significant effort and come up empty-handed. Perhaps if we could find the truth to the stories, we could damp down the expectations of anyone still here in Britannia Prima who might, somewhere in the back of their mind, still be weighing up collaborating with the Astrebani."

"You mean Drusus and the boy."

"Milesia too. She's not without resources and influence."

I could understand that. I have to confess that Milesia had remained in my thoughts long after the wagon she was riding in had departed, and in my dreams, too. I was haunted by her eyes and the sound of her voice. It was foolish, very foolish, but no reasoning, no conscious effort, could put an end to it.

"You who always have your nose in a book," said Hypatia, when I finally broached the subject. "How did the emperors solve the kind of problem we have with Drusus?"

"They sent a messenger to the exile and told him to kill himself, which he inevitably did, at least according to the histories."

"It's a myth," said Hypatia. "I bet that never happened. Those weren't messengers. They were assassins, and they put a knife to the throat of the victim and told him to kill himself or they would do the job much more slowly and painfully. That's what Drusus deserves. Until he's gone, we'll never be able to live in peace."

"That's all well and good, but I don't have any assassins at my command," I pointed out.

She looked at me coldly.

"Deacon Baxter would make a very good assassin. There's something in his look that tells me he's done that kind of job in the past."

"I can't very well send a churchman to kill my enemies," I protested.

"Then you will just have to do it yourself. You're a man, aren't you? You spend time every day exercising with your weapons. Use them."

"Hypatia, I think that would be very risky. Gaul's not entirely at peace, and my absence here…"

"We can manage without you for a month or two!"

"But what if something were to happen to me, if he manages to kill me?"

"Marcus, the problem you do not appear to see is that that could happen any day while Drusus is on the loose, stirring things up. You could be walking through the forum tomorrow and someone steps out from behind a column and sinks a knife into you."

"I've thought of that," I said, "all too often."

"Well, the victim could be me or one of the girls or even your sister – any one of us. Does that make you feel any better?"

"No."

"Then the man has to go, the same way as his brother. And if you want my opinion, that witch Milesia and her son should suffer the same fate. I don't trust any of them."

"Hypatia, I can't go around ordering women and children to be killed. That would put me in the same category as Nero or Caligula."

"Then at least you need to deal with Drusus, one way or the other."

I was still hesitating about what course to take when Aurelius caught me a few days later, my eyes seemingly focused on a dark spot on the wall of my workroom.

"I don't want to upset you, Marcus, since you already seem worried, but I just received a letter from one of my acquaintances in Treviri. Drusus Astrebanus has been there, talking very bravely and trying to recruit a group of men to sneak over here and murder you. He was promising Umbrosa Farm to the man whose sword put an end to you. I suppose he had plans to keep Verdaris for himself."

"Damn it, Aurelius. That man's becoming an obsession with me. I keep wondering what he will do next. I feel have to make a move myself, and no option looks like a good one. Hypatia was trying to persuade me that he should be killed."

"That would be my advice, too, though I wouldn't do it too openly."

"What do you mean?"

"Suppose you were to march over to Remis with a couple of hundred soldiers, announcing that you planned to round up your enemies and put them to the sword. I suspect you would meet with some resistance, and not just from people who might think they were on your list."

"The precedent isn't good," I admitted. "The last governor of Britannia who crossed to Gaul proclaimed himself emperor, started a civil war and ended up being executed."

"Constantinus."

"I don't intend to proclaim myself emperor."

"Nonetheless, you wouldn't be welcome."

"Suppose I asked Baxter? Hypatia thinks he has an assassin's look about him, and the bishop has already suggested he should be sent to find out what happened to Publius Julius."

"Alone?"

"It doesn't sound sufficient, when you put like that."

"Cull would step up for you."

"I couldn't ask Cull if I wasn't prepared to risk myself. It's a personal matter, you understand?"

"Not really, Marcus. You are the governor, and he's just a farmer."

"He's a friend, and he has family just like I have."

"That's misplaced loyalty."

"No, it's not, Aurelius, it's what I stand for, if anything, and what my father stood for. You don't ask your friends to take risks you wouldn't take yourself. You don't sacrifice others while you live in comfort and luxury yourself. You've just made up my mind for me. I have to go myself. Hypatia was hinting as much already. I have to stand up for myself, Aurelius."

The lawyer frowned.

"I'll go in disguise, a provincial landowner visiting Gaul, taking care of family business. No one knows me there. I'm not a threat to anyone except Drusus Astrebanus."

Aurelius grimaced, obviously thinking I was an idiot, but he could think what he liked. I had to face my wife. I had to live with myself. Perhaps it was stupid, but so is a lot of what we do in life.

"Let's take up another example of misplaced loyalty, Aurelius."

He looked alarmed for a moment, until I laughed.

"Am I misplacing my loyalty in asking you to look after the province while I am away?"

"I would hope not," he answered. "I only hope you will return, unlike your predecessor."

"You'll have support from the bishop and Hermanus. I'll just have to persuade the captain he must stay at home instead of coming with me."

Aurelius smiled.

"And I would be leaving my wife and children in your hands."

❧ Chapter 20 ☙

The four of us, Baxter, Cull, a young stable hand named Jarmi and I, slipped away from Verdaris, heading across country, avoiding villas and towns where we might be recognised, until we reached the port of Dubris. I did not publicise myself as being the governor of Britannia Prima, but stuck to the identity of a small-time northern landowner, Lucullus Silvanus. It was who I really was, who the Astrebani had accused me of being, after all. Once at the port, we took a boat to Bononia. The town had been a major harbour in Roman times, the headquarters of the fleet, but now it had a sad, run-down air. A few cargo vessels were tied up along the quay, but it appeared to be overgrown and abandoned. We did not intend to stay but immediately left for the provincial capital, Remis. The inns in Gaul are notoriously poor, as we soon found out, and I had already begun to wonder why Publius Julius and his family had not done as any wealthy traveller would normally have done and stayed at the houses of friends. But I had learned that there were few of those amongst the exiles, for Publius Julius or for me and my companions. Instead Fabiansson had given us the name of a lodging-house keeper, a man he could trust, where we could stay quietly while we searched for Drusus Astrebanus. We arrived, took a room and then began to gather what information we could.

Remis was a town teeming with exiled Britons. I avoided them. One wrong word and I would have been given away, but Cull and Baxter could play the parts of curious and ignorant visitors with pleasure. I did take a stroll around town, the hood of my cloak well pulled down. It was immediately obvious that Roman customs remained much stronger there than in Britannia. The basilica was humming with business, the forum was filled with townspeople at the market stalls and there was a fine Christian church. I was told that the city had been invaded by Vandals a few years before, but it seemed to have taken little harm and resembled the bustling Corinium I had visited as a child. I felt a little ashamed at the conditions at home, with our shabby, run-down administration and not even the excuse of a barbarian invasion. When I looked carefully, I could see amongst the tunicked men with short-cut hair talking Latin a sprinkling of rough-looking, long-haired individuals with trousers and cloaks and drooping moustaches, speaking a language I did not recognise. I concluded that these must be the barbarians, the feared warriors who had so recently ridden in from the east, devastating the countryside, burning towns and murdering the inhabitants in cold blood. But here they were, now sitting peacefully in the forum at Remis with the other citizens, drinking wine and laughing amongst themselves. I passed an obvious barbarian at one table heatedly discussing in broken Latin with a Roman-looking gentleman about a lawsuit he was bringing. Clearly, this was one invader who was taking his case to court rather than relying on brute force.

The rest of the time, with the help of the lodging-house keeper, I sat like a spider in the middle of its web and collected news. Drusus was not in town, we quickly learned. He had been on the eastern frontier, where men and lives are cheap, trying to recruit a gang of murderers. He was expected back at any time, our sources suggested, though he would probably stop in the city of Treviri, about two hundred miles to the east. It would take us several days to travel there, but making a move would be better than waiting in Remis for a man who might never turn up.

Treviri had a status in Belgica equivalent to that of Corinium in Britannia Prima, but it was far more magnificent, not least because the city had been the home of the emperors for several generations. We rode into town over an impressive bridge and through the ornate west gate, but we were not there for sightseeing. First, we had to find lodgings and then begin our search for Drusus. Baxter would be the best person to do the scouting since he was the least obviously a Briton. Cull and I would have to act a little more circumspectly, locate a tavern where foreigners were to be found, play simple farmers and ask about people who were known to maintain contacts with Britannia. Our northern accents, normally so carefully tempered in my case, would no doubt help.

When we compared notes in the evening, we were embarrassed to realise we had discovered one consistent fact. Britannia was considered a joke in Treviri. Cull and I had propped up the bar in a tavern.

"Sure, there were merchants and officials who had relationships with Britannia in the past, but now, what's the point?" said the owner. "Londinium and Camulodunum are finished. The only flourishing trade's in captives and ransoms," he chuckled, shrugging his shoulders.

"As for Britannia Prima" – he shook his head – "it's a backwater, that's all I know. The best I can say is it seems to be at peace, but I could say the same of a field of grazing cows. Wait until a pack of hungry wolves comes by," he added, "then we will see how long they last, and I have heard the wolves are gathering."

He grimaced and asked where we were from.

"Walcastrum," I said.

He looked puzzled for a moment and then smirked.

"Someone has to be, I suppose," he laughed. We thanked him, downed our drinks and moved on.

Baxter had better luck. He had located a lawyer called Apollinarius, some sort of agent in the town for British interests, not just merchants and traders but also the exiles and refugees who had fled from Britannia Superior.

"He sounds like someone we should talk to," I observed.

"Let's keep watch for a while and see if we pick anything up before we reveal ourselves," said Baxter with an air of experience. "If Drusus is in town, then he'll probably find his way to the lawyer sooner or later."

"We don't know that he's here," I pointed out, "only that he could have business here."

"That sounds like the kind of affair this Apollinarius would be involved in. All the more reason to stake him out, but also not to act prematurely."

"Fine," I said. "Tomorrow I will find out where Apollinarius lives, pretending I'm in town to make a deal, and you two can do a bit more asking around."

It was not difficult to locate the lawyer's house. He was well known in town but approaching Apollinarius in a clumsy manner would only risk alerting Drusus. Baxter and Cull decided they would do a tour around the city gates and come up with a strategy for surveying Apollinarius' house without being too obvious. They departed on their mission, and I was left alone to figure out a way to investigate Drusus' schemes. I decided that a drink and a meal would help my thought processes, so I made my way to the forum, sat down under one of the colonnades and ordered a jug of wine, diluted according to the Roman custom. I had not been sitting long, and was deep in thought, when a shadow fell over my table. I was startled for a moment and looked up to see two women eyeing me. Their heads were covered with hoods, making it difficult to see their features.

"Lucullus Silvanus," said the nearer one, in the voice that had haunted my sleep.

"Milesia, what are you doing here?"

"I could say the same," she replied. "You're straying far from home, and in dangerous territory."

She bent down towards me.

"You must be crazy, Marcus," she hissed. "Don't you understand what would happen if the authorities found you?"

"Understand?" I stuttered, with a feeling of mounting panic.

"It would be a death sentence," she continued, "faster and with fewer scruples than you served my late husband."

"You are supposed to be in the West Country," I stuttered.

"Did you think you were going to keep me quiet so easily?" she continued in a semi-whisper. "If you place someone in a remote area close to the coast with little to occupy themselves, don't you think they might develop a longing to visit the other side? In any case, am I forbidden to see my son?"

"Well, y-yes." I still found it hard to speak clearly.

Milesia straightened up and turned to her companion.

"Bryna, my dear, why don't you return home and I'll join you in a little while? Master Lucullus and I need to exchange a few words."

Her companion bowed her head, lifted the hem of her dress in a slight curtsey and slipped away across the forum.

"She is a dear girl," said Milesia, in an entirely different tone, watching her companion depart. "I should introduce you to her father now that you are here."

"Her father?"

"Apollinarius, yes. He was a lawyer in Londinium for many years and served my father-in-law. Isn't he one of the men you are trying to locate?"

"I see."

"Aren't you going to ask me to sit down?" she continued, as if we were a normal couple having a friendly meeting in a public place.

"Of course," I stuttered. "Would you like some wine?" I could just about manage coherent speech.

"Very much," she said, taking a seat and waving to the tavern servant at the same time.

"What are you doing here in Treviri, Marcus?" she said, leaning once again over the table in a conspiratorial manner. "You have to admit it seems an odd place to find the governor of Britannia Prima, though I have to assume you are incognito. I can't imagine you would have reached so far from the coast alive otherwise."

I was still trying to grapple with Milesia's sudden appearance and her apparently friendly tone. I decided that discretion would be a better strategy.

"I'm trying to find out what happened to my father-in-law. Do you know anything?"

She looked bemused.

"Still wondering?" she said. "I wish I knew, and so do many of my acquaintances."

Of course, her acquaintances would be amongst the enemies of Publius Julius, my enemies, too.

"You know nothing?" I said, fear once again creeping into my heart.

She shook her head.

"I know they've been searching. He owed many of them money, large sums. They would like it back. He's not in Remis, not in Treviri, not in Arelate, as far as I have heard." Her voice remained strangely warm.

"His family?"

"Nothing. No one has heard anything."

"His daughter, the grandchildren?"

"Not a squeak since they left Britannia. I wouldn't lie to you, not right to your face, Marcus."

I wondered how true that statement could be.

The servant returned with a second glass for the wine, and I poured some for her.

"That can't be the only reason," she stated, looking at me over the rim of the glass. "No one ever claimed Publius Julius made a diversion to Treviri, so why are you here?"

"He could have been taken here."

She laughed, not pleasantly.

"Please, Marcus, I'm not a fool."

"Very well, I am searching for your brother-in-law, too."

"Why?"

"To kill him." I felt like a fool as the words came out, a weight like lead inside me.

"I see," she sighed. "Well, he's not here either."

"He's rumoured to be on his way."

"I have heard that too, but you must understand, we take care to avoid one another. I think he still blames me for the fiasco with Vito." Her tone had a hint of sadness.

I looked at her more closely now, and her grey eyes met mine, the ones I remembered from Agridurnum. It was true that it had been a while since she had appeared in one of my dreams, but sitting across from her, I was again falling under her spell.

"I don't want to be associated with his schemes, Marcus. I have a child to think of."

"Constantinus? Where is he?"

"My son is here in Treviri, under the care of the canons," she said, looking away for a moment.

She turned back to face me.

"I heard a rumour," she continued, "that a Lucullus Silvanus, a British chief, had arrived in Treviri with three companions, and at first I was inclined to ignore it."

She looked at me carefully.

"And then a little bell rang in my head, the insulting name that Vito always used for you: Silvanus, the man of the backwoods. As opposed to himself, of course, the sophisticated man of the city, with all his clever plans, his hopes for the future when Constantinus – the general, of course, not our son – became emperor."

She took a sip of her wine.

"It's a small town, and I have friends here. It didn't take long to track you down and then to watch and wait until your companions were elsewhere. I recognised Deacon Baxter immediately, of course."

She paused.

"I could've killed you, and you would never have known who had done it. I could still kill you right now," she said, reaching inside her cloak, pulling out a nasty-looking dagger and laying it on the table. "Your companions would return to find a corpse and the province of Britannia Prima requiring yet another new governor."

She laughed.

"You've gone quite pale," she said.

If I were as pale on the outside as I felt sick on the inside, I could have easily been taken for a corpse.

"That's just a little taste of how I felt when I heard you had executed my husband." She held me with her gaze. "But I told you then, I'm not interested in a quarrel. I'm not even interested in killing you, although most people would think I had the right to do so."

"The vengeful widow?"

"Perhaps. Or the bitter, brooding exile, robbed of her fortune and her future."

"It doesn't seem your exile and lack of fortune is hampering you much," I observed, my spirits raised by the fact I was not dead when I could have been.

"On the contrary, it's very peaceful at the holy house, and I feel I am useful, building up the little community. I'm quite a little princess there, as I used to play at when I was a child. Providing that the watch is not too close and restrictive, naturally. Deacon Baxter's also quite useful and discreet most of the time."

She refilled her glass. I was glad I did not have to do it for her. My hand would have shaken too much.

"The monks, however, leave a little to be desired," she added, as if as an afterthought.

"What's that?"

"They are abstemious," she offered as an explanation.

I must have looked confused.

"They abstain from women," she clarified with a smile. "It's part of their religion."

"Isn't that what they are supposed to do?"

"Them, yes – me, no." She laughed, placing her hand on my forearm. "I don't mean from women, I mean from men, of course, in my case!"

I was beginning to feel a little uncomfortable. Some of the fantasies that had plagued me after we met for the first time began to come into my mind.

She must have seen my expression. She laughed again, quite loudly, attracting an irritated stare from the neighbouring table.

"Don't tell me you have never thought about me, Marcus. I remember how you looked at me when we first met in Agridurnum. I won't lie if I tell you that I have thought about you sometimes. When I have been feeling lonely and far from holy, surrounded only by monks and little Bryna, of course."

Words failed me.

"Do you know I once saw you, before that day in Agridurnum, years before, when you were still a boy?"

"Really?"

"Yes. Publius Julius held a party at Verdaris for his contacts in Londinium, and I was there. You don't remember?"

I shook my head.

"You were very quiet, watching everyone. Just like you're sitting quietly now. What was going through your head, I wondered even then, even though I was just a little girl."

"Did you figure it out?"

She laughed aloud, picked up her glass and took a deep drink.

"No. But I can guess this. You weren't thinking about marrying Hypatia Ursina and becoming governor."

"Far from it," I said. "I felt perpetually out of place at Verdaris."

"And do you feel out of place now that you are such an important man?"

"Sometimes."

"And need to escape?"

I smiled for the first time in our conversation. "To Treviri, you mean?"

"Amongst other places."

"I don't plan to enter a holy house to escape from the world," I said.

"Thank goodness. There's still hope."

"Hope of what?"

"I'm staying at the Red Dragon, Marcus. It would be a way to seal the peace between us."

I was unsure what she meant… dinner, perhaps.

"And your companion?"

"Bryna? This is her home town. She's staying at her father's, Apollinarius', house."

She saw a hesitating look in my eyes.

"You don't trust me? Here, take the dagger." She pushed it across the table to me. "It's not the only one I have, but it would even up the odds if it did come to a fight. I could even claim self-defence." Her outstretched hand clasped my wrist, and her eyes fastened on mine.

"It should have been me," she said suddenly, no longer warm but a little desperate, I thought. "He, Vito, should have had Hypatia, and you and I should have been together."

I was shocked.

"That would never have happened, Milesia. Our paths would never have crossed. There's no point in imagining the impossible," I stuttered truthfully.

"Our paths have crossed now," she said with a sigh. "No matter how hard you struggle, you can't avoid fate. So far from home as well…"

We sat in silence, each contemplating for a moment.

"I suppose you're right," she said at last. I felt her hand stroke mine for a moment, almost as if an insect had walked across it, and then she leaned back.

"Your friends are coming, Marcus." She suddenly let go of my arm and flipped up the hood of her cloak. "You'll give me my dagger back, this evening, at the Red Dragon inn, won't you?"

Cull found me at our lodgings in the morning. There had been a great deal more on offer at the Red Dragon than dinner, and I had much to think over, but it was quickly clear that this would not be the best time.

"We've located him, chief," said Cull.

For a moment I was confused, my mind still on the events of the night before.

"Drusus Astrebanus," he insisted.

"Where is he?"

"Exactly where we thought he would be, at the house of the lawyer, Apollinarius."

"Wait a moment. Are you sure?"

"Yes, we tracked him there last night."

"Tracked him?"

"It was just by chance. We were waiting by the east gate when we spotted him riding in. We followed him through the town and watched him enter a certain house. Then we hung around in a local tavern asking questions until we found out who lived there. Baxter's still outside keeping watch."

Now I was seriously worried. Had Milesia been telling the truth when she said he was not in town? Had she been leading me into a trap which failed to close for some reason? Was she really interested in making peace? Had she even been protecting me by ensuring I was out of the way when Drusus rode in?

Cull must have noticed me lost in thought because he nudged me.

"Come on, Marcus. We have him cornered."

We found Jarmi in the stable and set off together through the town, across the forum and into a quarter made up of wealthy-looking homes. As we rounded a corner, we spotted Baxter lurking in a doorway. He quickly waved us to stay where we were. In a moment he pulled a woollen hat down over his head, turned and, seemingly nonchalantly, made his way along the street towards us.

"Get down that alley," he hissed as he walked past us, "and stay there until I come back."

We stood looking blankly at each other, wondering what to do, until Baxter appeared at the other end of the alley and came towards us.

"By Christ," he said, "what a den of thieves!"

"What do you mean?" I asked.

"I couldn't believe my eyes," he said. "She walked past me just now, without a care in the world."

"Who?"

"The woman – Vitellus' wife, Milesia."

My knees suddenly went weak, and I had to steady myself against the stone wall to stop myself falling over.

"Are you alright, chief?" said Cull.

"Yes, yes, just the shock. I thought she was supposed to be locked up in Britannia, under guard in the holy house?"

"So did I," said Baxter. "I've even been down to check on her a couple of times. God knows what she's up to here in Treviri."

"I can't imagine," I said. "She's a dangerous woman."

Baxter and Cull glanced at each other and obviously came to a silent decision.

"There's four of us. That should be enough if we take him by surprise. Come on, keep your heads down and look like you belong here."

We ducked out of the alley and started to make our way along the street, Baxter in the lead. As we reached the place where he had been hiding, he motioned to us to step into the doorway and huddle there for a moment.

"This is the house," he said in a hoarse whisper, pointing upwards. "The main gate's just along the street."

Above our heads was a window, and we were startled when the shutters flew open and we could hear the voice of a woman yelling. I recognised the voice immediately, hiding my face in my hands not to give away my emotions. Then there came a man's voice, softer.

"Leave!" shouted the woman. "Leave right now! I told you not to come."

"But I need to speak to Apollinarius. I need the money."

"I don't care. I'll deal with it if I have to. Just go now. Leave, before I call the watch."

"But the money."

"Give me a forwarding address. You can send it to the Red Dragon. Take your horse and go. You are causing trouble for everyone: for me, for Bryna, for Apollinarius even."

"But Milesia, listen…"

"No, I won't listen, Drusus. I came here to see my son. I came here to give Bryna a chance to see her family, and now I find you, putting all of us in danger."

"There's no danger."

"He's here."

"Who?"

"Marcus."

"Silvanus? He can't be!"

"Ursinus, Drusus, the governor, whether you accept it or not, and there are three men with him. I recognised one of them, a henchman of Bishop Matthias."

"What're they doing here?"

"They're looking for you, you fool, to kill you, and if you don't leave, you might end up getting us all killed. I've had to take precautions myself, look."

"Oh, my God. Put it away, Milesia, before you harm someone."

"I'll put it away when you leave. If you don't, I might be tempted to put it in your stomach, just to end all this."

"No, no, I'll leave, Milesia, but I'm not giving up. They killed Vito, stole our riches, destroyed our home and lives. I won't be finished until I'm even."

"You're a fool, Drusus," came Milesia's voice again. "You'll ruin us all."

"Perhaps. I don't care. Our lives are ruined already. How can they get any worse?"

The man's voice died away.

We stood for a moment, looking at one another, then we heard another woman's voice from the window above.

"Mistress, I heard shouting, are you alright? You're crying? Can I help you?"

"No, darling Bryna, I'll be fine in a moment. It is just that idiot Drusus was here."

"I know, mistress. I passed him on the stairs."

"I wish he would go to hell and leave us alone."

After that there was nothing but silence from the room above.

"What're we going to do?" I whispered.

"He went in by that gate last night, so he must come out that way again," said Baxter, pointing to an opening a little further down the street.

"Wait here, you two. They don't know me," said Cull, and he began to inch his way along in the shadow of the wall. Baxter followed him, while Jarmi and I peered around the edge of the doorway. Suddenly Cull straightened himself up, stepped out into the street and walked past the opening leading into Apollinarius' house. A moment after he had done so, there was the sound of hooves, and a horse appeared in the gateway. We could guess who it was. Cull and Baxter were standing in the street on the far side of the gate, and after a moment of hesitation, I stepped out from the doorway.

"Stop, Drusus!" I yelled. The horseman looked back and forth and then kicked his mount. The horse skidded on the cobblestones for a moment and then took a jump towards me. I tried to draw my sword, but it was too late. I had it half out of the scabbard when I was hit by the horse and dashed against the wall. When I came to, Jarmi was standing over me.

"Thank God he's coming round," he said, apparently to Baxter and Cull.

I blinked a couple of times and tried to sit up, my head spinning. I could barely make out the shape of Cull standing in the street.

"He got clean away again," he said.

Jarmi and Baxter helped me to my feet. I held my head in my hands for a moment.

"Come on," said Baxter, "they'll have heard us inside. We'd better clear off before someone raises the alarm."

They half dragged me down the street, and by the time we returned to the lodgings my head had begun to clear.

"What do we do now?" said Cull.

"There's no point in staying here," said Baxter. "The speed he was going when he passed us, he'll be halfway to Remis by now."

"Let's head back there and see if we can catch up with him. Even if we don't find him again, we've learned something." Me more than anyone, I thought.

❧ Chapter 21 ☙

The first part of the journey had taken a peculiar and unexpected turn. I had complicated feelings about my interlude with Milesia. I did not want to meet her again. Drusus Astrebanus was no longer in town, and there was plenty of potential for trouble if we stayed any longer. It was a pity that we had not met Apollinarius but, knowing Milesia and Drusus had been in his house, the risk was too great to approach him. We headed west, and by the evening of the fourth day we were back in Remis. We agreed that Cull and I would continue the search for Drusus, while Baxter would use his links to the Church to enquire after Publius Julius. In the morning the deacon set out with his letter of introduction to Eusebius, the bishop of Remis, while Cull and I took a walk in the town, keeping careful lookout for anyone resembling Drusus.

Presently, Baxter caught up with us.

"The bishop will see us in the afternoon."

At the appointed time, we arrived at the palace, a building reminiscent of Villa Verdaris in the old days, servants hurrying in the shadows, clerks scribbling in alcoves, throngs of applicants and supplicants, religious and lay people.

The bishop was very gracious, clearly more of an intellectual than our own Bishop Matthias.

Baxter introduced me.

"This is Master Lucullus Silvanus, Your Excellency. He is a British lord seeking news of the former governor."

"I had the honour of meeting Governor Ursinus at the time of his visit," the bishop smiled, "as well as his beautiful wife and family. It was a pleasure to meet such a cultured and educated gentleman. They are unfortunately few and far between in these troubled times."

It was quickly evident that Cull and I did not match those standards, and we were promptly dismissed.

"My clerk, Master Asgard, will help you with your questions. Good day, Master Silvanus, and God bless you in your search." We bowed and retired, accompanied by the clerk who fortunately turned out to be more practical.

"Bishop Matthias wrote to me some months ago, and I made enquiries in the city. I was able to confirm that Governor Ursinus and his family left a couple of days after the date that the bishop provided me."

He paused and looked a little worried.

"I must say that my enquiries sparked a deal of interest that I didn't expect. It seems that you're not the only ones interested in the fate of the governor and his family. There's a merchant in the city, a certain Tullius, who claims to be an acquaintance of the governor. He implied that he might be able to provide more information."

We'd have to tread carefully, I reflected. Who knew what connection this Tullius had with him.

The clerk hesitated for a moment at my silence, but then continued.

"If this Tullius cannot help you, I suggest you try the southerly road to Tricasses. That's the route taken by most travellers to Lugdunum, and it's the one the Ursinus party took, to the best of my knowledge. I have written you a letter of introduction to the bishop of that city which should open the door for you if you choose that road."

We thanked Asgard profusely and left the palace a little heartened by the guidance we had received. We had not been back at the hostel for long when a message arrived saying that the merchant Tullius would see us that evening at Comenius' tavern. As dusk fell over the city, we made our way to the meeting place. We entered through an archway leading from the street into an inner courtyard. When we asked for Tullius, the servant indicated a table to the side of the court where a man was sitting alone. Baxter and Cull stepped forward, but caution made me hesitate. The silhouette of the man hunched over the table seemed familiar. Where had I seen him before?

I tapped Baxter on the shoulder, and when he turned I asked him to go forward to the table with Cull and engage the man in conversation. I would follow in a moment. He looked a bit confused but did as I asked, while I shifted back into the shadows. When my two companions reached the table, the man stood up and I took a better look at him. I had seen him before, but not recently. In clear view, the hair was thinner and greyer, and the face fatter, but there was no doubt about it: the mysterious merchant Tullius was none other than Tullianus, the former tax collector of Britannia Prima. While Baxter and Cull talked to him, I slipped around the far side of the courtyard, keeping to the shadows as much as possible. While I had recognised him, I wondered whether Tullius would recognise me. I do not think I had ever been introduced to him, only ever seen him at a distance when I was just a boy. However, Tullianus must have known my father, who I had come to resemble more and more as I got older. Eventually, I was behind Tullius' back as he chatted to Baxter, who then stood up to introduce me. As Tullius turned, I saw a slight tremor pass across his face, almost as if he had seen someone who could not be there, the ghost of a dead person. For a moment the shock dissipated and his professional look returned, until Baxter innocently used my old patronym that I had adopted as my disguise. This was one man with whom that was a bad mistake. Tullius recognised it at once. In an instant he knew the entire story, his face went white, his hands reached for the table to steady himself.

"Tax collector Tullianus!" There was no point pretending. I could see my cover was blown, as was his. "I don't believe we have met before in person."

Tullius or Tullianus gasped, beads of sweat appeared on his brow and different shades of colour passed over his face in rapid succession. All at once, he began to shout.

"Help, help, robbers! I'm being robbed!"

Heads turned from neighbouring groups, but for a moment no one moved. Then Tullius found strength in his legs and took off, dodging between the tables, across the courtyard, through the archway and out into the street. I sat down heavily in his place. Baxter and Cull looked amazed and shocked. Baxter, of course, was a stranger to Britannia, and Cull had never been to Corinium in the old days, so neither of them had any idea of the previous identity of the merchant. As I explained to them, Comenius, the tavern owner, came over to find out what all the trouble was.

"I'm sorry," I said. "Merchant Tullius seems to have mistaken me for someone else, someone he had done business with in the past."

Comenius looked grave. "Gentlemen, I don't like to have trouble at my tavern. I suggest you finish your dinner and leave. Merchant Tullius has many friends in this city, and if you have offended him then I must warn you that you could have severe problems if you remain."

We returned to our lodging, wondering whether to take the tavern keeper's warning seriously. By the time we reached our room, we had decided we would sleep first and review our plans in the morning. We did not get a chance.

I was awoken by a cry and the shout of a man's voice.

"That's not him, you fool."

In an instant I was alert and struggling to get out of the bed. Cull, who had been sharing it, was already awake and scrambling to his feet. Baxter and Jarmi had been sleeping closer to the door, and now, in the dim light, I could see three or four men clustered in the doorway, one bending over the bed. The bending man staggered backwards. I caught a glint of metal in his hand as he received Baxter's foot in his groin. Cull and I were half up when the other two rushed towards us, drawing daggers, but the room was so small that we were on them before they could use their weapons. Cull put his shoulder to the first man, while I grasped the sword arm of the second. His fist landed in my stomach, and I stepped back, flailing. As I did so, I knocked off the man's hat, and even in the semi-darkness I could make out the figure of Drusus Astrebanus.

"What are you doing here?" I spat out.

"Do unto others what they plan to do to you," he hissed, ever ready with his words.

There was no use wasting mine on him. I gripped him tightly, trying to keep close so he could not use his blade. Baxter had already managed to disarm the first man and now had his hands around the villain's throat. Drusus kept trying to pull back from me to give himself more room, but as he did so, I followed, as if we were in a strange sort of dance.

Our thumps and bangs, shouts and screams started to wake the other inhabitants of the lodging house, and I could hear footsteps on the stairs, cries of "Thieves!", "Call the watch!" and so forth. While his companions may have been of tougher material, fortunately for me, Drusus was no fighter, and between him pulling and me pushing and misdirected blows and kicks from the others, we found ourselves edging out of the room and towards the balcony which ran round the courtyard. I do not know how long our struggle lasted, but it was enough time for torches to be lit and for several people to be looking up at us from the yard below.

Suddenly Drusus pulled himself free, took two steps back and managed to draw his sword. He stood, panting, not quite sure what to do now he had the upper hand. Just at that moment there were shouts from the yard below.

"Who called the watch?"

"What's going on here?"

Drusus was distracted for a moment and glanced down. I desperately threw myself at him while he looked away, landing my fist in his face, and a moment later my foot hit his knee. He took a step backwards, lost his balance and tumbled down the stairs onto the flagstones of the yard with a thud. He did not get up. Two armed men stepped over him and gazed up the stairs.

Suddenly, I was pushed aside by the other intruders, who leaped down the steps two at a time. One of them grabbed hold of Drusus where he lay senseless in the yard. With an expertise born of practice, the fleeing man heaved Drusus onto his shoulder before anyone could react and, using the dangling body as a weapon, cleared a way through the watchers and vanished into the night.

"Let them go," said a voice from below, and a stout man began to climb the stairs. "What the hell is going on here?" he enquired as he reached the top.

"We were attacked in our room," I panted, still shocked by the assault. "You let the assailants go."

"Are you telling me how to do my job?" sneered the man. By now, his comrades had also reached the top of the stairs. "I don't like it when strangers come into town and cause trouble," he announced.

"We haven't caused any trouble," I protested. "We were attacked."

"This is the second time you and your friends have been involved in an incident today," he said, watching as Baxter dragged the body of the last intruder out of the room. "I had a complaint earlier this evening from Master Tullius that three Britons had assaulted him in Comenius' tavern. Now I find this. No coincidence that you match his description, I conclude."

The watch captain pointed down at the unconscious, possibly dead, man.

"Take him away," he said to his deputies.

As they did so, he stepped closer and put his face up to mine.

"I don't know who the hell you are, and I don't want to know, but if I see you here tomorrow, I will have you arrested. The men you have insulted have influence in this town. Way above my head, do you understand?"

"We have already been told that," I said.

"I'm doing you a favour by giving you a chance to leave with your skins intact, so don't push it," said the man.

"But what about my man here who is injured? He can't travel," I pleaded. Baxter had Jarmi in his arms, blood seeping through his shirt.

The watch captain looked down at him. "Just a servant, huh?" he sniffed. "He can stay, but he must leave as soon as he can," he continued, "and I can't answer for his safety or his upkeep."

"Don't worry about your servant, sir," said the lodging keeper who had joined us at the top of the stairs. "There's a lady who's been staying further along the street who's a wonderful healing woman. Just now she's away, but I'm told she'll be back this evening. You leave your servant here with me, and I'll ensure that he's well taken care of."

"Thank you, that's very kind, but how'll we find him again? We daren't return here. The watch won't allow it, and our enemies are after us, too, so it seems."

"I know who your enemies are," the lodging keeper said, "and I'll make sure your friend comes to no harm. Send me a message, sir, telling me where to direct him, and I'll be sure to do so."

"Just keep your nose clean, Festus," scowled the watch captain.

He gave me one more look and turned to follow his comrades as they manhandled the invader's body down the stairs.

"If I see you in this city again, I won't be responsible for the consequences." He paused for a moment. "Actually, I will, because it'll be me who's dealing them out. Understand?"

I did, and so did Baxter and Cull. Before dawn the next morning, we were already waiting for the south gate to be opened at the end of curfew, and as soon as it was, we rode off without even breaking our fast, leaving young Jarmi at the mercy of the lodging keeper and his mysterious healer.

ೲ Chapter 22 ೞ

The road south to Tricasses was a good one and well-travelled. Once we had made a few miles, we stopped at a roadside inn, had a meal and began to arrange our thoughts after the events of the night.

"Fuck it," I said. "We were fools not to think that Drusus and Tullianus would be in cahoots. Birds of a feather flock together. He must have tipped him off."

"He didn't look in too good shape, boss, when his friend carried him away," said Cull.

"Could have been dead, even," added Baxter.

I sighed.

"If he isn't, then we are properly screwed. They know I'm here, and they'll be on the alert."

"What do we want to do, clear off home?"

"Let's put a few miles between us and Remis. We still have the tip from the clerk Asgard to follow up. We would look stupid to go home empty-handed, beaten in a single fist fight."

Baxter looked doubtful and Cull looked worried, but at the end of the day I was in charge, so they acquiesced.

We tried to estimate how fast the Ursinus family could have progressed during a day, probably in the company of a convoy of traders and other travellers. They would have been much slower than three fit and experienced riders with little baggage. When we had gone as far as we thought reasonable, we stopped at the next hostel and took a room. Having established ourselves as bona fide travellers, we started making enquiries about the Ursinus family. At first the clerk was suspicious and called the host, but when we showed him the introductory letter to the bishop of Tricasses, he softened and began to search through his old records.

"It's a good job I keep this rubbish," he muttered. "People are always coming in here wanting to know who's been where and when."

Sure enough, at the end of August that year, a group of travellers, including the Ursinus family, had stayed overnight at this hostel. A feeling of relief spread through us. We were on the right track at least, and we now had an additional piece of evidence.

After a disturbed night, taking turns on guard, we left in the morning and set out on the next stage of our journey. At the next hostel the result was the same. The Ursinus party had arrived and stayed one night and then moved on. So it was until we reached the city of Tricasses. Cull and I were eager to press on, but Baxter took the letter of introduction to the bishop and went to find his secretary. We were close to his old home of Senones, and I guessed he would have liked to take a side trip, but I simply hoped to confirm we should continue on the road south. Fortunately for us, Baxter and the secretary had friends in common, so he generously agreed to accompany us to the headquarters of the city watch to check the records of travellers entering and leaving the city.

"People seem to think it's our job to look through these old records for their missing relatives," they grumbled. A small gift was offered, and after a pause some dusty rolls were pulled out and consulted. From what we could make out, the Ursinus family had joined a group which arrived safely in the city. However, several of the merchants had chosen to remain, so a smaller group had set off to the south in the direction of Autessiodurum two days later. We took the same route the next day.

Autessiodurum was another bustling town. It was not the provincial capital, but it still put Corinium to shame, with fine public buildings, a splendidly decorated church, a palace for the bishop and an impressive bridge over the river. When we took the road south the following day, however, we could see that we were entering wilder country. The well-tended fields on either side gave way to woods and then thickening forests. The prosperous farms disappeared, and only a few isolated cottages could be seen, some of which appeared to have been abandoned. At nightfall we reached a small town, really a village, surrounded by a rough wooden palisade. We entered and sought out the travellers' hostel. As we had done before, once we had settled in and ordered food, we began to enquire about the Ursinus family. The host seemed very reluctant to dig out the old records until we had passed him a couple of coins. There was no entry for the evening of the day that we knew the Ursinus family and their fellow travellers had left Autessiodurum. Other guests had arrived a couple of days before, but for that specific day, there was nothing. Had they turned back? In that case, surely there would have been a record with the watch at Autessiodurum, although we had to admit we had not thought to check such a possibility. Had they taken another road? But we had seen no other route suitable for long-distance wayfarers during the day. If they had left Autessiodurum in the morning on the same road we had, they must have reached this town in the evening. There was another option. They were in a smaller group, so perhaps they had been able to progress further and bypassed this halt for the next one. We would check that out in the morning.

As we headed further south, the country only became wilder and more desolate. The road curved through a narrow valley alongside a river with forested slopes on either side. The paving was in good condition, and clearly there must have been many travellers, but the surroundings still felt lonely and threatening. Around midday we could hear a noise in the distance, voices and the sounds of horses: a group coming along the road in the opposite direction. Baxter saw a footpath a little way ahead, which led up into the trees, so we decided to pull off and let them pass. We would take the opportunity to have our midday meal. We dismounted and led our horses a little way up the path to find somewhere for them to graze and where we could find fresh water. We spotted a grassy clearing, tied the horses to a tree and sat down to stretch out our legs. We could still hear the group approaching, much closer now, when suddenly new and different sounds reached our ears. Where there had been talking, there were now shouts and screams, where jocular chat, cries and yelling. We put down our bread and ale and stole quietly through the trees until we reached a point where we could see down to the road.

The band of travellers were passing the place where the path turned off, but they were no longer moving forward in an orderly manner. Some of them had stopped and were looking back; others were trying to push forward past their companions. The road was completely blocked by an ox wagon which could not make any progress in the confusion. At first we could not make out what they were saying, but then we heard the words "bandits" and "robbers". One of the travellers unsheathed a sword, and another reached into the wagon for a spear. The shouts grew more urgent and the screams shriller, and then, to our horror, we saw horsemen begin to push their way through the crowd, cutting at people with swords and stabbing at them with spears. Through the trees, we could see that they were long-haired and untidy. Some of them clearly looked like barbarians while others were wearing assorted pieces of Roman armour, helmets and breastplates. All of them slashed viciously at the travellers. When the man with the spear aimed a strike at one horseman, he was felled from behind by an axe-blow from another who had come up along the riverbank. The traveller with the sword struck out at one of the riders. The horse stumbled, but as it did so the man on its back aimed a heavy blow down onto his opponent's unprotected head. We could not see the result, but the traveller disappeared from our view while the horseman rode on. By now the caravan had come to a complete halt and was surrounded by the robbers. We crouched in silence and prayed that our own horses would not give us away. Even if we were well armed and trained to fight, we would not stand a chance against so many savage ruffians.

The travellers had been helpless against the assault, and soon the shouts died away, although the shrieks and screams did not cease immediately. The bandits ranged back and forth along the convoy, searching in the wagons for valuables, food and wine, and when they found what they were looking for, they loaded it into bags which they fastened over the backs of the horses they had seized. Several of them then joined together and, with an effort, tipped the ox-wagon off the road and down the bank towards the river, where it lay half submerged. Once they had cleared the road, they roped the women and children, tied them behind the captured horses and, with clouts and curses, began to drive their booty back along the way from which they had come.

We crouched in a state of shock for a long time without saying anything. Not least, we were still afraid of making any noise until we were sure the bandits were well out of hearing range. We stayed hidden for a long time after the sounds had died out down on the road, and then slowly we stood up. We were grown men, but we were trembling from what we had seen. We said nothing, but we had enough imagination to realise we could – really should – have been lying dead on the road along with the others. Instead, we unsheathed our swords and took the path back down to the highway. An awful sight met our eyes. A dozen dead bodies of men lay where they had fallen, struck down by the bandits. Several women and children had also been murdered. The contents of the wagons lay strewn across the road, baskets and boxes smashed open, clothes and other personal items lying in the dirt. We stepped around the debris, and by each body Baxter knelt, said a short prayer, and made the sign of the cross. One man lay still alive but severely injured. His eyes looked up at us, and as he tried to speak, Baxter took out his cross and placed it in the man's hand.

"Bless you," said the deacon, and he sat with the injured man until his breathing faded. While he did so, I searched along the road for any other signs of life, and Cull scrambled down to inspect the overturned wagon.

After a short while the deacon came up to me.

"He has passed on to a better place," he sighed.

Now we were the only living people on the road. We looked at one another, each hoping that someone else had something to say until I broke the silence.

"We can't stay here," I said, "in this place of death. I don't suppose the robbers will return, but if other travellers were to come by, they might think we were the perpetrators of the violence. We certainly look like we might be – two Britons and an African."

"We can't go on," said Cull. "We would just be taking the same road as the bandits."

"We just have to go back now," I said. "We've seen enough. I'll fetch the horses."

I climbed up the path and into the clearing where the horses stood grazing peacefully. I led them down to the road and we mounted. We made our way slowly to the north, back to the village we had left in the morning.

It was dark when we arrived, and wattle barriers had been dragged across the gaps in the fence that served as gates. We looked up at the dark palisade. There was no one to be seen, and perhaps that was just as well. Who would be glad to see three rough men at night in country like this? Baxter decided to try to bang on the gatepost with the shaft of his spear.

"Cut it out and clear off!" shouted a rough voice from inside. The tone was not friendly and the words more curses than advice. We noticed a derelict stable at the end of a path that led around the fence. We secured the horses and crept inside. It was dark and smelly, and we had little appetite. We stretched ourselves out and tried to sleep. I lay awake for a long time, with the scenes of the slaughter going through my mind. Finally, a fitful sleep overtook me until the rays of dawn began to creep in through the holes in the stable roof.

There was little sign of life when we got up. The gates of the village were still firmly closed, and when we approached, several men peered over the top of the fence. They shouted at us in a hostile manner. I could not make out what they were saying, but apparently Baxter could. He shouted back, and immediately the villagers began to threaten us with their weapons. Baxter spoke again and began to pull us back.

"Get out of range! They're threatening to kill us if we don't go away."

"Do they think we are bandits?"

"I'm more concerned they might be in league with the robbers we saw yesterday," said Baxter. "Let's take the horses and leave before they find enough courage to come after us."

With that we retrieved the horses, who had had a better breakfast than we had, and set off around the village to reach the road north. All the way we were stalked by the men behind the fence, who shouted down threats and jeered at our backs as we departed.

Once we had gone a little way, Baxter came up close alongside me.

"I'm sorry, chief," he said. "I should have thought more or said something, but I didn't want to."

I looked at him questioningly.

"About the bandits."

"What do you mean?"

"You know I lived in this region before. This has always been a territory where there have been bandits. Sometimes worse on this road, sometimes on the Aquitaine road. Usually they stay away from large groups, but if they band together like the ones we saw yesterday, then anyone can be at risk. Some of the villagers pass on information, tip them off about suitable targets."

I began to realise what he meant. Had the Ursinus party been overtaken by bandits like the group we saw yesterday? I could scarcely grasp the thought. Publius Julius and Lucius cut down like the men on the road? And Marcella and Ophelia dragged away, perhaps to a worse fate, captives like the women we saw yesterday? People whom I had grown up with, whom I had loved, even? And Ophelia's children, Lucia and Titus? Could the same have happened to them?

We rode on in silence until Cull, who was a little way in front, called out and stopped his horse. He pointed to the side of the road. He had spotted something half hidden by vegetation. Baxter and I dismounted and went over to what turned out to be a small cross, crudely made of wood. There was nothing written on it. Although it looked quite abandoned at first, we saw there was a small bunch of wildflowers placed at its foot. We had no idea who was memorialised by the cross, but someone had come this way and must have died at this place, someone who was not entirely forgotten. Cull had dismounted from his horse. He stood with me, his head bowed, while Baxter knelt in front of the cross in prayer.

We remounted with heavy hearts. Our horses, not knowing or caring about the troubles of human beings, began patiently putting one hoof in front of the other, making their way along the road and perhaps wondering why their riders did not urge them on as they had done the day before.

After a slow and dismal ride, the outline of the city of Autessiodurum emerged once again ahead of us. We rode up and passed in through the gate, relieved not to be challenged or met with hostile words and looks. As we dined, we considered what we should do.

"It seems a pointless risk to go on," I said. "Travelling south is just to venture into bandit country. We would be no match for a gang of armed and mounted thieves."

"They'd be ready to kill us just to get our weapons or horses," confirmed Baxter.

"We could wait for a large enough group of travellers so that we feel safe," suggested Cull.

"That could take a long time once the news spreads that bandits are active on the Lugdunum road," said Baxter. "Who would be foolish enough to take the risk?"

"You're right," I said. "I think the best we can do would be to double check that the Ursinus family did not return to Autessiodurum and leave by another route. If not, then we have to accept that the trail runs cold here." I sighed. "We've seen what could have happened with our own eyes, and maybe that's where the truth lies."

In the morning we visited the headquarters of the watch. They shook their heads in sympathy when they heard of the attack.

"We'll send a couple of men over to the Lugdunum gate to place a notice of warning," said the captain. "No one should take that route until we are sure it's safe."

"Someone should deal with those bandits," I suggested, my disguise slipping for a moment. He shrugged.

"There's a new man arriving soon, a Magister Aetius, who's all enthusiasm, I've heard, so maybe there'll be some action, but would you want to go up against those brutes?"

We searched through the records to see if there was any trace of the Ursinus family returning. To our consternation, there did not appear to be any northbound travellers arriving from Lugdunum for several days around that time. There was no record of anyone by the name of Ursinus leaving by the Aquitaine road either. The family had set out, but they had certainly never come back. They had left on the road we had taken, but there was no trace of them reaching the village where we had stayed.

Baxter paid one more visit to the bishop's secretary, and together they examined the monastery chronicle.

"The chronicler noted serious activity of bandits, thieves and other servants of the devil on the Lugdunum road throughout that summer," reported Baxter sorrowfully.

There seemed little more we could do but offer up prayers for the souls of those who had perished at their hands and hope that the Ursinus family were not amongst them.

From Autessiodurum we made our way to Senones. The bishop of Senones was overjoyed to see his old friend Deacon Baxter and catch up on the news of Bishop Matthias.

"To be honest, Brother Baxter," he said, "I have been shocked and rather ashamed to hear of Brother Matthias' difficulties in Britannia. The authorities there seem to have offered no support to Christians and allowed unbelievers to run wild!"

I avoided his gaze.

Baxter's friends tried hard to entertain us, but there was little they could do to lift our spirits. It was time to be on our way home, and after receiving much good advice on how to avoid returning to Remis and risk another encounter with Tullianus, we said farewell and headed north again.

From Senones we made our way to Parisius and from there to the port of Rotomagus, a thriving trading town on the Sequana River. It was not the shortest way back to Britannia, but we did not dare use a route that would take us through Remis. We had been told there was regular traffic from Rotomagus between Gaul and Britannia Prima, but that did not guarantee that there would be a boat leaving in our direction immediately. I was also growing concerned for Jarmi. How would he catch up with us before we left?

We found lodgings under the shadow of the amphitheatre and made our way down to the port. As we walked along the quay, we passed men unloading cargoes from riverboats. Stacks of wood, barrels and boxes lay on the dockside, while bales of cloth and sacks of grain were being readied for shipment to the towns and cities upstream. Towards the downstream end of the quay, several seagoing vessels were moored. Perhaps one of these would soon be heading out, hopefully bound for Litorina, Dubris or one of the smaller ports along the south coast of Britannia.

I noticed a group of seamen sitting on some upturned barrels outside a tavern. A fourth barrel served as a table where flagons of ale were visible. As we approached, one of the seamen facing us nodded to a companion who had his back to us, and the man turned around and stood up. He was tall, and his face looked tanned and weather-beaten, with long dark hair drawn back into a horse tail. A pair of long mustachios fell from his upper lip. Despite his rough appearance, his clothes looked of good quality, even expensive, and his belt was fastened with an ornate jewelled buckle.

When we drew close, he spoke to us.

"I would say you fit the description I was given," he said. "Three men: one African and two obvious Romanised Britons." He held out his hands in greeting and introduced himself. "Laurentius. Very relieved to see you, Governor."

You could have knocked me down with a feather. We had only been in the town for an hour. How did this man know who I was? Laurentius, Laurentius, I muttered to myself, and then I recognised the name. Laurentius, the mysterious merchant, the business partner of Fabianus who was never present at the council meetings. Was this the man?

Seeing our surprise, Laurentius called for more ale and asked us to sit down.

"We've been looking for you up and down the coast for a week," he said. "I heard you had given Tullianus a nasty scare in Remis, so I didn't think you would come back that way. He had men lying in wait for you, by the way, so it was just as well you didn't. I don't like the man, but he has money, and sometimes I just have to do business with him."

The ale was delivered, and we offered our thanks to the merchant while he spoke on.

"I heard you were in Senones, and so it seemed most likely you would turn up in Rotomagus sooner or later. A trader like me, I must have eyes and ears everywhere. And I have to understand people, what they are going to do, where they are going to be, sometimes before they know it themselves. We came in on the tide yesterday evening." His men smiled into their flagons but said nothing.

We three sat in silence too. We had been stumbling about Gaul, scarcely knowing what we were doing. Had we had eyes on us the whole time?

"With your contacts, do you know anything more about Governor Ursinus?" I asked the merchant.

Laurentius shook his head sadly.

"I was in Frisia at the time when the family crossed over, and after that I went up to the land of the Jutes. When I arrived back in Bononia, there was a rumour that the governor of Britannia Prima and his family had passed through, but by then they had left for the south. On the mainland, people are travelling all the time, Romans and barbarians, rich and poor. I didn't think any more of it until Fabianus filled me in on the empty treasury. I should have caught on earlier, I confess. My trade is along these shores, I think you know. We were bringing goods into Britannia, and there never seemed to be a shortage of ready money. How much business would I do if I had to worry about where it came from? Gold and silver are all the same whoever has them."

More ale was served.

"Tullianus had been doing business on the side for years," Laurentius continued. "There's nothing surprising in it. They all do, government officials. Tax money has to be spent, and sometimes it's spent for the public good, and sometimes it's diverted to personal use. It's a matter of proportion, that's all."

I did not like what I was hearing. Laurentius must have noticed my expression of disapproval and taken it personally.

"I know it might seem strange to someone like you, Governor, with land, a house and a farm. This is my life, from one port to another, and that means I know a lot of people, and I see a lot of what's going on. I'm sorry, though. Governor Ursinus slipped through while I was elsewhere."

He stopped talking and took a drink.

"Now I have a charge to fetch you back to Britannia," he continued after a moment, "but you'll have to be patient for a couple of days. There's a cargo of wine coming downriver I'm waiting for and" – he pointed to the sky – "in three days we'll have a favourable breeze for the crossing, and it won't be too rough so you gentlemen feel seasick."

Laurentius' expectations were fulfilled. The following day a heavily loaded riverboat made its way into port. For the afternoon, the merchant and his men, a gang of quay labourers and the crew of the boat offloaded barrels and amphorae, manhandled them along the quay and stacked them carefully in Laurentius' vessel.

He was right about the weather, too. Later in the day a storm blew up, rain pelted on the roofs of Rotomagus and the sky grew prematurely dark. Baxter, Cull and I retired to the lodgings, anticipating a dull evening, but we had not settled long before a boy appeared at the door with a message for my companions. They hurried away without explanation. I was left alone, about ready to turn in for the night, when the landlord knocked on the door of our room.

"There's someone downstairs asking to see you. Should I show them up?"

"Of course," I said, wondering who could be out looking for me in this weather. I should probably have been suspecting ill will. There were footsteps on the stairs, and a hooded figure stepped into the room. I let out a gasp when the hood was thrown back. It was Milesia.

"Marcus, please don't stand there with your mouth open. Help me get this wet cloak off. The landlord will be coming in a moment to take it and hang it by the fire to dry."

Dumbly, I did as I was asked, and in a moment the man appeared and relieved me of the soaking garment.

"I suppose we could have the same cross-questioning as last time," she said, "but I'll cut it short. We're both here because we have to return to Britannia. We have a friend in common, and that friend is assisting my companion and me to return to the comfortable but isolated quarters you and the bishop have arranged for us, just as he's assisting you to return to your wife and home."

I must have looked uneasy, which was not difficult in the circumstances.

"Don't worry, we're not taking the same boat. For God's sake, Marcus, sometimes I think you are hopeless," Milesia sighed.

"How did you know I was here?"

"I've only been following you halfway across the Empire."

I pursed my lips, giving her a questioning look.

"Very well," she said. "I'm exaggerating. It was luck. Our friend told me you were here when I arrived, but Fortuna may have had a hand in it as I have a letter for you. I had intended to send it from the holy house, but now I can give it to you directly."

She reached inside her gown and pulled out a waxed writing tablet, tightly tied shut.

"It's from the lawyer, Apollinarius – the lawyer in Treviri, my companion Bryna's father."

I opened the tablet and read down. The message was short and to the point.

From: *Magistratus Apollinarius*
To: *Governor Marcus Lucullus Ursinus*

Drusus Astrebanus has left Remis for Rome. He plans to make a personal plea to the imperial authorities. I have advised him against this, but he has insisted on claiming his rights as he sees them. He has set no date for his return.

"Was this written before or after his accident in Remis?"

"Before, but I'm confident he will stick to his plan."

"He's not dead, then?"

"I haven't heard that he is."

I glanced up at Milesia. "I had some experience of the road to Rome. I can't say I recommend it."

"Apollinarius said the same."

"I'm just wondering, Milesia, are you giving him money?"

"Drusus? Me? No! I need it all myself. I have a community to support. In any case, I don't need to give him any. He has sufficient funds, and he's no fool. He and Vito never entirely parted company with Tullianus. The man's sons were childhood friends of his. They had investments together. You should ask our mutual friend to fill you in."

"You are referring to Laurentius, I take it?"

She smiled. Another worry came to my mind. "Does Tullianus know that I am here in Rotomagus? I mean, if you found me?"

"I found you because I came to Rotomagus myself. I need to return to the holy house before the harvest starts."

"I can't imagine you in the fields gathering crops." It was tactless I suppose, but I could not help myself.

"You would be surprised," she said with a smile. "But I have to admit, it's Bryna who needs to return for the practical work. I have a more supervisory role."

"So you don't think Tullianus knows I'm here, and this letter's not a bluff on the part of Drusus?" I could not escape the thought it might be Milesia's bluff.

"Marcus, didn't we make peace and seal the deal? Do you think I came here just to give you the letter and to dry my cloak?"

"Are you planning to stay?" I asked, a little doubtfully.

"I had thought to… for a while. The weather outside is unpleasant. It's rather cosy here, and I like the company."

"But Baxter and Cull?"

"I assure you they'll not be returning any time soon, and I have to be at the quayside early in the morning. We could order a little dinner and some wine first, though."

Baxter and Cull reappeared around noon the following day. They were reticent about where they had been, looked slightly green and neither of them commented on the scent of perfume that filled our chamber.

Overnight the wind had died down and the rain had passed, and in the morning Laurentius' crew assembled at the dock. We were preparing to board ourselves when a small cart, drawn by a single horse, rolled along the quay and came to a halt close by. The carter stepped down from his seat. The young lady sitting beside him watched as he went around to the rear. To our astonishment, the man reached out and assisted Jarmi to the ground, and though the boy was limping, he made his way towards us with a broad smile.

"Jarmi!" I exclaimed. "How did you find us?"

"The lady brought me here along the river."

"You look well, youngster," said Cull.

The boy's eyes teared up.

"Such a wonderful lady," he said, pointing to the young woman seated on the cart. "She took good care of me, and I've felt better every day."

I did not recognise her immediately, but as soon as she spoke, I knew who she was: the lawyer's daughter we had heard through the window in Treviri.

"Master, he should recover well," she said. "He's been very brave."

"Thank you, mistress. We are grateful to you."

"My lady wishes you a safe voyage." She laughed and turned to the carter. "Come, Jacobus, our mistress is already waiting for us. We have to catch the breeze before the tide turns, and we don't want her to leave without out me."

We helped Jarmi to our ship, threw our own bags onto the deck and, with a shout, the moorings were cast off, oars were slid out, the sail was hoisted and presently we were bumping and lurching our way through the waves back to Britannia.

The journey to Gaul had left me disconcerted. A society had arisen in which people in the cities could go about their usual business undisturbed, trading, worshipping, making love even, while just a few miles away on a busy high road, travellers could be attacked and disappear without trace. I was determined that would never be allowed to happen in Britannia Prima.

We made our way together as far as Corinium and then parted company. Cull headed north to Walcastrum and Umbrosa Farm while I turned off for Verdaris to provide some sort of news to Hypatia. It was difficult to know exactly what to say. The truth was we had taken a lot of risks, but we were not a lot wiser than we were before I left. We still could not be sure what had happened to Publius Julius, though now I feared the worst. It did not seem likely that the Ursinus family would be returning. Drusus Astrebanus had escaped again, but we could hope that he would not be bothering us for some time, if the letter from Apollinarius was to be believed. At least now we seemed to have a few friends who could warn us if he returned. One of those, perhaps, was Milesia. I did not tell Hypatia about my encounters with her. It would have been difficult to hide my embarrassment. My only way to justify my behaviour was that it was transactional, just business mixed with a few moments of pleasure.

❧ Chapter 23 ☙

Drusus Astrebanus had not died. He had recovered from his fall in Remis with little more than a sore head, but he had been badly frightened. He had suddenly grasped that he was as vulnerable to assassination as I was, especially now we had located him. A month after my return to Britannia, I received a lengthy letter from Apollinarius confirming the short message I had been given by Milesia. He wrote that Drusus had left Belgica for the south, claiming urgent business in Rome and no doubt hoping to keep out of our reach. However, Drusus was not our only problem. The ill omens were many, and the world round about us appeared to be growing darker and darker.

"I can't help feeling that the stupidity and self-destructiveness of the citizens of Britannia Superior and their friends in exile actually make my task a lot easier," I remarked to Aurelius and Hermanus. "They provide a perfect example of what will happen to us if we don't remain united."

The island of Britannia had always been vulnerable to attacks by pirates from the east. The Saxons, Angles and Jutes were only the latest. The Empire had built a series of forts around the coasts to deter these interlopers. Nevertheless, Britannia Superior remained a tempting target for any mainland chief interested in filling his treasury, and generations of ambitious marauders had boosted their prestige by leading raids on the coastline.

"You would imagine the inhabitants of Britannia Superior would band together to oppose the intruders, but far from it. All I have heard is squabbling and disorganisation," I complained.

"Once the Romans left," observed Aurelius with a wry smile. "Before that, the Empire kept the screws down tight."

"Now it's every man for himself. Everyone sees an opportunity to grab a share of power."

"And even they can't agree amongst themselves what to do with it."

"Except to enrich themselves at the cost of the others."

The possibility that the disorder in the east would spill over into Britannia Prima was one of my major concerns as governor.

"It only seems to be getting worse," said Hermanus. "Since they don't have an organised military force, each side is hiring thugs as support in their internecine quarrels."

"I can see that it makes sense to the thugs," I said, "if they can be invited ashore to welcoming arms. Why should they fight if they can get help to steal and loot and sail away in peace? If they leave at all, that is. What I can't see is how the local leaders are benefitting."

"Things are so bad now I don't think they do benefit. If the terms offered by one man aren't favourable, then next time the mercenaries make an alliance with his enemies. The paymaster of today becomes the victim of tomorrow," sighed Hermanus. "It's a vicious circle. We can't let it spread here."

"We are fortunate that it hasn't so far, but I am surprised that Drusus, Tullianus and his gang have not tried harder to exploit the situation," said Aurelius.

"It's only a matter of time," I said. "We should be thinking of strengthening our defences. We should probably find additional recruits for our auxiliaries."

"That shouldn't be difficult," said Hermanus. "There is a constant stream of idle warriors after the disturbances in Germania and Gaul. All I need is sufficient money."

"We can manage it, and I think the landowners will contribute if we explain the need."

"Do you think these new barbarians will adapt to the auxiliary lifestyle without the example of the Roman army?" I wondered.

"I still have enough of the old guard to show the way," said the captain. "The newcomers will be fine when they are trained. A bit of old-fashioned discipline will do them good."

"I'll put forward the proposal at the next council," I said. "We should build half a dozen forts between us and Britannia Superior to block the obvious routes from the east, the valley of the Tamesis, for example. That would force anyone with ill intent to face a detour through the woods at the very least."

Some omens were more ambiguous. It must have been late spring the following year, and I was in the east yard at Verdaris talking to the blacksmith when I saw Fabiansson striding along the field road, followed by one of his servants.

"Stop!" I called out promptly, "It's muddy here – I'll come to you."

I quickly finished giving my instructions to the blacksmith and crossed the yard to the merchant.

"They told me I could find you out here," he said, slightly out of breath. "I have something I thought I should show you," he added, pointing to the servant who was carrying a rough sack over his shoulder. "I was looking for Hypatia, too."

"She should be in the house," I said. "Tread carefully, and we will go in through the tower door."

Fabiansson placed his feet cautiously as we crossed the farm-yard and entered the house through the rear door, past the entrance to new bathhouse, under the tower and into the gallery which surrounded the garden. I saw Hypatia supervising one of the gardeners, so I called her over.

She was as surprised to see Fabiansson as I was.

"This is the first time for ages," she smiled. "Come inside and have some ale. You must be thirsty after the journey, and your man, too. You can come with me to the kitchen," she continued, turning to the servant.

"Thank you, mistress," said the man, looking to his master for permission. "What shall I do with this?"

"Let me have it," said Fabiansson, taking the sack and gesturing to his servant to follow Hypatia.

In a moment my wife returned, accompanied by a maid with three beakers and a jug.

"Just what I needed," said the merchant, raising a beaker to his mouth, "but now down to my business."

He untied the sack and took out a silver-coloured goblet.

"What do you think of that?"

Hypatia's brow wrinkled, and she slowly extended a hand to touch it.

"It looks very like one of the goblets that Father used to have," she said tentatively.

She picked it up and gave out a gasp as she examined it closely.

"It is one of Father's goblets, one of those he took with him when he left," she said, with a tone of amazement in her voice. "Look, that's my father's seal stamped in the metal on the foot. Where did you find it?"

"It's a long story," said Fabiansson, "but in short, Laurentius sent it to me."

She put the goblet down on the table and took a step back, as if it were a threat.

"How did he get hold of it?"

"He was given it by one of his associates in Belgica, a man who recognised your father's seal, someone who was aware that you were still searching for your father."

"Did he tell you where his friend found it?" I butted in. "I know Drusus and his cronies have been trying to get their hands on Publius Julius' property."

"It wasn't from them. As I heard it, it was a soldier who brought it in, an officer who had been serving with Magister Aetius, hunting outlaws."

"You think the man could have looted it from the brigands?"

"I don't know any more than that," said Fabiansson. "I'm sorry. It's a bit garbled, but it seems the officer offered the goblet for sale. Laurentius' friend bought it, and only later realised it had belonged to your father, long after the soldier had left."

"So we still can't be sure where it came from?" I felt frustrated.

Hypatia picked up the goblet again, turning it in her hands.

"If only it could speak," she said. "I wonder where it's been." She put it down again. "Thank you, Fabiansson. It isn't much, but it's something I can show the girls, something I can pass on to them from my family."

"If this one has turned up, there could be more," I said. "We would be so grateful if you could ask Laurentius to tell his friends to keep their eyes open."

"I've already done that," he said. "Now where has Actus gone?" He began looking round for his servant. "We should be leaving so I can get home before it's dark."

"I'll draw my father's mark for you," said Hypatia, "several copies, and you can send them to your business partners, even those who didn't know my father. They might spot the mark if they know what they are looking for."

Over the months, Hypatia's effort began to bear fruit. Several more objects that had once belonged to Publius Julius were delivered to us: two plates were found in Belgica, another goblet in Senones, and a decorated bowl made its way from Aquitania, from Fabiansson's business partner in Burdigala. We could only surmise that Magister Aetius' offensive actions against the bandits had turned up treasures that had long been hidden by the thieves. The robbers had, in turn, been robbed, and their booty was once more in circulation.

Other omens were more obviously threatening. I have often reflected that the solution to one problem eventually becomes the cause of the next. It may not happen immediately, which simply serves to instil a false sense of success. Construction of the forts along the border with Britannia Superior was completed, the outposts were garrisoned with troops, and so, we thought, that problem had been dealt with. But the forts were far away and the occupants all too often left to look after themselves. It took time, but complacency and the proximity to temptation eventually took their toll.

"I have bad news, Marcus," said Hermanus, looking grim. "Someone has been trying to suborn the garrisons of the eastern forts."

"Pirates or Saxons?" I asked, thinking only of the most obvious culprits.

"Someone with silver to spread around," said the captain. "Neither pirates nor Saxons have money for extravagances like bribing soldiers. They have more direct methods. The edge of a blade is their best persuasion."

"Outsiders, do you think?" I frowned.

Aurelius joined us, almost as if he had been eavesdropping.

"I have an unhappy idea where the silver might be coming from."

"Go on," I said, with growing misgivings.

"Tullianus' health has been failing. The man was a crook, but he was also shrewd. I heard he made a fortune and is still sitting on it."

"Married? Children?"

"His wife died years ago, before he left Britannia, but he had two sons, and rumour has it they have gone into partnership with our old friend, Drusus Astrebanus."

"I thought he had travelled to Rome."

"That was a while ago, and a bad *denarius* always returns," said Aurelius.

"There are more than *denarii* in circulation," said Hermanus, "but what does Drusus' return mean for us?"

"I think it means that you now have three men with money that they can use to support their ambitions," said Aurelius.

"And you think they have been trying to subvert our garrisons?" I asked.

"Maybe," replied the lawyer.

"What did you do when you found out?" I turned to Hermanus.

"I rotated the troops, brought the cohorts who had been serving in the east back to Corinium where I can keep an eye on them and moved new troops out to the border."

"Let's hope that's solved the problem."

"I'll see that it does," said Hermanus.

In the face of omens, it is seldom a good strategy to remain passive. Every action demands an equal reaction.

"We need to start looking for a husband for Silva," I said to Hypatia, shortly after our daughter's sixteenth birthday.

"I've been thinking about it for years," said my wife, putting me in my place with a kindly glance.

"And your conclusion?"

"It's like this, Marcus," she sighed. "Back when I was Silva's age, marriages were made to cement ties between the leading families in Britannia."

"We should be doing the same."

"I understand," she replied, "but we must take care not to make the same mistake my father almost did. Sometimes an enemy will always be an enemy."

Talk of Silva's need for a husband reminded me that governing is often a matter of balancing opposing forces. The Welsh were peaceful now, but if they got the idea that we were threatened from the east as well, they might be tempted to take advantage. A plan began to form in my mind that would put an end to that risk for some time, a variation of the plan my father had hatched a generation before, although it would require a great deal of careful diplomacy with the northern lords, and within my own household.

Merwyn, the younger son of Prince Dewi, was not yet married. An engagement between Silva and the prince could secure peace on our western border, assuming the northern lords could swallow a Welsh prince as their neighbour. When I broached the subject with Hypatia she looked thoughtful but was not entirely negative. Of course, she did not have the same ingrained mistrust of the Welsh as we who had lived beside them. I rode north during the winter and consulted with Chief Gallius and his allies. Slowly, they came around to the idea, so I dispatched Deacon Baxter into Wales with my proposal, and after several rounds of bargaining, the deal was struck. The south of Wales and the west of Britannia would be tied together with Hymen's bands, as the poets call them, and in theory at least peace and harmony would reign.

"Have you met him, Father?" my daughter asked.

For a moment I chuckled, which was unfortunate.

"I have," I said. "But then he was only a baby."

Her face brightened for a moment and then fell.

"How do you know we will be compatible?" she asked.

"I don't know," I said. "But I have met his father, and I can say that he's an honest and decent man, and I've no doubt his son is too."

That did little to cheer her up, so I tried to be more encouraging.

"Silva, my dear, I don't think Prince Dewi would agree to the match if he did not think it would work. He must want the best for his son, and you are the best."

"I'll obey you, Father, of course," she said, "but I wish I could feel more confident."

To be honest, a young girl's feelings of confidence should only play a minor role when the peace and prosperity of a province is at stake.

Deacon Baxter, who had met the proposed husband, was encouraged to employ his powers of persuasion on behalf of the bridegroom. He must have done a good job, since there were no tears and no protests when, three days after midsummer, I set out for the second time to Wales. That first time I had been a young man, amongst the retainers of my father. This time I travelled as the governor of Britannia Prima with my eldest daughter, the proposed bride of Prince Merwyn. The entourage had to match the occasion. In place of the dozen farmers of the previous occasion, fifty soldiers headed by Captain Hermanus led the way, followed by another fifty mounted retainers pulled together from Verdaris and Umbrosa Farm or contributed by Chief Gallius and his friends as a gesture of goodwill. Behind us lumbered wagons loaded with gifts and comforting necessities for the journey, together with Hypatia and the young princess-to-be. Not long ago such a column of armed men would have been seen as a threat by the Welsh. It was a tribute to my father's foresight that we were welcomed as friends.

We were met by a splendid escort at the border, headed by Prince Dewi himself, and no expense had been spared when we arrived at Caerberg. In the twenty years since I had been there last, the old legionary fort had taken on the features of a palace. Now it was thronged with Welsh chiefs, especially those who needed an example of fraternal peace. Although Prince Merwyn was older than Silva, I thought the pair were well matched. Their eyes certainly shone as they swore the oaths of engagement. Bards and poets filled the hall, proclaiming the virtues of the bride. Christian priests showered blessings on the couple. Oxen were roasted, ale was drunk, and everyone had a jolly good time, with surprisingly few fistfights. In private the young princess-to-be charmed the Welsh ladies by showing that she, too, could play the harp, and she reduced them to tears by singing one of their own melodies in Welsh. That was a skill I had not suspected! However, I thanked God, and when I returned to Corinium, I donated a large sum to the Church for prayers for the young couple without even needing to be reminded by Hypatia.

Nonetheless, perhaps I still had not donated enough to assuage the malevolent forces. Shortly after, when I had returned to the basilica of Corinium, I happened to walk past Flavius' office and overheard the treasurer in a heated discussion with one of the tradesmen from the town. When Flavius noticed me, he called out.

"Governor, come and take a look at this."

He passed me a coin, and both he and the tradesman watched me with great expectation.

"It looks like a coin," I said, puzzled by their interest.

"But what sort of coin?" asked the tradesman.

"It seems like a perfectly ordinary coin to me," I said.

"It's a foreign coin," said the tradesman, with an air of defiant expertise.

"To be more precise," said Flavius, "it is one of the new coins issued by the Frankish rulers on the other side of the sea."

I still did not understand the point of the discussion.

"How much is it worth, then?" said the tradesman, eyeing the treasurer.

"Let me see," said Flavius, pulling out a small, portable balance from under his worktable.

"Hold this in your hand," he requested the tradesman, placing the coin on one side and beginning to pile small weights on the other.

"I would say it is worth ten of the wretched, clipped and debased lumps of so-called silver you usually get in payment in the forum," he concluded.

The tradesman looked surprised.

"Didn't know what he was doing, then," he said.

"Who didn't know what he was doing?" I asked, still confused.

"The young soldier what give it to me."

"You got this from a soldier?" I asked.

"Yes, one of those young ones that the captain moved here a while back."

I looked at Flavius and he looked at me. The coin in his hand was worth a couple of weeks' pay to a soldier. He would be unlikely to be careless with it.

"Let me know if you see any more of these," said the treasurer, turning to the trader, "and if you are satisfied, I'll give you ten of the usual coins for it. Do we have a deal?"

"Certainly do, sir, and at that rate I'll be round to you every time I see one."

"You do that," I said. "Spread the word and bring in any other strange coins you come across."

The man went off, stuffing the familiar old coins into his purse.

Flavius flipped the new one so that it tumbled in the air, and then he caught it with his hand.

"How do you suppose this got here?" I asked. "From Germania?"

"Or Belgica. The Franks are spreading their influence."

"They're not planning to spread it here, do you think?"

"Too far away," said the treasurer. "No, I think this must be linked to the worries Hermanus had about bribery and corruption in the ranks. We need to let him know it's reached as far as Corinium."

"A shiny new coin which is worth so much more than those we have to dispense," I mused. "Even if the man did not know how much it was worth."

The treasurer frowned in reply.

"I wonder what other shiny objects are being waved in front of our auxiliaries."

With the engagement between Merwyn and Silva sealed, the marriage was celebrated in the spring in Walcastrum, in the presence of the tribal chiefs of the north. The delay gave me the opportunity to carry out some building work at Umbrosa and to renovate the old farm into a house befitting a prince, albeit a Welshman. I arranged for a new wing to be constructed, with rooms for entertaining and more comfortable living space for my daughter and the family I expected. I would have preferred to build it in stone, like the buildings at Verdaris, but I could find no one with the skills of a stonemason. I had to be satisfied with scavenging material from abandoned buildings in Walcastrum to construct the lower part of the walls and a flagstone floor, and the upper part from timber. Even with those compromises, the new building looked very grand, and I was pleased with the result.

Prince Dewi himself made the journey to the marriage ceremony. Bishop Matthias ventured north, in pomp and state, and blessed the marriage, and a great feast was held in the basilica of Walcastrum. I would be lying if I did not detect some grumbling and muttering in certain corners by those gladly accepting my hospitality. The truth is that with Merwyn in Umbrosa Farm, the northerners could sleep comfortably at night, and their cattle could graze in peace.

And I was a grandfather before a year had passed.

"I am grateful you were willing to travel to Walcastrum and bless my daughter's marriage," I said to the bishop over a glass of wine.

"I am afraid it may be the last time that I will be able to help you that way, Governor," he replied.

"How so?"

"I have just received a message that my old friend, the bishop of Senones, has died."

"That's sad news," I said. "I remember him very positively. But, Bishop, have you been selected to replace him?"

"It's not quite so simple. In the Church there is always a certain game of musical chairs, as each man and his family jockey for every position of influence."

"I see."

He held up his hand.

"But I have not been forgotten by the clergy or the influential lay people, and my sister has been able to speak on my behalf."

"So a seat has opened up for you?"

"Indeed it has. I shall be returning home as bishop of Tricasses."

"Congratulations," I said, and I meant it. "You've been a great support to us here, and the Church has flourished under your leadership like never before."

He had been, above all, a friend and comforter to Hypatia. I watched him depart with a heavier heart than when I had seen him arrive. He left his flock in the hands of a newly arrived priest, Father Felix, a learned and devout man of faith, but one lacking the bishop's charisma. The church in Corinium stood complete, and the reach of Christianity had begun to spread from the town out into the countryside, but, despite the occasionally lively sermon from Deacon Baxter, something of the spirit of the Church disappeared with Bishop Matthias.

❧ Chapter 24 ☙

The weather was clear and frosty the night I was awakened by the sound of hooves in the yard. If the bards had been telling this tale, it would rather have begun on dark and stormy night. Probably that is one reason I have never heard a poet sing this story from start to finish. The beginning involved little courage or honour, but a large helping of short-sightedness and bad decision making, and so lacks the elements that would make it attractive to poets. And the end, we'll come to that…

Since there was little business to be done in winter, I was staying at Verdaris most of the time. The house people had retired for the night when I was disturbed by shouting from the stable yard. I got up from the bed and put on a thick gown. The floor was still warm under my feet, but the corridor was cold and stairs. A freezing blast came from the door to the yard being opened. A dishevelled figure entered, followed by a stable hand. The figure gestured to the man to leave and, drawing off a thick woollen hat, was revealed to be Optio Gracchus, sweating and dirty.

He dropped briefly to one knee.

"Governor, I'm sorry to disturb you, but the captain… Hermanus… is dead."

My heart must have stopped for a moment. My throat tightened as if gripped by a man's hand. A vision of Hermanus' grizzled face came to my mind, but I did not have time to reflect further as the optio continued.

"And I have further bad news," he went on. "The young men in the auxiliaries have revolted. They elected one of their own, Deric, as leader. Yesterday most of them left together on the east road to Agridurnum, though some of the older soldiers have stayed behind with their families. I don't know what the rebels intend to do, so we thought it best to consult you."

"Just a moment, Optio," I said, suddenly wide awake and trying to sound calmer than I really felt. "This sounds a little confused. Come and get some food and drink. Warm up a little and tell me slowly."

I took him by the arm and led him into my study, as sleepy house servants, woken by the disturbance, appeared in the corridor.

"Bring food, warm if possible, and clean clothes," I ordered them, and I ensured that Gracchus was seated. "Now, explain to me what has happened."

The optio took a deep breath.

"Hermanus collapsed three days ago, just when he was getting up from his bed in the morning. He had been complaining of a headache in the evening, but it's winter. It's not unusual. Nautila, his wife, came running to me, calling me to come. I found him still alive, breathing, but only staring ahead, unable to speak. The *medicus* came from the town, but there was nothing he could do. Hermanus was almost unresponsive, just the corner of his mouth seemed to move occasionally. He died that afternoon."

The optio fell into silence, staring at the floor. I was stunned. Hermanus had been a faithful companion for many years. Together we had worked hard to keep peace and order in the province. I do not think I could have managed without his help. We had eaten and drunk together many times, shared our troubles and joys. I cannot say we always agreed, but our view of the world was sufficiently similar that our differences could be overcome.

"But Gracchus." I broke the silence. "You said the auxiliaries have revolted. I'm confused – what did you mean?"

Gracchus cleared his throat, glancing up at me.

"They heard that the captain was sick and that there was no hope for him. Straightaway they began talking about who would replace Hermanus as captain. It's always been the tradition that the auxiliaries elect their own leader from amongst the other officers. But, aside from me and old Parens, the quartermaster, there are no other veteran officers in the detachment. The older men put my name forward, although they knew I didn't really want to be captain. Honestly, Governor, I hadn't thought about it." Gracchus sighed. "Hermanus always seemed so healthy and full of life. I always imagined he would grow old as captain."

The optio stopped for a moment. I thought I saw a tear in his eye as he struggled to conceal his emotions. After a pause to collect himself, he went on.

"I wasn't there for the election. I was in Hermanus' house trying to comfort Nautila. I heard that a young man, Deric, put himself forward as leader. I know him. He hasn't been with us for long, but his father had been a tribal leader in Germania. He felt that gave him the right to be a leader, too, I suppose."

"After the election, some of the veteran soldiers came to me. They had been in the minority. Most of them left the camp as soon as they saw where matters were heading. They met in a tavern in town to have a discussion of their own. They said I should put a guard on the door of the commander's house to prevent the young soldiers taking it for their new leader. I needn't have bothered," he added with a sigh, before continuing.

"Before dawn we built a bier. We carried Hermanus' body to the Christian church. Father Felix and Deacon Baxter respected him. A good man deserves a proper funeral. Afterwards, the veterans told me they wouldn't serve as auxiliaries with Deric as leader. They didn't want to join a band of robbers."

Gracchus looked at me anxiously, seeking approval. The servants had brought in a bowl of gruel and some bread.

"Eat some of the food, Gracchus," I said, "and then go on." By now, Hypatia had joined us, wondering what had kept me up. She sat beside me, wrapped in a blanket. Gracchus took a drink and a few spoonfuls and continued.

"I heard a rumour that they considered marching here and taking you by surprise." He looked uneasily at Hypatia and me. "Instead they set off for Agridurnum, counting that it would be poorly defended."

"So what did you do then?" I asked.

Gracchus took another drink. He had begun to seem a little hesitant.

"I'm sorry, Governor. We were still just thinking about protecting ourselves, not what could happen to anyone else. It was only when a couple of countrymen told the men on guard at the south gate that they had seen soldiers marching along the east road that we had any idea what was going on. I found a couple of cavalrymen, and we galloped across country to check. We hid in some trees and saw the auxiliaries marching east, if you could call it marching. They had about twenty horsemen at the front, and they were armed to the teeth. They looked a shambles to me. There was nothing I could do to hinder them, even at the cost of my life. After watching until they were out of sight, we trotted back to town."

"Why didn't you send me a message?" I interrupted.

"I thought it was a military matter. I thought they were probably on their way to the eastern forts. They had served there before, most of them. I thought it best to secure the camp so that they could not get back in. The gate nearest the town was shut and a stout bar closed across it. We closed up the other gates of the camp and piled earth against them. No one was getting in or out that way."

"And how long did that take?" My tone was getting sharp. "How long did it take for you to conclude the rebels were headed for Agridurnum, since you seem to think that is where they have gone?"

I was beginning to feel a little angry. While they had been so busy shovelling earth, no one had thought of sending me a message. Gracchus continued in a monotonous voice, as if he had not heard my question.

"The following morning we began to feel a little better. It didn't look like the rebels were coming back. About the middle of the afternoon, a farmer and his family arrived at the town gate. They lived by the east road. The rebels had reached their home around sunset on the previous evening, they said. He told us he and his wife had been beaten and their cattle and pigs slaughtered. In the morning the family had managed to escape while the rebels were sleeping. They had hidden long enough to see the men set fire to their house and barns. Then they fled to Corinium as fast as they could."

The optio began to sound hesitant once again.

"Then we started to get seriously worried."

"I should think so," I commented. Hypatia put her hand on my arm, her expression telling me to keep quiet and let Gracchus finish.

"Towards evening a couple of riders came galloping down the east road. They were two stable boys from Agridurnum. They sounded desperate. The rebels had reached the estate in the night. They had struck down Father Justin and hung him in the courtyard. They had rounded up the women and girls and closed them up in a barn. Everyone else was driven out of the villa into the freezing night. The boys had managed to catch a couple of horses that were loose in a field. At the crack of dawn, they had ridden for their lives. As we listened to them, we realised we had been foolish. We had to get help from outside. I blamed myself for not doing so earlier. I got a horse, and I came here.”

“We?” I asked. “Who is this ‘we’?”

“Me and Aurelius and” – he stuttered – “and the mayor… Fabiansson. We were reluctant to disturb you.”

I put my hands to my head. This was hard to hear, and my friends had kept me ignorant until the situation was so bad. I felt angry and frustrated, and those feelings had almost made me forget my old friend Hermanus.

“Thank you, Gracchus,” I said with a touch of irony. “At least you have come and told me now.”

“You need to ride to Corinium and take charge,” said Hypatia. “But there’s nothing you can do tonight. You and Gracchus need to get some sleep. Ride in the morning.”

“You’re right,” I said. “Something needs to be done. We need to hurry, but to do what?”

“You’re not going to solve those questions in the middle of the night with tired minds. Wait until the light of day,” she replied.

Gracchus had fallen into an embarrassed silence, spooning the gruel and chewing on a piece of bread. Once he had finished the food, I took him to a guestroom.

“Get some sleep, and we’ll start on a plan in the morning.”

I don’t suppose the optio slept any better than I did. Here was a disaster beyond anything we had imagined or prepared for, and my old friend Hermanus, the one man who would have known what to do, was gone, dead and quickly buried, and his memory had already been desecrated.

In the morning I rode down to Corinium with Gracchus.

“I’ll take care of Verdaris,” said Hypatia, seeing me off. “I’ll send a message with Jarmi to the surrounding farms and tell them to keep a lookout for trouble. If the rebels thought of coming here once, they could do it again."

To say I was angry would have been an understatement. I was absolutely furious and disappointed, not just by Gracchus – he was clearly in over his head – but by Aurelius and Fabiansson. They had let me down. However, a couple of hours' ride in the crisp morning air helped calm me a little. I realised that it would not make the situation better by pointing out their shortcomings and quarrelling with them. We were in desperate circumstances, a military catastrophe and no one with military experience to take charge.

Aurelius, Flavius, Theo and Fabiansson had congregated in the basilica offices, knowing that Gracchus had ridden out to Verdaris the previous evening. They greeted me miserably when I came in, the optio on my heels.

"I thought it would be alright if the guards opened the town gates to allow the people to go out to their fields and workshops," said Fabiansson, "providing they came back in by dark."

I gave him a hard stare.

"Now that the rebels have marched off," he added feebly. I had not seen him embarrassed before.

"Fabiansson, gentlemen," I said, "it's no good standing around here thinking everything's fine just because Corinium looks like it's safe. What about the people at Agridurnum, and what if the rebels burn down more farms or begin massacring people throughout the Durovenes lands? How much will it take before the southern chiefs turn against us? What if the garrisons in the eastern forts join the rebels? How are we going to stop these people?"

"My brother has a villa not far from Agridurnum," observed Aurelius sadly. "Could he be in danger?"

"We have no idea what the rebels are planning," I pointed out. "So how can any of us know what might happen to your brother? We need to get a better idea of what the rebels are thinking."

"You could ask the men who stayed behind at the camp," suggested Gracchus, the first sensible thing he had proposed since riding into my yard.

"A good idea, Optio," I said.

I turned to the administrators.

"I need a full idea of what we have available in the treasury. I need to know how many loyal auxiliaries there are spread around the province. I want couriers here, this afternoon, ready to ride to the four corners of the province, but first I need a little time to decide what message we should send."

I left the town by the south gate, with Gracchus in tow, to examine the state of the legionary camp and question the men who had stayed behind.

I found the camp pretty much abandoned and in a mess. There were smashed amphorae, drinking cups, plates and bowls scattered everywhere. Fires were still smouldering, and the half-eaten remains of slaughtered and roasted animals were strewn around. There were about a dozen sorry-looking young men making a feeble attempt to tidy up. They hung their heads when they saw me. The sight of them reminded me that the penalty for deserting was execution.

Gracchus sighed. "If I began executing the boys who stayed, how would that help matters?"

I called over a couple of older men who appeared to be supervising the clean-up.

"Tell me what happened," I ordered. They looked at each other before answering.

"When they heard that Hermanus was dying, and that Optio Gracchus was likely to succeed him, the young men became angry and agitated," said the first.

"Most of them were new and joined recently, after the captain began the new recruitment," added his companion.

"I think they mainly joined for adventure. The army way, sir, it's a lot of cleaning, some patrolling and no fighting, not so much battle. Especially here in Britannia."

"I have been trying hard to avoid having battles in this province," I emphasised grimly.

"We know, sir, but they claimed they were sick of being led by old men. They were sick of living in the camp. They had heard of auxiliaries who had also become rich and powerful, but they said Captain Hermanus had always held them back."

"It don't sound good, sir, but they wanted riches, food and drink, girls and slaves, and with their weapons they think they can just take them. There isn't anyone to stop them."

I could see Gracchus listening to the men, a hopeless expression on his face.

"Of course, we were horrified," the first soldier quickly added. "We have wives and children, homes, gardens and our animals to look after. Captain Hermanus was a good chief, and you too, sir. No one's died in battle, no one's lost an arm or leg or been blinded since Hermanus became captain. We don't want to be fighting unless we have to."

"I'm sorry to say, I think there's going to be some hard fighting soon," I said.

"We'll be ready, sir!"

"I hope so," I said. "What happened next?"

"Well, they voted for Deric, didn't they? Promised them the world," the first soldier nodded.

"He's been handing out money in the camp, too," said the second man with a disapproving look on his face.

"Don't know where he got it from," added the first.

"Luckily for us, they were too busy celebrating and drinking to the health and success of their new leader."

"Then they left," I filled in testily. "I know all that. Do you know where they went and why?"

"Agridurnum, I hear, but we weren't there when they decided. You need to speak to some of those boys who are cleaning up. They'll tell you."

Gracchus and I thanked them and made our way over to a pair of young men who were digging a hole, apparently to bury several half-burned animal carcasses. They stopped their work when we approached but failed to meet our eyes.

"Good work," I said. "I'm glad you're helping to clean up."

"We're sorry, sir," one of them muttered.

"Sorry?"

"Sorry we made this mess, sir. We had a big party, sir, to celebrate Deric being elected captain."

"In the morning they decided to march off, but we didn't go."

They did not need prompting to tell the story.

"First, they was going to rob the town, sir, but we heard the old men had already shut the gates, and anyway, sir, there's too many people in the town to take on."

"Then they set about thinking which rich villa they could rob. They said there was one up the road, sir, Verdaris, belongs to the governor, someone suggested."

"Then Deric spoke up in the end and said we should march to Agridurnum and rob the villa there."

"He gave everyone who was ready to follow him a share of silver coins and said there would be more when they got there."

"What sort of coin?" This was the same story I had heard earlier.

"One of those that his friends have been showing off, a shiny new one."

"He said that there was a store of food and wine and riches that was poorly guarded by a priest and a few farm hands. It was the richest estate in the south, he said. He knew all about it because he had served in the eastern forts, previous."

"So the others marched off, and you stayed here?"

"Yeah, we begun to think it probably wasn't a good idea. You know, just didn't seem right."

"And you?" I asked turning to the other.

"I've got a girl in town, and I didn't want to leave her."

"Do you know where Deric and his friends got the coins?"

"No idea, sir. Wasn't pay money, that's all."

This talk of coins was disturbing. I was reminded of the discussion I had had with Flavius the previous year. Was it just that the frontier had been leaking and some of the stolen goods from the east had found their way to Corinium, or had someone been bribing the auxiliaries?

On the way back to the basilica, I reflected on the situation we faced. Optio Gracchus had never fought a war. Britannia had been at peace all of his career. He had never led the auxiliaries. That had always been Hermanus' job. Gracchus had drilled the men and trained them to use their weapons. All of this he had learned by rote, by being trained by optios before him and following Captain Hermanus. Suddenly he had been faced with a situation where he needed to take the lead, and he had failed. There had been men expecting orders, and Deric had stepped in to give them, but why and to what end?

"Friends," I said, as joined the others back at the basilica, "I'm afraid there could be more to this than meets the eye. Gracchus, I want you to gather half a dozen good men and ride east. I need to know exactly what's going on at Agridurnum. Call in on Chief Bredonius. His estate is the closest to Agridurnum. Warn him to arm every man he can, however hopeless, and be prepared to defend himself. Tell him to gather in all the food and fuel from outlying barns as well to keep it out of the hands of the rebels."

I turned to Aurelius.

"Send a messenger to your brother with the same instructions. We need to tighten the noose round these deserters as soon as we can."

Fabiansson spoke up.

"We should warn Litorina, let the mayor know what has happened. There are more goods worth robbing there than at Agridurnum, and the port is far less well defended than we are here."

"Litorina is a long march from Agridurnum," I pointed out. "But very well, we'll do it anyway." It was as natural for a merchant to be concerned about warehouses as I was for farms and villas.

At the end of the day, I rode back to Verdaris. The message I had sent to Agridurnum's neighbours applied equally well to my own home, especially as it had been a possible target of the rebels. It was bitter, but there was little we could immediately do for the victims at Agridurnum. My thoughts were on the women and children of Verdaris.

Since the time the quarrel with the Astrebani had begun in earnest, I had continued to train my men to use weapons and keep discipline. The following morning I called together all the farm hands and the domestic servants and sent out messages to the tenants of the surrounding farmsteads. Without explaining the details, I informed them that a group of marauders had invaded the province and that we needed to be ready to defend our homes and those of our friends and neighbours. We set up a picket line across the road which ran over the hills and, many miles further on, close by Agridurnum. Half a dozen young men were sent out with instructions to hide up along the road and keep watch. Under no circumstances were they to get involved in a fight. Any sign that rebels were moving in our direction was to be reported back to Verdaris immediately.

With my home under guard, I had a little time to take stock of the situation. The men I had at hand were really only farmers, not warriors. Would we be ready to take on trained auxiliaries? How much could I count on neighbours and the provincial leaders? They were landowners who lived on and took care of their agricultural estates. As far as I knew, their retainers had not even had the instruction with weapons that mine had. Would it make sense to call out a horde of labourers to fight against soldiers? The Romans had clearly shown us what the result of that would be. Even though the rebel auxiliaries were hardly the calibre of legionaries, they were not just riff raff. They were well armed, and they had exercised for years. For the moment even threatening them with a fight was not realistic. And, even if I appealed to the provincial leaders right away, it might be weeks or months before sufficient good men were assembled to create a viable threat.

I still thought it was strange that Deric had so deliberately led the rebels to Agridurnum. Of course, there would be plenty of food in the storehouses there, and even though we had destroyed the main house years ago, the walls around the villa enclosed sufficient area for his men to find shelter. Worryingly, it was also in easy reach of the anarchy in the east of the country, a great recruiting ground for anyone with money to spread around and troublemaking on their mind.

I voiced my worries to Hypatia.

"Do you think Drusus is involved?" she asked.

"It would make sense. He would want his family lands back."

"He would want good access to his friends on the continent, as well."

"But there is no evidence! Just the Frankish coins, and any ambitious warlord could be handing those out."

I had to anticipate what the rebels would do next. Gracchus had described how thoughtless and destructive they had been in the camp. They had wasted food and drink. They had damaged the buildings and left valuable weapons and even the cohort's pay chest behind. Most likely they were doing the same at Agridurnum.

However well the unfortunate Father Justin had filled the stores, before long, the rebels would need more food, more to drink, more fuel for fires to keep out the cold. I had to hope that with time, they would become more vulnerable too.

Gracchus and his scouts returned with bad news. The forts on either side of the River Tamesis had gone over to the rebels. That left them controlling a good chunk of the river valley, as well as giving them direct access to the unruly areas to the east.

"I'm worried they could get reinforcements from Britannia Superior, Gracchus," I told him.

"I left a handful of men at the ruins, sir, to keep a watch on them."

For a moment I was puzzled.

"The ruins… ah yes, you mean at Old Calleva." The town was a former garrison post, lying between Corinium and Agridurnum. It had been abandoned by all but a few local farmers when the legions left and had been slowly decaying.

"I thought it would be bad if the rebels were lodged there, sir, and people from the farms and cottages around Agridurnum have started gathering inside the walls. They're frightened by what might happen."

"Are they planning to stay there? Do they have any food with them?" I asked, not quite sure what he meant.

"Some of them, sir, but I don't know how long they can stay there. The water supply doesn't work properly. That's why the town was abandoned, from what I have heard."

❧ Chapter 25 ☙

Nothing further appeared to happen as the first days turned into a week and more. Gracchus kept up his surveillance from Calleva, reporting that more and more people were crowding inside the old town walls. Some were trying to repair the tumbledown buildings. Others were constructing shacks amongst the ruins. Bredonius and Aurelius' brother reported that the rebels had been ranging the countryside, but with limited success as so many people had fled. The proximity of the rebels kept those two landowners and their followers on their toes. It was more difficult to maintain a consistent state of alert at Verdaris when we were so far away and the weather was so inhospitable. The men on the picket line were in a particularly miserable and exposed position. It was an unpopular responsibility and one I had to take myself now and then to set a good example. Otherwise, I spent the time checking the defences round the villa, making sure there were no vulnerabilities. The blacksmith worked overtime forging iron grilles so that all lower windows were secure, and we reinforced the gates so we could bar them effectively.

A strong defence was necessary, but like it or not, sooner or later we would have to take to the road and move south, if only to show ourselves to our friends in Corinium. Weapons were brought out, cleaned and sharpened. Provisions were packed into baskets and leather bags for easy transport on horseback. We were almost ready to leave when we found out it was not necessarily the need for food or drink which was going to drive the decision making of the rebels.

About a month or maybe six weeks had passed since Gracchus had come to me with news of the revolt when one of the young farmers from the picket line cantered into the stable yard. He was bleeding and battered, sweaty and exhausted from riding hard, and his horse was in little better state. The man stumbled from his mount and was immediately carried into the kitchen to the care of the maids, despite his protests that he needed to speak to me at once. News of his arrival reached me nonetheless.

"What has happened?" I asked the wounded man.

"Horsemen, boss, riding along the Agridurnum road," he gasped. "About a score of them, and they were dressed in old-style uniforms."

I pointed to his injuries.

"I thought I told you to avoid any fighting."

"We did, boss," he said. "We followed from the edge of the woods. The riders were in a hurry and didn't stop along the route. They passed by several small farms which they could have easily robbed and plundered."

"How did you end up like this, then?"

"I'm just coming to that. Me and the lads were dropping back, keeping to the forest paths like you told us, when suddenly three other men rode out of a thicket and attacked us."

"Were they part of the group?"

"I don't know. They didn't have any uniforms. We managed to fight them off. Clyd was wounded, but I think he's going to make it. I came as quick as I could by the back roads. The other boys are following behind, keeping themselves out of sight of the big group. They're bringing Clyd with them."

"Well done. You get yourself patched up and, ladies," I said, turning to the kitchen staff, "be ready for more wounded."

Twenty armed cavalrymen were a serious threat to us. From the household and the tenants from the surrounding farms we could barely muster twenty fighters ourselves. If the mysterious ambushers were part of the group, then they also knew they had been detected. I called to Barnulf, and we walked together around the outside of the buildings and double checked all possible ways someone could get in. I suppose we were trying to calm ourselves rather than do anything useful. If we were careful, we could probably withstand an attack. In the last few weeks Verdaris had become a fortress As the light began to fade, the rest of the pickets trotted into the yard, including the wounded Clyd.

"The rebels have stopped about three miles up the road," they told me. "They've been taking it easy since we got past Oak Hill."

"Maybe they're intending to wait out of sight for nightfall," suggested one of the men.

It seemed a likely possibility.

"Go and get a hot meal," I said, "and get Clyd patched up. We're going to need him if he's capable."

I went and found the relief pickets, who had ridden in from the surrounding farms and were assembling in the yard to take the night watch.

"There are enemies hiding somewhere along the Agridurnum road," I said. "We need to change the plan. Instead of heading over to Oak Hill, I want you to go and hide in the copse up the slope behind the villa."

They nodded.

"If Verdaris is overrun, you must spread out far and wide with the news and call together the tribal leaders. If that happens, you, Jos, are to ride into Corinium and rouse Gracchus and the remaining soldiers. You understand, only if we get overrun. Otherwise, stay hidden in the wood until you hear three calls on the hunting horn, and if you do, then hurry down to the house and hit the enemy from behind. Clear?"

They nodded. I paused.

"Jos, repeat what I just said," I ordered, remembering a tip Hermanus had given me. The man turned red and began stammering out a passable version of my instructions. I thumped heartily him on the back and sent them off.

As night fell, the fires were damped, the lights put out and an uneasy quiet descended over the house. The women and children huddled together in the upper floor of the tower while the men spread throughout the ground floor of the villa. A thin moon and a few stars cast a bare glint of blueish light over the frozen landscape. We knew there was a group of horsemen out there, presumably intent on attacking us. An owl hooted in alarm, alerting us that the rebels were trotting down the old road. Barnulf and I, watching from an upper window and taking care to keep in the shadows, could just make out their shapes in the starlight reflecting from the snow-covered fields. They halted for a moment where the roads met and then turned towards the villa. They could probably make out the light of a lamp through a window or the red glow of dying embers. They would surely calculate that the house was occupied, but we hoped they would conclude we were slumbering in peace. We saw the riders reach the yard gates, and then the dogs began to bark. One of the kitchen maids, posted in the yard, shouted at them to keep quiet. The hounds lay restless, their ears raised, as the shadowy figures probed outside. We were listening as carefully as the dogs.

Someone pushed at the yard door. The thick beam we had drawn across did not give way. The agitated dogs began to bark again. The maid shouted once more.

"Stop disturbing the house."

Another woman answered her.

"It must be the wind banging the gate that's set them off."

We tried to imagine what the rebels outside must be thinking. Had they caught us by surprise? Were there only women inside?

Had all the men gone away? We caught glimpses of the horsemen milling about, indecisive. Clearly, they were not going to get into the stable yard so easily. Would they begin to search for a different way in? Everything should be locked. It should be impossible.

A moment later there was a stifled call from the front of the house. One of the enemies had been creeping around and found another entrance. They were at the garden gate. Barnulf and I exchanged looks. Had we checked the gate was locked? Had one of the women been out for vegetables since we did our inspection? With our hearts sinking, we heard the gate creak as it swung open, and a shadowy figure stepped inside the garden. Someone must have forgotten to lock the gate.

"Damn the gods," I muttered. "Now we are in trouble. We can't let them get into the house."

I beckoned half a dozen men to follow me into the passage that led through the building; a couple more were crouching behind the low wall of the colonnade. The rest I sent upstairs, as quietly as possible, to spread along the gallery overlooking the garden.

As we waited, first one rebel and then another dismounted and slipped through the gate. The garden was in darkness, surrounded on three sides by high buildings. The moon had not risen far enough to sharpen their shadows. We could not see the intruders' movements, but we could hear them. One cursed as he tripped over a low-cut hedge. Another crunched on a patch of gravel. A whispered voice told the company to avoid the pond. One of the rebels must have visited Verdaris before. Now they were amongst the buildings and ahead, up a short flight of steps, lay the entrance.

As the intruders approached, we could begin to make out their shapes creeping through the garden. Some were wearing pieces of armour and now and then they would be exposed by a glint of metal. There was a sound of swords being drawn. Although we could not see very well, we would not need to. Our own weapons could hardly miss their targets in the space below. I gave a shout, and spears and sling stones rained down on the invaders from upper windows on all sides. Cursing and shouting, realising they had lost the advantage of surprise, and were confronted by an alert enemy, the intruders began to mill around, some trying to make their way back to the garden gate and others rushing towards the building, pushing up the steps into the portico where they were met by the defenders stationed there. In an instant there was confusion as men slashed and stabbed at one another in the gloom. The air was filled with yells and groans, the clash of metal and the barking of the dogs tied up in the yard.

I turned to the man next to me. I had had an idea.

"If there's no one outside the yard, open the gate a moment and let the dogs out!"

He vanished up the passage towards the stable yard. I could hear the yard gates squeal open and the sound of barking increase as the hunting dogs slipped out. We could hear them yelping as they raced around the villa to where the intruders' horses had been left outside the garden gate. The rebels could hear the melee too and began to press us less fiercely, conscious that their retreat had become more perilous. We had the advantage in the narrow entrance at the top of the garden steps since the attackers could only reach us two or three at a time. One man hauled himself over the low balcony, further round the cloister, to try to outflank us. He was quickly spotted as he struggled over the wall and cut down before he could get his feet on the ground. I was beginning to feel we were gaining the upper hand when I heard a call from the man who had got back from letting out the dogs.

"They are calling from the tower, boss. Something about fire."

"Take my place," I said, backing away from the fight and retreating through the passage into the stable yard. From high up in the tower, I heard a voice calling.

"Fire, Father, fire!"

Looking up, I saw it was my daughter, Amanda, standing on the upper floor of the tower. Seeing me, she called out again.

"Someone is throwing burning torches onto the outbuildings in the east yard. The bakehouse is already on fire."

For a moment I felt a sense of panic. How could we fight a fire and defend the house at the same time?

"Amanda, tell them to blow the horn three times."

"I will, Father, but how are we going to fight the fire?"

I wish I had an answer, but before I could offer an encouraging word, the girl called down again.

"We'll do it, Father, don't worry. Mother and I will manage."

"Stay there. A fight is no place for women!" I yelled. Then Hypatia's figure came into view over the parapet.

"This is my home too, Marcus. It is home to all of us, and I'm not going to let it burn."

Just then, I heard the horn blow three times. Hopefully, the sound would bring the men down from the copse, and they could take the attackers in the rear.

Barnulf appeared from the passageway next to me.

"We've got them on the retreat in the garden, boss. We should do something about that fire. We can't let it spread to the house."

There was another shout from the tower, Amanda again.

"Father, now they're trying to light the stables, three men!"

A flame arced over the stables and settled on the tiled roof above us.

"We have to stop this," said Barnulf, "I'm going out through the yard gate."

"I'm coming with you," I said, my heart pounding.

We ran across the yard, looking up at the stable roof. There on the tiles lay a flaming brand. While it could not do much harm there, if it rolled down into the yard, there was enough hay and straw that the blaze could spread.

"Open the gate and then close it behind us," Barnulf said to a bewildered stable boy, "and then watch that burning stick, and look out for any others that come over the roof."

The boy nodded anxiously. I wondered how useful he would be if a torch did tumble into the yard.

As we rounded the corner to the rear of the stables, I could see, a little distance away still, the party we had sent out earlier, running as fast as they could towards the house. I could also make out three figures hunched over, busy lighting a new torch, preparing to hurl it skywards. As we rushed towards them, the men glanced up and saw us. There was a flash of metal as they drew their swords. Two of them turned to face us while the third braced his arm and threw the blazing faggot up into the sky where it described a slow arc and disappeared behind the ridge of the stable roof. We hit the two men facing us as hard as we could, swords clashing. Barnulf and I had exercised daily since the revolt, but the men we were facing were skilled fighters. The third intruder would have shifted the odds desperately in their favour, but he was having trouble with his sword, distractedly looking towards the farm track to where our helpers were fast approaching.

The third man yelled something in a language I did not understand and, instead of advancing towards us, started to retreat. The man facing me glanced behind him in response to his comrade's shout, and he too began to back away. Their horses must be out there in the darkness, I thought. My loss of concentration was sufficient for my opponent to land a blow, and all at once I felt a sharp pain in my side as he struck home. I staggered and saw him preparing to strike again when a shadow pushed past me, hitting the man in the chest, knocking him off balance and onto the ground. It was Rufus, one of the hunting dogs. The man struggled to rise, but now I leaned over him panting, with my sword against his throat, and he lay still. A second dog, Blackster, galloped past us on the trail of the third villain who was now vanishing rapidly amongst the trees. His companion, facing Barnulf, backed away slowly, then turned and fled after him. By the time the ambush party reached us, the two men had disappeared into the darkness.

"Chief, are you alright?"

"I think so," I said, wincing. "Now get round the house to the vegetable garden and finish off the others."

Rufus growled down at the captive, who had given up any attempt to escape. He let go of his sword and lay panting on his back, his eyes fixed on the dog.

"Well, brother," I said, speaking British. "Get to your feet, slowly."

He looked at me uncomprehendingly. I wondered whether he was planning some trick, but then it struck me that he did not understand what I was saying.

I repeated my command, speaking slowly in Latin. He nodded to show now he understood. I commanded the dog to back off while the man first raised himself on his elbows and then straightened up.

"Hands on your head!" I ordered, turning to Barnulf. "It might be easiest to kill him, but I think we need to keep him alive for now and try to find out what's going on. We'll tie him up and then we can concentrate on putting out the fire."

The steward returned in a moment with a length of rope. We bound the man's hands behind his back and marched him into the stable yard, followed closely by the growling dog. There, we quickly tied his hands and feet to a hitching post. I gave his sword to the stable boy.

"If he tries to wriggle free, stab him."

I turned to the dog, probably a more reliable attendant than the boy.

"Guard!" I said, pointing to the captive.

As the dog lay down, growling softly, its eyes on the prisoner, we could see flames and embers rising into the sky beyond the kitchen wing. Barnulf and I rushed through the scullery and out into the east yard. The bakehouse and the smithy were well ablaze, but the women of the household were doing a gallant job. Hypatia had organised a bucket chain from the bathhouse. We would not save the outbuildings, but we could stop the fire spreading to the main house.

Hypatia had command for the moment, so Barnulf and I returned to the passageway leading through to the garden. Beyond was a jumble of dead, injured and exhausted men, friends and enemies.

"What do you want us to do with the rebels?" asked one of my men.

"We can't afford to take prisoners," I said. I recalled Cicero's opinion that pirates and rovers were common enemies to all and could expect no justice. We had heard how the rebels had treated the inhabitants of Agridurnum. Now, they had ridden for miles across country with one thought: to attack my peaceful home and put us to death. These were no innocent men. They had forfeited all their rights by attacking us. I was in no mood for mercy.

"A couple of them got away," said one of the men. "Do you want us to chase them down?"

"No, let's make sure we put the fire out. Go round and pull down the outbuildings in the east yard and do your best to douse them."

The man departed, and several others followed him.

Abruptly, I felt weak and sat down on the garden step. I put my hand to my side and felt something sticky. When I lifted it up again there was the unmistakable smell of blood. One of the men came by and looked down at me.

"By Christ, chief, you're wounded. Stay where you are and I'll fetch the mistress."

Hypatia came running a few moments later, followed by Amanda. My wife, for all her good qualities, was no medicine woman, but Amanda had spent her time around the kitchen and quickly called for help. In a moment they were joined by a pair of servants, and I was carried back to the house to be patched up.

In the morning I felt weak but not so much that I could not count three men dead and six wounded, not including myself, one badly enough he would probably die. Clyd, too, was in worse shape than he had seemed at first. One of the dogs had been killed: Blackster, the hound that had chased after the fleeing intruders.

"We found him round by the pigsties," said Barnulf, "stabbed in the chest."

"There were bloodstains," said the man with him, suggesting Blackster had not surrendered his life in vain.

"And the marks of feet being dragged in the snow."

"We followed them to the road."

"They disappeared in a welter of hoofprints."

The attackers had come off much worse than we had. We did not know how many had escaped, but six lay dead outside the passageway and another two by the garden gate. Another half a dozen had been captured uninjured and, after spending the night tied up in a stall, were led up to the copse and hung from a high branch. The only man who was left alive was the mysterious foreigner whom I had captured myself. He had been marched up to the copse along with the others, but I did not have him hung. I let him see what happened to his comrades. I hoped the sight would convince him to be cooperative.

With the intruders dealt with, I could inspect the damage. Resting on Hypatia's arm, I did a tour of the east yard. The blacksmith shop and the bakehouse were completely destroyed.

The bathhouse and kitchen were scorched, and charred remnants, ashes and cinders covered the roofs of the buildings around the stable yard. If there had been an unfavourable wind, the whole villa could have been burned down. As it was, the food stores and the animals, now housed for the winter in the stone buildings of the old east wing, had survived. At least we would not be going cold and hungry.

Discarded weapons were gathered up and the armour stripped from the corpses. The horses that had avoided the dogs were rounded up. Now we had mounts and good weapons for everyone and armour for those who wanted it. The frozen ground made it impossible to bury the bodies. Instead a huge pyre was built the next day from the charred timbers of the damaged buildings. The corpses were thrown on top and we set it alight. The stack burned long into the night.

The farm lads were pleased with themselves. They felt they had been transformed into battle-hardened warriors, recounting stories of what they had done in the fight. You would have thought we had been attacked by one hundred men from all the tales of skill and bravery. I admit even I sent a self-satisfied report down to Corinium. My estimate was that we had practically eliminated the auxiliary cavalry. Instead of the rebels being mobile, the tables had been turned. The odds shifted further in our favour three days later when Merwyn rode down from the north with a score of men. Some were farm hands from Umbrosa, but he had brought with him a handful of his own retainers. They might be Welshmen, but they were family now, and family would stick together, united against a common enemy.

Before they arrived, once the worst effects of my wound had passed, I settled to the business of questioning the captive. I had not seen him since the moment I had left him tied to the hitching post. He was taken from the stables where he had been held and escorted to my study. Barnulf and Jarmi remained in the room in case of trouble.

"Have you been treated well?" I asked, speaking in Latin, since that seemed to be a language we both understood, although his accent was a little strange to my Greek-trained ears.

"As well as could be expected."

"Your name?

"Does it matter?"

"To me, yes. You are a person, not a thing."

"Liutmann."

"Well, Master Liutmann," I asked, with exaggerated politeness, "by your dress you do not seem to be one of the auxiliaries, the rebels?"

"No."

"Perhaps you could tell me why you came here?"

"And if I don't?" He tried to sound defiant.

"You saw what happened to your fellows. They were strung up. That will be your fate if I choose it."

"And if I cooperate?"

I sat still for a moment, my elbows resting on my worktable.

"What do you say, Barnulf?" I asked the steward in British, assuming that the prisoner did not understand. "If he cooperates, should we let him go or hang him?"

"We could make him rebuild the smithy and the bakehouse, chief, before we hang him," said the steward.

I turned to the prisoner.

"My friend suggested you should remain here and help us repair the outbuildings you burned down. Are you much of a builder?"

"No, sir."

"Then, let me suggest an alternative. In return for your cooperation, I will send you away, together with one of the horses your comrades so thoughtfully left us and enough food to ensure you disappear from my sight once and for all. Does that sound like a better deal than a quick hanging?"

"Yes… sir."

"You can start by telling me why you came here."

"I was paid."

"Paid to do what?"

"I think you already know. To burn down your house."

"Why did you set it on fire while your comrades were still fighting to take it?"

"They were meant to rob it, and then it would burn down. The boss wanted it burned down."

"The boss?"

"Chief Drusus, who paid us."

"Was Drusus with you?" I could not hide my astonishment.

"Yes. I haven't heard he's dead, so he must have escaped."

So Drusus was the third man, the one who had run away without putting up a fight.

"Were you at Agridurnum with the rebel soldiers?"

For a moment the prisoner frowned, as if considering how much he should tell.

"Yes."

"How did you get there?"

"We came with Chief Drusus."

"We?"

"About a dozen of us, fighters from Germania."

"Is Drusus friends with the rebel leader, Deric?"

"They work together, from what I have seen."

"Did Drusus stir up the rebellion?"

"I don't know, sir. I wasn't part of that."

"Did he pay the rebels?"

"I don't know."

"But you were at Agridurnum with him. Why?"

"Chief Drusus said Agridurnum is his family home, which was stolen from him. He wanted his home back. The rebels helped him."

"And they helped you here?"

"Yes. It was the chief's idea, not Deric's. Deric just went along with it in the hope of getting some booty. The chief wanted to move quickly, to take you by surprise."

He looked at the floor for a moment.

"So only cavalry?" I asked.

"Yes, foot soldiers would take too long, he said. You could get tipped off and prepare. We had to sneak up on you before you expected it."

"You weren't planning to raid supplies?" I was curious about the rebels' stores of food.

"No one said anything about that to me. I was told to help the chief light the fire, nothing else, no fighting, no looting, no stealing, no nothing except burning the house."

"But there were only two of you with Drusus? Where is the rest of your band, the mercenaries?"

"They haven't arrived yet. The chief paid us and arranged to meet in Bononia. I was one of the first there, me and a friend. Chief Drusus was caught out when we heard the captain had suddenly died and the men revolted. He wasn't ready. We three came over on the first ship that was available and hurried to Agridurnum."

"But the others are on their way?"

"I suppose so, if the chief goes back to pick them up. I mean, I've never set foot in Britannia before. I just do as I'm told."

"Thank you, Master Liutmann. That has been useful," I concluded in a respectful tone. "Now my men will take you back to the stable, and if I have not thought of some other questions by this time tomorrow, I will set you free. Unlike some others, I stick to my deals, do you understand?" The prisoner nodded.

"Take him away and tie him up again," I said to Barnulf.

The following day we untied him, provided him with a bag of food and one of the captured horses and escorted him over the hills and out of sight. Barnulf though I had been foolish to let him go. Barnulf turned out to be wrong, thankfully.

❦ Chapter 26 ❧

When news of the attack on Verdaris spread, and I made sure that it did, expectations rose that I would take immediate steps to end the rebellion. Since I could not defeat the rebels alone, of course, it was necessary to convene the provincial council, though it was still the middle of winter. The announcement brought many leaders from all over Britannia Prima to Corinium despite the icy winds and frozen landscape. The men who lived close to Agridurnum were angry because their tenants were being terrorised and their property was being destroyed. The merchants and townspeople across the south were scared of the prospect that the disorder would spread, though most had not been directly affected. The leaders who lived further away, and thus nearer the frontiers of the province, were beginning to fear that other troublemakers would hear of the rebellion and try to take advantage, with their own property as the target.

The basilica was as cold inside as the world was outside. Passions were high, though largely as misdirected as the warmth from the braziers that had been placed throughout the council chamber.

"The rebel cavalry may have suffered a defeat, but that does not mean we have beaten the rebels," I emphasised once the assembly had settled down and complained about the awfulness of the weather, the difficulties of the journey and, ultimately, the despicability of the rebellious auxiliaries. "Unfortunately, there's no way that we can risk a head-on assault on Agridurnum with the forces we have today."

"Why not?" came several voices.

"We need to clean out that rats' nest!"

Bredonius, at least, was calm but concerned, and his voice carried weight.

"We need to get the people who have fled to Calleva back to their farms before planting time, otherwise there will be no harvest, no food. A famine."

"They are already desperately short of food," said Gracchus. "It's freezing and their supplies are coming to an end."

"It'll be worse when the hot weather comes," added Fabiansson. "All those people packed together in unsanitary conditions. It's only a matter of time before the miasma envelops them all and disease begins to spread."

"While I sympathise with those seeking refuge, and implore all of you to send whatever assistance you can, it does not change the calculation that we do not have enough trained men at hand to mount a full-scale assault on a such well-defended compound," I repeated. "And when it's time for ploughing and sowing, even the men we do have will be needed at home, otherwise there will be no harvest for any of us."

I did not want to reveal my hand too clearly. I did not wish to emphasise that Merwyn's Welshmen, together with the men from the north who had accompanied him, made up an already substantial force, though probably still insufficient. I did not want the other leaders to conclude that they could avoid being drawn into a fight altogether. It would not be good policy to appear at the provincial council with a retinue of Welshmen. In any case, I was worried that Drusus was still at large and that he had an unknown quantity of reinforcements on the way. I had left the Welsh and the northerners to guard Verdaris.

The chiefs knew the reality well enough, though that did not stop them discussing back and forth for three days. They could not agree who should provide how many men, who should pay to house them, who should provide food or how long their retainers would be away, not to say the uncomfortable possibility that some of them would not return. In fact, on every detail there was long and rancorous debate which achieved nothing.

On the morning of the third day, Fabiansson interrupted the talk by thumping a leather bag on the table in front of the assembly, one unmistakably full of coins.

"As mayor of Corinium, our provincial capital, may I take the floor for a moment?" he asked. After silence had fallen, he continued, "I propose to solve the problem and to do it my way." I saw the Litorina merchants nodding in agreement, from which I concluded they had contributed to the contents of the bag. He gave a quick glance towards me but then directed his attention to the provincial leaders.

"Since we cannot agree amongst ourselves how we will provide the men and means to rid ourselves of these rebels, the merchant guild proposes to pay someone else to solve the problem for us."

There was an apprehensive silence in the room.

I held up my hand to interrupt my friend.

"Fabiansson, I admire your initiative, but if we hire mercenaries from outside, we're hardly better than Drusus and Deric."

"I'm sorry, Governor," he responded in an impatient tone, "but we merchants have listened to the discussion for the last three days. We want peace and order restored as much as anyone. We agree that something must be done. We have the money, and we know how to use it."

He glanced around the room, daring anyone to contradict him.

"We've seen it done this way in Gaul and in the lands to the south. There are many trained warriors who are willing to fight for good pay. Even the emperor has hired men for many years. I have associates in Frisia who can place us in contact with trustworthy leaders, and I propose to reach out to them. In fact, gentlemen, a messenger from the guild is already on his way to Germania."

"This is exactly how we got into this trouble in the first place!" complained someone sharply, above general murmurs of dissatisfaction. It was Statorius, I think.

"Bribery and corruption," the voice continued, "recruiting foreigners, paying strangers to fight for us. Whatever has happened to honest government and well-trained professional armies?"

I suppose I should have been grateful that he had bothered to show up. It was a long way on winter roads from Stationum, and he was an old man.

Further shouting broke out around the chamber. Loud complaints and curses, contradictory cries of "Betrayal!", "Sold out!", "Go for it!", "We're with you!" and such comments filled the room. I let the babble continue for a while, hoping they would talk themselves to a standstill. What was the point in showing disapproval? I was frustrated with the landowners. They had had three days to arrive at a solution themselves, and they had just talked in circles. Each one wanted to benefit from the expenditure of others and keep their own risk to a minimum. I had begun to despair of finding a solution. I had not known what Fabiansson was planning, and I was exasperated with him for causing an uproar with his sudden intervention. Nonetheless, I was grateful that the deadlock seemed to have been broken. After a moment the hubbub died down somewhat, and I called for silence.

"Gentlemen. Friends. I think we should give the merchants a chance. Let's see what sort of man they can recruit, and then we can make a decision whether their plan is acceptable, or perhaps in the meantime one of us can put forward a better one. For my part,

I think I will ride up to my father's lands and consult with my son-in-law, Prince Merwyn, about whether the Welsh would be willing to supply us with fighters for a similar sum of gold. They are our neighbours, after all."

As I suspected, if there was absolutely anything that the provincial chiefs did not want, it was armed Welshmen given free rein to wander across the country. Angry leaders shouted that I was not fit to be governor and that I was more interested in protecting my own property than leading the province and such like. I had no choice but to persuade everyone to clear the room.

The furious group surged out into the street, still hurling objections and saying they would immediately go home to their own estates and gather men together and force me from leadership. Since this was exactly what they had refused to do for the last three days in a better cause, I was not especially alarmed by their threats and frankly only glad to see them disperse. Once the council chamber had been cleared, Fabiansson was waiting in the governor's office.

"You should have warned me," I said sharply. "I thought we were allies, working together?"

"We are," he said. "I didn't mean to come to this meeting to cause trouble."

"Well, you just did," I pointed out needlessly.

"It came up over dinner yesterday," he said, holding his hands out. "We were talking. We'd seen the message you sent about Drusus, and someone suggested recruiting men of the same sort for our side."

"I'm the governor – at least I'm supposed to be. I'm supposed to be in charge, and I need to know about matters like this plan. That quarrel would have been completely unnecessary if it had been handled differently."

I had begun to realise that I had not made matters better by losing my temper and threatening them with Welshmen. I wondered how many knew that there was already a band of traditional enemies at Verdaris, not half a day's ride up the road.

"Two weeks," I told him. "I give you two weeks to find a trustworthy mercenary, a professional, not some kind of rabble."

"I understand you very well. The continent is overflowing with trained and experienced warriors. You've already seen that. It's how they do things over there. Whoever pays the most…"

"I was not joking about the Welsh," I reminded him. "Merwyn and his men are already guarding Verdaris. I doubt it would be much trouble to recruit plenty more if they think they have a chance of earning fame and fortune in our lands. The Welsh are no different from anyone else in that regard… and neither are the Hibernians."

Fabiansson gave me a grim look and shook the leather bag of coins.

"I understand. I have the money. I'll fix things with the other merchants. There'll be no need for more Welshmen. If you call on them, it will be the end of the province as we know it."

I let him go, wondering how long he had been conspiring behind my back. I thought of his friend and partner, Laurentius. There was a man who had contacts on the continent, reputable and disreputable. A quiet word dropped here, a few coins there, a flagon of ale on the dockside in Litorina; they could have set this in motion long ago without me knowing anything about it.

Fabiansson was as good as his word. I suppose you must be if you are to be successful as a merchant in this troubled age. A promise is a promise in those circles. I received a message at Verdaris that Fabiansson and his candidate could attend the council at Corinium within three days. There was little time, so I quickly called all the local chiefs and the town leaders from Corinium and Litorina. I particularly wanted to include those with estates close to Agridurnum. I deliberately omitted to invite those who lived far away, not only because of the short notice we had been given, but because I calculated that the men most at risk from the current situation were most likely to want a quick solution, and I was determined to stack the dice in my favour.

We gathered in the council chamber once again, a considerably smaller group, and as we were seating ourselves, Fabiansson came in, followed by a large, fair man. From his looks, I guessed he must be a Saxon. He was a good hand taller than most people in the room, and perhaps double the bulk where the bulk should be – on his arms, legs and chest, not his stomach. His long blond hair flowed to his shoulders. He wore a rough leather jerkin and trousers. A short dagger hung from his belt, which was closed by a jewelled clasp, and a brooch in the form of a bear held his cloak in place. The man appeared the very epitome of a warrior. Everything about him exuded power and rough strength. He was followed by a lank youth of similar height but half the volume. It was not hard to infer he must be the big man's son.

Fabiansson gestured to the pair to sit beside him as he took his place alongside the merchants of Litorina. The Saxon occupied at least one and a half seats, and the merchants had to edge along the bench in a slightly embarrassed way to accommodate him and make a place for the son. Once the buzz had settled, I asked him to introduce his guest.

"Governor, you gave me two weeks to find a candidate to lead a war band against the rebels who have taken over Agridurnum, attacked your own home and threatened the lives and livelihoods of our friends gathered here. I would like to introduce Chief Gisla, who heard of my proposal and has come to discuss terms. Chief Gisla does not speak Latin well, but he has served in the auxiliaries in Gaul, as have many of his followers. The young man with him is his son, Edwulf."

"Welcome to our council," I said, speaking as slowly and clearly as I could.

"Thank you," replied the chief in heavily accented Latin, and then muttered something to Fabiansson in his own language.

I might have predicted Fabiansson would understand Saxon. I wondered for a moment what other hidden talents he had.

The merchant stood up and beckoned the Saxon to do the same.

"Chief Gisla has asked me to translate his words. He can speak more freely and clearly in his own tongue."

The Saxon, interrupted now and then by Fabiansson's interpretation, began to describe his understanding of our problem.

"He is telling us he has been the leader of a war band. He served in the auxiliaries for the emperor in his youth, as did many of his men," Fabiansson started.

The chief nodded while the merchant spoke and then pointed to himself.

"He says age is beginning to take its toll on all of them, and they would like to earn one more decent fee and then settle down."

The chief nodded and smiled round the room.

"After that it will be up to younger men to take up the sword and live the warrior life."

He gestured to the youth sitting next to him and continued speaking.

"He already has two sons serving in Gaul, but his youngest son, Edwulf, is still learning from his father, and he has a lot to learn," said Fabiansson.

The chief assumed a serious expression for a moment.

"He understands that there has been a lot of trouble in Britannia from Saxon pirates, but he swears he is no pirate or raider, but an honest man, a professional soldier, and when not employed in fighting, he tends his farm."

I was willing to give him the benefit of the doubt.

"His men follow his leadership in this," added Fabiansson, with an unconvincingly innocent expression. The Saxon flashed another smile and then looked grim again.

"He has heard that we have just lost the beloved leader of our soldiers. We must understand the bonds between fighting men and a chief they have served with for many years. We should know we can trust his men to follow his orders."

He seemed to have forgotten that the very reason he had been invited was that our "fighting men" were not obeying orders.

Fabiansson looked around the room to try to judge the effect he was having on the audience.

I interrupted before the Saxon had a chance to continue his recitation. I had had enough of these polite phrases, and though I realised it was not good manners, I wanted to get down to business. I trusted Fabiansson knew me well enough.

"What are your terms?" I asked.

Fabiansson frowned, did not relay my question to his companion and quickly began to speak without consulting him.

"Chief Gisla has accepted the silver offered by the merchants, but he has heard that the estate occupied by the rebels is good farmland and the previous owners have been rich and prosperous. An estate like that would need men to defend it, particularly when it's in such a vulnerable position."

There was a hush in the meeting room.

"He has told me that he and a select few of his followers are looking for a new place to live, away from the fighting in Gaul. If he is successful in removing the rebels, he proposes he could take over the estate and farm it for himself. He would be obedient to our laws and customs. He would pay any taxes and rents that are due, even to the Christian Church. He promises to live in peace with his neighbours in his old age and to assist them in any future conflicts whether with Britons or Saxons."

"Or Welsh!" someone called out. I scowled around the room but could not see who had spoken. I did not like the direction this discussion was going, even without the facetious interruptions.

"Some people might have difficulty in seeing a Saxon chief in Agridurnum." Not only Drusus Astrebanus, I thought. I had, after all, already donated the property to the Church.

Fabiansson whispered something to the Saxon, and he murmured in return before the merchant spoke up again.

"He says he understands that it might be difficult to trust the word of a stranger from another land," continued the merchant. "This concern is not groundless, he admits, especially when so many of his fellow countrymen have provided good reason to be distrusted. For that reason, he has brought his youngest son with him to offer as a hostage for his good behaviour."

All eyes turned to the seated youngster.

"He hopes that the supreme chief of the Britons, a man known far and wide for his learning and wisdom as well as his skill in combat, would be willing to take on this green youth and educate him, not just in fighting and farming but the finer skills as well."

The chief stood, carefully watching us. Then he spoke up himself in halting Latin.

"Simple man," he said, pointing to himself. "Farm boy, not read, not write, no school. All the time tricked by lawyers, merchants, moneylenders." He looked towards Fabiansson, and I could have sworn he gave him a wink. "Son get educated, read, write, clever man, not tricked the same."

At this, the chief looked around the room in all directions and then abruptly sat down. Fabiansson remained standing. I also looked around the room in all directions, anticipating comments or questions. They sat like birds along a house ridge in the autumn, each watching the others and waiting for another to make the first move.

"Chief Gisla," I said, "how many men do you propose to contribute to this venture?"

Fabiansson bent down and exchanged a few words with the Saxon and then straightened up and faced the room.

"The chief will need to see the site of the proposed attack. He will need to understand how many men we can provide and we will have to agree on how the assault will be carried out. He's not ready to make an estimate sight unseen."

"Chief Gisla," I said, fixing a smile on my face and speaking in carefully enunciated Latin, "your judgement of value of the estate at Agridurnum is quite accurate. You may have heard that as governor of Britannia Prima, that estate has become my responsibility since I confiscated the lands from a traitor some years ago. If you take over the estate, will you be ready to swear loyalty to me as your chief?"

More words were exchanged between the merchant and the Saxon before Fabiansson turned and addressed me.

"He understands that that will be necessary. He's a man of honour."

"My boy, to you," said the Saxon, butting in. "My precious boy!"

"That is why he is offering his son as a hostage for his word," explained Fabiansson.

"First win battle. Perhaps all dead. Only crows lords of place," the tall blond man interrupted once again.

Too damned right, my friend, I thought. And if we sit here bargaining in public, then the crows' hopes of getting a good feed will be rising. I turned to the council and asked whether they accepted Chief Gisla's offer.

I could see their reluctance. No one especially wanted a Saxon chief as a neighbour. On the other hand, their present neighbours, the rebel horde, were entirely intolerable and had to be removed.

"This man certainly looks up to the job," said Bredonius.

"His offer should be accepted," proposed Aurelius. "We need to deal with this problem before the spring advances too far. Even if the man can't read, I will put together a written agreement for the records."

We retired to the governor's office to seal the bargain with a toast and suitable words of honour and praise all around. I assume that the bag of coins changed hands discreetly.

❧ Chapter 27 ❧

The following day Gisla, Edwulf, Gracchus and I took the road to the east. We passed through Old Calleva. For the first time, I saw the appalling conditions of the people who had fled from the countryside: crying children and half starved, hollow-eyed men and women living in shacks. Gracchus had set up an advance camp for his men in a few of the better preserved buildings, as much to keep order amongst the refugees as to support an assault on Agridurnum.

"This is as bad as anything I saw during the invasions in Gaul," said Gracchus.

"I don't need more persuasion," I said, "but good wishes alone won't get these people back to their homes."

We took an ancient path winding up to the ridge line until we reached Breedon, the home of Chief Bredonius. Our dismal mood limited small talk, but Gracchus had dealt with many Saxons in his time, and he knew enough of their speech to converse a little with our new ally on the journey.

We spent the night in the hospitality of Bredonius, and then, before dawn the next morning, we mounted and rode on towards Agridurnum. From a distance we saw the fresh ramparts the rebels had thrown up to fortify the villa compound. Gisla insisted on dismounting and ordered his son to follow him.

"You stay back, friends. No need for risks," said the Saxon, speaking rather more fluent Latin in private than he had displayed only recently at the assembly.

Gracchus and I watched over the horses as Gisla and his son crept on their bellies as close to the fort as they dared. They lay for a long while, observing the rebels coming and going, and then crawled back into cover. Gisla's accent may have been thick, but his knowledge of military terms was more than adequate. In a mix of Latin and Saxon he explained his proposal while Gracchus made notes.

"How many men? Rebels, good soldiers or bad? This Deric, good leader or fool?"

He thought for a moment and then answered his own question.

"Maybe I met his father one time? Big fool, that man."

He turned to me.

"How good your men, chief?"

"We've been training for a long time, but they have never had to fight seriously, expect the few who were involved in defending Verdaris."

He murmured to himself.

"They good to climb ramparts and wall?"

"I doubt they could do it under a rain of spears," I confessed. "The veterans are no longer agile, and my men are really just farm hands with swords and javelins."

The Saxon rode in silence all the way back to Breedon, but a meal and an ale loosened his tongue.

"I fight rebel Romans before," he started, looking thoughtful. "I watch these people in fort. They not good soldiers, no order, easy to beat."

That sounded optimistic, but the chief frowned again, scratching at his beard.

"Can't do frontal assault. Too many dead people. My men not happy die. Your men not happy die."

I had to agree.

"Need to trick, make thinking some other plan."

"Do you think we can do that?"

"Not difficult. These people easy fool."

"What about the mercenaries that Drusus has hired?"

He shrugged.

"Not see them. I know those guys. They not here. If here, not too many. We beat them easy."

I was not entirely convinced by his assessment. Drusus had probably sounded just as confident when he persuaded Deric to send his cavalry to attack Verdaris, and that had not turned out so well. But then, I had Fabiansson's word that Gisla was a professional, and Drusus, I was grateful, was not.

"Now we go back to your town. I speak to Master Fabiansson. I go back to my country. I come back in fourteen days." He smiled. "God willing and good winds."

"How many men do you think you need?"

"I bring maybe thirty, maybe forty, see who is around."

He looked at me seriously.

"Not too many, else they not be tricked. You guys, you got to do the fighting, yes? All the guys you can find. Hundred, two hundred, everybody. Hide in the woods. Come running at right moment. My guys, we put on good show. Everyone looking at us. Not see you."

As the evening wore on, we found that Gisla's son Edwulf had a good voice, and when someone found a harp, he played a fine tune, too. In the morning, when Gisla made ready to depart from Litorina, he pushed his son over to me.

"You go with chief, boy. Stay here until Dad gets back."

The deal had been done, and young Edwulf had to commence his role as hostage.

While waiting for Gisla to reappear, our daily routine continued as much as was possible in the circumstances. I returned to Verdaris, taking Edwulf with me. The villa was more like an armed camp than a farmstead. Hypatia was already having to ration the food to make sure there was enough for all the newcomers. Edwulf may have been silent during the negotiations, but I soon discovered he was a sharp lad. Not speaking any language other than Saxon, he was forced to stay silent when he first arrived. Until then few of my people had ever heard that tongue spoken before. Nonetheless, as his singing and harp playing showed, he had a good ear, and he had willing teachers in the form of the women of Verdaris. The men were understandably more suspicious of this tall, blond outsider who spent an hour each morning exercising with his sword and spear. After a few days, the braver of them noticed how skilled he was and, by gesture and a few broken words, persuaded him to let them join his training. In the evening I sat with him and tried to teach him a few British words useful for soldiering. For Edwulf, bounding around the yard and stave fighting with the farm hands was clearly easier than reading and writing. On reflection, it could have been that he was more valuable as a teacher to me than I was to him, as I slowly began picking up some rudiments of Saxon.

Fourteen days passed, and Gracchus moved most of his veterans from Old Calleva to Bredonius' farm where they pitched camp in one of his barns. In their place, I began the slow process of moving my men from Verdaris down to the jumping-off post in Old Calleva. Each group had to take its own supplies and more, since there were none in the ruins of the old settlement, and, however short we were ourselves, we could not ignore the hungry refugees. The fifteenth and sixteenth days passed, and then a favourable wind brought news that Gisla had returned with his men. According to the plan, his band was not to join us directly but to come ashore along the coast to the east of Agridurnum, masquerading as a gang of sea raiders, which did not pose any great difficulty. Gisla and his band were to march ostentatiously westwards, taking their time, exactly as a pack of pirates would. Each nightfall they were to camp and light a huge bonfire to advertise their presence. This signal was picked up by patrols sent out by Gracchus, who hurried to Breedon and on to Verdaris with the message that the Saxons had arrived.

Gisla had to move slowly. He had to leave enough time for the rest of us to travel from Verdaris, Calleva and Corinium to rendezvous at Bredonius' estate. While we did so, his group sauntered along the west road in the vague direction of Corinium, that would eventually take them past Agridurnum. As they approached the target, a small group broke away to burn down some cottages which Bredonius had reluctantly agreed to sacrifice. Our hope was that this would convince any observers of their piratical credentials, but it also gave cover for a meeting to coordinate our forces. Before dawn the following day, my men and Gracchus' veterans made our way from Bredonius' farm towards the rebel stronghold. Our progress was slow as we had to trudge through fields and woods carrying long ladders until we were concealed behind a low ridge not far from the back side of Agridurnum compound.

Lying as we were behind the fort, we could not see how events unfurled in front. However, since then I have heard the tale so many times in one or another hall that I can almost feel I took part. No doubt the singers embellished this part of the narration; I am no poet to employ their flowery language, but I can give some taste of the story.

Gisla and his men approached from the east, singing and cheering and generally making a great effort to ensure they were noticed. The villa of Agridurnum was situated well back from the main road so that the civilised Romans who had built it would not be disturbed by passing carts and herds of animals being driven to market. Gisla and his band marched loudly along the road as if they had not noticed the compound of buildings but made enough noise to attract the occupants and draw them into a false calculation of our allies' strength and organisation. Just as the company appeared to have passed by, they pretended to notice the villa, and all of a sudden and in a disorganised manner suggesting a disagreement, they turned back. They ambled towards the gate and halted just out of javelin range. The defenders, curious, began to climb up onto the ramparts, and the two groups began to trade insults.

It was at this critical point that Gisla had to take a personal risk. He stepped forward and called out in a loud voice in a mixture of dog Latin and agricultural Saxon, "This is a nice-looking fort, just suitable as a base for pirate raids. It would be a pity for anyone to lose their lives in a fight. If the inhabitants could just give up, they would be allowed to go free!"

That, of course, brought a derisory reply.

"Do you take us for fools?" the rebels called back in a contemptuous tone. "Fat guy, clear off with your miserable band before real soldiers come out and massacre you!"

Gisla gave the impression, so he said, of carefully managed anger at these insults.

"You're only making threats because you're hiding behind these walls. Any real Saxon is worth three of you."

"We're as good as any Saxons," the assembled rebels shouted back belligerently, "but it's beneath our dignity to waste our time on a rag-bag gang of robbers."

Insults of this type and worse continued to be traded, becoming more personal as time went on. After a particularly malicious exchange of insults relating to their respective fathers' mothers, their manhood and fighting ability, Deric felt obliged to accept a personal challenge from Gisla. The fort gates swung open, and he rode out at the head of his closest supporters. At that, the

Saxons began to bang their shields and shout loudly. One of them made a show of raising a horn and blowing with great fury, to derisory jeers from the watchers above.

The rebels would not have been so amused if they had known the horn was the signal that Gisla's ruse had worked, their leader had been lured out of the fort and it was time for us to break cover and run as quickly as we could across the open fields towards the rebel camp. We threw the first ladders over the ditch which surrounded the compound, then the ramparts and walls above. Carefully, we crossed the ditch and anxiously scaled the bank, not quite knowing what would greet us when we reached the top. We need not have worried as most of the occupants of the fort were distracted by the show at the front. The men from Verdaris began to spread around the ramparts. Bredonius' farm hands clambered down into the yard, followed by the army veterans, and spread amongst the farm buildings of the Agridurnum villa. Behind them came Merwyn with his northerners and the Welshmen. I had not been able to keep them away when they realised there was a chance of battle and plunder. I had not done much to dissuade them either. Every able-bodied man was needed in the assault.

Suddenly, a sharp-eyed rebel noticed strangers in the camp and began to shriek and yell in alarm. For a moment the men on the ramparts were bewildered to see us creeping up behind them. It took a critical moment for them to realise they were under attack from the rear, then they began to shout and turn towards us. It was too late. We were on them. We were armed, and many of our opponents had left their weapons in the yard below when they had scrambled up to get a good look at the entertainment playing out beyond the front gate. In their desperation to defend themselves, they seized what materials they could or leaped from the ramparts into the courtyard. Those that stayed put were squeezed together more and more, and one by one they were struck down by my men. In the yard, the battle was a more equal contest. A few cooler heads amongst the rebels had never been lured onto the ramparts and had weapons to defend themselves. Bredonius' tenants and labourers were a poor match for them.

As we had been climbing in at the back, the single combat in front of the fort had begun. Deric was young and well trained but had no experience of real battle. Gisla was older and slower, but he was experienced and knew how to fight for his life. As we crept along the ramparts, the combatants cautiously circled one another to the cries and cheers of both sides, but before any serious exchange of blows could take place, the tone of the shouts and yells from above shifted as our attack drove home. For a moment Deric was distracted, and that was all Gisla needed. With a well-aimed blow, the rebel leader was knocked to the ground. At the same time the rest of the Saxons charged forward. The men outside the fort were stunned for a moment as the tables were turned, but they had brought their weapons with them. Though they were badly outnumbered, they quickly recovered their senses and took up a defensive position. The Saxon assault pushed them slowly back towards the fort entrance, but further retreat was blocked by the desperately fighting rebels who had remained in the fort. Then events took an even worse turn.

Bredonius' men had been beaten back and began searching for shelter. In doing so, they forced open a door to a barn, intending to creep inside for protection, but from the darkness, they heard hushed voices speaking in British. They called out to ask who was hidden there, fearing more rebels. Instead they discovered women and children and their families and relations who had been captured when the rebels took over Agridurnum. As the bedraggled women and half-starved children emerged into the light, the farm hands' spirit was renewed. With a roar, they turned, ran back and rejoined the fight. They were followed by the screaming women who picked up anything they could use as a weapon: knives, farm implements, axes and hammers. The children armed themselves too, boys and girls, and rushed behind their mothers and aunts, each one with whatever they could seize, to revenge themselves on their tormenters. The strongest and angriest women joined in the fight, regardless of the danger and the suitability of their weapons, while the rest took out their fury on the injured and dying, stabbing them and beating them, gouging eyes and cutting off body parts. In an instant the yard was a maelstrom of Britons, Welsh, Saxons and rebels, men, women and children hacking at each other with whatever they could lay their hands on. I clambered down a staircase into the yard and stood for a moment transfixed by the horrendous sight, wondering which way to turn. That was the last thing I can remember doing that day.

❧ Chapter 28 ☙

I woke up with an aching head, in complete darkness. I had expected to find myself in the midst of the battle, but instead I was alone and in silence. My hands felt itchy and swollen, but as I flexed my fingers, the feeling slowly returned. I tried to move my arms and legs, but I could not. I could feel rope biting into my wrists when I struggled. I gradually realised I was lying, bound, on an earthen floor inside a darkened room.

I could not remember what had happened. One moment I was involved in a chaotic struggle, the next I was seemingly a prisoner, but of whom and how? I managed to wriggle around to change my position and could just make out a rectangle of bright light, the outline of an ill-fitting door, apparently with daylight outside. I could see nothing else except the indistinct form of the room.

I heard voices beyond the door. I did not recognise them, and I could not make out what they were saying. Then the door was flung open and dazzling light flooded in, so bright that I had to shut my eyes.

I heard, or rather felt, footsteps coming towards me. Someone was standing over me.

"Governor so-called Ursinus!" said a mocking voice.

I recognised it immediately: Drusus Astrebanus.

"Delivered into my hands!" he continued in the same tone.

I could not think straight.

"How?" I muttered.

He crouched down low. I could make out his shape against the light of the doorway.

"How? You were blundering about, not paying enough attention, and I was not planning to be caught so easily. You walked right past me, and it was only a moment's work." He chuckled to himself and straightened up again.

"Now we shall see what kind of show I can put on." He backed away a couple of steps. "It would be a pity to waste this opportunity with a sordid secret murder the way you did with my brother."

I could hear him breathing.

"We'll see how you like being kicked down stairs. We'll see how you like being attacked by dogs."

He stepped nearer to me again.

"Do you see what it did," he demanded, "your dog?"

I could just about discern him pulling up his sleeve.

"I can't see anything," I protested.

"You need to be punished for all the trouble you have caused me and my family, and your people have to know you have been punished."

His outline revolved, filling the rectangle of light for a moment, and then vanished as the door was closed and the room sank back into darkness.

I was baffled and confused more than frightened at that moment. I do not think I could reason well enough to understand his threats more than vaguely.

The voices outside died away. Drusus' intervention had woken me up, and although my head was still muzzy, I realised I should try to do something to improve my situation. Lying on the ground was humiliating and uncomfortable and left me vulnerable. I began to worm my way across the floor, away from the door. At the far side of the room there must be a wall, and if there was a wall I could at least sit up. Foot by foot I squirmed, until I felt something rough behind me against my head. I bent my arms as far as I could, feeling back and forth until I was convinced it was the wall. Then I tucked up my legs and with an effort rolled myself into a sitting position.

My wriggling and writhing progress had left me exhausted. The wound I had received at Verdaris began to hurt. For a moment I sat leaning my back against the wall, catching my breath, biting my teeth together to block the pain. It was not particularly comfortable with my hands still trapped behind me, but it was a great deal better than lying on the floor. Where could I be? The wall felt rough, as if the builder had not taken too much care with the plastering. The floor, I already knew, was beaten earth. I could hear murmurs and occasionally the loud resonating footsteps of a person walking above. Another time, I heard an odd treading sound which could have been someone climbing a flight of stairs, taking uneven steps. My first thought was that I must be in some sort of outbuilding, one that was more than one storey high, a barn or a stable. There were no other sounds, no women or children or animals, so I could hardly still be at Agridurnum. Whatever the result of the battle, my last vision had been of mayhem, and it could not have died away into silence. The building I was held in must be isolated, out in the countryside, I guessed, where Drusus and some companions were holed up.

The door opened again, and now I could clearly see the shape of a man. It was not Drusus this time, but a stranger. I could see his head turning as he tried to spot me in the gloom. I said nothing and sat as still as I could, watching to see what he would do.

He stepped into the room, still looking around. With the additional light which streamed in once he had moved away from the opening, he finally spotted me.

"Water," he said, coming towards me with a beaker and a jug.

He bent down and offered me the beaker. I gulped down the contents.

Close up, I could see that he was wearing civilian clothes, similar to those I was wearing. He was evidently not one of the rebel soldiers.

"More?"

I shook my head. "No."

He stood up, gazed down at me for a moment and then turned and left, closing the door behind him.

When he had gone, I had time to think again. There was something strange about him. He had only said two words, but on reflection I thought I detected a foreign accent. I had started to get used to the way the Saxons pronounced British words. He was not a Saxon. He was not Welsh either. I had heard that tone before. I struggled to recall, and then suddenly the prisoner we had taken at Verdaris – Liutmann – came to mind. This stranger had a similar accent, and now, come to think of it, his clothes were similar to Liutmann's too. Luitmann had said he was from Germania. This stranger probably was as well, and that meant that Drusus reinforcements must have arrived, though we had not seen them at Agridurnum. Somehow I had fallen into his hands.

I sat alone, sunk in thought. I began to wonder what Drusus had in mind for me. I was to be punished, he had said. Anxiety began to take hold of me. I could see my death ahead, and not an easy one. I thought of Hypatia and the children, of my friends – Cull, Barnulf, Baxter, Fabiansson and the others. Did they realise I had been captured? Were they doing anything to find me? Should I try to do something to escape? What could I do? I was tied up, in a dark and apparently empty room.

The light faded outside. Where there had been daylight, there was now an uneven orange glow. Someone must have lit a fire. Outside the room must be the open air, and Drusus and his men were not concerned about being observed. After a while the door opened again, and I was sure I could see flames in the yard outside. The same man came in, the supposed German.

"Water," he said again, offering the beaker.

"Food?" I asked. He grunted to himself.

"No food," he said.

"No food?" I wondered.

"Me no food, you no food," he replied, taking the beaker back.

What did that mean? That they had no food? My mind wove all sorts of theories about what could be going on, but as these were of no consequence, I will not repeat them. Instead, I rolled over and tried to fall asleep.

When I woke up, I could hear voices outside speaking in sharp tones, words I could not understand. I could see the outline of the door sharply demarcated by the sunlight. It must be day again, and the men outside were clearly on the move, agitated by something.

The door swung open violently, and three men stepped into the room. One of them was Drusus. He gave an order, and his companions came over and hauled me to my feet.

"Marcus Lucullus Silvanus, self-proclaimed governor of Britannia Prima, in the name of the emperor, I condemn you to death," he pronounced, in as haughty a tone as was possible in the circumstances. He sniffed.

"The sentence will be carried out immediately: public beheading as an example to the population how traitors are penalised in the Empire."

He said something more to the men that I could not understand, and they began to drag me towards the door.

The light outside was almost blinding after the darkness of the room. I closed my eyes, and that led to me stumbling over the threshold. The two men gripped me tighter, forcing me upright. As the orange blaze of light shining through my eyelids slowly faded, I cautiously opened them and looked around. At last I could see where I was, though that did not give me much hope.

The space outside the room was an open yard, surrounded on all four sides by a high wooden palisade. In the yard, along the palisade, were several buildings, also made of wood. In the centre was the place where the fire had burned the evening before. A little to the left of the building where I had been imprisoned was a set of wooden stairs leading up to a walkway which ran around the palisade. The walkway ran above my prison, forming a small platform, and it must have been these stairs which I had heard men climbing and the platform which I had heard them walking along. I could not see the entrance to the yard but assumed it must be on the other side of the building. Taking all this in as I stood blinking in the sunlight, I realised I must be in one of the forts which we had constructed on the eastern frontier of the province, the forts which Optio Gracchus had told me had gone over to the rebels.

Now I could see Drusus and eight or ten similarly dressed men, long hair, moustaches, ill-shaven faces, watching me.

Drusus spoke again, waving to the stairs.

The men said something in return. Drusus cursed and nodded.

They bent down and untied my ankles. At last I could stretch my legs and totter along.

"Up the stairs," he said. I did as I was ordered, my feet still clumsy from being tied up.

When we reached the walkway, I could see out over the fence. I could see trees, a small meadow, a river – the Tamesis perhaps – flowing slowly by with a couple of white birds, swans, swimming on it, and alongside it a paved road stretched into the distance. It was a beautiful day in Britannia. I was glad to be able to see it instead of dying in that miserable cellar.

"Now we wait," said Drusus.

One of the men gripping me muttered something under his breath, then spoke aloud. Evidently they did not want to keep holding me since, in response to Drusus' reply, they found a length of rope and tied my ankles together again. With a rough push, I was forced to sit down, now leaning against the rampart. At least I was in the open air and not the darkness, but my fate seemed to have been sealed. After a while the remaining men climbed the stairs from the yard and ranged themselves along the parapet, looking out along the road. From the angle of the sun, I could conclude they were looking west in the direction of Agridurnum.

Presently, I could make out the sound of horses' hooves on the road, men on horseback, trotting, faint voices on the breeze. One of the ruffians on the walkway picked up a javelin, and after a moment's calculation hurled it out into the open. The hoof beats stopped. The voices grew louder.

Drusus yelled something I could not make out. He looked down at me then, peering out over the wall, and pronounced my name several times. This obviously did not have the desired effect, as he waved to the men standing nearest me who immediately grabbed me, turned me round and propped me against the barrier. My head cleared the top of the wall, and in front of me, standing some way away, I could see four horsemen.

"A bunch of fucking Saxons," said one of Drusus' ruffians.

From their general appearance, I could see they must be members of Gisla's warband.

Drusus called out, pointed at me and once again repeated my name. Ironically, he was forced to call me Governor Marcus Lucullus Ursinus, since the newcomers would never have recognised any other name, though he did manage to pronounce it in a sneering tone.

The men called something back in Saxon. I could not understand what they said, but it was sufficient for the men holding me to turn me around again and force me to sit down.

"That should get us the right audience," said Drusus to me, now in British. "A few miserable Saxon farmers would not be enough. We want your friends, your real followers, so they can see the final moments of their leader." He smiled in a nasty manner.

I caught a glimpse of the men on the parapet exchanging glances. They seemed uneasy. One of them spoke to Drusus, gesticulating and pointing to the east. He pointed at me, drew his hand across his throat. Drusus shook his head.

Another man spoke up. Then another. Drusus looked back and forth. I could see he was beginning to get nervous, and small beads of sweat appeared on his face. His voice rose.

The first man spoke again, pointing down to where I guessed the gate was, gesticulating. Someone from the far end of the line came over.

"I don't understand why it is so important, Drusus," he said, this time in accented Latin. "You are just going to get us trapped here. The only way out is on this side. If they block it we are doomed."

One of the men who had spoken earlier gave voice again in Latin.

"It's not my fault we have no food. I thought there would be supplies here."

The other spoke again.

"Of course I want to get the fuck away, but he's in charge."

Now several voices could be heard. The Latin speaker switched to the foreign language I did not understand, waving his arms to calm the men down. I could see them standing sullenly, sometimes glancing out to the road and sometimes giving Drusus doubtful looks.

The Latin speaker crossed his arms and looked up the road, too.

"I don't see why we can't just kill him here and leave. They'll find him soon enough."

"It has to be a public execution. That's what traitors deserve," said Drusus.

"They are not going to see it anyway if you kill him behind the wall."

Drusus looked thoughtful for a moment, then barked an order. Three or four men scampered down the stairs and came back manhandling a couple of benches. With a great deal of effort, they carried them up the stairs and set them down on the platform.

"Stand on there," he ordered me. It was impossible, of course, with tied feet. He yelled at the men, and they hoisted me onto one of the benches and then climbed up beside me.

"That better?" he said, glaring around.

"Marginally," the Latin speaker replied. "I still don't like these theatrics. After all the effort we have made, we could get clean away, and you want to risk it with this show. It doesn't make sense."

"It makes sense to me, Alwynn," said Drusus firmly. The man looked around, his gaze scanning along the line of watching men.

I was still standing on the bench when I felt my companions tense. One of them said something, calling down to the walkway. Looking hard, I thought I could see movement up along the road and hear the faint sound of horses.

The men along the parapet looked at each other and at Alwynn. As they did so, the first clear sign of their enemy appeared far away on the road.

"We go!" shouted one of the men. Drusus screeched in reply.

"Drusus, this is your show, not ours," said Alwynn. "You paid us to fight, not to commit suicide."

As he spoke, the two men beside me on the bench lifted me down to the ground and then let go.

"I'm staying," said Drusus, though he sounded nervous. "I'm going to see this through."

"Good luck," said Alwynn, with an insincere tone.

He shouted something at the men, and they began to shuffle along the walkway and bounce down the stairs to the yard. Then came the squeaking of the gate being opened, and I glimpsed shapes scurrying past below me and around the corner of the fort, a couple of horses whinnying. I was alone on the platform with Drusus.

"Stand by the parapet, Marcus. I want them to see you die."

I stood still.

"Move!" he screeched, pulling a dagger from his belt. "Move!" He prodded me in the back with the weapon, and I had to hop forward to avoid being stabbed. I had no way of resisting, bound hand and foot.

I looked out over the wall and could see a troop of horsemen approaching, my friends and comrades, Drusus' audience. We watched them coming at a slow walk.

There was a step on the boards behind us. We both turned. One of the mercenaries was standing there, a leather helmet pulled tight over his head.

"I thought you had all gone," said Drusus.

"All but me," said the man hesitatingly.

He looked at me and pulled his sword.

"You go, chief. If those men catch you, they'll certainly torture you. Leave him to me. I kill him."

I saw Drusus hesitate. The horsemen were getting quite close. He was torn between waiting and taking his chance to flee.

"Very well," he said suddenly, stuffed his dagger in his belt, turned and vanished down the stairs.

"Just you and me," said the soldier, as he watched Drusus' departing back. He pulled out his sword and rested it against the bench.

As he did so, he loosened the helmet with his other hand and then, seizing it firmly, pulled it off.

"Liutmann?" I exclaimed.

He took a deep breath and placed his hands on his hips.

"Yes."

He looked out over the parapet, standing still.

"Governor," he said finally. "Once you save my life and now…"

My knees felt weak and my legs sagged.

He began to count under his breath.

"Eins, zwei, drei, vier, funf, sechs, seiben, acht, neun, zehn…"

He picked up the sword.

"Blood for Drusus," he said, grasping the sword in both hands and, before I could react, swung it at my head.

For a moment I thought I had died and gone to hell. Two grim masks looked down at me. Long moustaches and beards sprouted from the edges of metal helmets which covered most of their faces. Slowly they came into focus, men or devils.

One of them shouted, his fetid breath enveloping me and spittle spattering my face.

I could hear steps and running, more confused shouts.

"Thank God!" A voice I dimly recognised. The two figures backed away and another face loomed into view.

"Marcus, Marcus, look at me!"

"Oh, shit!" said another with a singing tone, "what have they done to him?"

"It's me, Marcus," said the first again. "It's Cull, don't you recognise me?"

Slowly the face began to coalesce in form, and a memory came back to me of my friend.

"By Christ!" the one said to the other. "He's bleeding, but do you see anything broken?"

Another figure joined the two, almost blocking out the sky.

"Just flesh. No bones! We take. Back to camp."

"If you say so, chief. Do you think it is safe?"

"I seen wounds, Prince. These not bad. Just hit on head. Bang, knocked out!"

"I think you're right, chief," said the first man. "You two, come and give us a hand."

The two devils came into view again. Their hands seized hold of me, and I was carried away.

Later, when my head cleared again, I found I was in a farmyard. There was a woman washing me. Men clustered round, went away, other men came. They spoke to each other. Some words I understood; some I could make no sense of. Some faces I vaguely remembered; others, I had no idea who they were.

"We're going to move you again, master," said a voice. I was hoisted up and carried through the ruins of buildings, smoke curling, the stench of dead bodies, the smell of horses, and I was swaying, floating through the landscape.

"Marcus, you'll be alright. They said so," said a man walking beside me.

I was in an unfamiliar room. Lying on a bed. It smelt clean and fresh. A young woman came, offered me water.

"Would the master like something to eat?"

Her calm and friendly voice woke something in me. I was hungry. I felt as if I had not eaten for days.

"Yes," I whispered.

Water and food gave me a little strength. The young woman helped me to sit up, placed cushions behind my back.

"I'll tell them you are feeling better," she said.

I was left alone for a moment, awake now, struggling to put together what had happened. Only an outline, a hazy memory of a darkened room.

Three men came in, treading quietly. They were smiling. I tried to smile in return.

"Marcus, thank God! You look better sitting up." Now I remembered the voice.

"Cull," I said. "I'm glad to see you." I turned, and the features of the second man came back to me.

"Merwyn, my friend, it's you!" The prince smiled, but I could see a tear in his eye.

The third man I could not place. I knew I should know him, but I could not put a name to the face.

"Chief Gisla's here as well," said Cull, pointing to the stranger. The big man bowed. He looked down at me.

"You not know me. Bang on head," he said. "Not remember a thing. Seen it before. He be alright. Come back soon."

"Thank God we found you," said Cull. "We didn't know where you were. We thought you'd been killed. You were there one moment, and suddenly you were gone."

"We looked all over," continued Merwyn. "We found a tunnel, out under the wall and the bank, an old water conduit from Roman times. Drusus must have known about it and used it to escape."

"Then we got the message that he had you. First, we didn't believe the warriors, but since we couldn't find you anywhere, we had to believe it was true."

"I don't remember," I said. "Just a dark room."

"In the fort."

"Perhaps your friend is right," I said. "Perhaps I will remember what happened one day."

ଊ Chapter 29 ଓ

I still do not remember much of the days after I was rescued from the fort. My head hurt; my body hurt. I could not tolerate light shining on my face and had to lie in a room with a blanket fixed over the window. There were nights when I was back in that dark cellar, with the figure of Drusus leaning over me. In my delusions Drusus did not leave me with Liutmann, but it was his blade which slashed down, and not with the flat side. On those nights I woke up sweating and trembling and could not fall asleep again. There were times when I believed I had died and arrived in some private and bizarre afterlife. Gradually, I suppose, my injuries began to heal. I began to have a vague recollection of the events leading up to the attack on Agridurnum, or at least, I began to understand the stories my friends told me. After a while a sense of sadness began to grow in me, though I should have been glad I had survived. My old friend, Hermanus, the first ally I had had before I even became governor, a man I trusted and relied on, who had always seemed permanent, was dead. My own home had been invaded and part of it lay in charred ruins. I had been incapable of acting as governor, and as my senses returned I began to feel that I did not want to be governor any longer.

Hypatia had little patience with me when I complained.

"You can't just give up. People rely on you. You gave your word."

"To whom? Everyone has gone."

"To me. I haven't gone."

"I can't help feeling that being governor is simply a threat to us. That it's like a red rag to a bull to Drusus and his friends. Perhaps if I gave up being governor, he would leave us alone."

"Would it un-execute his brother? Would it give him Agridurnum back? Don't you think he would go on blaming you for those?"

I shook my head and an instant later regretted I had done so. Hypatia ignored my discomfort and continued.

"As long as you are governor, you have the means to defeat Drusus and his companions. They know that now. You command the forces of the province, not just our own followers, and you have friends across the land. It's those people you can't let down."

"I've been governor for twenty years," I insisted. "Maybe it's time to move on, give someone else a chance."

Hypatia frowned and took a breath.

"And who else is going to do it? Who else is going to be governor? Aurelius, Fabiansson, Marcellus? No, Marcus, you swore you would take on this responsibility, and you have to continue."

I understood her passion, but I was not convinced by her arguments. There was also something more gnawing at me than my personal problems, a feeling that had grown on me while I lay in my darkened sickroom. There was enough evidence to convince me that it was not entirely a melancholic fantasy. The defeat of the rebel soldiers did not feel like a victory, however enthusiastic the men who surrounded me sounded. Before the revolt we could delude ourselves that the Roman way of life was continuing, but now it was impossible to keep on pretending. The last vestige of the Roman army had died with the rebels. We had even had our own bishop once, a man who could pick up a pen and write to the bishop of Rome himself. We had bravely declared our independence, but as we did that, we had fooled ourselves that the old ways could continue. In my misery and discomfort, I had concluded I was governing a shell, a make-believe. The Roman ways had gone for good and would never come back.

"We sat in this chamber and talked when thieves and traitors stole and ravaged our countryside," I began, when I called the provincial council in the spring. "We argued about who was ready to contribute to the effort to defeat the rebels, who felt it was some other's task, someone else's money to be used."

I paused and looked round the chamber.

"I'm grateful to those of you who did contribute, in hospitality, in providing supplies and in putting your lives and livelihoods at risk. I want to remind you that the last remnants of our professional army, the Roman army, died in that fight. From now on, it will be up to each man, each family, to defend themselves."

There were loud grumblings of denial.

I banged my fist on the podium.

"Gentlemen, don't forget that we received a letter from Emperor Honorius years ago stating that Britannia was responsible for its own administration and defence. We have all heard distressing stories from eastern Britannia, and perhaps we imagined the same could not happen here. This winter we saw that it could. We saw anarchy on our own doorstep."

As I spoke, a strange feeling came over me. If I wanted my fellow leaders to begin to think and act like Britons, then I would have to find a way to shake them up. It had always been the tradition in the council chamber to speak Latin, a leftover from Roman times, but while I continued to speak in Latin, everyone, including me, was falling into the trap of still thinking as Romans. I stopped speaking and looked around the room. Then I took a breath and continued, this time in British.

"My father did not rely on Rome," I began, watching the expressions on the faces of the men opposite me. "Those of you from the north know this. Circumstances forced us to take care of ourselves. However, my father still thought of himself as a loyal Roman, serving the governor who in turn served the emperor. This winter we worked together – we fought together – to defeat the rebels. We weren't following some law or custom handed down from far away by an alien ruler. We didn't do it because we serve a Roman. We did it because it was in our own interests to destroy these rebels. They threatened our homes and our families. That is how we solved the problem, and that is how we are going to have to solve similar problems in the future. There is no one out there to help us."

I pointed to the leaders sitting in the council chamber, picking out some of them individually.

"This is what you are going to do. I'm not giving you orders. I have no authority to do so. It's in your own best interests to do it. You're going to go home, each one to his own estate. You're going to prepare to defend yourselves. You can train your men on your own, reading from a textbook. I have heard Vegetius is the most up-to-date writer on this subject. Or you can get practical training from the experts we have amongst us. I'm sure Chief Gisla or Gracchus and their men would be happy to instruct your farm boys and stable hands on how to fight more like warriors than tavern brawlers."

I paused, and there was silence in the room.

"Together, working together, continuing to cooperate, talk and discuss – argue if we must – we can maintain the peace and prosperity of this region of Britannia. If we don't work together, we will suffer the same fate as our friends in Britannia Superior. The strong and prepared will survive, at least for a time. The weak and unprepared will go to the wall sooner than they expect."

I let my words sink in for a moment. I looked around the room and was met with blank expressions. Despite my words, were my friends and colleagues still stuck in the view that things had not changed, that they would not change? I felt increasingly desperate.

"Let's put an end to this pretence that we are a province of the Roman Empire and that I am governor of this province. It is just a way to ignore the changes that have been taking place. This will be the last meeting of the provincial assembly of Britannia Prima. I am not continuing to serve as a so-called governor. What comes after, we can still discuss, but we must find another way to rule ourselves, another type of leader, another form of rule suitable to our present situation."

I took off my governor's regalia and bundled it in my cloak.

"Who will be our leader now?" came a worried voice.

"That's up to you," I answered and began to make my way out of the hall.

"You can't just walk away!" said Marcellus in a slightly desperate tone, suddenly stepping forward. "Everyone who cares about our province should meet here tomorrow, and we'll thrash this out. Everyone must come back here tomorrow."

I admit, I would have liked to walk away. I would have liked to collect my horse from the stables behind the Ursinus town house and ride out of town, to Verdaris, to Umbrosa even, and leave all these responsibilities behind. I felt that I had done enough. In the old days of the Roman Republic, or ancient Athens long before that, a man could be appointed to rule the land in times of difficulty, war or catastrophe, but when the hard times were over, he was expected to relinquish his position and retire to his former life as a farmer or a landowner. Surely I was allowed to leave the stage and return to my farm and my family? As I walked through the forum after the meeting, I was struggling with myself. How much had my words in the council chamber been a sincere reflection of my real desires and how much a theatrical gesture intended to shock? I was not sure myself, but I began to have the uneasy feeling that Hypatia's judgement would not be lenient.

The news of my actions spread faster than my walking.

My wife was waiting for me.

"Now you have really put the cat amongst the pigeons, Marcus," she said. "You didn't choose your words very well, I hear."

"I chose them as well as I could," I said, a little defensively. "I just don't want everyone continuing as if nothing has happened, pretending that we are Romans, following Roman customs, trying and failing to do things the Roman way. It won't work anymore!"

She gave me an exasperated look, which still contained a modicum of sympathy. "Why didn't you say anything to me before doing this? I know how hurt you have been. I know you sleep poorly, that you worry. I know that. It's the price you have to pay. I could say the reward will come in heaven, but I don't have to. Just look at this town, this house, the countryside, the people going about their business in peace. Isn't that reward enough for some stress and worry?"

We had invited Marcellus and Gallius' eldest son, Questus, to dinner. Questus had recently taken over from his father as leader of the north.

"Marcus," said Marcellus. "I think I understand what you mean about not acting like Romans, but people are used to seeing you as leader now, even if they don't always like what you say and do."

"Besides," said Questus, helping himself to meat, "let's be realistic. You are the leader with the best warriors now. It was mainly your people, your family and men loyal to you who fought at Agridurnum." He chewed a mouthful of food for a moment. "This is good. You even seem to have the best cook, too."

Hypatia gave me a serious look.

"Tomorrow I am going over to the basilica before your council starts, and I will talk to Aurelius and Fabiansson," she said.

I slept better than I had for a long time. I had said what I had been struggling to put into words, and it felt good to have said it.

There were a few curious glances when the chiefs assembled the following afternoon and found Marcellus and Questus on the podium where they had been used to seeing me. Marcellus was still wearing his Roman-style tunic, but Questus had pointedly discarded his in favour of work clothes. I sat in the place in the chamber which my father had used to occupy in Publius Julius' time.

"This is an urgent situation," began Marcellus. "We heard Chief Marcus yesterday telling us that the government we have been used to for years, tens of years…"

"Hundreds of years!"

"…is no longer functioning. He described the problem, but unfortunately he offered no adequate solution. Today, before we close this council, we must find one."

I won't describe the tedious discussion that went on for hours. I sat in silence, listening. As time went on, I began to detect the influence of Hypatia. As a woman, she had no place in our assembly, but I recognised her handiwork. She was always more patient than me. She had not wasted her morning.

"Let me outline the proposal," said Aurelius eventually, when everyone was tired of talking. "We need a clear leader. We need a man we can turn to in an emergency. But we also need men who can carry out the administration in times of peace. These don't have to be the same people. Some of us spent some time together this morning thinking about this. Our proposal is that this council should follow our neighbours in Gaul. We have all heard of Magister Aetius' triumphs against bandits and malcontents. Now our friend, Marcus Lucullus, has shown us the way to deal with our own troublemakers. We should appoint a master of our military forces to take care of any threats to our defences, but we should also have a master of officials to take care of the day-to-day administration. It's true we would be copying practices from the Empire, but…"

There were a few murmurs of approval, none of dissent.

Fabiansson got to his feet.

"Friends, it's not for me, as a mere merchant and town mayor, to dictate who should be our leaders, but I would like to nominate our friend and former governor, Marcus Lucullus Ursinus, for the office of master of the military forces."

And so the words of praise began to flow. I am sure you have heard such phrases when there is a task to be done which offers more trouble than honour, when the men speaking do not wish to take responsibility themselves but are unwilling to admit it. I felt an uncomfortable dissonance between the high praise and the image I carried of myself, huddled in the dark room at the mercy of Drusus, little pride, even less self-esteem. I thanked each of my friends and colleagues for their kind words and, sighing to myself, accepted their proposal.

❧ Chapter 30 ☙

At the end of the summer, just after the first frost of autumn, Gisla arranged a feast to celebrate the completion of his hall and the harvest which he and his followers had managed to gather from the fields around Agridurnum thanks to a mild and warm summer. He wanted to thank neighbours and friends for the help they had given. I would, I reflected, be eating and be warmed, in part, by corn and wood I had contributed myself from the Verdaris estate. I did not travel alone. It was a family affair, too, with Hypatia and Amanda joining me.

I was returning from a visit to the stables on the evening after we arrived, after checking on the well-being of the horses. We would be hunting in the morning, and I wanted to ensure that they had recovered from the journey. I met Gisla by the entrance to the hall, and we stood side by side for a moment, watching the low clouds scudding across the skies, momentarily hiding the stars and the crescent moon.

"We should have good weather tomorrow," he said.

I had hunted frequently when I was young. It had been necessary to keep the wild beasts down, the wolves that lived in the hills, the foxes and martens. It had been necessary to provide food for the table, deer and boar, to supplement the animals we raised ourselves. Now I had become a townsman, sitting behind a desk in the basilica, writing and talking. I had left eradicating vermin and supplying meat to the men of the estate. For me, hunting had become an occasional pastime, something I did when I was visiting

Verdaris or when arranged by thoughtful hosts on my travels around the province.

"How is the hunting? Did the rebels leave you any game?" I was proud to be able to speak to him in his own tongue, clumsily but carefully, thanks to his son.

Gisla chuckled as he always did when I spoke Saxon. It probably sounded strange to his ears.

"A little. They cut down most of the cover, but they couldn't do much with the forest. The animals are beginning to trickle back. Not as good as at Verdaris, I'm sure," he laughed.

"We were spared, largely," I said. My tone must have betrayed my feelings. Gisla glanced at me with a concerned expression.

"Are you still worried about Drusus and his hired men?"

"They are out there somewhere," I said.

"We haven't seen them for months," said the Saxon. "They couldn't survive for any length of time in the east. There is too much unrest."

"I think he still has friends there. And in any case, they still come to me in my dreams," I added, rather feebly.

"Ghosts," said Gisla, "mere ghosts."

But I saw that he shivered. Ghosts could still harm people. Everyone accepted that.

"Will he never give up?" he asked.

"I doubt it," I replied.

"Looking for revenge for the death of his brother?"

"That, and more," I reflected. "For the loss of riches and power. For a gamble that did not succeed and the loss of honour that comes from that."

"And you? You have won. Don't you feel honoured?"

"I should, I know," I said, "but I don't. There are many days when I feel I don't deserve the honour I've been given. I think of the men who have died – even Vitellus Astrebanus. Drusus is a constant reminder, like the slave who was supposed to have stood behind Caesar at his triumph."

I saw Gisla look puzzled for a moment. Perhaps my Saxon words had failed me. Then he shook his head.

"Now you're feeling sorry for yourself, Marcus. Come on, there's ale waiting for us in the hall and a good day's hunting tomorrow."

I remained for a moment, watching the clouds drifting across the sky and vanishing one by one behind the trees. Perhaps we were like those clouds. We were adrift in the world, just a group of people who happened to be blown together in the same direction. I heard laughter from the hall. I saw the light from the doorway. I needed company. I left the clouds to their fate beyond the trees and turned my attention to my dinner.

❧ Historical Note ☙

There have been many advances in archaeology in recent years, and our view of life in Britannia in late antiquity has been evolving. Once it was thought Britannia was in a long decline before the Romans left, and when they did, it plunged almost immediately into an era of chaos and brutality: the Dark Ages. Our view of this period was illuminated only by the stories of Hengist and Horsa and King Arthur. Now our view is changing. Britannia was, like many other parts of the Roman Empire, subject to incursions from neighbouring enemies, but it was otherwise still a relatively prosperous province, still capable of supporting a candidate for emperor in Constantine III. It is beyond doubt that the province eventually became a post-colonial "failed state". The towns and the great villas fell into ruin, and it took many years for a new governmental structure to evolve. However, that does not mean that all was anarchy. Archaeology suggests that much of the lower-level social structure continued, especially in agricultural areas, and modest local leadership was capable of imposing a certain amount of order.

As a psychologist, it occurred to me that there must have been people living long into the post-Roman period who had grown up under the influence of the Romans, remembered them and lived their life accordingly. Only when these people died and their children and grandchildren forgot, ignored or abandoned their elders' attitudes and behaviour would Roman influence finally have died out.

I was close to finishing this book when I came across the work of Stuart Laycock. Call it confirmation bias, but I was glad to see that another writer, with a great deal more expertise than I have, reasoned in a similar manner. Laycock was present during the collapse of post-communist Yugoslavia and saw how ancient demarcations could be whipped up into new hatreds and conflicts. In his book, *Britannia – The Failed State: Ethnic Conflict and the End of Roman Britain*, he argues that a similar process could have taken place in post-Roman Britain, that pre-Roman tribal loyalties persisted during the Roman occupation and re-emerged after the imperial power had departed. I am not in a position to judge the accuracy of his reasoning and I deliberately chose not to use the tribal names cited by Ptolemy. There is no evidence that these names persisted into post-imperial times, and in any case, it is not necessary that they did so. Rather, I have assumed there was sufficient trace of old identities remaining and these, through myth building and selective use of history, could be exploited later to create a "them and us" which had more to do with personal ambition and control of territory than proto-ethnicity. I have chosen to present the problem as one of a group of men who managed to preserve and control the remnants of the imperial order versus a few who felt they missed out. This is a common pattern of conflict we see around us today in a post-colonial world where the majority of conflicts are not between states, but within states, for land, riches and influence left behind by the receding empire.

I have considered the towns and the villa estates as actors in this story, too. My Corinium bears only limited resemblance to the archaeological remains that have been uncovered, but I console myself that the complete map of Corinium still remains largely speculative. Similarly with Londinium and Verulamium. Archaeology and the historical record suggest that some religious and probably civil administration struggled on after the departure of the legions, but for how long and to what extent is largely speculative. In that spirit, the other towns are fictional, but located in places where there really were towns during the Roman era. The villas and farms, Umbrosa, Verdaris and Agridurnum, are based on excavated exemplars, though, of course, their life stories are as much fictional as those of the human characters. These sites may outlive their inhabitants, but like the humans, with a few exceptions, the villas and the towns will also ultimately die.

❧ Bibliography ☙

For anyone wishing to read more about this period and the debate amongst historians concerning what happened and what could have happened, I have consulted the following books:

Bell, Tyler (2019) *The Religious Reuse of Roman Structures in Early Medieval England.* Middleton, DE, USA

Blair, John (2018) *Building Anglo-Saxon England.* Princeton University Press, Princeton, NJ, USA

Collins, Roger (2010) *Early Medieval Europe, 300–1000, 3rd Ed.* Palgrave Macmillan, London, UK

de la Bédoyère, Guy (2013) *Roman Britain, A New History, 2nd Ed.* Thames & Hudson, New York, USA

Fleming, Robin (2011) *Britain after Rome.* Penguin, London, UK

Laycock, Stuart (2008) *Britannia – The Failed State: Ethnic Conflict and the End of Roman Britain*, Kindle Edition. Tempus Publishing, Stroud, UK

McWhirr, Alan (1986) *Cirencester Excavations III: Houses in Roman Cirencester.* Cirencester Excavation Committee, Cirencester, UK

Oosthuizen, Susan (2019) *The Emergence of the English.* Arc Humanities Press, Leeds, UK

Pitts, Mike (2019) *Digging Up Britain.* Thames & Hudson, London, UK

Wickham, Chris (2009) *The Inheritance of Rome.* Penguin, London, UK

ℰ Acknowledgements ℭ

I would like to thank some of the people who have helped me through the transformation from scientific research to historical fiction. These include my professors and teachers in the history programme at the Delaware County Community College for challenging me to conduct historical background research and write about it, the members of the Brandywine Valley Writers Group, for their encouragement and practical knowledge, Andrew Noakes, Jenny Powell and Cecily Blench of The History Quill Ltd for their editorial assistance, and lastly my wife, Marja, for suspending quite reasonable disbelief.